I0638215

SILENCE HER

DOUGLAS FETTERLY

STORY MERCHANT BOOKS
LOS ANGELES
2017

STORY MERCHANT BOOKS

ISBN 10: 978-0-9991621-0-1
ISBN 13: 978-0-999162-0-1

Story Merchant Books
400 S. Burnside Avenue #11B
Los Angeles, CA 90036

http://www.storymerchant.com
http://www.storymerchantbooks.com

Cover Design by IndieDesignz.com and artist Chris Steitz

Chapter number font: Love My Tattoo, by Mirko Carcereri
Interior body font: Bookman Old Style

https://www.facebook.com/Silence-Her-1908626176016781/

*Dedicated to my Sweetie
—my wife, Sheryl Shook—
whose unwavering support,
wisdom, and love made
this book possible.*

ACKNOWLEDGEMENTS

My appreciation goes out to the following people (and everyone who continually expressed support along the way): Ellen Anderson, James Center, and Stacey Cook for their editing, suggestions, and friendship throughout the process; Ken Atchity and the staff at Story Merchant Books for their unwavering support; Pam Houston for leading an enlightening fiction workshop at the Aspen Writers' Foundation Summer Words Conference; Michael Neff of Algonkian Conferences for his provocative direction; Debbie Zakerski, Karen Kunz, Margaret Sanders, Teena Michael, Margherita Molnar, Keith Thompson, Diane Carlson, the Clevelands, the Yamashiros, and Dave Raney for checking in along the way; Chris Steitz for his artistic support; my wise and delightful sister, Gretchen, who continually inspires me; daughter Angie for her loyalty, and her thoughtfulness in giving writing books to me when I began my literary journey twenty-five years ago; son Doug for his inquisitiveness, forthright comments, and love ; daughter Mary for her spirited encouragement; and to Sheryl—my muse—for the abundant joy, inspiration, and love she brings to my life.

Silence Her

Silence Her

1

Lishan Amir sat at her desk, feeling pleased. She began re-reading her exposé against Senator Libby and his cronies, the ink on the newsprint barely dry. Sitting with legs crossed between her charcoal knit pencil skirt and black, stylized Harley boots, she raised her head, surprised, when her desk lamp unexpectedly shut off.

She looked up to see Executive Editor Jerry Hanson, the lamp's pull chain still in his grip. His other hand held the afternoon edition, a Page A1 headline circled in red. "Truth Be Known: Senator and FDA Collude With Food Kingpin to Seduce Public."

"Got a minute?" Jerry asked as though there were a question mark. But it was merely rhetorical. His face was contorted and taut.

His Xanax must be wearing thin, Lishan thought.

"Of course, Jerry." Standing, she smoothed and checked her button-back blouse. She liked the raglan sleeves, but the ecru color was a little too revealing for a close-up meeting with a guy she couldn't stomach. Still, it would have to do.

Jerry was already heading to his office.

It was early afternoon on Monday, well after *The Washington Mirror* had hit the streets. Lishan's exposé had made the front page. She always did enjoy a little hyperbole when exposing dishonest CEOs and government officials.

Still, she had been mildly surprised when it passed through the city desk editor's hands unchanged. The various editors in the hierarchy had strict orders against certain brands of controversy, nearly always finding a conservative replacement before the paper went to press. Jerry was unbending in this arena, especially if the official under fire was a deep-pocket business ally.

Lishan continued to push back against these restrictive guidelines. Today she was in luck. It was the city desk editor's last day. For some reason, Jerry had let this editor handle final-page signoff on her last day of work. It must have been an oversight—perhaps one-too-many prescription hits.

1

1

Douglas Fetterly

"Tell me where the fu...where you think you're headed with this *truth* thing of yours, or where you *were* headed," Jerry barked as they entered his office. "It's a fun read, Lishan—a departure from your usual torturous writing. But we don't want to make Senator Libby out to be an immoral servant of the people, now do we, like when you wrote about our country's new president and dissed him for what you called his '"sophomoric referrals to *fake news*?."'" Again, not a question.

Jerry reached out on his desk and straightened the photo of the president—the inscription, "You and I both know the real news."

"And Conner, whom you've accused, along with our beloved senator and the FDA, is an outstanding CEO. If it weren't for Conner, our country would have a food shortage, not to mention a lack of pharmaceuticals!"

Jerry fidgeted a furrow along the hardwood floor. Years of pacing was caving it in, like a piece of old plywood left out in the sun. Breathing deeply to regain composure, he continued, "I think they're doing a fine job."

Jerry, self-described in his adulterous singles ads as a handsome DWM, had an imposing presence in the newsroom. A head taller than Lishan's five foot eight, he was a towering figure, barely fitting through the X and Y of the doorframe. He wasn't what most would call fat. Hefty was more like it. His flat-top hairstyle was military-fashion, short enough to allow sunburn. The office grapevine pegged him as a fascist, acting as though he were in command of a battalion of missionaries. He had the subtlety of a bouncer. Handsome he was not.

Lishan stood near the door, neither intimidated nor overly confident. She found this to be the best stance when faced with Jerry's self-righteousness.

"Jerry, I'm a journalist. I get the news out, good or bad. That's my job. Facts are facts."

"You're forgetting a major component. We're also a business. Profit and loss statements complete with advertisers, and government officials who audit our books. Remember the IRS last year? *Remember?* And if you could think outside of your liberal-minded box, you would know that our senators are working hard to provide democracy for the people."

Lishan had heard it all before. He pressed—hard—any time she or any other reporter stepped on one of his friends' toes. The question was, how far could she push?

And, yes, the IRS. How could she forget? She saw Jerry as the one needing a reminder—the investigation, the audit narrowing to Jerry's court with his undeclared monetary connections to certain government officials. At mention of the IRS, Lishan just shook her head. She knew what the *real* issue was.

"Are we going to be true to the people, or just print what the Associated Press gives us alongside recipes for Grandma's favorite pudding, next to Home Mart ads? Senator Libby has broken nearly every promise to the public. He wasn't well liked to begin with. The promises, and likely some kickbacks, were the only ticket that got him elected. And Conner Foods, Conner Pharmaceuticals, do you have any idea how many people have become sick or died at Jack Conner's hands? The toxic fillers and empty calories he gets away with in the foods he manufactures? The drugs that never should have been fast-tracked through the system? Do you..." Lishan stopped to take a breath. "We can't, in journalistic faith, support this."

Jerry's face seemed to expand, pressing outward against the invisible seams that held his face together. He didn't like Lishan, but he respected her work. He knew she was a top-notch reporter. She had a following. The problem was that Lishan was often too damned good, probing into matters that could cause trouble for Jerry's friends, and Jerry.

"Yes, Lishan, we can. And we will."

"What? Support hypocrisy? Support decisions that favor liars and cheats and their high-paid lobbyists, at the expense of the public?"

"No, dammit! We *are* true to the people."

"Like the time you put a spin on the RU-486 'morning after' story, the day after Bush fired Jane Henney? We made it look like Henney got fired for defying FDA ethics. Ethics my glutes, Jerry. Everybody—and I mean everybody—knows it was because she violated the political football. She *was* following the guidelines. And as far as this newspaper, as the story goes..."

"I *know* how the story goes."

"As the story goes," Lishan pressed, her voice elevated, "*you* had been in support of Henney, until Bush's press secretary paid you a friendly visit. Night and day, Jerry. One day you're a professed representative of the people. The next, you're a born-again..."

The editor slammed his fist on the desk, knocking his NRA trophy on its side.

"*Don't* question my principles, Ms. Amir!"

3

Jerry could hear himself lose control, his voice carrying beyond the walls of his office. He straightened to his full height, closing the short gap to where Lishan stood.

The trophy survived his temper, but Lishan didn't feel so solid as Jerry charged her. Her instinct for self-preservation would have had her bolting out the door, but then she might as well bone up on writing about which kind of chocolate made the best ganache.

Jerry slowed, taking a deep breath. Another. He sidled up to Lishan, putting his arm halfway around the reporter's shoulders. He didn't want to add to his list of incidents with the publisher. It could be his last.

"Lishan, you're a good reporter," he said, patronizing. "A troublemaker sometimes, but good. We both know this. I won't beat around...well, you know. There's so much injustice in this world. We can't take it all on." Jerry had eased into a gentle, grandfatherly voice. "Aren't you twenty-three?"

"No, Jerry. I'm half your age—fifty-four, aren't you?"

Jerry stifled a bristle. He had lost that round of jabs, knowing he looked older than his forty-six years. "I'm asking you, as a *compadre*, to just cool it. Don't be so offensive. They are all good people."

Jerry gave a couple of pats and then removed his arm. As he opened the door, it was clear the meeting was over.

"Lishan, think about it. Oh, and one more minor item. Your insubordination has finally nominated you for the probation list. Sign here. If you don't toe the line for the next six months, beginning today, I have the authority to purge you from my employee list—and we both know I would be devastated if I was forced to do that. You should take tomorrow off."

Lishan looked Jerry straight in the eye. "You were born before frontal lobotomies were outlawed, weren't you?"

"What do you mean?"

"Never mind, Jerry. Just never mind."

As Lishan walked off, Jerry's assistant, Maria, called out to him. "Senator Libby is on the phone."

Jerry grimaced as he looked out at Lishan, who merely turned her head and smiled at the mention of Jerry's golf buddy.

Heading to her desk, Lishan could hear her desk phone ringing. She picked it up just before it transferred to voice mail.

"This is Lishan."

The reply followed what felt like a measured pause. "Yes, I know." The gruff male voice said nothing more.

"Hello?" Lishan prompted, unsure of the caller's intent. She waded through the silence for what seemed like a dozen heart-beats. Before she could prompt again, the caller hung up.

19th Street NW, D.C.

The sound of breaking glass came from Jack Conner's posh office. It was the $2,000 mirror he used to frequently inspect his tall, 220-pound European-American frame and the shaved head he felt gave him a look of power. Six months prior, when Charlotte first took the Executive Secretary position, she would have sprung up to attend to his needs.

But no longer. Conner was known for his anger. It was no surprise when his fury would send one of his arms in a sweeping movement across his desk, clearing everything in sight onto the floor. Important documents, a half-empty wine glass—it didn't matter. Charlotte once found a journal, buried in the bottom drawer of her desk, with entries from the previous six secretaries. The journal was filled with comments on his violence. It was never physical toward the employees, but there were emotional hits. Charlotte questioned how long she would last. The six secretaries spanned a mere two years.

"Who in Christ's name does she think she is?" he spewed, from a face that had borne years of tantrums, as he reread Lishan's article. One hour prior, he had stepped from his private jet to his limo, then straight into his office. A filtered stack of mail and newspapers, accumulated in his five-day absence, lay scattered on his desk. His Caribbean junket, sponsored by Senator Libby, hadn't tempered his peevish nature in the slightest.

Conner, fifty-six, as President and CEO of both Conner Foods and Conner Pharmaceuticals since their inception eighteen years ago, was not accustomed to losing. He bore an ego the likes of a few scornful politicians Charlotte had met—self-absorbed and contemptuous. His MBA piggybacked on his law degree, which gave him a solid sense of what he needed to achieve his goals and how to stop those in his way.

He buzzed Charlotte.

"Why in the hell didn't you tell me about this article? I don't care if it was just hot off the press. Damn, Ch..."

The intercom monologue was drowned by a loud, screeching sound.

"What the...?"

"It's okay, sir. If you lower your voice, it doesn't happen. Feedback, I think." Conner was unaware of the small device, from a game and joke shop, that created the screech. A previous occupant of Charlotte's desk had picked it up, finding it extremely useful in temporarily halting Conner's tirades.

"Damn! Can't we get that fixed?"

"It doesn't seem so, sir. We've replaced the entire intercom twice. It must be something in your voice. I don't believe it happens when you speak in a normal tone." Charlotte had to hold back a laugh.

"I *am* speaking in a normal tone." Conner cut off the conversation, leaving Charlotte to her work.

His office occupied the top floor of a window-encased highrise overlooking the heart of D.C. As his empire expanded, early on, million by billion, it became increasingly clear he needed to be near the decision-makers that would affect his businesses. Senators and various agency administrators topped the list.

Conner's father had been a senator—in fact, previously the richest senator in U.S. history.

His father hadn't amassed his fortune by being kind. Treatment of his only son was no exception. Conner tragically internalized, at a young age, that getting what he wanted— wealth and power beyond imagination—required ruthless means. He had mastered the paradigm flawlessly.

Conner had no real interest in oil or any fickle market. That left, in his mind, food and drugs. The world needed both, he felt, prompting the creation of his two multi-billion-dollar businesses.

Over the years, only two other power mongers dared challenge Conner's CEO status. The first became institutionalized in short order, dying several years later. A drug habit was the story that surfaced, but only Conner and his abettor knew the truth. The newspapers made light reference to *One Flew Over the Cuckoo's Nest*. The second disappeared altogether, with only whispers linking it to Conner. No body, no crime.

Charlotte buzzed the intercom. "Commissioner Schuler is on line one, Mr. Conner. Shall I tell him you're unavail..."

"Arthur, did you get that box of Caribbean rum I sent you from the islands?" Conner had no patience for anyone, let alone his secretary whose sentences were always too long for him.

"Yes, Jack. Thanks. But, dammit, that's not why I called. How in the hell can I get Congress to fund my requests when you keep giving the press fuel to make me look bad?" Schuler

7

was furious. "You told me those last Fast Track documents for that whatchamacallit drug were legit. That Amir reporter said I allowed my agency to cut corners for Conner Pharmaceuticals, and now people are getting sick. Dammit, Jack."

Conner knew the commissioner *did* cut corners for him. He had the half-a-million money transfer document to prove it. But Conner wasn't going to push that point. This was one individual Conner didn't want to anger. He needed the FDA's support to fast-track the expensive foods and drugs requiring FDA approval.

"Arthur, I'm thinking if you check your personal bank account by day's end, you'll see enough money to help you smooth this over. Blame one of your scientists. Fire someone if you have to. I'll take care of Amir. If that works for you, I should let you get back to running the Agency. The country needs it." Conner smiled to himself, holding back his condescension.

The commissioner balked at first, something about wanting to do the right thing by the public, but money talked in the end.

After the call, Conner reread the exposé that drew a triangle of complicity connecting him to Senator Libby and Schuler. He boiled over again. *Shouldn't that ruddy-faced Southerner, or wherever he came from, be calling me about what* he's *going to do about this?* he bellowed to himself. With nothing left on his desk to sweep clear, he yelled into the intercom.

"Get Libby on the phone. Now!"

There was no reason to stick around the newsroom after her run-in with Jerry. Lishan decided to head home. It was 2:30 when she arrived. Throwing herself down on her bed, arms and legs extended like a snow angel, Lishan imagined taking a short nap. Ten minutes into her rest, her irises grew fully visible as she remembered a significant event that evening.

The D.C. Media Gala.

The inaudible words formed on her lips. She hadn't forgotten, but the run-in with her editor had dominated her thoughts.

The party would begin at 6:30 p.m. in the atrium of the Ronald Reagan Building. Dignitaries from every niche would attend, given the importance of the schmooze and lobby tactics that greased the skids for nearly all deals struck between the various magnates of government, news, and industry.

Lishan rifled the back-end of her closet where lesser-used clothing was relegated. She found a backless dress of black silk. *Tempting*, she thought, questioning whether she would be more powerful in her alluring femininity or her less-revealing business attire. *Maybe the pinstriped gray suit I wore to my* Mirror *interview?*

No, she thought, *not the suit. It's a formal affair, after all.* Still, she didn't want her sexuality to eclipse her business stature. She had a reputation to uphold. Then she saw her one outfit by designer Salman Kabir. It was an off-white brocade dress, backless yet sophisticated, contoured from breast to ankle. *Yes, this will do.*

Showered and dressed by 6:00 p.m., Lishan was nearly ready to venture out. She brushed her shoulder-length, black hair, adding a small dollop of lightweight conditioner to soften the waves. She called her close friend Erik to see if he would chaperone her out the front door of the apartment building and into a taxi—her way of showing off being dressed to the nines, which he rarely saw.

"I thought this gala deal was going to be at the Fairmont. What happened?" Erik asked as they headed toward the exit.

"It was. But the chair had some chauvinistic issue with the Fairmont's founders back in San Francisco—sisters Tessie and

Virginia Fair. Can you believe it? That was a hundred years ago."

"Some prejudices run long and deep," Erik said. "Rancorous, in my mind."

She blew a kiss to him as she stepped into a taxi. Erik didn't return the kiss. She could see tension lines in his face.

Before the cabbie closed the door, she asked Erik, "Is something wrong?"

Erik hesitated, his mouth tight with irritation.

"Yes, actually. You found a way to take me to the last two galas. It just seemed odd that you didn't invite me this year. Are you meeting someone there?"

Lishan capped her anger as best she could. *Dammit, Erik, you always weave in your jealousies.*

"No, Erik, I'm not meeting someone." Lishan's breathing became audible. "Look, it's always been a hassle getting you in. It's against the rules. I told you two months ago, when I received the invitation, that I couldn't take you this year. I tried. Maybe you tuned me out when I told you."

"Maybe I did. Anyway, have fun Lishan." Erik turned his back as he headed inside, his insincerity having done its damage.

Great, just great, Lishan said to herself. She cast a meager smile to the cabbie, a "thank you" for his patience. She decided to let the altercation go and focus on the gala. Erik didn't seem to be changing anytime soon, and she had to be in good form for the event. Still, she wished she understood why his jealousy was so charged.

Lishan managed to regain her smile by the time she arrived. She thought back to the two previous Media Galas, which her editor took delight in calling Media Balls. All three invitations had come at the request of her publisher, since Jerry would never have invited Lishan.

After she passed through security, she heard a woman call out "Mrs. O." Turning, she saw Elizabeth Walker, publisher extraordinaire.

"Ah, Michelle, it *is* you," Elizabeth said with a smile. "How's the puppy?"

Lishan dipped her eyebrows, confused that her publisher clearly knew her and yet seemed to have mistaken her for someone else. Then it struck her—the White House. Lishan broke into a grin.

"I forgot how closely you follow fashion. This gown, as you so aptly discerned, is by a designer the former First Lady used. In fact, I believe he's here tonight, though I'm not certain just why."

"He happened to be in town, and media socialites deemed it appropriate," Elizabeth said. "My, my," she quipped, admiring Lishan's backless gown as they entered the atrium. "It does look good on you! I must be paying you too much. I wish I had the courage to wear such an artistic statement."

Lishan blushed. "Oh, you have the courage."

They both smiled, walking arm in arm until they entered the "circus," as Erik occasionally referred to such events. There they parted, Lishan understanding the publisher had lobbying to do.

Lishan chatted briefly with an assortment of media folk she knew, mostly journalists and editors from newspapers. She got numerous compliments from her colleagues on her front-page headline, along with a few playful warnings to watch her back.

Half an hour into the party, a sudden eruption of camera flashes got everyone's attention. Four men and their wives, with one couple in tow, entered nearly as a pack.

Lishan immediately recognized Jack Conner, Senator Libby, and the FDA commissioner. Several seconds lapsed before she identified the fourth—a trim, white male in his late forties, the look of the country club set—Nathaniel Ferrali, *the* uppermost echelon U.S. Attorney for the District of Columbia. The lesser couple bringing up the rear included none other than her editor, Jerry Hanson, appearing nearly as an attendant to the group. It was clear that Jerry attempted to blend in as though he were a key figure, but his antics, his waving and smiling, only made him look ridiculous.

Lishan made herself less conspicuous. She knew their gossip about her wouldn't be flattering. She imagined the commissioner and Jerry would see her as a mere speck of agitation. As for Ferrali, she couldn't be sure. Yet, for Conner and Libby, perception management was key to them if reputations were to remain fully intact along with profits and a checkmark at the polls.

She kept the troublesome group in her periphery until they settled into an area close to the bar. Lishan maneuvered to one of the many hors d'oeuvres tables, peering at her options, when a gentleman's voice said, "I love your gown."

She looked up to find an exquisitely dressed Indian-born man looking warmly at her.

"My name is Salman Kabir. How do you do?"

Salman Kabir, Lishan repeated to herself. Barely containing her delight, she finally said, "My name's Lishan Amir," extending her hand. "This is your dress."

"In a manner of speaking," Salman smiled. "You wear it very well."

They talked of fashion and world affairs. Ten minutes had gone by when Lishan felt an icy hand on her back. She recoiled sharply, turning to find the group of ten standing there, gazing at her attire. Conner withdrew his hand.

"Nice frock," Conner laughed. "A little sleazy though, don't you think?"

"I'm not surprised," chimed Senator Libby. "A backless dress of such poor quality at a formal affair. Really, Ms. Amir. I must agree with Mr. Conner. Sleazy."

"Sleazy," Lishan mimicked. She turned toward the designer. "Do you find this gown sleazy, Mr. Kabir?"

Salman put his hand to his chin. "Hmm. Honestly? I can't say I do. But perhaps these gentlemen are more expert than I about fashion."

Conner's wife Loren gasped as she recognized the designer and his work. She tried to get her husband's attention, but to no avail.

"So, are you an expert on sleaze, Senator?" Lishan said.

The senator grew red. "Ms. Amir, you don't know me well enough to insult me."

"But *I* do." The soprano voice, coming from behind the group, caught everyone's attention. The men and their wives turned to find a tall, slender, African-American...female? The intruder's attire included a snug-fitting shiny black skirt, halting six inches above the knee. The top was a matching black long-sleeve blouse, with two lines of purple sequins—like two reversed parentheses—suggesting a 6-inch waist. The neckline plunged shamelessly.

Ah, it's JoJo, Lishan said to herself, delighted. The FDA commissioner also recognized him, but he chose to keep silent.

JoJo continued, shocking nearly everyone as he changed to his deep baritone. "Hello, Senator. And Jack and Nathaniel, how nice to see all of you again. I should add, as to sleazy, you boys just don't recognize artful clothing when you see it, unless of course it's being taken off by some—if I may borrow a word you boys seem to freely apply—bimbo."

JoJo nodded to the commissioner, then turned his attention to Salman, shaking his hand. "Mr. Kabir, I just *adore* your work," JoJo said admiringly, running his fingers along the fabric of Lishan's gown. JoJo scanned the faces of the five men. "See you again at the club, sometime this week?"

JoJo smiled, then turned to Jerry.

"I don't know you, but you *really* should have those amalgam fillings removed."

Jerry responded by closing his mouth, hiding two silver-colored fillings that were, unfortunately, prominent when he spoke. He glared at Lishan.

JoJo continued. "You do know those mercury fillings are killing the few brain cells you have left? Too bad the FDA still succumbs to the amalgam lobby."

By this time, the scowls on the faces of the angry wives had knocked the wind out of the five men. The men backed away, tight-lipped, tails tucked.

Conner was the only one to flash a threatening look before he departed.

JoJo winked at Lishan, then sashayed into the crowd.

Salman's face brightened. He loved a good skirmish. "The shenanigans of self-important men. Fatuous comes to mind." He paused. "And who was that tall, beautiful gentleman?"

"You do understand beauty."

"Hmm. The whole of humanity, with its myriad of tragedy, its effervescence, its pulchritude."

"His name is JoJo. A sweet friend of mine—scientist with the FDA by day, dancer and performer by night. I met him when I wrote an article about him and how he could pass as a top female model and dancer." Lishan paused, then added, "I'm sorry you had to witness that nastiness with Conner and the senator."

Salman waved his hand in a gentle gesture. "No doubt they are still stinging from your fine article today."

"You saw that?"

"Of course. I imagine most of Washington is looking at those...gentlemen a bit differently this evening, thanks to your work. They are of no import, Lishan. That much is clear."

Compliments and hugs exchanged, Lishan excused herself and wove her way to JoJo.

"Thank you. You were marvelous," she said.

"Conner and Libby deserve to be behind bars. The U.S. Attorney as well. And to treat someone like you with such disdain, and in public."

13

"They feel threatened by me. By the way, have they actually been to your club?"

"Of course. More than once. Some of the performers, like me, are in drag. Some aren't. The likes of Conner and Libby are difficult to miss. Loud and obnoxious, with egos the size of elephant balls. No doubt to compensate for other...shortcomings."

Lishan laughed out loud. They spoke for another ten minutes before Lishan realized she was tired. The day had taken a bit of a toll. It was time to head home.

"Ms. Amir?"

Lishan took a deep breath as she turned to face what she feared might be another intruder.

"Yes?"

"Howard Perkins. I..."

Lishan brightened, jumping in. "Howard Perkins. I know exactly who you are. It's truly my pleasure to meet you."

"I didn't know I had such an enthusiastic following," he said.

"Any investigative reporter worth her career knows who you are. Your reputation in our field precedes you." Lishan was glowing.

Perkins matched her glow. "Kind of you," he said. "I only have a moment, but I wanted to meet you. I appreciate your work, especially that last Truth Be Known article of yours."

Their conversation lasted fifteen enjoyable minutes. Howard produced a business card from his wallet.

"Can I give you my card, Ms. Amir?"

"Please, call me Lishan."

"Excellent. I'd enjoy chatting sometime over a glass of wine, or an espresso?"

"I'd like that, Mr. Perkins."

"Please, it's Howard. Take care, Lishan—and give me a call any time. At the moment, I've got a few shins to kick."

The warmth in Howard's smile was enough to chase away the October chill. Tucking the card in her bag, Lishan headed for the exit.

On her way out, she saw that JoJo had cornered the president's new press secretary. Since the recent S.N.L. skits, he had become fodder for ridicule. JoJo couldn't resist.

A line of taxis was ready and waiting when Lishan reached the outside air. During the ride home, Lishan skimmed a few notes she had made, making a mental memo to further investigate some of the FDA-related comments Howard had mentioned:

14

When using accelerated approval, Subpart E, drug skips certain safety data.

Did the Roche Corporation know of unresolved deaths that occurred during clinical trials but still submitted the drug for FDA approval?

Warner-Lambert and Pfizer – Rezulin – 63 deaths, liver failure, lawsuits? Did the FDA know? Was a questioning reviewer stifled?

Lishan found herself driven to dive deeper into the truth.

4

Johnny Mazzini was a scrawny kid in the Bronx. In the fifth grade, his lack of bulk didn't buy him any favors, especially with the school bullies. Johnny was sensitive, always seeking the approval of others by any means possible. By chance, he found that baking helped his situation. He began taking cookies to school, gaining a false sense of friendship with other kids. The bullies would take their share and still beat him up.

He remembered one time when he must have grabbed a wrong ingredient, or one that had become toxic. Nine of the ten kids who ate the cookies became very sick – including the bullies. After that, the bullies never bothered him again. Johnny never forgot.

5

Tuesday morning—the day off she had earned from her run-in with the editor—was just two weeks past the autumn equinox. The air was crisp and full of promise, but the week ahead felt like it had too many ingredients for Lishan to keep track of—at least until her French press had finished its brew. Lishan's intellect seemed to sharpen in direct proportion to the number of cups of strong coffee she consumed.

Her life had taken on a seemingly increased complexity as she sought to balance the rebuke from her editor against recent keystrokes he hadn't approved. She pulled out her calendar.

Lishan wasn't unhappy with the unpaid day off. It gave her an opportunity to attend a Senate hearing she had in mind. The FDA commissioner was speaking before the Senate Committee on Health, Education, Labor, and Pensions. After two cups of black, single-origin coffee, she caught a taxi to the Senate building.

FDA Commissioner Arthur Schuler stood before the committee, his speech notes in front of him. The hearing was titled "Ensuring Public Safety: FDA's Determination of Obesity Relative to Artificial Sweeteners."

He began, "Good morning, Chairman Hinkle and members of the committee. I'm Dr. Arthur Schuler, Commissioner of Food and Drugs at the Food and Drug Administration, which falls within the Department of Health and Human Services. Thank you for the opportunity to discuss food safety with you today and for your longstanding commitment to food safety."

The commissioner spent the next seven minutes trumpeting the FDA's accomplishments, a display Lishan had noticed in other hearings. It reminded her of the antics of male animals when courting.

As the hearing continued, various senators spoke up, asking the commissioner questions—mostly pertinent—usually with respect, though commonly traceable to the party line. The central theme focused on how the FDA viewed the correlation between artificial sweeteners and the rise of obesity in the United States, specifically regarding the aspartame-like sweetener Connulose that Conner Foods had introduced five years earlier.

Twenty minutes into the hearing, a commotion occurred at one of the ornate double doors. Two men entered loudly. Lishan's eyes widened. Senator Libby and Jerry Hanson.

It was barely mid-morning, but the two appeared inebriated. When they realized they'd become the center of attention, they simply smiled and waved to the group. Senator Libby took his empty seat at the dais, while Jerry stood, given standing room only. Lishan noticed Jerry nod and smile toward the center of the room. She followed his gaze to Commissioner Schuler. *Another friend.*

One of the democratic senators, Maria Sanchez (D-NM), referred to national health studies that indicated a direct relationship between obesity, neurotoxicity, and the consumption of Conner's chemical sweetener.

"When James Schlatter, a G.D. Searle chemist, happened upon an exceptionally sweet-tasting chemical—marketed as aspartame—while researching an anti-ulcer drug back in 1965, he unknowingly unleashed on the world one of the greatest food debacles of all time," Sanchez said. "The FDA initially denied approval, given evidence of neurotoxicity. However, certain events paved the way for its approval; events like the sudden acceptance of a position in Searle's law firm by Samuel Skinner, the U.S. Attorney in charge of investigating Searle's reported criminal misconduct. That stymied the investigation until the statute of limitations ran out. Donald Rumsfeld's new position as Searle's CEO also helped. A little over two decades later, Jack Conner created a competitive sweetener—three hundred percent sweeter than aspartame—called Connulose. Ladies and gentlemen, today, nearly three decades later, these dangerous additives are still adversely affecting the health of all users. Only one year after soft drink companies began using aspartame, the Center for Disease Control began fielding hundreds of complaints for headaches, cardiac and liver problems, and neurologic symptoms. All of you who drink diet sodas and who add this chemical—yes, a chemical, not a food—to your coffee need to be aware of the toxicity of these sweeteners and their direct influence in the rise of obesity in our country. Look around you." Most of the audience shifted uncomfortably in their seats. "Again, I urge the FDA, once and for all, to quit bowing to the demands of the food and drug lobby. It is a disgrace."

The Democratic senator had barely put a period on her paragraph when Senator Libby seized control.

"I would like to remind everyone of Dr. Robert Brackett's testimony in a November 2006 hearing. He was the Director of the Center for Food Safety and Applied Nutrition. In his superb delivery, true to the reputation of the Bush administration..."

There was a murmur in the chamber, a few smiles and soft chuckles. Senator Libby raised his voice. At five foot seven, his soft chin supporting round cheeks, he looked more like a sagging marshmallow than the powerful senator he had become. As he peered through his thick glasses, his massive, balding head still managed to dwarf his overweight frame.

"Dr. Brackett made it eminently clear that obesity is a result of lifestyle and overconsumption, not Connulose. And, it was determined, my honored colleagues, that the argument against Connulose is moot, since it has been unequivocally shown to be a *natural* substance, utilizing constituents from high-fructose corn syrup. I ask you, what could be more natural than corn in the good ol' U S of A?"

The commission chair—Senator Dade—took the opportunity to clarify a point. "As a reminder, the FDA still has on its plate a future agenda in which it will decide the precise parameters of what it means to be 'natural.'"

"Yes, and in the meantime," Senator Libby boomed, "I can assure you that Connulose *is* all natural and not in the least responsible for any obesity, or neuro...tosis, or whatever, in this fine country."

A distracting hubbub had broken out. Many of the senators looked toward the sidelines, their eyes focused on one key figure—Jack Conner. Conner just smiled, nodding to those who were on his side. He appeared completely unruffled.

Lishan took note of Libby's comments, of Conner's attitude, writing them in her five by eight Moleskine. Ideas were forming quickly in her head.

The hearing lasted another hour. The commissioner closed by suggesting meetings with the public and industry groups. As the meeting adjourned and people filed out, Lishan held back, disappearing into a less conspicuous part of the room. She was curious about how Jerry and Schuler would interact. She didn't have long to wait.

Conner and the senator were speaking privately. The two men simultaneously made eye contact with Lishan before turning their backs on her.

Jerry had walked over to the table where Schuler had made his presentation. The two men walked out together, chatting and smiling.

As Lishan exited the building, she felt a fist push into her back, but there was something more, almost like a nasty bee sting. She turned to find Conner, his earlier smile still plastered on his craggy face. Lishan was resolute to be unshaken, or at least not to let it show, though Conner's 6'3" frame reeked of the excesses of power and strength.

"Hello, little girl."

Lishan narrowed her eyes. "Ms. Amir to you." She tried ignoring the pain in her back.

"I always did enjoy your feistiness. In any case, it's a pleasure, you can be sure." As he turned to walk away, he put a small pocketknife back in his pants pocket, the tip covered in fresh blood. He looked at Lishan, smiling. "Good luck with your career...or finding a new one."

As she began to leave, Lishan felt her back where the sting was not diminishing, not at all. The spot was moist. When she checked her hand, Lishan's eyes grew fully round. There was blood.

She proceeded to the lady's restroom where a young woman took a look for Lishan, confirming that it appeared to be a puncture of some kind, about the width of the woman's tiny pinky finger. Lishan always carried a spare Band-Aid and a small, square gauze pad. With her acquaintance's help, and a couple of minutes of applied pressure, the bleeding subsided.

Lishan's fury was rising, as was her fear.

She stopped at one of her favorite coffee shops, one with a Bohemian flair. She couldn't help but consider the thick connections and good ol' boy influences in this town. With an Americano in hand, she sat in a deep, comfy chair and pulled out her laptop. Typing in help.senate.gov to get to the Hearings section, Lishan skirted through the various listings until she found the collaborations she was looking for.

Jerry, Schuler, and Conner went back a number of years, well before Schuler became commissioner.

The puncture in her back still hurt, but the pain was subsiding. The bleeding had indeed stopped, so she wasn't worried about the wound itself. But the fact that Conner wouldn't hesitate to inflict pain—that worried her. *Damn him.*

- - -

The air was unusually cool, prompting Lishan to clear her head with a long walk home instead of taking public transit. It gave her time to think, time to contemplate her next story, and time to listen to her music. *Cherish the Day* streamed through her tiny Bose headphones. Sade's lyrics and soulful voice always added to Lishan's resolve.

Lishan had learned one consistent truth in her investigative reporting: where profits and food magnates were concerned, virtually any case could be made to fit an agenda. Any product could be "tested" so the results were ascribed to the desired end-point. Skewing lab findings or statistics toward a particular outcome was a highly developed art and science.

She remembered remnants of articles she had read. One, from a supposedly prominent journal, repudiated the claim of danger in trans fats. Lishan recalled digging, peeling back the layers until she uncovered the truth. Not in black and white, to the casual observer, but there, nonetheless. The food processing company had, surreptitiously, through the subsidiary name game, funded the study. The presiding scientists were not available for comment.

Lishan stopped just short of her apartment complex. To hell with Jerry, with the Conners and Libbys of this town. Inside her apartment, a glass of chardonnay, Camembert de Normandie, a baguette, and a movie ended all aspirations for the rest of the evening.

The following morning, Lishan returned to work at *The Mirror*. After a couple of hours, she realized she wanted to be elsewhere, prompting her to head out for a cup of neighborhood coffee. As she left *The Mirror* and passed through the elegant, manually-operated, three-chambered door of brushed bronze, she was greeted by the bright sun, a slight chill, and the intense stare of a taxi driver standing by his ubiquitous, illegally parked Yellow cab. Turning right on the expansive sidewalk, she noticed the driver hurriedly getting into his cab.

The streets and intersections were wide in this part of D.C., with traffic and pedestrian signals geared toward the professional on the move. Lishan smiled as she remembered her time in Honolulu, where, just when a mainland driver's patience ran out waiting for the light to turn green, a glance at the 'walk' signal revealed another twenty-five seconds to go. Lishan briskly stepped out into the second of five intersections she needed to traverse before arriving at the café.

An alarmed voice shouting "Look out!" and a strong hand wrapped around her right arm were her last recollections before she fell to the pavement amid the sound of squealing tires.

"Miss, are you alright?" Hearing the caring male voice was reassuring. At least her hearing and other senses were likely still intact. "Don't move just yet. When you're ready, let me help you up, if nothing feels broken."

Lishan slowly sat up, brushing off bits of miniscule stone fragments and grime as she took stock. Her right thigh hurt, but it felt no more than a bruise.

"What happened?" she muttered.

"You're quite lucky," the voice offered.

Lishan shook off the fog and focused on her rescuer—a dark brown-skinned male, nearly black, perhaps thirty-five, with beautiful facial features.

He continued, "That taxi driver ran the light, and not by a slight margin."

Lishan could do little more than blink as the reality sank in that she may have just narrowly avoided being killed, perhaps murdered. As the small crowd dispersed, she stood, slowly. She felt a slight limp in her right leg as she tried to walk. Gradually, the limp eased.

"I...I can't thank you enough. I believe you saved my life. My name is Lishan." She extended her hand.

"I'm Osiris," the man said.

"Can I buy you a coffee, or lunch?"

"Kind of you, but I'm running late for a meeting—unless you could still use my help."

Lishan gave herself another once-over. "Just a scrape or two. So how can I thank you?"

"Your well-being is all that matters. Thank you, though."

As Lishan began to walk off, she thought to turn and ask if he thought the taxi driver had tried to hit her, but she brushed off the thought. Then she remembered Conner. *He wouldn't go that far, would he?*

She wrestled with the possible answers, finally convincing herself that the cabbie had simply been in a hurry. *Aren't they all?* she asked herself. Lishan was shaken enough that she decided to head back to *The Mirror,* sans coffee.

- - -

Her desk was neat and organized—not the norm in the newsroom. Nobody understood this quirk in her otherwise typical journalistic nature. Everyone remotely connected to the business knew that journalists were slobs at their desks, with stacks of newspapers that caused even the most seasoned fire marshals to shake their heads during inspections.

The plaque on her desk read, "We create our own conflict." To Lishan, it wasn't a suggestion to lie low. She framed it as a philosophical view of the world and how it came to be.

The gray cubicle walls surrounding her were only four feet high, ensuring that no one could easily hide from Jerry's view. This was where Lishan allowed her clutter. Her wall space was filled with none-too-flattering articles about various senators, governors, or the FDA. As she sat back in her squeaky, low-grade ergonomic chair—the product of a tightening budget—she replayed the words delegated by her supposed boss.

Dammit, she thought. *It's the journalist's job to keep the country running smoothly, to prod honesty from those government officials with unspecified vacations to the Bahamas, those CEOs whose frosted seven-figure bonuses were just never enough, the shareholders who measured their stock gain without regard to who gets hurt.*

Conner Foods and Conner Pharmaceuticals were at the top of Lishan's Public Enemy list, along with eight other companies that dominated food and drugs in the U.S. Lishan knew most people were surprised by the holdings of these companies, thinking the brand names they knew and loved were still wholly-owned and produced by the original companies. Few knew these ten companies dictated over ninety-five percent of the two behemoth industries. Lishan was determined to remove the blindfolds.

Then there was Senator Libby with his notorious reputation for bending legislation that smoothed the way for much of Conner's shenanigans. Lishan paused and shuddered as she recalled the morning's close call.

The afternoon was disappearing. Lishan looked ahead at her assignments for the week, always considering them "tentative" since news didn't align itself in neat, tidy packages. The world was too disorderly and dynamic to submit to a weekly timetable.

She noticed there was nothing controversial on the list, nothing remotely connected to government. This was usual when Jerry felt like exercising his ego, but the list did seem conspicuously clean this week—not a polemic in sight. Heading down to the lunchroom to get a cup of the dregs, she noticed a new product in the snack vending machine: potato chips with "zero trans fats" clearly marked in the upper right-hand corner. On a reporter's whim, Lishan dug in her pocket for the sixty-five cents. The six-ounce pack spiraled forward, but it stopped just short of its intended fall.

"Doomed," Lishan muttered to herself. Digging again, she found only sixty cents. Another expletive. Calculating its importance, and not wanting to be seen with two bags of chips, she stood there for a moment, curling her toes inside her Timberlands, fidgeting.

"Lunch or dinner?" It was her publisher. "Chips at that!" she grinned.

"It's for an article I'm writing." Lishan felt sheepish. *Of all people to run into.*

"Right," Elizabeth chided. "I think I'll buy a Snickers. The editorial board wants the low-down." Noticing Lishan's dilemma, she dug out a quarter and gave it to Lishan. "For your research." She grinned as she proceeded to another vending machine to buy a guava juice.

Lishan took in the ingredients list on the bag of chips. There was the usual flair, speaking to the cravings, the need for instant gratification. But, *caveat emptor*, Lishan thought. Highly paid professionals stood behind the claims and allure in most every packaged food. The question she often sought to answer was how much the food companies weighed share prices versus consumer health. And what about that FDA?

In the past six months, the marketing contingents throughout the greedier food companies had caught on to the public's growing awareness of trans fats. She imagined, though, that not every consumer made the connection between trans fats and the hydrogenated or partially hydrogenated oils in the ingredients list. But Lishan did.

On her new purchase, there it was: partially hydrogenated oil in the ingredients. "Zero trans fats" on the front of the bag, right-hand corner. Mutually exclusive. *How can they get away with this?*

"*Merde!*" she muttered, an angry breath finishing her thought.

The problem gaining momentum in Lishan's mind was that the FDA wasn't being straight with the public. The Agency could stand behind its belief that a small quantity of a harmful ingredient, like trans fats, was not harmful. But to intentionally mislead the public, allowing statements on the front of packaging that an ingredient did not exist in a food, when in fact it did—that was an injustice. Deceit with a dollar sign. She could feel the next exposé forming. Perhaps "The Hydrogenated Oil Caper."

The publisher had returned. Catching the drift in Lishan's demeanor, with a nod toward the chips, she said, "So, do something about it." Leaving a smile to underscore her support, the publisher disappeared through a set of double doors.

With two bags of chips in hand, Lishan headed back up the single flight to her desk.

- - -

Settling in, she grew contemplative. She recalled her father—Jemal—a tall, good-looking Ethiopian man whose genes influenced Lishan's height and skin the color of creamed coffee. They once lived in the Bronx, having left Ethiopia when the Derg came into power, threatening intellectuals like Jemal and his family. Lishan was ten. Nightmares of the escape through Kenya plagued Lishan throughout her teen years. Her two brothers had died at the hand of a juvenile Derg soldier before her father overpowered the youth.

When she was nearly twenty-four, her parents were shot as they were coming home from a literary event. Her mother, Anne, of Czech and New England descent, died instantly. Her father died three days later. Lishan had already moved to D.C., where she remained after finishing her bachelor's. She felt so alone.

Immediately, Wayzero Niesha—a very close family friend and sage, mostly known to Lishan as "Auntie," who watched over Lishan in her early childhood in Ethiopia—became Lishan's protector. Niesha had moved to the U.S., along with Jemal's family, at the age of thirty, working in the Ethiopian embassy as an economics advisor. She was well respected, having earned the Wayzero title for her wisdom and compassion in all manner of political and humanitarian efforts in her homeland.

Lishan had grown up in a culture where one's word, one's promise, was as binding as any legal contract. When she thought of the likes of Jerry, with his hypocrisies and self-serving ways, her nostrils flared in annoyance. His imperious nature led to exactly the kind of injustice Lishan couldn't stand—big business and elites working their intimidation so no one would interfere.

- - -

"What are you doing, Lishan?" Jerry stood behind her, a commanding stance. Perhaps he'd been there more than a few seconds. Lishan couldn't be sure.

"I hope you're just eating those. They won't be Exhibit A." Looking up, as though contemplating a ship on the horizon, he addressed another reporter, having inflicted his intended damage on Lishan.

"Hey, Jody, what's the status..." Jerry's voice trailed off, following his body as he headed over to provide guidance to another lost soul.

Lishan opened a drawer in her gray metal desk, a carryover from the old days before desks were made of compressed sawdust. Removing an unmarked hanging folder from the rear of the drawer, she thumbed through its contents, finding article after article referencing failures, intentional or otherwise, where the public's health was compromised.

Extracting a PBS interview with whistleblower Dr. David Graham—a former FDA Associate Director for Science and Medicine in the Office of Drug Safety—she perused his comments aimed at setting the public straight on where the FDA stood. Lishan had highlighted a few graphs, settling now on one quote she especially remembered: "As currently configured, the FDA is not able to adequately protect the American public. It's more interested in protecting the interests of industry. It views industry as its client."

Her desk phone came to life, a distraction she wasn't in the mood for. "This is Lishan."

"Lishan, this is Jody at the front desk. I have a Ms. Reed here to see you. She's from Senator Libby's office."

Don't they ever bother to make an appointment? Lishan knew this was an intimidation visit. Making an appointment would have been too cordial. *No, this is about power.*

In the lobby, Lishan extended her hand. The handshake was not reciprocated.

"Justine Reed. I'm an attorney from Senator Libby's office."

"Would you care to use a conference room?"

"Your desk, Ms. Amir, will do just fine, if you don't mind."

It wasn't a question. Lishan knew the attorney wanted her to back off, so any public humiliation or patronizing behavior would put Lishan on the defensive.

"How can I help you?" Lishan's smirk was barely visible. She had no interest in placating anyone today, especially some mid-level enforcer from Libby's stable.

"My purpose..."

"Is to intimidate." Lishan was pointed.

Reed just smiled beneath stylized lips. "You know we don't operate that way."

"No, in fact I don't."

"We are here to help, regardless of your belief. Look, we're getting off on the wrong foot—and my shoes are quite a bit larger than yours."

"They fit your body," Lishan smiled.

The attorney leaned forward, her features hard and focused. "I'm here because Senator Libby's office has its hands full without having to fend off inaccurate, sensationalistic stories."

Lishan didn't budge. She wasn't about to be outdone. "I'm confident you're absolutely correct."

"Your sarcasm is unnecessary, Ms. Amir. Listen, I stopped by, hoping to have a pleasant visit with..."

"Excuse me," Lishan jumped in. "Don't patronize me. Some may see Libby—Senator Libby—as a humanitarian. But we both know better, now don't we?"

The attorney bristled, taking a breath to regain composure—part of her training. She knew she would lose this round if she displayed uncontrolled anger.

"As I was saying, I hoped to have a pleasant visit with a suitable outcome..."

"That I should capitulate? Please don't waste your time."

"Your reputation precedes you." Reed stood. "Here's today's *New York Times*. It's a newspaper. After you see your name in print, infamously, perhaps you'll consider a redrawing of your so-called exposé—one that paints the senator in the light he deserves."

"Gray?"

Reed just blinked, then turned to leave. Over her shoulder, she delivered her parting comment. "If you're interested in the truth, and not theatrical bullshit, we strongly suggest that you consider recasting him as, shall we say, a public defender?"

"And if I don't?"

Justine Reed drew a long breath. She turned and leaned in, whispering, "If you only knew what we're capable of."

"Dolt." Lishan smiled as the word eased through her lips. "Read my..." Lishan's eyes were piercing. "Don't. Threaten. Me. Good day."

The attorney started to speak, but thought better of it. She turned and left—speechless, defeated, hatred in her eyes.

What was it about the senator that could get a journalist like herself in trouble? Rhetorical question, she thought. There were too many millions, or billions, at stake. And, in today's world, where politicians and CEOs were beginning to get jail sentences, Lishan knew her own welfare was a mere pittance to pay if it meant some VIP's safety from the cell. She didn't expect the government to do her in, though the Warren Commission came to mind. The worst she would have imagined was being boycotted from the newspaper, but that was before the near *accident* this morning.

She opened the *Times*, heading straight to the op-ed page. There it was:

WASHINGTON JOURNALIST

PRONE TO LIBEL
By Senator Libby (R-NY)

Two days ago, a bright-eyed, yet brain-dead young reporter, from a usually prominent Washington, D.C. newspaper, wrote what she called an exposé about me and CEO Jack Conner. It included references to improprieties within the FDA.

She no doubt intends to set the world straight, and somehow believes that I'm irresponsible, a portal through which she will readily find injustices to be corrected.

Unfortunately, her efforts have consequences that cannot be overlooked, as they are damaging and false. Libel is never to be trifled with.

The op-ed continued, but Lishan had seen quite enough. She was mildly curious about the possibility of facing a libel suit, but that was extremely remote. For one thing, Libby was a highly visible public figure—fair game, usually. For another, everything she wrote had been checked and double-checked, and truth was an unbeatable defense against libel. Libby was playing his intimidation card.

Good, she thought. *He's getting desperate. I must be too close for his comfort.*

7

Charlotte pressed the key. "Mr. Conner, I've got Henry Krager from Krager Grocers on line one."

As he summarily dismissed Charlotte, Conner shifted from gruff to his dripping sweet marketing voice as he answered the call.

"Henry, how's my favorite grocery king?"

"This isn't a social call, Jack. That exposé on Monday—you know, the one that makes anyone doing business with you look like they are in cahoots with crooks—let's just say the board is up in arms. I've kept you from getting booted off of our preferred list on more than one occasion, but this time I might not be able to."

"Henry, you can't be serious. You know my products are the..."

"Are the what, Jack? I'm well aware of how many lawsuits you've had to skirt out from under due to shortcuts you take to increase your bottom line—shortcuts that resulted in kids getting sick from tainted baby food, for one, or getting FDA approval before one of your harebrained oils had been fully vetted, despite hundreds of reported cases of intestinal damage. And now, this crackerjack reporter is getting the public to pay attention. What the hell, Jack?"

Conner held back his temper, at least from Henry's ears. There would be time later for his tantrum. Right now, he had to salvage the situation. This was how empires were lost: one key player at a time. He would lie and distort—whatever it took.

"Henry, yes, I've had a few products that didn't pass muster, but they are not representative of the whole."

Krager paused before responding. "Look, Jack, I don't want to strong-arm you. We go way back. I know this. But the board members don't. I'll do what I can to calm the storm, but you've got to quiet that newspaper, no matter what it takes—if your business matters to you."

A moment later, Conner was left to himself. The calculating and conniving part of his brain had kicked in, seething. He pressed the buzzer he was so fond of.

30

"Get Jerry Hanson on the phone, and I don't mean tomorrow."

When Jerry heard it was Jack Conner himself, he was quite pleased. Conner never called him. Conner always went through Senator Libby. Jerry already imagined the praise Conner would lavish on him. *Yes, this must be good.*

"Hi Jack. How's..."

"Listen, you little weasel. I'm not accustomed to being dragged over the mud by some fish-wrap. Don't you call the shots on what gets published and what doesn't? Take lessons from Fox if you don't know how to run the show. I want that Amir girl muzzled. I don't care how you do it. People who bad-mouth me don't live very... Let's just say, it's not good for her health, or yours. Do I make myself clear, Hanson? And my name, to you, is Mr. Conner."

Jerry couldn't get off the phone fast enough. His hands were sweating and shaky. His eyes narrowed as he spotted Lishan at her desk.

𝄞

At a quarter to five, with a few calls under her belt to day-care facilities about their choices in toys—safety versus cost—Lishan headed to her flat. It was renovated student housing, serving Georgetown University. Her place was on the third floor of a five-story brick building, a corner unit with inviting views of the Potomac.

Her friend, property manager Erik Andersson, had managed to see that Lishan was given her preference when she was looking for a place to live a couple of years ago. Erik, who doubled as a government affairs professor, was quite fond of Lishan. He had met her a year before she moved in while she was a top student in his political science seminar. She was then twenty-four, having gone back for a master's in journalism. He was twenty-seven. Though the housing was earmarked specifically for current students, Erik bent the rules in order to have her nearby.

Lishan enjoyed living in her old stomping grounds, close to where she'd done her undergrad and graduate work at Georgetown. She found the eagerness of the students refreshing. The first-floor study lounge, next to the lobby, was always ripe with opportunity for intellectual conversation as the students represented a diversity found typically only in places like New York City, Berkeley, or San Francisco. There, she often ran into Erik, a daily objective of hers after returning from *The Mirror*.

The building had been renovated seven years ago—a tasteful renovation that retained the charm of aging architecture, including the fixtures. The kitchen seemed an anomaly, as it was fully modernized, leaning towards art deco but finished with modern appliances.

The apartments were comfortable. Windows and balcony sliding glass doors were double paned, walls and ceilings insulated. It was a quiet and peaceful retreat.

Lishan's apartment contained a master-sized bedroom, complete with associated bathroom and walk-in closet. She had a variety of wall hangings, mostly batiks from Africa, reminiscent of a segment of her family's origin. The oddest decoration was a fifteen-foot African rock python skin draped along one wall. The animal had squeezed the life out of one of her cousins

32

when Lishan was a young child. Her uncle found and eradicated the threat to the rest of his family. The skin reminded Lishan of her early childhood with its dangers and hardships that never seemed far away.

For the past two years, 4:00 p.m. was Lishan's theoretical quitting time—theoretical in that, as any reporter knew, reporting assignments were at the whim of editors and events that needed reporting. Early court cases, late city council meetings, an unscheduled public appearance by some celebrity or politician—each was a common occurrence. Lishan, however, had a fairly regular schedule. It probably had something to do with her walking in on an interview between Jerry and a young female interviewee, Jerry's hand well above the knee of the soon-to-be reporter. Jerry knew that the publisher would have severely admonished him and that Lishan was well aware of the codes surrounding HR violations. Lishan wouldn't have resorted to such blackmail, but Jerry didn't take unnecessary risks, unless he knew he could win.

Before heading down to the lobby, Lishan changed clothes, consciously separating her day job from the rest of her life. Hanging up her khaki pants, she reached in the closet for her stack of jeans, pulling out her favorite: a belled European brand made from hemp. They were all size 8, as Lishan decided long ago that she would never buy larger pants. Her waistline was a benchmark to keep her from gaining any significant weight. She did have one loose-fitting pair, though, for a week when she enjoyed one-too-many celebrations over pizza and a Hefeweizen or two.

Approaching the lobby, she heard a desk phone ring. *Something familiar about that ring*, she thought. Then it stopped her, the feeling of dread chilling her entire body. *The hang-up call from Monday morning. Am I in danger?* Now, with the taxi incident, she began to question her safety.

Erik spotted her. "Hey, Lishan. Are we all good about the Media Gala?"

Lishan nodded. It did help that he asked.

He paused. "Something on your mind?"

Lishan looked serious. "I...I may be in trouble. My safety." She hadn't seen him since he walked her to the taxi Monday night. She proceeded to tell Erik of the morning's taxi incident and the hang-up phone call on Monday. His alarm was evident and his smile disappeared as they discussed what it meant. Perhaps it was nothing, but they didn't know.

From a young age, Lishan felt compelled to deal with injustice. As a budding teen, after listening to the political discussions her mother, father, and their friends would have, she decided to go after the politicians and others who interfered with justice.

She also had an axe to grind as a result of her father losing his job as a scientist for the FDA. Lishan had turned thirteen on the day her father came home from work with a sad, angry look on his face. Her parents chose not to spoil her birthday party, and the FDA issue was not broached.

When Lishan was college age, her parents had pressed her, gently, to continue her education. She chose to wait a year. She had an Uncle Joseph who had impressed her with the value in seeing a little of the world before continuing her education. Within three weeks of graduating from high school, Lishan landed a six-month assignment covering food and nutrition alongside failures and advances in malaria programs in Nairobi, Kenya with an African journalist. The experience added realism to the dreams Lishan developed as a teen. The internship increased her insight into world poverty. Downtown Nairobi sported a business population dressed in slacks, ties, and stylish dresses, while half-a-mile in any direction found shacks with tin roofs and no running water. Africa expanded and amplified her views of humanity, of the U.S., and of her life.

After the assignment was over, she nabbed a four-month work-study assignment with a Parisian friend of the Kenyan journalist. Paris broadened Lishan's worldview with a perspective that gave her sophistication uncommon among American nineteen-year-olds. But it wasn't altogether different from the Western culture she grew up in, unlike Africa where the soul of the earth was exposed. When she returned home, she was ready to continue her formal education. Her journalistic calling to make a difference was stronger than ever.

When it came time to apply to universities, she found herself conflicted. As she imagined the coming years of her life, it was important to her to be exposed to the world, to the outspoken, to those who would not idly accept the status quo. *Send me to Washington to buck the politicians, or Berkeley to join the remnants of the hippies and radical poets*, she thought. *Or the Middle East, or Africa.* But she felt a need to mature just a bit more before going out into the world again. She didn't tell anyone, but her recent six-month stint in Africa had been frightening at times. She just wasn't quite ready to immerse herself again. Not just yet.

Philosophically, she had her parents to thank for instilling a Bohemian bent in her nature, a liberal view of life that nearly eliminated prejudice and included a concern for the wellbeing of all creatures. This made Berkeley a temptation, but it was too far from the tight-knit culture and family that she came from. Four to six months was one thing, but not four to six years. She was in no hurry for that much physical distance from them.

This left D.C., the hub of politics for the wealthiest and most powerful nation in the world. Georgetown University was just the environment in which she could meld together her youth, the catalysts of her experiences in Africa and Western Europe, and her burning passion to bring change. This would be the era of transformation, of an upward thrust towards the heavens of justice. The honest politician. She knew it was a road strewn with obstacles. But she could do it. She just knew.

The next four years found her immersed in the study of journalism and politics. Lishan blossomed as her shell unraveled, revealing additional layers of her lust to make change, the compassion that drove her headlong into writing, with a nature predisposed to the exposé. She embraced the populist tradition.

Alongside her formal schooling, she worked as an intern for *The Capitol Review* editing obituaries. This was the drudgery of journalism, as she saw it. She knew other interns who could not get past the seemingly compulsory initiation of calling the families of the newly deceased and attempting to make heartfelt bios of somebody's grandmother, or someone's son, who had just died. And the obituary was seldom just right for the grieving families, who let her know as much. She was told the newspaper never quite captured the essence of that important individual who no longer baked a cake, held the grandchild, or chased the ball into the street. Lishan felt relegated to a spot at the fringe of the action. It reminded her of when she played goalie for her high school soccer team. Some days she hardly got her hands or feet on the ball.

Then there was James, a previous intern who commiserated with Lishan about her tasks. He had "been there" already, having edited scores of obits. In the process of one of the critiquing sessions, he asked Lishan if she would like to go dancing some time. Not a date. Just dancing. She didn't see any harm in it, putting aside the stories of the risks of dating someone in the office. But it wasn't a date, she told herself.

They went to The Speak Easy, a hot nightclub in Georgetown. James had on his sexiest outfit—snug, black jeans and a gauzy black long-sleeve shirt, unbuttoned halfway down, a style a hot Broadway dancer might employ. They bedded one another that night, much to her delight. But memory of the elation faded the next morning when she began hearing whispers while getting sly looks from some of James' buddies. When one of the young women in the lunchroom took a sideways, lingering look at her crotch while whispering something about pleasure, Lishan guessed what had happened. As she approached his desk in the newsroom, his neighbors giggled, pretending to return to their work.

"Hey, James," she had said. "Is there something I should know?"

He had seemed embarrassed, discovered. "What do you mean?" She clearly remembered his attempt to disarm her questioning.

"Does everyone know?" She was still soft in manner, for she did enjoy him, and the evening had brought a hot sweat to both their bodies. "What are all those five-dollar bills on your desk?"

It hit her. Her voice was no longer quiet. "Was I your prize last night? Did you bet you could fuck me?"

His silence and withdrawal answered her question.

"Jesus, like I was just some trophy? Fuck you, James."

For the next week, a strained atmosphere hung in the newsroom whenever she and James were in proximity. It was an uncomfortable feeling. Both wished they hadn't indulged their fantasies that night. Lishan swore: never again.

But "never again" occurred much sooner than she imagined. One month after James won his bet, Lishan was assigned a temporary beat assisting Nels, a seasoned reporter, covering the county police. Rafael, a new intern, came onboard to take over Lishan's obit role. Lishan was given the task of getting him up to speed with the intricacies of obituary writing.

Looking back, Lishan wasn't exactly sure what she emitted, but she ended up in bed again—a bed complete with an aspiring intern who clearly wanted her attention. She could see, or feel, it coming, since within two days of sitting next to Rafael, he began brushing his leg against hers as they sat in front of the comput-er screen. It seemed innocent enough, with the apparent focus still on the monitor, but she still found her breath quickening more often than not. One week after his arrival, he approached her at the end of the day with a proposal to get a bite. He was built much like James. *Do all male interns fit a certain model?* she thought.

Lishan couldn't hold herself blameless for the evening, but, later, she did feel as though she was again the prize. It wouldn't be so bad, not bad at all, if it weren't for the fact that, here again, he worked in the very same newsroom that she did. She did manage to maneuver out of a full overnight. At least, she thought, she had the presence of mind to hold back a little, min-imizing further implications.

The next day, Rafael was cozier than ever whenever she sat next to him. She tried to keep appearances professional, but he just wouldn't have it. His arm was around her neck; his hand was much too personal on her thigh. He was making a state-ment. At twenty-two, Rafael had made his mark in the news-room. Lishan couldn't be absolved from her part in the affair, but she did have a strong desire to be discreet. She didn't mind people finding out. She just wanted to keep her professional side professional.

Her sense of doom was compounded when James walked by, lingering for effect as he touched her hair, saying "Hey, Lish-an" in a sultry manner before sauntering off.

Rafael caught the innuendo, standing abruptly, towering. "Damn, Lishan," his voice a little too loud as he gathered his pride. "Who else?" Embarrassed in front of his peers, he stormed out. He wasn't seen the rest of the day.

The entire newsroom had gone quiet. Some of the women wore an expression of sorrow for their comrade, taken down in action.

Lishan just sat there for what seemed like an hour, though it was a mere moment. And exactly what had she been think-ing—or not—when she slept with him that evening? This was the very thought that continued to cross her mind. Couldn't she rein in her hormones, at least at work? She decided this would be a good time to manage her life just a little bit better.

One of the editors—Beth Atkinson in Lifestyles—had been watching Lishan mature in the organization, noticing her pain and how she handled herself. After Beth put in a good word, Lishan was moved to a paid assignment as a reporter in Beth's

37

department, with a probationary period of three months. Lishan managed to survive the three months and became a full-fledged member of the newsroom.

Though Lishan was delighted, she knew the Lifestyles department wasn't her game. She could see the value in the features dealing with the arts, music, literature, performances, or the human elements of the community. But Lishan felt she was geared more for the dirt and grime. She knew her passion was aimed at the corruption in Washington, in the world. A position opened as a city reporter, and Lishan made the move. Just what she was looking for.

Within a couple of years, she had earned a reputation in the D.C. area for being a no-nonsense reporter with an eye for deceit, for finding the telling fingerprint that was often missed.

But Lishan's reputation came with a price. She also became a target, and she began to receive an increasing number of hate letters and warnings. "We know where your sister lives"—threats designed to get her attention. Lishan doubted her assailant knew anything of her family, but the inference was clear.

Her first principal target-to-be arrived in the form of an article in one of the underground weeklies she read. Jack Conner—CEO of both Conner Foods and Conner Pharmaceuticals—was a blight in the world community. The more she read of Conner, the more infuriated she grew. She felt the conglomerates, especially those run by the power-hungry elite, were responsible parties in a world too often dictated to, rather than run by, the people. "Connered" was practically a verb, as when Clinton was "Lewinskied." A verb associated with fear in certain circles.

Lishan had heard Conner's name often in her years in journalism. Yet the head editors had always managed to direct the feisty reporter away from this extreme capitalist.

- - -

Many of the articles that spurred Lishan into action early in her career were written by Janet Swenson, a seasoned reporter for the alternative paper *The People's Advocate*. Swenson had peeled back the layers of the likes of Conner until the stench behind the façade was revealed. The newspaper's relatively small circulation and Swenson's sixty-five years allowed her to take on such dangerous territory without too much fear of retribution. The paper, and the sage reporter, were both looked upon by the conglomerate CEOs as a nuisance, but not worthy of any concrete action. Only activists and those keeping tabs on the activists read papers of this kind. *Too bad,* Lishan thought. Those who veered to the far right were the ones who most needed to read the liberal viewpoints, to open their eyes.

Research on Conner left her with two distinct images of this behemoth financier. One was of a giant of a man, creating huge, pseudo-benevolent empires where only dirt and trash had existed before. The other was of a gangster who stopped at nothing to increase his profit margin and guard the turf he considered his, to do with as he wished.

Lishan couldn't help but note these two reputations were clearly delineated across newspaper lines: the mainstream newspapers, with their Republican, economically-based viewpoints, slanted him as a corporate goliath worthy of the business world's utmost respect; the more liberal papers—those advocating in favor of the people and the environment—easily found the Mafia godfather in him, a godfather bragging a trail of death and destruction.

- - -

It was four years ago when Lishan dug in, Conner fully in her sights. The stack of goods she had on Conner made Lishan's normally neat desk look like the cluttered chaos of most of her colleagues. It was a stack that had grown into a tower without approval from the editor. Lishan hadn't bothered to tell her yet.

"What's this? Are you a Conner fan?"

Amy Reardon, Editor-in-Chief of the *Review,* made a habit of tossing feeler questions at her staff. She found it gave her insight and often advance warning of the adventuresome, if not troublesome, meanderings of the Pulitzer Prize wannabes on her staff. "Planning to lay bare the bugger, are you?"

Lishan was younger then. It showed in her surprise at how quickly the editor had her pegged. Lishan was nervous in her presence.

Amy Reardon was formerly of *USA Today* fame before she left to "explore other opportunities," the standard public statement made when "fired" was the underlying reality. No one seemed to know just why she had left. The editor was powerful; of that Lishan had no question. The principals of large organizations, and many a politician as well, were often seen in her office. Planned Parenthood, Teamsters, senators, AFL-CIO, the vice president. The list was long. Yes, Lishan was nervous.

"I've been thinking it's time to do a little piece on Conner. I thought...."

"You thought? It would appear you've acquired enough info to choke a *little piece* to death." Unceremonious and effective, Reardon continued. "And just when were you going to spring this gem on our glorious newspaper?"

"I, uh..."

"As I thought. I want a synopsis on the city desk editor's desk by 9:00 a.m. tomorrow. No, make it 4:00 p.m. this afternoon. Do it on your lunch break. After all, it's not an official assignment, now is it?"

Amy wandered off, checking other desks as a sixth-grade teacher might meander among the children to ensure proper oversight. Perhaps two desks away, Lishan could hear her mutter, "Taking on Jack Conner. The arrogance of youth."

Lishan knew there wasn't much time to pull together a convincing proposal. Still, she was a journalist, often with fewer hours than this to write a late-breaking story. She wasn't completely sure about the editor's stance, though it had been made quite clear it wasn't a reporter's job to just go off on their own. She understood.

What did she have so far? Conner was known in the courtroom, in the Fortune 100, in the press. He was not easily intimidated. Conner's first few indictments ended in displays that made the judicial system look inexperienced and childlike. He had a fleet of attorneys, headed by the grandson of Ben Milani of worldly fame. Thomas Milani took after his grandfather in his extraordinary ability to convince judges and juries to interpret the law to his client's benefit in over eighty-five percent of the cases he represented—an unprecedented reputation. He also had a flamboyance he loved to flaunt. Each time he won a significant case, he donned his bright gold tuxedo and flew up to the Village to take in a jazz performance at one of several venues he adored.

There was the case in 1999 in which Conner was acquitted when the star-witness in a food safety case went quiet. The witness was a supervisor on one of Conner's innumerable production lines who complained to the local health department and the press about sanitary problems on the line. He was never mistreated, but shortly after the indictment he received a cordial visit from one of the attorneys who thanked him for pointing out a flaw in the operation, and offered him a $250,000 check to settle out of court, along with a job offer at a small fish packing plant up on the Chesapeake. Not surprisingly, he dropped the charges, leaving the health department and the courts with nothing to substantiate a continuance. Four months later, he died in a car accident—a catastrophic failure of the steering linkage in the new car he had purchased using Conner's settlement.

Lishan uncovered five other cases that took place between 2000 and 2003, each similar to the 1999 case. Conner was the common denominator.

At 4:00 p.m., she slunk into the editor's office. To her surprise, the city editor was also in the office, notepad in hand.

"I hope you don't mind, Lishan. I invited Josh, since he's responsible for you and your work."

"No, I..."

"Let's get started. Josh, do you have the document, the one that Lishan signed, stating that she's read and understands the rules and regs for the reporters?"

"Yes, it's right here."

"Lishan, do you recall that a reporter is not to take off on their own, spending precious company resources on an article or project that hasn't been approved? I'm not talking about writing down a few notes for a lead you have. I'm talking about a continued investigation, spending hours of company time, on a topic without approval. Worse yet, in your case, possibly days spent without a peep to the city editor. What do you have to say in your defense?"

"I thought..."

"Again?" Her voice elevated. A few daredevils in the newsroom looked up, but then busied themselves with non-distracting tasks while the audible pickings were ripe. "You thought. If I hear one more reporter tell me what they thought was in the best interest of this newspaper, without so much as an ounce of respect for what those of us who run this paper think..." Amy stood up. "Okay. We're done. I'm sure you have *other* assignments to deal with."

"But, my proposal? All my hard work this afternoon?" Lishan was at a loss, deflated. Her arguments and justifications were not going to be heard.

Amy looked her square in the face, unwavering. "This isn't the first time you've been in my office for prima donna behavior. The waste of time is your doing, not mine. Give this some serious thought, Lishan. I will *not* have a newsroom full of runaway journalists."

After Lishan left, the city editor and Amy continued their conversation. An hour later, Lishan had her assignment for the next two weeks—covering the bakeries in town.

For the next six months, Lishan played it straight, gradually earning back her credibility with the city editor, and, she hoped, with Amy. She took a backup position covering meetings at City Hall, which ultimately led her to a position as a judicial reporter.

Then came the opportunity she dreamed about, though she was unsettled about taking the risk. Amy was out of the country—a holiday in the tropics. Jack Conner's name came up on the agenda. Indictment. Food safety. This coming Tuesday, 9:00 a.m., courtroom C-3.

Lishan wouldn't let go of the thought that this was her chance. She could be impetuous to a fault where her passions were concerned. *Amy will never know*, Lishan thought. *She's gone for two weeks, with more than enough other issues to attend to when she returns.*

The hearing took place as scheduled, and Judge Feinsted was residing. Feinsted. The name lodged in Lishan's mind. She knew that name. Digging through her desk, she uncovered the material she had buried nine months earlier. Sure enough. He owned stock, twenty-three percent in fact, in one of Conner's companies. Somewhat removed, of course, so no threads would easily appear. But Lishan had done her homework. There was a clear conflict of interest. The next morning's paper included Lishan's summary of the first day's proceedings, which were continuing into day two. But she managed to sneak around the copy desk editor's final page approval and add a comment questioning the potential conflict of interest, now lay bare.

By 11:00 a.m., Amy's phone had begun to ring. Her assistant, fielding the calls, forwarded a few of them to the city desk editor. He was not amused. The hearing had been put on hold.

"Lishan, got a minute? Conner? Feinsted? So?" Josh was furious.

"Feinsted is a worm. This had to be disclosed." Lishan was practically pleading.

"Feinsted is a personal friend of Ms. Reardon's. We don't hide the truth here, Lishan. But we do consider our allegiances, our loyalties, the damage we should and shouldn't do. All you can hope is that she'll understand. I think you're in deep trouble. Besides, you are making my desk look bad. How did you get this through, anyhow?" He paused. "No, don't tell me. I heard you were at a pagination station at deadline. No, this isn't good."

Within two weeks, Judge Feinsted stepped down from the case, sidestepping the conflict-of-interest issue as best he could. Within two days of Amy Reardon's return and briefings, Lishan cleared her desk.

That time in her life burned a path to Conner in Lishan's brain. She had to stop him from getting away with whatever he damn well felt like.

14

A perpetual drizzle and dark gray clouds gave an ominous overcast, stated the television weathercasters with their hyperbolic and judging comments about nature. It was Thursday morning. Lishan began her usual task of sorting through her mail at *The Mirror*—an array of junk and invitations to various events seeking news coverage.

A foot-square package caught her attention. At first, nothing appeared unusual, but the return address was peculiar:

Socrates
P.O. Box 399 BC
Washington, D.C. 20008

With minor hesitation, she opened the box, finding six cupcakes in a bakery box she recognized from her favorite boulangerie. A printed letter was neatly folded inside a blank envelope.

> "Dear Ms. Amir. I don't know if you remember me. I said hello to you several years ago at a county meeting you attended. I very much admire your work. You did an excellent job of exposing Conner in your most recent exposé. I was buying cupcakes for my grandchildren when I saw your newspaper in a rack. I decided it was time to send you a gift. I hope you enjoy these. Socrates is not my given name, but my close friends have called me by it for many years. Take care. Socrates."

This wasn't the first time she received gifts in the form of food in the mail. However, she could always recognize the sender. She tried placing this Socrates fellow but couldn't, chalking it up to the vast number of people she had met over the years. She hadn't decided what to do with them when she heard a small voice behind her. Turning, Lishan saw a young girl, perhaps eight years old, standing next to Kathy, one of Lishan's peers.

"Can I have a cupcake?" the little voice said.

"You have to say 'please', Jennifer. Hi, Lishan. Forgive my daughter. She saw the cupcakes. It's her favorite treat."

"Please?"

Lishan hesitated, only because she hadn't decided the fate of the sugary treats.

"Please? They're my favorites. Especially that chocolate one with the smiley face on it."

"Jennifer, don't..."

"It's okay, Kathy. They're my favorite, too." Lishan turned toward Jennifer. "Of course you can. What about you, Kathy?"

"Oh, no thanks. My jeans are getting tight. Say 'thank you,' Jenn."

"Thank you," the small voice said.

After they left, Lishan set the box aside and returned to the final paragraphs of the piece she was working on.

Two hours later, a scream from the other end of the newsroom stopped everyone in their tracks.

"Jennifer, Jennifer, what's wrong dear? *Jennifer.*" Kathy yelled out, "Call 911. Somebody call 911." She burst into tears. Her daughter had vomited and fallen to the floor, unresponsive.

One of the sports department interns rushed over. "I've got EMT training. Let me through."

Within seconds, he determined the girl had shallow breathing, with a heart rate double what it should be. Eight minutes later, after an ambulance screeched to a halt in front of the building, three EMTs burst into the newsroom with a stretcher. As they quickly asked for any information that would help, Lishan timidly spoke up.

"I think she may have been poisoned. I received these cupcakes in the mail today. She ate one."

"Do you know who they came from?" said the EMT issuing the orders.

"I'm not quite sure. Someone named Socrates, who says I met him at a meeting. It has an odd return address. 399 BC."

"399 BC?" a voice from a few desks away spoke up. "That's the year Socrates drank the poison that ended his life."

The head EMT relayed the information to the ER doctor he was in contact with.

"Are these the cupcakes?" He grabbed the box without waiting for a reply.

All eyes, especially Kathy's, focused on Lishan as the EMTs loaded Jennifer on the gurney.

"How could you let her eat it, not knowing where it came from? How could you?" Kathy was beside herself.

"I...I didn't know."

"You just eat anything that comes in the mail to you? And you're a reporter who pisses people off."

"I...I didn't think it through. The cupcakes were in a bakery box. I've been to that boulangerie so many times. The box was so familiar, I guess I just let my guard down. I'm so sorry, Kathy."

Kathy just glared, saying nothing more as she headed to the elevator, her daughter barely hanging onto life.

A Metropolitan PD cop, who arrived after monitoring the emergency scanner, came over to Lishan.

"Ma'am, we need to fill out a report."

- - -

As soon as the newsroom quieted down as much as it could, Lishan went out into the cool air. Her life suddenly felt in shambles. What should she do? She knew that checking on the child, the one who was laughing and playing only an hour ago, was the proper thing to do. She also knew she should never have let her have the cupcake.

Howard University Hospital. She found Kathy pacing the floor. Her daughter was in ICU. At first Kathy wanted nothing to do with Lishan, understandably. But as the minutes went by, Kathy broke down, her tears falling like daggers in Lishan's mind. Lishan approached her with an embrace. It was not refused.

It seemed like an hour had passed before a doctor came out to talk with Kathy. Jennifer's vitals had stabilized, but she had not woken up. Her EEG suggested a coma, but it was not unlike when someone is given a general anesthetic. The doctor was hopeful the coma-like state would pass, but another significant concern was that her kidneys appeared to be failing. The lab hadn't yet returned the results of the breakdown of what was in the cupcakes. The doctor said she would let Kathy know the minute they had more information.

Lishan stayed until some of Kathy's family arrived. She decided to return to *The Mirror*. As she entered the newsroom, a few of her closer friends came over, offering support. They knew Lishan had made a mistake, but not beyond the realm of error they might make someday.

- - -

Lishan's fury began to overtake her sorrow, though the sorrow was never far behind. She decided to head to the library, a place she hadn't visited much since the Internet took top billing. But there was still much to be garnered from its authoritative shelves. Besides, she needed to clear her head, and a strong coffee along the way would help.

One of her favorite cafés was on the same block as the library. Choosing a seat away from any windows, Lishan began writing notes in her reporter's notebook. The Americano was comforting. She wanted to get to some decent bandwidth and track down everything she could about poisons and comas, but there was little point to it until the lab finished its probing.

Her life was indeed being threatened. Not just a minor threat. There was no question. She shuddered involuntarily. One last sip and she continued to the library.

Shutting down her cell phone, Lishan entered the library, heading straight for the reference desk. Of the two staff members nearby, she chose the fellow with the long dreads.

"Hi. I need to find out everything you have on Jack Conner, the food and drug CEO. Also, anything on the FDA and Senator Libby."

The librarian rolled his eyes, but juxtaposed the gesture with a sharp smile. "The library isn't big enough, once you include the FDA. As to Conner, not much of the truth has made it to print. However...here, follow me." They wound their way to the political section. The librarian reached up to a top shelf, retrieving a book that had been pushed back out of sight. Before he handed the book to Lishan, he stopped, measuring up the client before him.

"How do you vote?" he asked.

"Let's just say the new administration is attempting to quash civil liberties and give us air we can't see through and water the color of industrial waste," replied Lishan.

"Let me guess." The librarian paused, contemplating. "Okay. Alan Frazier. This guy's in prison, framed under the pretense of unlawful surveillance, but it's known that libel is what irked Conner. We were ordered by the publisher to remove all of his books, but, hey, freedom of speech. The management doesn't know we still have it."

Lishan barely focused on the book at first, thinking about the author in prison. Jarring herself back to the present, she took a close look. *CEOs & Senators: Bedfellows With Your Food & Drug Administration.* It seemed full of pertinent data.

"Prison. Hmm. Can I check it out? Sounds like just the info I'm looking for."

The librarian hesitated. "It's a loan. Nothing formal. Return it to me, personally." The librarian winked. "Just know I consider it a treasure. Don't make any waves that will bring it to anyone's attention. Are you writing about the FDA?"

"Yes. And a senator and Conner. At this point, Conner is getting top billing since he is trying to silence me. I'm a reporter at *The Mirror.*"

The librarian made a sound, as though he had just discovered something of interest. "And they're letting you write about this?"

"No, not really. I'm breaking the rules."

The librarian smiled, giving a hint of a nod. He took Lishan to another section where he handed her two books. "These will give you some background on Conner, but they read almost like an autobiography. That is, there's not much dirt in these pages. Your best bet for your purposes is search engines, which I hate to say, since I'm a librarian. Good luck," he said as he returned to his desk.

Lishan picked out a stuffed chair in a corner of the library. There was no point in returning too quickly to the newsroom. Jerry would be sure to sniff out the book. Her initial foray began with the author's page. Who was this risk-taker? How was this author any different from herself? Frazier. A Philadelphia journalist with two non-fiction books about the government under his belt.

She checked to see who the publisher was. Undercover Press. *Ah,* she remembered. There was a small story in one of the publishing magazines. Undercover Press had narrowed its field two years back, profitable though the publishing house had been. Children's stories seemed to be their specialty these days. She imagined the sedative, an injection from Conner or Libby straight to the bottom line.

The kudos on the back cover were, not surprisingly, few and unfamiliar. It must have seemed a risk to have one's name listed in conjunction with this author. She did recognize one name, though: Howard Perkins.

The contents page. Lishan could feel her heartbeat quicken.

1. Who's on the payroll?
2. The elitists and their food monopolies
3. What's in a pharmaceutical besides money?
4. The injustice of pills you can't afford
5. Does the FDA protect the public over industry?
6. Government vs. the public: whose dollar is it, anyway?
7. Government vs. the public: whose heart attack is it, anyway?
8. Isn't monosodium glutamate our right as Americans?
9. Trans fats won't kill you—if you don't eat them.
10. The senator who could.
11. Check your life vest as you rock the boat

Lishan's eyes were wide. She had to talk with this author. Would he agree? She would find a way. Prison, though. She wouldn't admit it openly, but it scared her a little.

A poignant film, *The Shawshank Redemption*, came to mind, kindling memories of her volunteer literary work with the incarcerated when she was twenty-one. She remembered the four locked steel doors she had to pass through, to get in or out. The memories were unnerving.

But she couldn't let go of her story. Especially now. *Someone has already gone to prison for speaking out.* Perhaps this would be her life's work. *My calling*, Lishan thought, *or undoing*, remembering the cupcake. No, she would be smart. And there was always Howard Perkins if the author was incommunicado.

Lishan perused the book. She was intent as she skimmed the pages.

After one hour at the library, Lishan realized she needed to get back to the paper. She put the book in her messenger bag, just in case. She didn't want Jerry discovering it on her desk.

"Hey, how are you, little girl? Where've you been, by the way? Getting more cupcakes?"

Lishan hadn't settled back into her desk for more than one turn of an egg timer. She turned to face Jerry. She wasn't sure which tack to take today. Acquiesce or raise her gun. She realized that Jerry was the one guy she almost always lied to. He was like a bulldog. There was no reasoning with him, with the truth at least. And *"little girl"*. Where had she heard this? Then she remembered Conner and Libby—the pack. It also reminded her of the tragedy a few short hours ago. Jennifer.

"Just a coffee run, Jerry. Checking on a lead."

"Tykes Day Care, I imagine?"

"How'd you know?" An edge of sarcasm rolled off her breath.

"You'll make a fine reporter, Lishan. Someday." As he walked off, he turned. Through his usual smirk, his voice elevated for omniscient effect, he said, "I'll need that daycare piece by noon, Lishan."

Lishan couldn't just let this interchange go. "Hey, Jerry."

He stopped, turning slowly. There was something in her tone that urged a caution on his part. He just looked at her, aware that others were watching.

"Don't call me '*little girl*.' It's demeaning. And don't ever put your hand on me, like you did when I was in your office. How could you stoop so low to ask me if I went out to buy more cupcakes, Jerry?" She started to turn back to face her desk, but stopped midway. "By the way, do you happen to know the extension for Human Resources?" She wasn't smiling as she turned away and ended the dialogue.

Lishan gathered up a daycare piece in the works that needed polishing. She kept it in the wings for just such an occasion. Dubbing in "Tykes" where needed, she zipped it off to the city desk.

Ten minutes later found her outside, thinking about Alan Frazier and how to garner the inside scoop from him. She decided to return to the library where she could do some additional research beyond Jerry's prying eyes. On her way in, Lishan sought out the helpful reference desk librarian.

"Pardon me." Lishan leaned over, whispering far below library standards. "What are my chances of talking with him, this Frazier fellow?"

Quietly, he replied, "I know right where that book is. Follow me."

Pretending to discuss a particular book, the librarian softly said to Lishan, "He's in upstate New York. Rockland Prison. It's been two years, so I don't know if they still watch him that closely. But I wouldn't put it past Conner. Just be careful. Notice if anyone is watching you. Maybe you can pass as someone else. A distant relative, perhaps. Just remember that Frazier's story was one of the many nails headed towards Conner's pine box. You can imagine how that went over. Again, be hyper-vigilant where these guys are concerned. Gotta run." He turned to head back to the reference desk.

"Thanks. Hey, can I leave you a phone number, or email address, in case anything...?"

The librarian never looked back, just shook his head, giving a goodbye sign over his shoulder with his hand. Lishan paused, acting as though she were intent on the pages in front of her. Then she proceeded to an Internet station to search the web. She didn't acknowledge the librarian after that. Not to be rude. Just pretense, in case. Just in case.

1×10^{100}. GOOGOL. Frazier and Rockland Prison. Three hits. October, two years ago. It was a local story, Rockland's, not too much press. Conner likely wanted no publicity at all. Lishan wrote down the URLs she needed, a few key dates, and a phone number for the prison. She also took note of the front-page photo that accompanied one of the articles. In the background, slightly out of focus, were the head of the FDA and Conner. No, this was no lightweight issue she was getting herself into.

11

Erik was two flavors of geek. He easily spent an hour or two, daily, reading about the cutting edge in gadgets. Anything that spoke of the latest technology was researched a to z. He also had an incessant craving to watch all things related to government that aired on TV, from senate hearings to judicial proceedings.

Erik called himself Scandinavian, but Norwegian was more precise. He traveled to the United States at nineteen, planning only an extended visit, but he found his Scandinavian good looks—his sandy blonde hair, chiseled features, and lean muscular physique—stood out and made him very popular, especially with the women, young and old. His hormones and ego ruled; permanent residency was his natural next step.

He was nearly as fond of the women he entertained as the art he admired, though he quickly discovered that posting photos on his walls—photos of the women he had dated—created far more tension than he could manage. This left considerable room for some Post Impressionists, the artistic movement that paved the way for Matisse, whose art was also on his walls along with other Fauvist painters.

Erik dabbled in displays of Picasso and Dali, but the surreal aspects, for some reason, didn't always sit well with most of the women he dated. This was a curiosity he had yet to understand about them, or himself. Lishan, however, experienced and soundly professed a delight each time she was able to settle into his art, no matter his choices. He always noticed.

Erik had the fit and lithe body of a twenty-year-old. He'd always taken exceptionally good care of himself. Erik had nearly married once, in his early twenties. His study buddy, Janie. But they were too dissimilar, ultimately. They thought the shared love of literature and art would have been enough of a draw. It wasn't. Janie was too caught up in money, an unlikely combination coming from an English Lit major. She confessed one day to a relentless need to have the fame of Updike, wanting the recognition of *The New Yorker* and *Harper's*, the money of Oprah. Erik didn't share her passion for money. Art and women were his captors.

Lishan was clearly a favorite of his, but he had self-imposed limits around going the distance with her. The reason went back three years. Her name was Etta, the first student to fully straddle the teacher-student boundary he had successfully maintained since he began teaching. At nineteen, she was eight years younger, with an upbringing in Barcelona that had been beneficial both to her artistic views on life and her allure. The arousal he felt from her sensual writing, and her body, clipped the padlock from the gate. They both sensed it.

One evening, as he stayed late to grade finals, Etta walked into his office long after the political science building was otherwise empty. Closing and locking the door, pulling the shades he occasionally used to gain solitude, she knelt in front of his chair. Erik thought to protest, but she gave the "shhh" sign with her finger, all the convincing he seemed to need. Her hands fondled him to a quick erection beneath his black cotton pants. No questions or words were exchanged. Erik just took a deep breath, hesitated, and went with it. Their sex was hot and quick. Ten minutes later, she was gone, a condom wrapper left on the floor. He might have forgiven himself, accepting the biological predispositions in his body, but the illicit affair didn't last only the week he envisioned. Etta had other plans.

She was a "C" student, a poor one at that, with an "A" in mind. Seeing his predicament, Erik managed to make a math "error," squeezing Etta into a "B." One week later, Etta joined the army, eventual deploying to the Middle East. Breathing a mixture of relief and tentativeness, he had hoped to be rid of her, but his hope was diminished two and a half years later. He was sitting on a bench on campus, reading one of Lishan's exposés, when Etta walked up and sat down. She was friendly in their brief encounter, a gleam in her smile suggesting she had a secret for sale. He knew his tryst with Etta had created uneasiness where he might have otherwise allowed inroads with Lishan.

As to Lishan, his body's reaction to her presence had always given away his true feelings. From the first day in class—when she smiled at him with those light brown eyes, and the sensation he felt when she stood next to him at the end of class, asking about an assignment—he felt her in his blood. Even the attraction other male students held for her only served to make Erik more desirous. But was that completely true? Erik knew his jealousy was beginning to gain the upper hand.

53

After she left the library, Lishan walked briskly. Her adrenalin caused her to pick up her pace before she realized it had taken hold. Any yellow cab that slowed near her made it worse.

She had no clear thought on how to handle the rest of her day or the rest of her journalistic career for that matter. Could she work for a mainstream paper and still tell the plain truth, regardless of the advertisers and political conflicts of interest? She thought about the FDA, about the commissioner, Senator Libby, and, of course, Conner. Whom could she trust, given that corruption and greed seemed to permeate most anyone who was obsessed with money and power? Thinking back to the hearing, she questioned just how much she knew about the FDA. Her mind raced with ideas.

And what of her safety? She couldn't ignore the attempted poisoning. She hoped she was wrong about the cupcakes, but logic told her otherwise. Regardless, she had to keep pressing forward, but with both eyes fully open.

She needed to talk with someone. On an off chance, Lishan decided to call JoJo to see if he had some time for coffee and conversation, perhaps an interview.

"Joseph," a sweet baritone answered.

"JoJo?"

"Joseph by day. JoJo by night. Hi, Lishan."

"How could you tell it was me?"

"I'm good at deception, which includes perception. I'm efficient at what I do."

A beautiful blend of Puerto Rican and Italian, JoJo used to perform at Finocchio's in San Francisco—a female impersonator club—while he was finishing his doctorate in molecular biology at UC Berkeley alongside a minor in political science. JoJo felt the performing balanced out both sides of his brain. Part of the act was singing, and the audience was never completely sure if the performers were truly male. He did look and sound all female—until, in a flamboyant move, he shed his blouse, revealing a definitely-male upper body. Finocchio's closed down, and JoJo, then twenty-six, moved to D.C., doctorate in hand; he found a job with the FDA in which he uncovered or verified the truth—

a job catering to his disposition, at least for now. Lishan took an immediate liking to this glamorous beguiler.

"Do I call you JoJo or Joseph?"

"JoJo to you, sweet brown-eyes."

Lishan could feel herself flush. He had real charm—this sweet male in feminine packaging. "I called to ask if you might have some time to talk. I've got a few things on my mind. Also, for one of my next exposés, perhaps I could interview you sometime about the FDA, about trans...." She stopped midsentence when a mother and young daughter walked by.

"Genders? Are you changing course, sweetie?"

"Fats. Trans...fats." She laughed as best she could.

JoJo chuckled. "*Avec plaisir.* I happen to have an opening, just for you. What would you say to Madame's Organ in 30? I just love that place, the community."

Lishan hadn't expected such enthusiasm. She was pleased. "As cute as you are, know that I've got some serious concerns I need to talk about. I hope that's not a disappointment."

"Lishy, Lishy. Not at all." JoJo tempered his enthusiasm to match Lishan's somber tone. "You *sound* serious. By the way, I read your exposé. I saw a Wanted poster with your mug on it in the lunchroom. I'm kidding...somewhat. Not to worry."

Lishan took a long breath and continued, "I want to thank you for your intervention at the Gala. Your wit was timely and welcome. And your outfit!"

"Again, my pleasure. I felt particularly impish that eve. See you in 30?"

Lishan navigated the Red Line to within walking distance of the neighborhood of Adams Morgan, just north of the Capitol. The two-story pub, with a rooftop covered patio, had made an impression on everyone she knew who had gone there. It had a Bohemian atmosphere, memorable in itself, but the name-play was what carried it from tongue to tongue. *Whimsical,* she thought.

She waited outside for only a few minutes before catching sight of JoJo's stylish figure striding in her direction. He was dressed in a white sundress with pink polka-dots, falling with a flare just above the knee. His matching sunhat had a large brim with colors reversed from the dress. The Gucci sunglasses, large and round, nicely bridged the distance between the hat and the bright, red-lipped smile. His smooth *dulce de leche* exterior, outlined against the dazzle of Hollywood fashion opulence, provided a stunning hit to the senses.

"Aren't you a darling to meet me, you beautiful girl, you!" He smiled, giving Lishan a grand hug.

Lishan managed a smile in return.

JoJo sensed that something was bothering her. "Let's go in. I'm quite famished."

"Is this an FDA-approved establishment?" Lishan asked, attempting to interject a playful tone.

"Thirty years ago, that might have meant something. Today, the FDA's reputation is tarnished—not beyond repair, but the trust has been damaged."

They went upstairs to the rooftop open-air patio.

JoJo ordered a butter-leaf salad with a side of cottage cheese. "Girlie figure, you know." He winked at Lishan.

Lishan followed suit, minus the cottage cheese but with a side of grilled salmon.

After sitting down, Lishan pulled out her Moleskine journal then reached over and felt the hem of JoJo's dress. "Do you always dress like this at the Agency?"

"I used to be more conservative. One sunny day, I wore a dress similar to this one and was threatened by a white-shirt-and-tie manager. Within three hours, my attorney had issued a cease-and-desist to the manager, the manager's manager, the FDA commissioner, and the FDA's HR department. I'm no slouch when it comes to these matters."

"Impressive. I didn't realize you traveled in such circles."

"Try stepping outside of the mainstream, and it becomes readily apparent what one must do to maintain a voice. It's unfortunate that some of our species only respond when the dollars in their pocket are threatened. We'd like to think humanitarian considerations take center stage, but it's not fully instilled, apparently." JoJo adjusted his dress and let his smile fade. "I gather you want to know the insider scoop on the FDA, but there's something else, isn't there?"

"Yes. Something else." Lishan's eyes welled up. "Someone—Jack Conner, I believe—is trying to shut me up. Murder is more like it."

JoJo reached over and touched the few tears that fell. "Talk to me. I'm here, for as long as you want."

"You know the exposé I wrote. Ever since then, I have been threatened. Until today, I wasn't sure to what degree. Now, I think I know, and it's not pretty." She proceeded to tell JoJo about the taxi incident, about the pocketknife Conner used on her. She managed a deep breath and then told him about the poisoning. It was difficult getting it out, as the emotional drain kept diffusing her words. When she had finished, JoJo reached over and took Lishan's hands.

"We'll get through this, you know. You're smart, and you have friends like me who have your back."

They spoke of the obvious—avoiding her usual hangouts; being hyper vigilant; possibly moving; putting Conner in prison, as difficult as it might be.

"Is my exposé really worth murdering me?"

"Lishan, I don't know this for a fact, but that exposé of yours may have caused problems in some boardrooms across the country—people whose livelihoods depend on reputations, on alliances, on perceptions. If Conner got just one call from a major client, one call threatening to pull up stakes if Conner couldn't get a lid on his notoriety, then a man like Conner would stop at nothing. Truly nothing."

Lishan took in the gravity of JoJo's words. She didn't speak for a couple of minutes. JoJo sat quietly, letting her unfold on her own time. After they exhausted the list of things to consider, Lishan finally sat back, looking out toward the trees.

"JoJo, I needed this. You have helped so much." Lishan shifted in her seat. "Could we change the subject? I need a break from this nightmare, at least for now."

"Of course, my dear. Of course. What would you like to talk about? You mentioned on the phone a possible interview."

"Yes, an interview." Lishan paused, taking in that she could focus on something besides her impending demise. "For one, I want our readers—the public—to know why the FDA doesn't put them first."

JoJo blinked to acknowledge the statement, taking a delicate bite of his salad before leaning forward. "You should know I'm on your side. I want the Agency to come clean. But I wouldn't suggest that most of the FDA's workforce isn't duty bound. There's an ethic that runs deep, one where the average Josephine in any department wants to protect and save the world. Unfortunately, certain FDA officials are prone to lobbyist persuasion. Then, of course, there's the ever-greedy industry, and a few complicit senators."

"But why allow the dishonesty? Why not promote the truth, with philanthropy at the heart? Something's wrong when eleven drugs are taken off the market in the short span of a few years— I believe it was 1997 to 2000. If I recall correctly, Baycol was one of them, causing thirty-one deaths before it was removed. And then there's the deceit about trans fats."

JoJo took another bite and sat back to deliberate. "I just think it will take a calamity of gigantic proportions, one that shifts people's views on life and what's important."

"And thirty-one deaths are not a calamity?"

"I agree with you. But some people would say that thirty-one deaths and a few less-than-perfect drugs don't compare with the benefits of what passes through the FDA's gates. You're familiar with Maslow's Hierarchy? Of course you are. It would take a catastrophe to get people—especially the middle- and upper-classes—to look below their lofty positions and see how much of the world lives at the lower levels from day-to-day. Until they do, they won't begin to really care about humanistic principles. So, it depends upon whether an individual is related to those thirty-one, or perhaps to the thousands in the Vioxx fiasco, as opposed to those whose lives were saved through the FDA."

"Or, as opposed to profits."

"Yes, profits. The almighty denominator. Makes me think of Conner."

Lishan liked what she saw in this sweet male before her. Her curiosity drifted to the possible number of FDA employees who cross-dressed.

Lishan asked, "Can I buy you a Redhook? ESB?"

JoJo's smile was all it took for Lishan to call out for two of her favorite beers.

"Would it matter?" Lishan chided. "Your agency spends only five percent of its budget on safety, as I hear."

"Now, now. Let's not be calling a spade a spade."

"You shouldn't use that expression."

JoJo smiled. "Ah, I see. You truly are negotiating a paradigm free of oppression. So no 'gypped' or 'lame'?"

"Exactly." Lishan paused. "Can we talk about trans fat labeling? Industry doesn't want the public to know the truth if it interferes with profits. And the FDA supports it."

JoJo's face lost its brightness. "I've gone head-to-head with my manager on this very issue. I'll send my latest letter to you." JoJo took a sip of his Redhook. "Industry lies to us, Lishan. Their lobbyists ply members of Congress, who squeeze the FDA. Industry's scientists—some, at least—are paid to make the product look good to the FDA, make it at least appear safe. If they do a study *showing* that a toxic constituent—trans fat, for example—is innocuous, safe, in low quantities, they often convince the FDA to let it be listed as zero quantity. Studies are often swayed when money, or one's employment, is at stake." JoJo sat back, drawing in a full breath. "It makes me furious. My apologies."

"Don't apologize. Getting worked up can be a prime motivator. Hey, maybe Libby should promote a law that'll allow these CEOs to put cocaine or nicotine in their food products so people will get hooked. The quantities will be below some standard, so they can be labeled as zero. What's half a gram of cocaine in a serving? Think of the money they would make. Maybe *that* would get the public's attention." Lishan followed her light smile with a grimace.

JoJo touched her hand. "You know, the FDA used to require a comment on the labeling: 'Intake of trans fats should be as low as possible.' Do you know who got in the way and had it removed? Members of the food industry. More specifically, large food processing companies represented by—at the time—the National Food Processors Association. Can't have the public's health get in the way of sales, now can we? But the FDA and Congress need to take the ultimate responsibility, unless of course we expect the public to stand up for its rights. In this country? I don't know. Apathy reigns."

JoJo enjoyed a healthy swig of his beer, intending to let Lishan steer the balance of the conversation. He let his gaze shift to the leaves shimmering in a nearby tree.

"Someday we should commingle our ideas on how the Agency should be run," JoJo said, his smile returning. "Perhaps we should change the name to the Food and Drug Cartel."

"Nice." Lishan lips smiled, but her eyes retained an underlying sadness. Raising her beer for a toast, she said, "To the FDC. Now, what else do you do—besides sing and save the world?"

"Ah. Here's a peek into my world. It can be dry, but it'll be quick, I assure you. We have the Division of Dietary Supplement Programs, the New Dietary Ingredient Review Team, the Clinical Evaluation Team, and the Infant Formula and Medical Foods Staff. All top-quality scientists, excluding Rafferty, a bought and paid-for manager. You should see the list of perks he has accumulated. I can tell you the FDA is no slouch organization to get into, minus nepotism and appointees who contributed to a political career or two...or three."

JoJo looked pensive. "More specifically, for your notes, I'm a regulatory reviewer—an interdisciplinary scientist for CFSAN.

Sorry—for the Center for Food Safety and Applied Nutrition. If you care to drill down a bit deeper," JoJo winked, "you'll find me in On-Lids. Don't you just love it! It's O-N-L-D-S, which is another way of saying the Office of Nutrition Labeling and Dietary Supplements. They require—at least on paper—critical thinking, evaluative and comparative analysis, classes on drugs and clinical trials, how drugs are developed, clinical pharmacology, and your basic chemistry and biology."

"Impressive. Left foot in science; right in dance. But I must ask, are *you* ever nudged to smooth the path of a food or label's acceptance? Perhaps an all-expense-paid weekend in Jamaica, or your continued employment?"

JoJo quieted, looking like a passport officer at the St. Petersburg airport in the former U.S.S.R.—stone cold. "When I first arrived at College Park, where CFSAN is, I had a bent to correct a flaw in a misleading label. I was younger, naive. It didn't take long to discover that seriously questioning certain past decisions was the fast track to the sup's office. I was hell bent..."

"You told me once, or at least inferred, that you're not a Christian."

JoJo's eyes sparkled. "There I was, atheist in full bloom, abusing the fundamental tenets of my maker—my FDA boss—in order to advance social change within the department. I wanted to steer these tenets away from pro-industry and into pro-public."

Lishan interjected: "The façade is that the FDA is all about the well-being of the public over industry."

"Yes. The veneer has been getting thicker. Industry became chairman of the board several decades ago, but the general public is unaware. The pretense in this case might be in the form of a label that states there are *no* trans fats in a jar of peanut butter, or a bag of potato chips, when in fact there are. Or it could be the label on a twenty-ounce soft drink container—one hundred calories per serving, it states. The unknowing consumer believes the entire drink equals one hundred calories. No—one hundred calories per eight-ounce serving; two hundred fifty calories in its entirety. Obesity is on the rise."

A searching look had overtaken the beautiful bone structures in JoJo's face. "You mentioned Christian. In one of my many letters to FDA management, I used the word transgression." Stroking his chin, he continued. "In college, religious studies consumed me for a couple of semesters. I recall, according to the King James Version, that transgression of the law is a sin, and the wages of sin is death. The scientist and philosopher in me, then, would equate the FDA's violation of ethics and morals, in order to satisfy the desires of industry, with transgressions—something like a parallel between physical and spiritual truths. I can see my book title now—*Death by FDA*."

Lishan smiled at the parallel.

"I digress," JoJo said. "Obesity. Those companies want you to purchase shopping carts full of potato chips and soft drinks. They don't want the consumer to cut back. How complicit is the FDA? Very. I was immediately moved to other projects due to my inquisitive, apparently threatening nature. I would have been fired, I'm certain, if it weren't for my panache and the newspapers crying foul on my behalf. The FDA avoids that kind of publicity. No doubt there are current explicit instructions to never let anything referencing a hydrogenated fatty molecule cross my desk."

"And the devil's advocate?"

"A Christian question?"

Lishan's cheeks lifted as she searched for a replacement. "How would the FDA argue its defense?"

"In the realm of food safety, it's a tough job. Industry wants to sell its products. Let me make mention of the Agency's stance in the drug world, which buys them a larger share of the jury's support and understanding. The Agency says that the public— notably special interest groups like those working with AIDs, cancer, and the like—wants those drugs with potential benefit to be available at the earliest possible date. Yet, this can create a situation where an increased number of people die or have significant side effects because a drug is released too early or isn't fully tested. If the Agency and the companies take the time they need to ensure the full measure of appropriate testing, then those groups—including Big Pharma, the shareholders of which want to recoup their investment and make millions as soon as possible—complain that it's taking too long for the drugs to hit the streets, allowing people to die prematurely or remain ill unnecessarily. Do you see? Of course you do."

Lishan jotted copious notes, careful not to miss a single nuance. "Then, rhetorically speaking, where is the FDA at fault if it has the odds set against them, odds like Senator Libby and CEOs like Conner?"

"Lishan, that's just it. The FDA does get a bad rap, somewhat—but only in part. It shouldn't allow any improper outside influence to govern its actions, though Congress has its way of interfering. That's where it goes wrong, not to mention that there's management within the FDA that's soft on science, focused on business. Remember when the Republicans took over Congress in 1994? They pushed reform bills that diminished the FDA's authority in order to push drugs more quickly out to the public."

"I remember. The commissioner at the time, David Kessler, was not a Republican puppet, and he retaliated. But the FDA Modernization Act was still passed. That was 1997, under Clinton's watch, I believe. The review process was shortened, be that good or bad. Bad, I think."

They stopped to fuel their contemplation. A moment later, JoJo continued. "Dear, I should go in about ten. No offense, lovely as you are."

He took a moment to look out from the rooftop patio where they sat at a picnic table. "I just love it up here. No enclosures—just open air. Somewhat rustic. I find it soothing compared to the sterile office environment."

Lishan nodded her agreement.

JoJo leaned in a little, briefly gazing into Lishan's eyes before he caught himself.

Lishan sat back, toying with her glass of water. "But isn't the public always ready and willing to do anything it can, take any risk, to mitigate one's own disease, one's own pain? JoJo, I agree with you, but I know that when people are in pain they'll consider any avenue."

"Ah, but if you try a drug purchased from a pharmacy or administered by your physician, aren't you placing at least a modicum of trust in the safety of that drug? And that potato chip package that advertises zero trans fats—aren't you trusting that our government wouldn't allow dangerous oils that have been scientifically and medically proven to clog our arteries, and worse?"

"Okay, but here's the difference. If I were given the absolute truth, then I could make an informed decision. If a physician or pharmacist were to say, 'Listen, your baby stands a fifty percent chance of losing a limb if you take this,' or your doctor had the training—another story—and told you that hydrogenated oils can ultimately cause a very early death...'"

JoJo's attention abruptly shifted.

"JoJo?" The tall, slender-hipped male approaching their booth had turned a few heads, including Lishan's.

"Michael!" JoJo slid from the booth, standing tall, fully embracing the newcomer.

Introductions were made. Then JoJo turned to Lishan. "I'm going to be bold and perhaps discourteous, but I have no doubt you will understand. I haven't seen this handsome boy in over three months. Can we continue our meeting on another day? I'll send you that FDA letter." JoJo stopped, his demeanor more serious. "Lishan, remember what we talked about. Your safety. You cannot make one slip. Not one. You have my number. Call it anytime, day or night. Anytime. Okay?"

Lishan forced a slim, understanding smile. "Of course." She turned to JoJo's friend. "So nice to meet you, Michael." Lishan stood to leave, but JoJo intercepted her exit, wrapping his every curve up against her in a hug that announced his body to hers.

More than a few seconds later, Lishan began her exit again, a scant blush to her cheeks. She turned her gaze toward Michael. "Have fun!"

13

As the sun arced toward its early wintertime setting, Lishan knew it was nearing her therapy appointment time—3:00 p.m. In her early childhood, she knew nothing of therapy, other than sitting and asking questions of aunties and uncles. Stateside it was different. One's issues were often entrusted to someone not of the family, someone unknown. She had her Auntie Niesha, but a few of Lishan's friends had spoken highly of the benefits of therapy, so she decided to give it a try.

Before heading up the stairs, Lishan called the hospital, hoping to get an update—positive news, really—about Jennifer. The nurse was cordial but stood her ground, telling Lishan that HIPAA regulations prevented her from compromising a patient's right to privacy. Lishan knew that going to the hospital was her only option. *After therapy,* she told herself.

Stella Fendwell, PhD, MFT—a medium height, forty-something, ten pounds overweight, edgy woman of British descent—carved out a portion of her weekly schedule to see clients through *The Mirror's* employee assistance program. Each could qualify for up to twenty visits. Stella's schedule seemed fairly open, while the alternate therapist—a kindly-looking African-American gentleman—was booked beyond the next two quarters. This did not bode well in Lishan's mind, but she had little choice if the free therapy was to be utilized.

Stella's office was on the third floor in a building next door to the newspaper. A view of the parking lot was all she could afford. In Stella's mind, if she were a writer like Thoreau, she might have found solace in the simplicity, but it was a far cry from the beauty of the woods, and she liked to think of herself as an upper crust Londoner. Being relegated to kitsch seemed to grate on her as she passed judgment on her clients.

Lishan had only her initial visit behind her, and those fifty minutes largely wrapped themselves around Lishan's childhood and the death of her parents. She had just started discussing Erik when the timer declared itself. Lishan sensed that Stella's attitude bordered on unfriendliness. Hopefully, it would pass.

Today, it was time to delve into her relationship with Erik, along with the seeming multitude of men she was involved with when she was nineteen and twenty and what some would call promiscuity. Commitment evaded Lishan, but she saw nothing wrong with her status. And promiscuous? Was that the label Erik assigned her?

Stella hadn't arrived yet. She was on the phone with Jerry. She knew Jerry had it out for Lishan. They were discussing a conversation they had several days earlier, when Stella told Jerry that Lishan already had one appointment with her and had made another. Jerry immediately saw an opportunity to make himself look good in Conner's eyes and had called Conner to discuss the opportunity, somewhat like the tattletale he was as a child.

"What did he say?" She could hear in Jerry's voice that he was pleased with himself.

"Conner agreed." Jerry didn't tell Stella that Conner hadn't treated him with any of the respect he had hoped for. "He said if we could use anything she divulges to you to help get her fired, it was worth..." Jerry paused for a mere second "...$5,000 to him." Jerry decided not to tell Stella that Conner had offered ten. *I deserve some of this,* Jerry had told himself.

"Five thousand!" Stella's eyes shifted to see if anyone had heard her exclaim. She was standing in the uncovered parking lot. She had also heard the pause in Jerry's voice, fairly certain he had taken the cream off the top of Conner's offer. "You know, Jerry, as a therapist I do have a creed that governs my work. I don't know."

Jerry laughed. "Oh, bullshit, Stella. I know you too well. Listen, if you want the five thousand—half of it—it's here already. Conner doesn't waste any time."

Stella already knew what tack she would take. "I'll see what I can do, within the limits of the law, of course."

Of course. Jerry just rolled his eyes.

"Besides, she did do Conner an injustice with that exposé of hers. It's only right. Listen, I've got to run. Lishan is probably wondering where I am. Catch up with you later in the week."

Stella arrived ten minutes late. Without apology, she simply motioned Lishan to follow her in.

Lishan sat down while Stella finished primping her short, bright red hair. "Let's see, where were we? You want to discover the reason behind your propensity for sleeping around, and why you don't want to marry Erik."

Lishan blinked. "Well, not exactly." *Who is this person?* Lishan asked herself. *No tact! How did she become a therapist?*

Lishan gathered her wits and proceeded. "First of all, I don't feel I have a propensity for sleeping around. Back then, I was finding my way as I became an adult, so, yeah, I slept with a few guys...then. And I don't feel it's wrong for me to not want marriage, with Erik or anyone else, at this stage in my life. More to the point, I want to know if there are any defects in my views of relationships that I would benefit from by uncovering sooner rather than later. That's why I'm here."

"Oh, I see." Stella shifted slightly in her chair, nervously sifting through her previous notes, wasting time by recapping some of what Lishan had talked about during their first visit. Leaning forward, Stella continued, "Would you like a relationship with Erik?"

"I don't know."

Stella smiled, motherly. "Are you sure? Often we know the answer, though we may declare otherwise. It lets us off the hook."

Lishan retained her poise, unsure of the supposed confidante before her. "Losing my parents in my early twenties left me questioning what I could count on. The pain was too great. And my boyfriends were too shallow for me."

"Fear, then, is a likely denominator. It's all right, Lishan. It often is...fear. About your boyfriends, were they in fact too shallow, or did you sabotage the potential depths?"

Lishan thought back over the past ten years. Rafael and James didn't quite constitute boyfriends. "I didn't have any real..." Lishan stopped.

"Yes?"

"I had a boyfriend when I was in juvie." Lishan stopped, wishing she had said nothing about her experience at the hall. "Perhaps it's nothing."

"Lishan."

Lishan looked up. Stella was looking straight at her.

"You, of course, know it's not nothing. Juvenile hall kept you off the streets for a reason."

Lishan felt uncomfortable in her chair, shifting noticeably. She didn't answer.

"Lishan?"

"Ms. Fendwell, what do you know of my reasons for being in juvie? Kids end up there for so many reasons, often just a minor infraction, or nothing to do with breaking the law at all. Sometimes it's about their parents and illegal immigration. Sometimes a kid is just surviving on the streets."

"Sometimes it's for murder, or..." Stella's voice trailed off, surprising herself as she heard what she insinuated.

Where did that come from? "I didn't kill anyone, Ms. Fendwell. A felony was..." Lishan stopped. She couldn't trust Stella Fendwell with anything further. She could feel annoyance building. Lishan looked at the door and then at her watch.

Stella took the opportunity to call the session quits. It wasn't clear if she saw her own blunder in her last comment to Lishan. "Okay. Let's close early today. Lishan, think about whether there are problems you have buried, past and present. I'm here to help. See you next week." The latter was not a question.

Lishan walked for the next half an hour, feeling caged. Finally, she saw a chain family restaurant, one she had never entered. Conceivably, she could find anonymity there. Choosing a booth in the back, she contemplated coffee and a breakfast special—sausage and eggs, hash browns, and a short stack. Breakfast late in the day always provided comfort. When she was growing up, her father would surprise the family with just such a breakfast, for dinner, if he sensed unhappiness in his brood.

"Hi. You can't sit back here. I'm short-staffed this evening and need you to sit up with the other customers." The fifty-something waitress turned her back to head toward the front of the restaurant, long and narrow as it was.

"Listen, I need some distance from people right now. I need to sit..."

"Look, honey. I don't have time for this. If you want service, you'll have to sit up front with the rest of the low...the rest of the customers."

Lishan stood. "*Low* life? Where is your manager?"

"Go for it. *I* am the manager. Do you see that sign, where we reserve the right? Maybe you should leave. You have just exceeded my quota of spoiled customers today. Look..."

Lishan put up both her hands. "No, you look. I..." Lishan heaved a sigh and felt her eyes moisten. Her breathing hardened, then began to quiet. "I'm sorry. I have just had one hell of a week, and my assigned therapist—who needs therapy—topped it all off. Can I buy you a coffee? You didn't deserve how I acted."

The waitress softened. "You neither, honey. My boyfriend was mean this morning, and I've been mistreating customers all day long. Rain check on the coffee, but I appreciate it. Here, will halfway back work for you?"

The two women shared a meaningful smile as Lishan proceeded to a midway booth. Sitting, she reached up and gently took the older woman's right hand in hers, smiled again, then ordered.

Warmed by a whiff from the cup of decaf in front of her, Lishan pulled out her notebook and began writing about the feelings that surfaced during the therapy session.

Lishan's breakfast special arrived, along with a side of fruit not on the menu. The waitress smiled, then whisked off. Lishan felt for the woman who was clearly burdened by the lack of help today.

Turning to her notes, she began to reflect and write about what troubled her. At the age of seventeen, she'd fallen in with a troublesome crowd through her boyfriend, Lucas. Her mother and father were leery of Lucas due to his disrespectful manner and lack of any thought regarding his future. It wasn't that he had to have his future plans nailed down, but rather that he was boastful about his street life and how it was going to carry him along. He had no expectations of living to middle age. This worried them.

Lishan was in a rebellious stage and was attracted to the renegade in Lucas, and her parents' aversion fueled it. Before this period, Lishan was a fairly easy child to rear, but this particular year brought fear into the family. Not only did she end up in juvenile hall for aiding her boyfriend in a small drug sale, but she was also pregnant. A significant concern was that she might be tried as an adult and sent to prison, as well as what she would do with a child at her age in prison. If Lishan pressed to have the baby, she would likely be in shackles during the delivery, a barbaric practice that many correctional facilities still employed.

Jemal and Anne knew their daughter was not a criminal. This phase was simply that: a temporary phase. But would the social workers and juvenile system listen?

Lishan had mixed emotions regarding keeping the child, but Lucas made it an easier question to answer by turning on her and treating Lishan as if she no longer existed. *Fine*, thought Lishan. *Just fine.*

Jemal made tentative arrangements for Lishan to have an abortion, if that was the ultimate decision—but it was not an easy one. Finally, Auntie Niesha and Lishan arrived at the choice.

Niesha came to the hall early that day. She had made arrangements with the administrators to spend additional time with her niece. The visiting room was spartan, sterile, and quite secure—three layers of security chambers, each awaiting the buzz that unlocked the door, made sure of it.

"How are you, Lishan?" Niesha asked with all the sincerity a caring auntie could muster.

Lishan had been holding it together, stoic at best, but feeling her auntie's love and concern melted the shield. Lishan broke down crying.

After consoling her niece, Niesha let Lishan know it was time to move forward, to make a decision. Lishan sat up straight, the adult in her overriding the child.

"There are several questions we can address that will help us to understand what to do, unless you already know what you want."

Lishan shook her head.

"None of these questions are asked without love for the child you carry. Yet, the world is quite unlike what it was a few decades ago. We must consider your life ahead, the child's outlook, and the community. Also, the father has left you as a single parent, one with virtually no adult skills."

Lishan could do no more than nod and grasp her auntie's hand, her lifeboat.

"One other compelling concern is that you were taking methamphetamines during your child's development. The risks to the child's normal physical and mental development are real." Niesha paused to stroke her niece's hand. Tenderly, she added, "You stop me if anything is unclear, okay?"

Lishan, again, could only nod. She wiped a stray tear with her sleeve.

"It's probably too early in your life to truly decide if you want children, but, if you do, do you believe you'll be able to raise this child well enough? Darling, it's time—you are going to have to answer this. I know it's tough."

Lishan looked up, straightening from her defeated posture. "No, Auntie. I know enough of life to understand that I'm not ready to bring a child into the world. Yes, I could give the child up for adoption, but I don't think that would be a fair beginning."

Niesha took a deep breath, as though she had been waiting to inhale. She chose her tone to ensure her question was not manipulative. "Are you thinking that you should have an abortion?"

Lishan's eyes began to moisten. Seconds passed before she could answer. "Yes. Yes, I should. It is what I believe is best. And you, Auntie?"

"I agree with you, but it had to come from you first. Your father has begun making arrangements, in case you decided. Lishan, how many weeks since your last period?"

"Eleven weeks." It was an immediate answer. Lishan knew the score—exactly.

"Okay. If it's all right with you, I'll see if we can make the arrangements to do this within the next week."

Four days later, Lishan experienced the pain that would postpone her motherhood.

Three weeks later, she was moved to a group home and then released to her parents four weeks afterward. She was absolved of any significant crime, given that it was a single offense and her adjunct role in the drug sale was a small one. Six weeks of community service would close the case. That time in her life was permanently etched in Lishan's memory, never to be forgotten. It was a time she used as a gauge for many of the questionable decisions she had to make, and it largely kept her out of trouble. That was ten years ago, but the pain from Lucas' abandonment, the pregnancy she was ill prepared for, and the loss of the new life she had created, lingered ever since.

14

Lishan was well aware of the walls she erected to protect her emotional self as a consequence of her past. Did this include an arm's-length approach to Erik? Perhaps it was time to dismantle the walls. But could she be sure?

This last thought nudged her back into the therapy session. What was to be gained by keeping her drug and abortion history in the past? She knew that it was a trust issue. Why should she automatically trust the therapist, especially one who was tied to her employer? And there was Jerry, with his staunch Christian right views on abortion.

An image of a child in a coffin bombarded Lishan's thoughts again, not for the first time today. She tried the hospital again. The same roadblock prevented her from getting a status. *What did I expect?* she said under her breath. *Why don't I just go down there?* It was a nagging question. She felt ashamed, but hiding from the reality wouldn't help. This she knew.

She arrived at the hospital. After making the inquiry, she was directed to the waiting room where Kathy sat, clearly exhausted.

"Kathy, hi."

Kathy didn't stand. She just looked up and nodded.

"You know I feel terrible. It's not the guilt that brought me here." *Why did I say that?* she thought to herself. "I'm here to help however I can. Anything."

"She's still in ICU. The doctor said her vital signs have improved, but she still hasn't woken up. The lab report came back. They're still working on just what caused this. They agree there is a poison, but because it was ingested, it's taking awhile to pin it down without any other information. They're also concerned about one of her kidneys. She's only eight, Lishan. Only eight." Kathy choked back the tears.

Lishan took Kathy's hand. "Can I stay with you awhile? However long you like."

"You know, that's kind of you. Maybe just a little bit. It might do me good to talk. My mother and sister were here earlier, but I was in such shock I couldn't talk much at all. I've had time today to relive our lives together. It reminds me of how important every day is. Not to let a single moment pass where we do less than our best, especially with how we treat one another." Kathy closed a journal she had been writing in. "Lishan, can you tell me, why would someone try to poison you?"

"Yes. Of course. You deserve to know." Lishan filled her lungs, exhaling her own fears as much as she could in order to make room for her friend's. "You know Jack Conner, the food and drug magnate."

"Don't we all. That sleazebag. My sister's husband was one of several hundred who got sick on one of Conner Foods products that was released to the public before it was fully researched. That was several years ago. We tried taking the company to court, but he seems to have the justice system sewn up in his favor."

"I didn't know," Lishan replied, waiting a moment. "You know my exposé that was in Monday's edition."

"Are you kidding? The entire newsroom knows. Everyone who's not management, possibly excluding Elizabeth Walker, was glad to see it hit the streets. Do you think he's the culprit?"

"Yes. I can't be certain, but there have been too many factors pointing in his direction ever since the article. He...."

Kathy's attention immediately shifted to the approaching doctor, who sat down next to Kathy.

"It's looking promising, but we're not on solid ground yet. The CDC and local poison control lab finally narrowed it to ricin, derived from the castor bean. This would likely only come from someone with an in-depth knowledge of drugs."

Lishan and Kathy glanced at one another. *Conner or someone in his employ.*

"From what I understand of the situation, the amount of the ricin toxin may not have been intended to kill an adult—just make you very sick. But to a child's body...you can understand. Jennifer has a strong constitution. Her vitals continue to improve. There was an earlier concern about kidney failure. We are still investigating. Rest assured she is our top priority." The doctor stood, gave a consoling smile, then left.

Kathy turned to Lishan. "I think I just need to be alone for now. I want you to know I appreciate your coming down. I know this weighs on you, too. Thank you, Lishan." As Lishan stood to leave, Kathy touched Lishan's arm. "Lishan, be careful. Conner will obviously not stop until you are no longer a threat."

Lishan nodded, pursing her lips. *Yes, until I'm no longer a threat.*

Fifteen minutes later, Lishan headed up the stairs at *The Mirror,* closing up her day before heading home.

15

Walking home—which she often preferred to driving—Lishan was deep in thought about her life, hospitals, and Jennifer. She chose only well-lit streets, since the darkness was a little too frightening tonight.

"Lishan?"

She swung around, startled, since she hadn't been aware of anyone close by. For a few seconds, Lishan peered at the helmeted rider straddling a dark blue twenty-six-inch Peugeot bicycle, one foot on the ground where he'd stopped. All she could discern was a mass of shimmering black hair flowing from under the Bell helmet. Sensing her confusion, the rider removed the helmet, shaking out his shoulder-length hair.

"Rafael? The intern from the *Review*?"

"It's been a few years." He paused, taking her in. "It's nice to see you. You're looking...good." Rafael smiled.

Lishan hesitated, fumbling for words. They never reconnected after that day in the newsroom.

"Do I get a hug?" Rafael wasn't waiting for an answer. He leaned his bike against a parking meter and approached her.

Lishan finally broke out of her trance. "Uh, yes. Yes, of course."

Rafael closed the gap, giving her a quick kiss on the lips and a hug that squelched any imagination.

"That was nice." Sensing she seemed reserved, aloof, he stepped back a foot. "How've you been?"

Lishan took in the form in front of her. Rafael had buffed out beautifully, assuming the stature of a vibrant young man exuding confidence and poise. He was only nineteen when they first met. Now, in his early twenties, he was a knockout.

"I'm, let's see. I'm doing okay. It's...it's been a full and challenging day," Lishan stammered, feeling suddenly shy.

Rafael picked up on her shyness. He gave her a friendly, slightly provocative, once-over. "Say, why don't we grab a bite? I'd love to know what's been going on with you."

"I've got to get home. I'm exhausted, and I've got a lot to process from the day. I should pass."

"Oh," he said, playing the disappointment card. "That's okay. Perhaps another night? Here's my phone number." He took a business card from his wallet.

As he turned to leave, Lishan hesitated, feeling the depths of the fears. She suddenly knew she didn't want to be alone. She blurted out, "You know, I do have to eat. Why don't you join me? I need to stop by my flat. I could take you out, or throw something together."

"I'd love to. I'm also pretty tired. Perhaps we could just stay in? Why don't I pick up a few greens? I could make a salad."

"I already have fresh spinach and butter lettuce. I could whip up one of my father's Ethiopian dishes. I think I've got it covered. Just come on by. Do you want to walk with me?"

"Tell you what. I've got one brief errand to run. I could be there in half an hour. Does that work for you?" Rafael attempted to attenuate his enthusiasm, but it was barely contained.

"Perfect. Here's my business card from the newspaper." Lishan scribbled a rough map on the back.

He looked at the card, and the map. "You're still at *The Mirror*. I know. I read your articles."

Lishan was pleased but conflicted, given all that has been tied to Monday's exposé. "Okay. See you in thirty." Lishan started to walk off, then turned around. "Rafael."

"Yes."

"It's been a rough day. I can't guarantee I'll be very good company."

He walked back toward her, touching her shoulders. "Not to worry. It'll be nice to just catch up. We'll play the evening however it's best for you, okay?"

Lishan nodded and continued her walk.

After putting on his helmet, he remembered the day she embarrassed him in front of his peers. In his culture, being publicly embarrassed by a woman ranked high on the offense list. He could not forget that day.

As Lishan strode off, she saw a taxi. Not a Yellow. Home in six minutes, with time to ensure that her apartment was not a mess. Enough time for a cursory check and a shower. She was reminded of the day's events when she found the Frazier book in her messenger bag.

Five minutes into the process, she heard a knock at the door. *Could he be here already?* Opening the door, she found Erik standing there.

"Erik, hi." Panic struck. She cared for Erik and certainly wanted to avoid hurting his feelings. She just stood there.

"Can I come in...or is this a bad time?" The next few seconds of silence stopped Erik's hint of forward motion.

"It's...it's a little of both. I have less than twenty minutes to get ready, but I always love seeing you. Oh, how thoughtless of me. Come in. Give me a hug."

Erik took in Lishan's awkwardness, the lack of assuredness she normally had. He stepped forward to hug her but didn't move beyond the arc of the door. He knew he wasn't coming in.

"You've got some hunk coming over, don't you?" He could see her shallow breathing. "It's truly okay. Look, I've got to run. I just stopped by on my way down the hall."

"Erik...he's just someone I used to work with some years ago." She drew another deep breath. "Okay, we dated once. I just ran into him half an hour ago. He's coming by so we can catch up on the last couple of years."

"Lishan, it's okay. You deserve these experiences. And look at you, you exotic female." He smiled, his attempt at levity barely relaxing the thickness in the air. "I doubt he's coming by just to 'catch up.' Don't worry. I'll see you later. Give me all the details, or at least a few of them." He was gone, waving over his shoulder.

"Erik, today...."

"Tell me in the morning, okay?" Rhetorical question at best.

Lishan felt uneasy at the interaction, but she had to let it go—at least for now.

地

"Damn." Lishan thought back a few minutes to the interaction with Erik. She liked him a great deal. Love? She didn't want to hurt Erik's feelings. Ten minutes left.

She squeezed in a three-minute shower, changing into her loose-fitting, drawstring, oat-colored Prana pants, and a gauzy, white, long-sleeve shirt. Barefoot. One last quick glance around the flat.

At the thirty-minute mark, she heard a soft knock. She knew it had to be Rafael, but a wave of nervousness jarred her equilibrium, given the close call with Erik.

"Hi! Come in. Any trouble finding the place?"

"None at all." Rafael opened his arms, inviting a hug.

Lishan felt nervous. *Is this okay? Am I wrong?*

"I like your pad," he said, his eyes settling back on Lishan after taking in the surroundings. "Prana pants. Gramicci shirt. Nice."

"I'm a yuppie masquerading as a hippie, or is it vice versa?"

"I've always enjoyed fashion." Rafael grinned. "Hey, can I have the tour?"

Lishan led him to the sliding glass door that opened to the balcony.

"Nice view of the river. How long have you lived here?"

"Oh, let's see. Two years. No, three."

They stood side by side, taking in the river's beauty.

"What else have you got?" He led the way, addressing the kitchen and his final stop—the bedroom.

Rafael threw his black wool coat on the bed, further exposing his trim body in provocative jeans and a Zara pullover open at the neck. Lishan noticed his deliberateness.

"What can I get you? Water, cabernet, Red Hook?"

"Please. Cab." While Lishan poured the wine, Rafael reached into his satchel and retrieved a reporter's notepad. A soft cotton pajama bottom fell out.

In her periphery, Lishan took it all in. She couldn't process it, deciding to cross that bridge later.

"I see you're going after Senator Libby and Conner, not to mention the FDA." Rafael raised his eyebrows. "Perilous territory. I'm surprised your editor hasn't admonished you for it." He watched her face for signs. "Oh—he already has, hasn't he?"

"You *have* been reading my articles."

"Yes, including your exposé this past Monday. I enjoy your work."

Lishan felt a knot in her belly. Rafael had an odd look on his face, contemplative, as though he was taking mental notes of things, of her apartment. She liked Rafael—was enticed by him—but was he keeping tabs on her? Was it just a chance meeting on the street today? Being stalked crossed her mind. And now she realized she didn't know him well enough to divulge anything private.

"Really? I'm honored. It's been a couple of years, so I didn't know how you felt about me. Who are you working for?"

Rafael paused. "Oh, I'm just doing a little writing."

"On someone's payroll?"

"Uh, yes. I'm still working for *The Capitol Review* as a reporter on the news desk."

Lishan flinched. She was curious about his secrecy—he was working for a competitor.

"What projects are you involved in?"

Again, Rafael fidgeted. "Oh, just the usual."

This elusive barrier to the truth bothered Lishan. She turned away from him, as though she had something else to do.

Rafael shifted in his seat, realizing he would be out the door fairly quickly if he didn't give her something to go on. But he had to do it without mentioning that he occasionally wrote positive stories about Conner. No, he couldn't mention Conner. He had to appeal to Lishan's sensibility, to her writing. "It's just a conflict of interest project," he lied. "Some muckety-muck plying both sides of the fence. Nothing of interest. Tell me more about your exposés."

Lishan felt uneasy, deciding to let the evasive action go, but knowing she would reveal next to nothing. She wove a limited story, promoting truths she believed in, but she also didn't mention Conner or anything that had happened to her.

"From my mid-teens, I read the labels on the foods we bought. My mother and father were big on truth in advertising, and on eating healthily. I began to learn about dangerous oils used in cooking, about the dangers behind artificial sweeteners. There is so much disease in this country. We have high rates of cancer, neurologic disorders, and others that I believe are directly related to...."

"What oils do you use?" he blurted out. "If you're the master, I should take notes."

Lishan felt a slight irritation. His interruption signaled an apparent lack of interest in her story, but she set it aside in the interest of adding some lightness to her life.

"Just olive oil—organic, expeller pressed—and water. Many mainstream cooking oil companies use solvents similar to gasoline to extract the oils. What do you mean, 'master'?" She attempted levity by throwing a sugar pea at him.

Rafael ducked, smiling. He studied Lishan's features closely, taking in the situation. He had a score to settle, but he would not pass up the sex, at least not this time.

Dinner became just snacking on veggies and chips, Pugliese bread and Gouda. Rafael finished his glass of wine within what seemed like two minutes, pouring its replacement, and topping hers off in the process. Another telltale warning—Lishan could feel that he was nudging her into submission. But she wouldn't have it. She slowed significantly, never finishing the second glass.

As the hour grew late, Rafael was clearly attempting to maneuver into an overnight with her. It all got to be too much for Lishan to deal with, but she didn't have the energy to outright oust him.

"Rafael, I've got to get some sleep. I've got an extra blanket and pillow for you if you want to sleep on the couch."

"I could keep you warm," he said in an alluring tone.

"I know. It crossed my mind." *Damn, stupid, stupid, stupid.* She tried to unravel her error. "I suppose sex crosses everyone's mind in these situations, whether they act on it or not. I'm just not in that place, Rafael. I hope you'll understand."

"Oh, of course." He kept his disappointment to a minimum, thinking she might capitulate during the night.

With the bedding on the couch, Lishan gave him a meager hug, then bid goodnight. As she closed the door to her bedroom, she saw the lock on the knob. She had never used it before, but she felt inclined. She locked it.

Sleep came at a price; the day had been filled with just too many events. Life-threatening events, and not just for her. An hour went by before her breathing began to slow, the beta waves giving way to alpha. She thought she heard the doorknob twist, which brought her fully awake. It had stopped, so she couldn't be sure. Still, she didn't want to chance it. Lishan lay awake for another hour before pushing a heavy box of giveaway books

against the door and tying a string from the knob to a tambou-
rine setting against the wall. She withdrew her camping knife
from its sheath in the nightstand, placing it next to the lamp.
Finally, sleep came.

17

Lishan awoke to filtered sunlight. The events hours earlier hit her full-on. After she dressed, she tip-toed from the bed-room. Rafael was awake, yawning, his clothes on the floor.

"Hey, bright eyes," he said.

"Hey. Did you sleep well?"

"Of course," he beamed. "I hope I didn't wake you in the middle of the night. I wanted to use the bathroom but your door was locked. I decided I could wait." He hoped his lie held. Truth was, he wanted to slip into bed with her.

Lishan felt confusion. Trust was not easy to come by with him, her intuition told her.

She managed a smile. "I hope you don't mind. I've got a full day ahead of me." She didn't want to lead him on.

"You know where the shower is. Take your time. Have fun today. It was nice to see you." Wanting to keep some distance, she blew him what would barely pass as a kiss as she gathered her messenger bag.

"Aren't you going to shower? I don't want those other men getting a whiff of those pheromones of yours."

All Lishan wanted was to leave her apartment and not of-fend him. Anyone, really. "No. The pheromones from last night arc minc to keep. I've got to go."

Outside in the hallway, she thought about her parting words.

"Damn, damn, damn," she muttered between her teeth. "What the hell. Why do I have to please everyone else? Where's *my* truth? I may as well have asked him to marry me."

"Marry who?"

Lishan swiveled to find Erik. "Oh, uh..."

"You don't have to tell me. I know he's still in there. And you probably don't want him to be. We can talk about it later, if you want to." The lines on Erik's face seemed a jumble of emotions.

Lishan was dumbfounded. *How in the world do they always know? How?* Sheepishly, she nodded.

Erik gave her a wink as he walked off toward the stairwell, the barest nuance in his face letting her know he was unsettled.

Lishan felt a little unsure of herself, absently heading toward the elevator instead of the stairs. Inside, an eternity passed before she pressed the 'L' button. How would she have felt if Erik entertained lovers? In the lobby, she proceeded to Erik's office but hesitated outside his door, not certain whether she should just let it go or not. But the glass windows betrayed her presence. He looked up and beckoned her to come in.

"Look. I want to say, 'How could you?' and 'I'm happy for you,' all in the same breath."

"Yes, I know." She hesitated. "Erik. I didn't sleep with him."

"But he stayed the night. Kept to his side of the bed? Look, I'm not at my best." A haughtiness overtook him. "I should get back to my work."

Lishan felt hurt, then angry. The anger won.

"That pisses me off, Erik." Her eyes had narrowed fully, the creases in her forehead deep.

"Yeah, well. Look, Lishan. You can do what you want. Perhaps we should talk later."

Lishan heaved a sigh. She thought to bring up the poisoning, but she just didn't have the energy to deal with anything more from Erik this morning. As she was leaving, a bright, pony-tailed young woman—all of nineteen—brushed past Lishan, calling out "Hey, baby" to Erik.

This wasn't the first young woman Lishan had seen treat him as though he were Eros. Probably love-struck students, she always thought. Still, he never seemed to protest. She tucked this one away with the others.

- - -

As Rafael showered and prepared to leave, he took a look around Lishan's apartment. He felt as though he were uncovering secrets, going through her drawers, checking her bookshelves. He had a surfacing feeling of revenge, a score to settle against this female who humiliated him. *How could she not fuck me?* ran through his mind. *Damned tease.*

18

At a quarter 'til nine, after a blueberry scone for breakfast and a cup of Mayorga coffee to spur him on, JoJo got off the Camden Line train at College Park, Maryland, then walked the third of a mile to the corner of Paint Branch Parkway and 51st Avenue.

Morning sunlight drenched the building that was home to the FDA's CFSAN. As JoJo approached, he couldn't help but notice the vertical architecture that adorned the array of windows, nearly appearing like prison bars when seen from a distance.

JoJo once briefly met the worldly architects—Kallmann, McKinnell, & Wood—at an awards luncheon, where he was tempted to broach the subject, but for some reason he allowed tact to overrule his oft-forward nature, letting the bars stand unquestioned.

JoJo's doctorate in molecular biology was key in his landing a job as an interdisciplinary scientist. He largely enjoyed his work, though it was difficult at times to answer to a manager—Bill Rafferty—who lacked the appropriate expertise for the job. Word had it that Rafferty was a step-nephew of Jack Conner, though he would never acknowledge it. *Nepotism—a potential web of inefficiencies*, JoJo thought.

JoJo felt secure in his life. He had plenty of money stemming from his education, his side job as an entertainer, and a trust fund left by his stepfather. His stepfather had been one of the few adult males who believed in him. But JoJo had often felt marginalized due to his deviations from social norms. He felt his position as a regulatory reviewer for nutrition issues—evaluating nutrient content, labeling, and health claims—would be a perfect opportunity to make a few things right in the world.

He stopped in the employees' coffee shop on the way to his office, wary of the supposed nutrition in any of the vending offerings. Samantha, one of his colleagues, caught his attention. She was eating from a brightly colored ceramic bowl filled with cooked spinach, her breakfast stop before duty called.

"Stop-and-Shop?" he quipped.

She raised her head, glaring through her smile. "Organic. Homegrown."

"Don't trust the FDA and USDA?" JoJo quipped.

"*Moi?* Honey, Johns Hopkins hit the nail. If I may quote: 'Food and nutrition policies are like sausage. You don't want to see how they're made.' You forget, I work here. I think a major multinational biotech firm influenced—overrode, shall we say—my last report. So, no, I'll grow my own, thank you very much."

JoJo nodded. Many of the FDA employees, aware of the oft-sought loopholes exploited by industrial lobbies, were exceedingly careful about their store-bought food. They kept an eye on organic standards and nutrition labeling, pressing to ensure the standards were not watered down. Homegrown was a much-touted subject.

"I'm with you," he said, departing without a morsel.

As JoJo approached his office, the phone rang. It was his boss.

"Joe, can you stop by my office in the next few?" Rafferty sounded prickly.

JoJo never did like to be called Joe, which is likely why Rafferty stuck by it.

As JoJo entered Rafferty's office, the manager didn't bother to look up. Rather, he tapped a finger at a letter he held.

"I've read your concerns, unfounded as they appear. But I didn't want you to think I don't care." Rafferty looked up, condescendingly. "Why don't I read this out loud, so you can hear what it sounds like? See if you can pick out the logic then explain it to me, if you can. I'll skip the formalities at the top—To Whom, yada yada."

JoJo half rolled his eyes, while Rafferty fussed with a few papers on his desk. Taking JoJo's letter in hand, Rafferty began:

As I review the stand taken by the FDA—specifically, CFSAN—I cannot fathom the...

Rafferty stopped and looked up at JoJo. "Skip the literary-speak, Joe. 'Fathom' is for Shakespeare. We are a government agency. Try 'understand' instead." He continued.

As I review the stand taken by the FDA—specifically, CFSAN—I cannot...understand...the allowance of labeling that misleads the consumer. Two cases in point: one is that monosodium glutamate—MSG—can be simply listed as 'spices.' MSG causes headaches in many consumers. Two is that producers are allowed to put a 'zero trans fats' label on the front of the package, when, in fact, the Principal Display Panel, with its net quantity of contents and ingredients, indicates the presence of hydrogenated oils, a.k.a. trans fats, albeit a small quantity. The loophole is an FDA regulation that allows industry to state zero grams of trans fats if there exists less than 0.5 grams per serving. NIH, in its infinite list of grants and studies on health, found that there is no safe, acceptable amount of these oils to be consumed. Not one gram. Not one tenth of one gram.

And just when did the FDA decide it could reinvent "zero"? Apparently, the U.S. government, at the undeniable behest of lobbyists—including Conner Foods—has decided to inaugurate a new mathematical concept. Read "The State of Pennsylvania v. Conner Foods, Truth in Labeling," a lawsuit stemming from CF's first foray into deceiving the public about trans fats.

I would like to draw upon quotes from our own FDA documents. One is from a budget file as part of a justification for the fiscal base. It reads, "The single most important factor in ensuring that citizens lead long, healthy lives and minimize the likelihood of chronic disease is the availability and effective use of science-based nutrition information."

Then there's the following letter, wherein we state unequivocally that no labeling is to be false or misleading. "However, FDA's research has found that with Front of Package labeling, people are less likely to check the Nutrition Facts label on the information panel of foods (usually, the back or side of the package). It is thus essential that both the criteria and symbols used in front-of-package and shelf-labeling systems are nutritionally sound, well-designed to help consumers make informed and healthy food choices, and not false or misleading."

I respectfully submit that the FDA is charged with ensuring honesty and truth in the labeling it supports and mandates, and that the transgressions I have mentioned need to be corrected. Additionally, my concern extends to the likelihood that these inequities exist in additional areas and should gain the attention of management without delay.

Regards,

Joseph Velázquez
Interdisciplinary Scientist
CFSAN

Rafferty rocked back in his chair, his excess forty-five pounds nearly tipping the scale of balance. He put his two hands together, rotating the thumbs around one another. "Joe. Joseph. JoJo. You're a good soldier."

"I'm not a soldier."

"A euphemism."

"Not exactly."

Rafferty poorly disguised his annoyance. Taking stock of JoJo's colorful clothing, he continued. "As I said, you're a good...employee. Since your arrival here, you've often made a point of informing management about your views regarding shortcomings within the Agency. Of course, there are *some* shortcomings. Every government agency has them. Look at the POTUS and..." Rafferty paused. "Forget I said that. I would just like to think we're better than average. But, Mr. Velázquez, you have pushed the envelope to the point of wasting time—mine and my superior's time. If you insist, I'll forward your complaint form and attached letter to our division management, a copy of which will be forwarded to the Inspector General of the Department of Health and Human Services. But I think you should reconsider. I personally like MSG, and every day I consume food that's laced—loaded—with trans fats. And I'm in good health."

JoJo held his teeth tight together, hoping to hold back the laugh that tugged at his face.

"I'm putting your letter in my 'hold' file, giving you a month to think about it. Your review is, coincidentally, due at that time. That is how we consolidate, how we make the best use of time here at the Agency. Now, I have a plate full of important decisions to consider. If you'll excuse me..."

14

Jerry's phone played "Life's Been Good," signaling a new text message. "Jerry? It's Stella. Have time for a beer?"

It was the morning after Stella's session with Lishan. She wanted the $2,500 and perhaps a roll in the sack.

"Let's see. It's just ten. When were you thinking?"

"Now."

Jerry smiled. He knew when Stella was feeling carnal. "I'll get someone to cover the final pages. Same place?"

Stella lived three blocks away—the third floor of a Hummelstown brownstone on a relatively quiet side street. It had served as a rendezvous for Stella and her escapades on many occasions. Jerry was likely unaware that he was one of many.

Jerry liked being on his back—a surrender, of sorts. Besides, being smothered in her bustiness thrilled him.

Afterward, donning one of two robes she stole from an Embassy Suites, she poured two Sam Adams beers.

"You *do* know I'm not supposed to share any of this with you. Client confidentiality," Stella said, sipping her beer.

Jerry reached in his pocket and pulled out the envelope with twenty-five crisp hundred-dollar bills in it. He didn't flinch when Stella counted every bill; he knew the company he kept.

"But it may have bearing on her employment, especially if she weren't forthright in her employment process. Did you know she was in juvie? Something about a felony." Stella leaned back in the couch, feeling quite pleased with herself.

"Nooo. Really?"

"She chose not to elaborate, which caught my attention. If she has a record as a felon and didn't report it on the employment forms..."

"I get your drift." Jerry grabbed a handful of pretzels from the ever-present snack tray on the coffee table. Stella enjoyed manipulating her friends and acquaintances into liking her, and, therefore, doing her bidding. Appetizers helped. "I've never liked her. She's a difficult employee."

Stella looked at Jerry, thinking of difficult employees. From her many clients, she knew Jerry had often crossed the HR line. But she would never breach the subject with him. He was too valuable an ally, having garnered HR file information for her on more than one occasion. They were complicit in one another's deceits.

An hour later, Jerry was back at his desk. Lishan walked past before he had a chance to view her files. He just couldn't help himself.

"Lishan. Got a minute?"

"Of course, Jerry. Anything for you." The sarcasm hung thick.

"Were you ever in trouble with the law? Just asking."

"Why would you ask?"

"Oh, I don't know. We always like to know these things about our employees."

"You ask everyone this question?"

Jerry's face hardened, nervously. "No. Well, yes. I do."

"Mind if I ask around, corroborating your story? Nothing wrong with that, is there?" Lishan was getting angry. She knew what had happened. But could she prove it? Unlikely, but she could stir the pot. "I have work to do. Anything else? Perhaps whether I belong to the Communist Party, or the Christian Left?"

Jerry furrowed his forehead. *The Left?* he asked himself. "No. No. You're free to go."

At her desk, Lishan called Jerry's assistant, Marie Elena, to confirm rumors that Jerry and Stella had some form of relationship. Lishan and Marie Elena had become friends over the past year, occasionally sharing war stories about Jerry. Marie Elena said that Jerry had received a call from Stella mid-morning, after which Jerry left for a couple of hours, returning with beer on his breath and a Cheshire cat grin.

Her next call was to Stella's office. "Stella, this is Lishan Amir. Jerry Hanson just confided in me that you shared my juvenile hall experience with him. I hope you have a backup line of work. By the way, I won't be needing anymore of your, shall we say, help." She hung up.

Within an hour, the entire newsroom heard "God dammit, Jerry" as his door was shut—more like slammed—by Stella. Jerry looked like a cat caught at 5:00 p.m. in the middle of a Manhattan intersection while Stella drove back and forth, arms flailing, Jerry in her sights.

The newsroom quieted over those next few minutes as every employee became curious about what the editor had gotten himself into *this* time. When Stella exited his office, she spied

Lishan and made a sudden shift in her direction, coming to within a foot of Lishan.

Leaning over, her jowls quivering, Stella whispered, "Don't you *ever* threaten me. Do you hear me? *Ever*. And, by the way, I *never* said a word to Jerry about you. Not a word. Nothing you could prove, anyway." Her high heels clacked heavily as she headed toward the elevator.

"Stella Fendwell," Lishan said in a normal tone. As Stella turned, Lishan continued confidently, "Look up ethics, when you get a chance. And karma while you're at it. Careful—the elevator is in need of service."

Upon reaching the elevator and noticing the impending service notice, Stella haughtily shifted toward the door and took the stairs.

Lishan looked into Jerry's office. He was seething, attempting to contain his emotions. In that single second of eye contact, Jerry picked up the handset to his phone. Lishan knew he was calling HR to see if he had any leverage.

Half an hour later, Lishan's phone rang. She was being summoned to the HR director's office. Jerry was nowhere in sight when she arrived.

"Have a seat, Lishan." The directive was not unkind, though not friendly. "It has come to my attention that you were once convicted of a felony, yet your personnel forms—that you filled out—state clearly that you never had such a conviction. You do know, don't you, that falsifying documents of this nature can be grounds for dismissal?"

Lishan looked at the director, not saying a word as she held his eyes. At fifty, Irish-born Ross O'Brannigan had long since let his health go—his suit jacket unbuttoned to accommodate the additional fifty-some pounds. He became skittish as the silence ensued.

"Lishan?"

"Yes, I heard you. I'm simply measuring my next steps, since you're approaching me with a false accusation."

The director's eyes opened fully. He chose his next words with caution. Attempting to place the blame elsewhere, he began, "According to my sources..."

"You mean Jerry Hanson."

"Yes. That is, no, I can't tell you."

"Reliable character, wouldn't you say?"

"Ms. Amir, his character isn't in question here."

89

"It should be." Lishan paused, then continued. "Have you confirmed what your *sources* say? I know the answer, since if you had, you wouldn't be accusing me now."

"I'm not accusing you."

"Pardon? Your direct insinuation suggests I have falsified documents. Do you mind if we ask the publisher to hear the rest of this?"

He took a long breath. "There's no need, Ms. Amir. She has more important items on her agenda."

"It's all right. I'll make an appointment."

"Ms. Amir, I can assure you…"

"No, no, no. It will be my pleasure."

Attempting to gain control, Ross pressed his pivotal question. "Ms. Amir, were you ever found guilty of a felony? Yes or no."

Lishan stood. "You should know that I intend to be fair and honest with you, that I respect the position you hold and your maintenance of a safe workplace. But I feel there's a petty conspiracy in the wings, of which I'm the intended target. That, I can't stand for. I believe I should be—in words our country supposedly stands behind—innocent until proven guilty, or has the new administration flipped that one, too? I feel the appropriate next step is for this newspaper to withhold allegations until it finds reasonable proof. Is that fair enough?"

The director already felt he was in over his intellectual head. He declined to push the matter until he could regroup. "Fair enough. Will you still be speaking with the publisher?"

Lishan simply smiled as she headed toward the door.

Friday afternoon, Lishan began setting her sights on the weekend—a much needed respite. As she walked up the stairs to her desk, her cell phone rang. It was Kathy.

Lishan couldn't answer it quickly enough. "Kathy. Is she okay?"

"They moved her out of ICU last night. We got a private room so I could stay with her. She woke up." Kathy's tears were audible. "We don't know yet the extent of the damage. Kidneys? Lungs? Brain? But the doctor was more encouraging this morning. I thought you should know."

Lishan's eyes filled. "Thank God. Kathy, I'm so glad you called. Can I bring you anything?"

"No, but thank you. My sister is here for the day. You take care of yourself, okay. I'll keep you posted. Go after Jack Conner. For all three of us."

Lishan stayed in the stairwell for several minutes, not wanting her tears to tell a story, any story, as she entered the newsroom. After several minutes at her desk, her desk phone rang. O'Brannigan needed to see her again in his office. Lishan took a breath and headed upstairs. She noticed Jerry's absence from the newsroom as she left.

Entering the executive offices, she headed toward O'Brannigan's and found the door open. There she found Jerry and the publisher, seated and waiting. O'Brannigan stood and closed the door.

Lishan could feel her adrenals kicking in. This was likely her last day at the paper, unless she was convincing.

Elizabeth Walker gave Lishan a weak smile. That told Lishan she was worried. Lishan hadn't filled in Ms. Walker about the incident, using her bluff with the HR director as just that—a bluff. She thought it unnecessary to follow through.

"I imagine you know why we're all gathered here?" A smug look spread across Jerry's face. He could hardly contain his glee, causing the publisher to give him a condemning glare.

Lishan finally answered. "Yes. You're attempting to fire me."

Jerry barely suppressed a nod.

91

The director continued. "Now, Ms. Amir, you shouldn't make such an assumption. I..."

"Why not? After our last meeting, you essentially accused me of falsifying documents, something about my leaving off a felony."

"Then you admit to having a felony in your record?"

"Did your findings prove that I was lying?" Lishan retained a level of confidence the others didn't expect.

"Well, yes." O'Brannigan began to perspire. He didn't like the feel of the proceedings. "We show here that you did a stint in juvenile hall, at the age of seventeen, as an accomplice in a drug deal. We have sources that indicate a felony judgment was entered."

"When you state *sources,* you must mean the confidential information I shared with Employee Assistance therapist Stella Fendwell, that she ultimately—and, illegally, I might add—shared with editor Hanson."

"That is quite an accusation, Ms. Amir. Can you prove it?"

"Do I understand that you merely have hearsay at this point? Can I see the document that states I was convicted of a felony?"

"Ms. Amir, were you or were you not convicted of a felony?"

Lishan paused, thinking.

"Lishan?" It was Jerry. "We just want what's best for all concerned, and we have our rules."

Lishan still remained quiet.

"Lishan." This time it was Elizabeth Walker. "All we're looking for is the truth." She was soft and kind in her delivery.

"Thank you, Ms. Walker. *You* are looking for the truth. The others present are merely seeking to prove my guilt, which doesn't exist." Lishan stood. Looking at the others, she continued. "My entire life—apart from perhaps six months at the age of seventeen—has been led with honesty and integrity. You have nothing—*nothing*—showing that I was convicted of a felony. Because I never was. All you have is word of mouth—a deliberate and inaccurate leak from Stella Fendwell to editor Hanson. She misconstrued my comment about a felony, because I hadn't finished my sentence. There was no felony. The authorities, at that time, questioned if my actions could be considered a felony, but there was a one hundred percent agreement that my small part in the affair was not felonious, that it was manipulated by a twenty-one-year-old adult, and that I, as a minor with an outstanding community service record, was to be released. I was never formally charged, never tried. End of story"

Elizabeth Walker stood, barely holding her anger in check. Looking at both Hanson and O'Brannigan, she asked, "Is this true? You don't have any verifiable documents showing that Ms. Amir was convicted of a felony? And, I might add, spending time in juvenile hall is not to be held against someone. I myself spent one month in a hall at the age of seventeen for running away from a dysfunctional home."

The two men shifted uncomfortably in their seats, looking toward the door.

"Answer me. Hanson?"

"I have nothing."

"O'Brannigan?"

"This was not my doing. Hanson..."

"O'Brannigan!"

"No. I have no documents."

The publisher headed toward the door. Stopping, she turned her taut face toward the two men, one at a time. "There will be repercussions. Mark my word. This issue—as far as Lishan Amir is concerned—is closed. Do I make myself clear?"

"Yes."

"Yes."

"Lishan?" The publisher motioned her to accompany her out the door. As they cleared the door, the publisher turned toward Hanson, who hadn't budged. "Well? Don't you have something...constructive...to do?"

Hanson stood and quickly squeezed past the two women, heading down the stairs and hopefully, he thought, out of sight.

"My apologies, Lishan. You shouldn't ever be subjected to such treatment. Close up shop for the day. Take Monday off. See you on Tuesday."

3:10 p.m. Lishan was back in her apartment. She wanted to spend time looking through the Frazier book, but it was nowhere to be found. Had she left it somewhere? If she'd somehow lost it, it would be hard to replace. She felt a little sick.

Text, outbox: "Erik. I have much to share with you. I'm not at my best this week, so if you're in a bad mood, I don't have enough energy for both of us. What do you think?"

Erik knocked on her door ten minutes later. "I'm doing okay. Not my best week, either. But I had to check on you. I know you tried to tell me something yesterday." He was annoyed by her "bad mood" comment, but somehow he managed to rise above it.

"And I wanted to this morning."

Erik said nothing.

Lishan still felt hurt by Erik's seeming lack of caring over the past forty-eight hours. She would bring up the poisoning when she was ready.

"Did I leave a book in your apartment? It was written by a guy named Frazier."

"Hmm. No. Tell me more about it."

The story about the reference librarian unfolded.

"It sounds familiar," Erik said. "Just a minute. I'll be right back."

Eric returned from his apartment, a book in hand. Sitting down close to her, he handed it to her without a word. It was Lishan's missing book.

Lishan was wide-eyed. "My God...dess! Where did you get this? Did I leave it at your place?"

"No. It was a front-page story in two metro newspapers a few years ago. I borrowed one from the library but didn't return it. I think the library forgot about it, and so did I. I didn't remember the author's name when you mentioned it. You can have it."

Lishan didn't know what to think. This was just too much coincidence for her. Was Erik playing her? Had she inadvertently left it at his place and then he decided to just shelve it without telling her? He had been angry with her recently.

"Well, uh, thank you." Lishan paused, her face muscles tightening slightly. "Are you sure this isn't mine?"

Erik stood. "Why would I tell you it's mine if it was yours, Lishan? Are you insinuating I lied?" His breathing quickened.

"Look, Erik, I wouldn't think you would lie to me, unless you were angry with me. There aren't many copies of the book in circulation, so I..."

"You *do* think I would lie to you. You know, I have some work to do. Why don't we meet up a bit later?" He glared at her, not believing what he was hearing.

"Fine. What time?"

Ice hung between them.

"Five thirty, at my apartment."

His departure happened quickly. They were both angry. *Now what?* she thought.

- - -

At 5:30, Lishan knocked gently on Erik's door. Erik stepped back to let Lishan in, giving her a brief hug to help break the tension.

"I'm sorry about earlier," he said. "I made a salad, and I have another favorite of yours—Potomac Pale Ale. Also, you're forgiven, about Rafael staying over, in case it was on your mind."

Lishan exhaled, then gave an accepting smile. She knew that other men—"extraneous," Erik called them—caused him a certain pain. She admired his strength. As she settled back into the loveseat, the pale ale and the pizza he ordered comforted her. He did know her, didn't he? He always had her interests at heart.

"Thank you. About Rafael. And the book. I'm sorry, too." The reappearance of the book, so quickly, still bothered her, but she knew she had to set her concern aside for now.

Within a few minutes, the earlier tension seemed to have quieted.

"Erik?"

His face drained. He had too much bad news delivered his way.

"I believe I'm in danger," she continued. "Someone tried to poison me yesterday."

A pallor replaced any remaining color. "Tell me." He was listening. Intent.

After Lishan told the salient points, they both sat back, quiet. Lishan looked around the flat. She had always liked Erik's taste in furnishings—Klimt's "Kiss" framed his headboard. Picasso's "Girl With a Mandolin," and a few Matisses rounded out his collection. Lishan was the first to break the silence.

"It may just be a warning. We don't know that Conner wants me dead. If I don't make any more trouble for him, maybe he'll just drop it."

"Maybe," Erik said, weakly. "Maybe not. The problem is, how will he know you won't make any more trouble? And could you live with that, letting him continue to get away with whatever he wants? Your well-being is my first concern, but we still have to ask the hard questions."

"I suppose we could see how it plays out in the days ahead. Weeks, maybe. But you're right. I don't plan on letting it go, but I would prefer not to pay for it with my life or the life of any of my close family or friends."

"Okay. So we'll play it safe for now. What do you think?"

They busied themselves devouring the pizza in addition to popping another couple of beers.

Erik wanted to forget about Rafael, to make light of what he thought was Lishan's philandering. It was an issue that was heavy in his heart, but he knew he needed to let Lishan relax, feel off the hook. Still, it was an itch.

Erik put on a smile, trying his best to be lighthearted. "Sometime I want you to tell me all about that gigolo who corralled you last night. I'll scratch his..."

Lishan just blinked, her way of not lending any weight to his comment.

Erik pretended to extend his claws, followed by a warm smile.

"Do you like seeing Rafael?" Erik decided to get it over with.

Lishan drew a long breath that resulted in an equally long exhale. "I thought I did, but I don't feel I can trust him. Can we address it later? I'm done with men, for now—except you, of course."

As a distraction, Lishan opened the Frazier book. She had brought it with her. They read passages from it, pulling up what they could from the Internet, trying to understand how the case against Frazier could have held water. In the process, Lishan presented her thoughts on writing a second exposé that focused more on the FDA.

"Okay, so I have some ideas about the FDA and why they sometimes wear the antagonist hat. But I need to think carefully about this," she continued. "That is, I'm grateful for their presence, but their inequities are just too glaring. In your opinion, where do I place the fulcrum?"

"Work from the premise that the FDA, the granddaddy food companies, and the conglomerate pharmaceutical CEOs are all in bed together—there's an image for a political cartoon. Throw in a few senators, perhaps more than a few. Then, draw the public in with who gets, uh—can I cuss?"

"Erik, you wouldn't! Girl that I am." Lishan smiled, as though she had just thought of something dreadfully funny. "Fucked? Isn't that it? Who gets *fucked*? No, you can't. Cuss." She stole a sip of his beer, grabbing a napkin as a couple of drops slipped through her smile.

For a moment, their laughter caught on, causing their eyes to glisten. Lishan could feel a slight flush in her cheeks. After all, he was her professor at one time.

Erik lightly touched Lishan's knee.

"Yes. By and large, it's common knowledge. But there's so much apathy in the States that the government pretty much feels immune to its own notoriety, to the negative publicity. They know most of the public just wants their oil, their TVs, their Internet connections, no matter the price. So the government isn't too worried. But I feel it's changing. Slowly. But changing. Look at Martha Stewart. Look at Liddy. There are some big names that didn't avoid the gallows. What irks me is the government still isn't too concerned. Yes, we see some purging, some tweaking, but it's largely surface. Same thing with the FDA, or Conner. It's just unfortunate that our species is so greedy."

"To a caring and compassionate species. Ours. Someday?" Lishan raised her glass again.

"To a dreamer, more like it." He laughed again, to the tink of glass. "Just kidding. Mostly."

After a notable silence, Erik thought he detected a drift in Lishan's attention. "Are you okay, Lishan?"

Lishan had grown somber.

"Hmm. Yes. It's just that I'm concerned. I've never before put my career, or my health, or my life in danger."

Erik didn't hold back. "We need to talk further about this. Not tomorrow. Let me get some snacks for us, then figure this out."

Erik stood and headed to the kitchen. "Care for a soda?"

Lishan opted out when she saw the can. "That has aspartame in it. Do you know how much obesity has been directly attributed to this artificial sweetener?"

Erik contemplated his options for a few seconds then returned to the kitchen and emptied the cola down the drain.

Erik came back to her side with just cheese and crackers. "I understand. This is important to you—as it should be."

She stood, pacing. "You know, the Delaney clause in the Food Additives Amendment stated that any additive that caused cancer in humans or animals had to be prohibited. But the public outcry against having its chemical sweetener saccharin eliminated caused the FDA to lose its case. Saccharin and other artificial sweeteners remain—unfortunately."

"I remember," Erik said, then redirected the conversation. "Can we talk about your safety? We can't overlook a thing."

Lishan spent the next half hour describing anything of relevance.

"Do you think you're safe in your apartment, given the poisoning?"

"I don't know. It seems risky on their part to come straight to my apartment. I think it's okay, for now."

Erik hesitated. "I don't know, either, but we can't take a chance. Do you want to stay here?"

Lishan thought for a moment. "I could, but what if we both go check out my apartment. If it looks okay, with the windows and doors bolted shut, I should be alright."

Erik wasn't completely happy with the idea, but he decided to go along with it.

After a few minutes alone in her apartment, Lishan began feeling edgy, almost trapped. On a whim, she decided it was time to head to the Cove, a retreat she hadn't indulged in since last spring. Her grandparents on her mother's side had left their cabin to remaining family. It was a small, two-bedroom log cabin and boathouse on Cook Point Cove, a somewhat isolated area off the eastern shores of Chesapeake Bay. There, amid a cluster of gulls, she would find the clarity she needed to determine her next steps in her career and her life.

A little over two hours driving time, plus a stop for a light dinner in Cambridge at Jimmie & Sook's, put Lishan at the cabin. It was dark. One hour later she was fast asleep.

Saturday morning. Lishan's favorite day of the week. She recalled watching cartoons as a child. It was always a special time in her mind, no matter how old she was. Here, at the Cove, she had no television, no phone that anyone other than family knew about. Her cell phone service didn't work until she was a mile down the road toward Cambridge, whose developments were pushing ever closer to the Cove with each passing year. Her writing and a good book were her Saturday specials now, after a brisk one-hour run followed by a fistful of nuts and some juice. This combination always got her day off to a good start.

Lishan had a runner's body. She rarely let a day go by without some form of exercise. Today's run wasn't as clearing as it usually was. She kept trying to meditate during the run, but her mind drifted. *Could Conner know I'm here?* The thought was troubling.

She knew she couldn't drop her case against Conner and his influence in government. The conviction in her heart as a true journalist, not some underling subscribing to an editor's ego, drove her decision to keep probing. As to the FDA, she would find a way to get the people riled up just enough to put pressure on the Agency to fully represent the health of the people, not the lobbyists for the food and pharmaceutical industries.

Lishan recalled reading the novel *Ecotopia Emerging*. The story involved an oil conglomerate and its threats to anyone who stood in the way of its profits. Oppression, death. Don't upset the rich and powerful. This was the message imbedded in the cupcakes.

She'd been following government agencies and their oft-sly maneuvers since she was old enough to care about the world. Lishan could no longer just write about local affairs without weaving in a pitch for social consciousness. The world had grown too small. The isolationists of the early twentieth century had lost their battle to keep the United States separate from the world, though the new POTUS was doing what he could to wall off the country.

Now, here she was, challenging greedy food and Big Pharma CEOs and shareholders, along with any FDA officials on the take. Lishan was insignificant in their scheme of things, a mere pest, an irritant that could be eradicated with little thought to morals and justice. The FDA had a job to do. Protect the public. But would it be at the expense of its corporate sponsors?

Lishan understood the conflict. As a journalist working for a mainstream newspaper, she knew what her putative limits were. The trouble was, she was and always would be an advocate for the people, with more interest in justice than the bankrolls of the upper class.

After a shower, she brewed up a pot of her favorite Pachamama coffee and sat in the breakfast nook.

The cabin had a certain warmth to it this morning. Lishan craved feeling cozy, prompting her to put on her pajamas—the light blue ones with the Dr. Seuss characters—instead of street clothes. Sitting back in the comfy breakfast nook her grandparents had added off the kitchen, she looked through the paned window, out over the shoreline to the slight chop in the water. She jotted down a few words that came to mind when she thought about the avarice in the world: compassion, dignity, and honesty, wondering how these came to be replaced by that selfishness within the egos of so many of the human species. She recalled a favorite quote by Benjamin Franklin: "Those who would give up essential liberty to purchase a little temporary safety deserve neither liberty nor safety."

She inscribed her next thought as a question mark on her notepad. *What's my next step?* She unpacked her messenger bag, smiling as she remembered that Erik had given it to her two years ago on her birthday. He playfully called it her metrosexual bag, mostly because he liked the feel of the words as they slid from his lips.

Amid the stack of papers, she pulled out *CEOs & Senators: Bedfellows With Your Food & Drug Administration*. Now, before her, it seemed she had the guidance she looked for. She would see if she could talk with Alan Frazier.

Rockland Prison was near Albany, NY, 370 miles from D.C. Was it worth her time to catch a train and pay a visit in person? Perhaps it was her only option. Nevertheless, she didn't know if her visit would be well received by Frazier.

Only one way to find out. Lishan got dressed and walked the mile to where her cell phone synchronized with a transmission tower.

"Hi. My name is Lishan Amir. I'm writing a story about food and our government. One of your inmates, Alan Frazier, came up in conversation. Is it possible to visit him, perhaps later today, assuming he's agreeable to a meeting?"

The clerk fielding the call was pleasant enough, offering to call Lishan back shortly. It wasn't long.

"Ms. Amir. This is Vice Warden Johnson from Rockland Penitentiary. I understand you wish to speak with a Mr. Frazier."

"Yes. I'm writing a story about food and our government, and I would like it to be well-rounded."

"You're a journalist, I understand."

Lishan hesitated. Was she getting herself in deeper trouble? "Yes."

"Hmm. I spoke with Mr. Frazier. He's agreeable, though he might not tell you much. Come on up. D.C.'s not that far from here. Just ask any crow."

Lishan could hear a muffled chuckle.

"Visiting hours usually end by eight, and, since you're a journalist, we won't make an exception." Another chuckle. "He'll be available at nine in the morning. Don't be late." The connection dropped.

Lishan realized the vice warden had hung up on her. And it bothered her that the prison had traced Lishan's whereabouts already. Why the scrutiny?

She was in a quandary. Lishan didn't mind butting up against the establishment, but she didn't want to be absolutely foolish about it, including not getting reimbursed for this trip. It would cost her a few hundred. She perused the Amtrak schedule. Total time, with a transfer at Penn Station in New York, was seven hours. Then there was the taxi to a motel and the prison.

One call to Amtrak booked her tickets, setting the trip in motion.

Back at the cabin, her feet tucked under her on the cozy bench seat, she opened Frazier's book. There was no doubt, no denying that she couldn't ignore this lead. Thirty minutes later, Lishan drove the two hours to her apartment building to drop off her car and catch a taxi to Union Station. She thought she might arrive at the prison before 8:00 p.m. but decided there was no point in pushing it. Tomorrow morning would do just fine.

見る

As the train whisked her along toward upstate New York, it seemed an excellent time to continue with Frazier's book. She thought about texting Erik, but she didn't want to risk any additional chaos just then. *I'll call him later* was a passing thought, one that disappeared with the mesmerizing sound of steel wheels on steel track.

Lishan skimmed through the chapters over the next few hours. Five minutes into the book, Lishan took out her notebook and began taking notes—there were innumerable references to Jack Conner, ones he wouldn't like. If a quarter of the allegations were true, it was no wonder Frazier was pegged as a prime target of Conner's. Two pages of notes later, Lishan arrived at her last stop. It was 7:30 p.m.

Before hailing a taxi, Lishan went to the restroom. On her way in, she noticed someone in the shadows, leaning against the wall near the door. Normally, Lishan would pay no particular attention, but the figure had taken a good long look at her. Leaving the restroom, Lishan didn't see the stranger at first glance. As she stepped into a taxi, she noticed what she thought might be the same person stepping into a taxi right behind her. She told herself there was nothing unusual about this, but a feeling of increased vigilance stuck with her.

"Where to?" The congenial woman in her fifties reminded Lishan of her mother.

"I just need a good, clean local motel, one where I can get a bite to eat nearby. I'm heading out to the prison in the morning, if that helps in your suggestion."

"Sure. Blaylock's Motel is just ten minutes from here, near the outskirts of town. There's a good restaurant at the motel, and it's on Highway 60, the road to the prison."

"Can I catch a taxi in the morning, out to the prison?"

"Hmm. Not easily. You'll need to call."

"Is it worth staying there? I don't need a resort, but someplace comfortable and clean would be preferred."

"Yes. It's a nice motel, well-known here. The restaurant gets high marks for its organic food—uncommon in these parts."

"Works for me. Say, how long is the cab ride to the prison from there?"

"Forty-five minutes. What takes you out there?"

Lishan chose her words carefully. She could feel the effects of the various cautions surrounding this inmate. Ultimately, though, she chose just to be open. *What harm could there be?*

"I'm doing some writing. There's an inmate who has some details I'd like to understand."

"I hope you're not a reporter. The vice warden can't stand 'em. He dreamed up some charge against one once. The poor fellow had to go through a strip search."

"Strip search! I thought those were virtually outlawed unless there's probable cause to believe a weapon or some illegal substance is being concealed."

The driver just nodded.

"You need to understand. The vice warden has friends in, uh, low places. He's one of the Conner boys. You're not going to quote me, are you?"

"As in Jack Conner?"

"The very one. This guy's a cousin. I think I know the fellow you're going to visit. Alan Frazier. At least I know him through the papers."

Lishan had quieted, lost in thought. Then she remembered the cabby's concern. "No, I'm not going to quote you. Anyone who stirs up trouble for the Conner clan likely ends up on a blacklist somewhere."

"Frazier was framed for unlawful surveillance, a felony. But behind the scenes, we know it was the libel in his book, which on its own wouldn't have sent him to prison. Frazier got four years. Some say 'only' four years, but that's still a long time in the clink. Him in Rockland, it's a fitting revenge by the Conner boys, don't you think? Be in a prison where a relative of the guy you accuse in your book runs the place? You sure you want to do this?"

Lishan paused, looking out the window. She could see the motel up ahead. Two stories. Bright and cheery looking. The neighborhood looked safe enough. "Green Gables" announced the restaurant.

"I think I'll still go ahead with it. What have I got to lose?"

The cabby gave Lishan a cautionary look. "Plenty. I would tell you I'm sure you'll be fine, but I can't." The driver stopped in front of the lobby. "Do you want me to wait for you?"

"No, but thank you."

The cabby looked out the driver-side window at a passing taxi. "I should tell you I think you were followed. This happened once before with a guy headed to the prison. You sure?"

Followed. Lishan could feel her heart rate increase. She thought she was just writing a few articles so these companies, and the government, wouldn't feel like they could run roughshod over the public. Perhaps those with a sense of entitlement would stop at nothing. No irritation was too small. When she thought about it, she knew it was no surprise.

"Yes, I'm sure. I have to go through with this. Thanks for the ride and the tips. Take care."

The motel did have a nice feel to it. Sitting on the outskirts of town, it felt like a gateway between the city and country. Lishan took a room on the top floor, settled in, and then headed down to Green Gables. She was taken with the extravagance of the menu. Her parents had always preached the benefits of organic foods during her upbringing, but she, of course, had to run the teenage rebellion until she was older.

She ordered vegetarian lasagna, built with layers of spinach noodles and a side of organic asparagus.

"This is quite delicious. My compliments," she offered to the waiter, who simply smiled. Some of her friends used to compare "health" food to cardboard. Her dinner was anything but.

As Lishan headed to the elevator to get to her quiet, and hopefully uneventful, room, she was approached by a medium height, well-built man, perhaps in his thirties.

"Yes?"

"I have an urgent message for you."

"From?"

"The vice warden."

The vice warden. Lishan didn't like the feel of this. "How did he know I was here?"

"He always checks up on visitors he's unfamiliar with. Can we talk?"

While she didn't think she was in any imminent danger, she wasn't sure where this vice warden was taking Lishan. Likely, though, this would be a wasted trip if she didn't talk with the intruder.

Lishan perceived a hint of Hawaiian ancestry, which meant he could likely have been of early Hawaiian descent combined with Filipino, Japanese, Chinese, Pacific Islander, or a mix of any or all—possibly European American as well. He wore linen slacks and a silk long-sleeve black shirt.

"My name is Beck," he said, extending his hand, "You no doubt already know my name."

He sat down on a couch in the lobby. "Please sit down," he encouraged. His demeanor was professional at least.

"The vice warden wants me to ask you some questions, all in the name of security. Surely you understand."

"Of course."

"My apologies for the hour. You didn't check in until late." He busied himself for a few seconds in his briefcase.

Lishan took in the high quality of the Le Donne bag. He had a business-like manner about him, but he did seem gentle enough. Lishan felt herself relaxing a little. "Are you hungry? I believe the restaurant is open until 11."

"Do you mind? I'll take care of it," Beck offered.

"We can dicker."

They returned to the same booth she sat in earlier. Beck ordered a couple of hors d'oeuvres and a bottle of Cabernet.

"It's been a difficult day, and I promised myself some wine before the day is over. Again, I hope you don't mind."

Lishan's guard tightened at the mention of wine. She wouldn't be the prey in a cat and mouse game. How much trouble could she get into, she wondered. Perhaps the cabby was mistaken, and the vice warden was just doing his job. Thoroughly.

"What questions do you have for me? You said...Beck?"

"Yes. You see, we protect the rights of our pris...our inmates. Your reasons for coming can't conflict with their well-being. I need to know a little about you and specifically why you are here."

Lishan's face tightened, almost unperceptively, as she attempted to accurately size up the situation. Worst case was that she wouldn't get the interview. At least that was what she imagined. Was she overlooking anything?

"Ask away. Don't get too personal, though." She smiled, barely, as though making a small joke.

Beck held back any response. With a baguette and Brie, alongside a bottle of California's Stags Leap Cabernet, he continued.

"Perfect," he said to the waiter who filled his, then Lishan's, glasses. As the waiter turned to leave, a five-dollar tip in hand, he winked a smile at Beck, likely wishing he were in Beck's shoes.

"So, you're a reporter."

"Uh, that's..."

"Ms. Amir, you're a reporter. We...I know this. I've done my homework. It's not a bad thing. But be honest with me."

Lishan straightened a little and came on just a bit stronger. "Before we proceed, I would like to know the nature of your work. You mentioned homework. It's appropriate that I know."

He took a bite of the soft cheese, followed by a long sip of wine. "My homework. I'm a detective. Private. The vice warden likes my work. I always come through for him." He let the tiniest of a sly smile escape.

Lishan could feel the tug of the alcohol. It was warm and disarming—a caution, given the nature of the conversation. "How did a man like you get hooked up with..."

"The prison? Ah, yes. I earned my MA in psych from Rutgers. My parents had a few bucks. I tried my hand as a family therapist for a few years, but I got bored. I wanted to reach out and shake some of my clients. I decided it was time to get out of Dodge. I had connections, one of them the vice warden. He needed a few people tracked down this past year. I've been snooping ever since. But enough about me."

"What can I tell you that you don't already know?"

"Okay. You can't tell me about your recent exposé. You can't tell me about your dislike for the government, at least regarding what you call its dishonesty with the public. I can tell *you* that you're just a speck in the ointment, just another wannabe out to change the world. But when you start interfering with the sources for revenue—be it a large company or a government official—then sometimes, just sometimes, they push back a little. Okay, more than a little. So, you *can* tell me...why bother with this interview, assuming Frazier will tell you anything and assuming your editor will allow any of this to go to print...which he won't?"

Won't print? The nerve, Lishan thought privately, suppressing a smile. She raised her glass. "To everything you think you know."

She could tell from his eyes that she caught him off guard. He smiled, but it was weak. In an effort to regain a footing, he offered a counter toast.

"Here's to life and getting what we want."

Lishan's eyebrows lifted. She refused to toast.

107

"Something I said?" Beck looked troubled.

"Getting what we want? I can't toast to that. Getting what you want—at any cost?"

"I didn't quite mean it that way." Beck knew he had lost control of the situation. He clearly didn't like it.

"Then how did you mean it? It sounded selfish. To hell with anyone else, you might say." Lishan looked as though she was going to leave.

"Listen, I..." Beck paused. "Can we..."

Lishan stood up.

"You can tell the vice warden I am simply a voice for the people. No harm will come from my talking with Frazier." Lishan motioned to the waiter. It was time to leave. "Beck, I'm tired. I'm sure you won't mind if we call it a night."

Beck was stymied. He reached for the check, but Lishan was too fast. Besides, she wouldn't have let him pay for her. Putting cash down for her portion, she put the waiter's American Express folder back on the table, opened.

"Good luck to you, Beck. Report whatever you want."

Beck just sat there, at a loss for words.

In her room, the clock on the laminated nightstand read 11:14. Up at 7:00 a.m.? How long did the cabby say it would take? Forty-five.

Lishan thought about the meeting she just left. *What a self-centered ass. No wonder there is so little unity in the world.* Containing her thoughts, Lishan moved on to tomorrow's visit.

"Hi, I'd like to have a taxi pick me up at eight in the morning."

"You'll have to call back in the morning. The dispatcher went home with a headache."

The voice on the phone was no-nonsense. Lishan decided pleasantries would be the safer bet. "Hmm. What time do you open?"

"Weekdays it's seven. But tomorrow is Sunday. Someone should be here by eight. Maybe."

"Maybe? That's not good enough. I need to be at the prison by nine." The line went dead.

Lishan called again. It rang eight times before being answered. The same voice.

"Hi. Sorry. I didn't mean to sound pushy," Lishan said.

"Yes, in fact you did. Don't you go to church in the morning?"

Lishan hesitated. An offense at this point could cost her a ride. "I never miss church," she lied. "I'll be going tomorrow evening. What church do you attend?"

"I'm an evangelical...herbalist." The woman, fifty in Lishan's mind, cracked up, her laughter filling whatever room she was in. Lishan's sensitivity was being hijacked. It took nearly ten seconds before the laughter died down. The woman sensed that Lishan was not amused. Finally, she offered, "I'm an atheist. Just pulling your chain. Okay, I'll leave a note. Where are you? The Blaylock Motel?"

"Yes. Does everyone heading to the prison stay here?"

"No. Most everyone stays there...at the prison." More laughter, cut short this time. "I'm sorry. I must be in rare form tonight. Yeah, everyone stays there, though we don't get too many people visiting these days since the incident."

"Incident. What incident?" Her eyes were now fully round.

"Don't you watch the news? About three months ago, a visitor—I think he was looking up that FDA writer guy—got shot. It was a mistake. Someone thought he was a prisoner escaping. He lived, but I hear he walks with a limp now. I'm sure it's fine, though."

Lishan just blinked. *So many reasons not to go.*

"It sounds ominous, but I've come far enough. I think I'll go ahead with my visit."

"Suit yourself."

"Just double-checking: I'll call at eight, then?"

"Yeah. I'll leave a note, but you should call. You know, just in case."

Her sleep was fitful. By dawn, Lishan felt as though she had slept no more than an hour. Dreams and reality sparred for first place. Was the flashlight beam on the motel's two-inch blinds part of a dream? She knew that the stretcher and ambulance at the prison, with psychedelic lights flashing off the disco ball, and the female stretched out with a bloody bandage on her left knee was a dream. It was not her. Not yet, at least.

She couldn't find any ease in her mind this morning. With no intention of staying the next night, and her return ticket on the last train out at 6:00 p.m., she packed her bag, leaving out her casual business attire. She imagined bone-colored pants and a dress shirt would do. A shower, breakfast, call to the taxi company just in case, and she'd be on her way.

Green Gables was as pleasant for breakfast as it had been for dinner. She considered the eggs Florentine, but another favorite of hers was available, one she nearly never found in a restaurant: Joe's Special, vegetarian style. Instead of ground beef, it used marinated veggie sausages. Half regular and half decaf would keep her adrenals from being any more agitated than they already were.

7:50 a.m. One call to the taxi company produced nothing. 7:53, the same. 7:58, no change. 8:00 a.m., the ninth ring, a voice. Lishan felt she was talking to a hangover, but she didn't quibble. No, the dispatcher hadn't seen the note. There didn't appear to be one. A taxi would be right out, perhaps twenty minutes. Forty minutes later, a slightly beat-up silver 1985 Mercedes 500 SEL taxi eased into the parking lot.

Right out, twenty minutes—Lishan repeated in her mind as she gauged the time on her watch. Nothing big-city about this operation. She just might make it in time for the 9:00 a.m. appointment.

The driver reminded Lishan of someone's Aunt Bee, one who watched the soaps and indulged in boxes of chocolate.

"Hi darlin'." She flung a smile Lishan's way, along with an up-and-down look. "Where to?"

Lishan thought to mention that she should already know, but it seemed counter-productive. "The prison."

"I'll have to stop for gas if we're going that far."

Lishan could feel the woman's foot stomping the accelerator as they pulled a U-turn, heading away from the prison toward a gas station, traveling just under the speed limit.

"Could you drive just a little faster? I have an appointment there at nine."

"Nope. Wouldn't be safe. You want to be safe, don't you?"

And that was that.

9:40 a.m. The prison loomed into view. The forestlands had been cleared for three hundred yards around the perimeter of the prison walls. To the south, a small community of ten duplexes—housing for the guards—and two Victorian homes—one clearly more expansive than the other—were held inside a high chain link fence, complete with razor wire.

"Who gets the expensive Victorian?"

"It's not as you might think. That's for the vice warden. He calls the shots here. The warden is just a, what do you say, figurehead. Don't anger the vice warden. Hey, should I wait for you?"

"I think not. Can you be back here in a few hours? Perhaps 1 or 2?"

"Sure, darlin'. You can count on me." She reached around the bucket seat and patted the inside of Lishan's right thigh, giving a gingerly squeeze before letting her go.

Lecherous old gal, Lishan thought.

囝
匤

At the gate, the guard made it clear the taxi would not enter; Lishan would enter on foot. It wasn't the distance Lishan minded, as it was short. It was the vulnerability.

Lishan was pointed to the vice warden's office. As she entered the office, the man behind the desk was not quite what she had expected. A military man of stature with a physique to match was in her mind's eye. Yet here was a small man, balding and homely. Lishan stood there for nearly a minute before she was acknowledged—a tactic of hierarchy, Lishan recognized.

"You're late, you know. You'll have to come back at one."

Lishan was stunned. "The taxi didn't come through as promised. Can't I just have that much less time for the interview?"

"Do you think we just squander time here, wasting the taxpayers' money? Frazier went back to work when you didn't show. He has a project that won't be completed until twelve thirty, then lunch. You get the picture. Or don't you?"

Lishan knew her place in this game. Subservience to the master. In as meek a tone as she could muster, fighting a strong desire to interject a marked sarcasm, she said, "Yes, I understand. Where would you like me to wait?"

"We don't have a waiting room. This is not a hotel lobby. You'll have to wait outside the prison grounds."

"Back out through the guard gate?"

Vice Warden Johnson didn't reply. The introduction was over.

Lishan was frisked, with only minimal boundary violations, as she passed through the guard gate. This was a complete 180 since she was not frisked on the way in. Once outside, she decided to walk the perimeter of the prison, just to get a look. Immediately after opening her notebook, though, she heard "STOP" via megaphone. It was a powerful sound, inducing a certain fear in the recipient, especially given the arsenal at each guard tower. Within several seconds, three guards, each with a loaded weapon, surrounded Lishan.

She was whisked around by one and handcuffed by another. She dropped her notebook in the dirt.

"Hey!" Lishan yelled.

"Hey what?" came the menacing response from the third guard.

"You've no right to treat me like this." Lishan was angry. "I'm here visiting an inmate, with the vice warden's permission."

"Didn't you know the prisoners are *inside* the fence, not outside?" The guards' cohesive laughter suggested this was an old joke in their world.

One of the guards called the vice warden's office on a two-way radio. But Lishan neither saw nor heard any indication that the radio was transmitting or receiving. In Lishan's book, she was being harassed and the guard just pretending to make a call.

"Okay, you're free. But don't be walking around. There's a bench over there by the bus stop. You can wait there."

After Lishan was uncuffed, she saw no point in trying to negotiate with these guys. At least the bus stop had a roof, providing shade.

She dusted off her notebook and proceeded to make a few key notes, though she knew her treatment was indelibly inscribed in her memory. How could she forget? She passed the time with a copy of *The Economist* she brought for just such an occasion. It was the one source of news she felt was the least filtered or biased.

As 1:00 p.m. approached, Lishan worked her way back to Johnson's office. Again, she was not searched upon entry. Nor was she treated any differently in the vice warden's office. Instead of responding with fury, Lishan just took a breath, barely suppressing a smile and a roll of her eyes as she wondered at the species she was born into.

"Are you ready?" Johnson bore a mischievous smile and made no effort to hide it. He led her through no less than six keyed steel doors, finally ending at the visitor's room. Lishan supposed she was taken the circuitous route, for effect.

"Okay, you've got fifteen minutes." The vice warden was at the point of uproarious laughter. Lishan could see it. She decided it was time to push back. She was angry.

"Fifteen? That's *not* okay. On the form you had me fill out and fax to you, I checked the 'one hour' box, and there was no mention from you or anyone else about a shorter time period. You can stuff your fifteen minutes. I'll come back with a court order prescribing at least three hours with your supposed prisoner." Lishan turned around. She was feeling hostile. "Take me out of here. Now."

Surprisingly, the vice warden was speechless. Lishan could see he was shaken, though every effort was made to hide it.

"I was just joshing with you. Didn't you know?"

"No, it wasn't apparent."

"Okay, one hour."

"And none of this glass in between us. I want a room where we can sit and talk."

"You journalists are getting mighty pushy these days. Sure, why not, Virginia. A room of one's own."

Lishan's eyes widened at the vice warden's literary reference. He didn't miss the implication.

"Thought I didn't read, did you? Tsk."

"Not at all," she lied. She was diverted to a small space, next to a water cooler. It wasn't completely private, but it had a small table and two chairs.

"Thank you." Lishan was barely cordial. Nothing in return.

The vice warden disappeared. Two minutes later, a disheveled, forty-something male, with shoulder-length graying hair, eased into the space next to where Lishan stood.

"You're the reporter," the man stated, barely asking.

"Yes, but I don't believe you should think of me that way. My name is Lishan. Lishan Amir. I work for *The Washington Mirror* in D.C., but the editor doesn't support the work I'm doing to expose injustice in the likes of Senator Libby, Conner, and the FDA."

"Why shouldn't I think of you as a reporter?"

"Can we sit down?"

Frazier complied. He seemed ill at ease with the gentleness emanating from Lishan.

"If you think of me as a reporter, you might just peg me as something inconsistent with who I really am."

He seemed to relax a little. "I'm Alan Frazier, as you know. I...say, are we being monitored, or recorded?"

"Not on my end. I can't speak for the room. It looks like a cubbyhole off a mini-lunchroom, but I couldn't say." In a lower voice, Lishan said, "Perhaps if we speak softly, they won't be able to listen in."

They leaned in closer, keeping their voices low. "Back to why I shouldn't think of you as a reporter," Frazier said.

"Ah." Lishan took a long breath. "Technically, I'm a reporter. But I think of myself more as a writer—of social justice—wearing a journalist hat. I hope that makes sense on some level." Lishan smiled an inquisitive smile. "May I call you Alan?"

"Alan, yes. And I believe I get your drift. You're not filling a nine-to-five space. What brings you here? Chasing Goliath?"

"If I'm not careful, I'll be in here with you, following your footsteps. Or dead."

Alan just nodded, a somber look consuming his face.

"So, you'd like to profit from my experience. No, that didn't come out quite right. You're hoping I have some inside tips, am I correct?"

"Yes. I didn't know what you might offer, but I knew I had to try. Besides, I don't feel so alone, knowing there are others—you, for example—who have been willing to take a stand."

Alan sat back, clasping his hands under his chin. He leaned in again as he continued. "Staying out of jail has a lot to do with how well connected you are—who you know—and who your connections know. I just didn't have, still don't have, anybody on my side who can conjure at least a little fear in these guys."

"I don't know that I'm in any better shape than you in that regard. Who do you believe was the kingpin behind your being in prison?"

"Hmm. Sometimes it's a bit difficult to know the true underpinnings. FDA top brass themselves would not have taken it this far. I shouldn't insinuate that they were blameless. It's just that Jack Conner is like the Mafia in my opinion. That is, he's behind the invitation that put me in prison. I've been here two years. Two to go. Conner wanted me in for ten, but the judge knew he was handing me a sentence I didn't deserve."

Alan paused, taking in the surroundings. Through a glass window, he could see the visitor's room twenty feet away. Within, there were several visitors, each on one side of a chicken-wire-impregnated glass separator, telephone handset in hand. Opposite each was an inmate. The room Alan and Lishan were in looked as though it was once a small office off a small conference room, but the larger room had become a mini-lunchroom for visitors, with a few tables, chairs, and vending machines. The smaller room had the door removed, but it still offered a semblance of privacy.

"How did you manage to get us in here? I'm not on their perks list, you know."

"I got lucky, I think." Lishan didn't want to lose precious time on unrelated details, but she did give him the gist of her brief confrontation with the vice warden.

"You did seem to intimidate the VW a little. Could be good. Could be bad. Just be careful. Now, I'm sure you only have limited time with me. How can I help?"

"I know you went after both the FDA and companies like Conner Foods in your book. Are there any particular avenues that worked in your favor or worked against you? Anything that will help me put Conner in prison?"

"The principals at the FDA were close-lipped. Not a peep from them. In my book, I listed... Say, do you have a copy of my book?" Alan suddenly looked around. "Don't answer. Just know I list my sources in it. Probably why the FDA—no, Conner's political pawns—had the books quietly retrieved."

They sat in momentary silence, likely considering their prospective fates.

"I'm known somewhat as a rebel," Lishan said quietly. "I speak up against the status quo in Washington. I'm sick of the lies spouted by the mega-corporations, the lobbyists, and the politicians who run this country. I do a series called 'Truth Be Known.' In fact, just a week ago I wrote an exposé that rather pointedly involved Conner, the FDA commissioner, and Senator Libby regarding their propensity to mislead the public, specifically with our food. It's not as though I've uncovered a spy ring or that Conner isn't abiding by the letter of the law—at least some of the laws."

Alan sat back, taking it all in. "Yes, I know." His eyes did a sweep of the surroundings—pensive, if not mildly brooding. "If your editor is against this, what do you plan to do? Write a book?"

Lishan gave a thoughtful smile. So far, her face had been somewhat featureless, worthy of the Stoics. But she began to open up to this writer who shared her passion.

"It wasn't foremost in my mind a minute ago, but talking with you does spark interest in writing a book. Think of it: how many writers could they imprison for making these improprieties public?" Lishan paused. "Sorry. Makes me think of Socrates. Okay, a book. It's on my list. But, to answer your question, I want to get these messages out to the public now, today. The paper I work for is well-known, well-read. If I can get a couple of good stories out there, perhaps acquire a readership, a following, that would make the editor see the value, then we can help effect change. One problem, though: my editor knows the FDA director, and Libby as well, so that creates a bit of a snag—an undertow, really. But whether I have to go underground to write this or find a way at the paper.... The publisher is on my side—that's a plus. I want to give it my best shot, which is why I'm here."

Frazier whispered, "There's a reference librarian at the New York Avenue Library in D.C. He's a tall Rastafarian. With dreads. Is that redundant? Buy him dinner."

"I think I've met him. Dinner is an excellent idea."

"I just remembered: there's a bodyguard you should be aware of. He appears to be on Conner's payroll, though good luck proving it. I was on the subway in D.C. This guy sits down next to me. Large, dark overcoat. Leather gloves. Substantial fellow. 220, with a slight belly—but don't underestimate his strength. All he said was, 'I won't allow anybody taking potshots at Jack Conner. Especially *you*.' That was it. He stood up, purposely stepping on my foot with his heel. I think he meant to break my ankle, but I had hiking boots on. It still hurt. He got off at the next stop. I don't know his name."

"When did this take place?"

"About two weeks after the book hit the streets. This prison sentence hit me quickly. Conner must have his boots on some influential necks. Say, what do you know about Kessler?"

"The former FDA commissioner?"

"One and the same."

"I believe that during his stint with the FDA he made progress for the people. He swore to enforce laws on food labels, for one. I think he was the kind of commissioner the public would hope for. Why?"

"I don't believe he's too accessible, but you can try. Perhaps you can cajole him for some insight."

Alan took a sip of water, taking a long look at Lishan as he did. "It's gutsy, you coming out here."

"So I understand."

"I imagine you're purposely not taking notes. Probably for the best."

"I'm absolutely taking notes—just nothing written. After the treatment I received earlier, I could see no point in handing over to the vice warden anything you might tell me. Say, as to your incarceration, do you think there's any way I can help you get out early?"

"By the time you could arrange it, I'd be due to get out. So, it's probably not..."

"No prison breaks allowed, you two." Johnson had just stepped up to the doorway. It was unclear how much he had heard. "You boys and girls aren't planning anything, now are you? We've got room here, Ms. Amir, if you need a place to clear your head for a while. Room and board. I hope you plan to write about our wonderful facility here. Make us look good in that fish wrap of yours. In any case, the party's over."

"I've been here just half an hour." Lishan was not pleading. She was stating fact, making a point.

"You looked like you were having just too much fun. Besides, Mr. Frazier here has a project to finish, don't you Alan?"

Lishan watched Alan stand, expecting that same dejected look she witnessed when they first met. But she was pleasantly surprised. Alan had a little bounce in his step.

"Whatever you say, VW." Alan's words were chipper. When he turned to Lishan, there was an air of confidence that had returned to his face, as though all was not lost. "Lishan, thank you. I wish you well."

Johnson had a twinge of the same nervousness that had surfaced when Lishan confronted him earlier. "Guard, take Mr. Frazier back to his duties. Ms. Amir, it's time for you to leave. We can't just cater to you reporters all day long, you know."

"Of course not. You have incarcerating to do. How else will you make fine, upstanding citizens of these men?"

The vice warden was a little uncertain whether there was an insult imbedded. Lishan had no doubt, applying her most patronizing voice in thanking the vice warden.

Passing out through the gate and once again frisked, Lishan was free to go. But where? There was no taxi in sight. "Did a taxi show up here for me earlier?"

"Oh, yeah," one of the guards said, suppressing a smile. "You weren't here, so I told her to just go on home. I hope you don't mind?" Lishan recognized the rhetoric.

"Is there a bus?" Lishan felt stupid asking the question.

"Weekdays only. Sorry."

Lishan tried her cell phone, but there was no signal. "I need to call a cab, then."

"There's a payphone next to the VW's office."

Lishan started back through the gate.

"Do you have an appointment?" The guard and his buddy practically doubled over in laughter. "An...appointment."

Lishan just kept walking, trying to shake her head without inviting a large caliber bullet.

"Five o'clock? That's the soonest you can be out here?" No point in arguing. She didn't want to offend the one cabby committed to picking her up.

As she walked back through the gate, toward the bus stop, she was again frisked. She made no comments this time, which sped up the process. She deduced it was no fun for the guards if she didn't protest. As she was leaving the guard post, one of them spoke up, "Here's your notebook. We found it outside."

Opening it, Lishan found the only pages left were blank ones. Her previous notes had been ripped out. "Hey..." she started to yell out. But the words stopped before her larynx, replaced with a short laugh. The notes were all about day care. *That should keep the VW and the encryption team working overtime*, she thought.

Three and a quarter additional hours in the bus stop shack. At least she had *The Economist*. Lishan wondered if the magazine ever did pieces on this part of the world.

She decided to write a few notes while they were fresh in her mind. She doubted the authorities would attempt to confiscate her work, now that she was outside their supposed jurisdiction. Lishan thought it best to be cryptic where Alan's comments were concerned, just in case.

The next memory she had was "Aunt Bee" waking her up. "Hey hon. Care for a ride?"

"I must have dozed. Yes, I do." Lishan rubbed her face a little. She had a sudden concern for her possessions. Had they been taken during her sleep, however long it was? Everything seemed to be in order.

Safely tucked into the cab, which seemed nearly an oxymoron, she decided to inquire about the afternoon schedule. "Say, what happened this afternoon? I know I was delayed."

"As pretty as you are, I couldn't just hang out for very long. Lost revenue, you know. And the guards encouraged me not to stay. I hope you don't mind, but you owe me for that trip."

Lishan felt miffed, but she caught her voice in time, realizing the charge was appropriately due. "Hmm. I see your point." Half to herself, "What time is it?"

"Five thirty. I know you requested five, but I got slammed."

"Five thirty." Lishan began waking up to the realities of the evening. "No way I'll make the six o'clock train, is there? And it's the last train."

"I've got a couch, if you don't mind a few cat hairs." Again, there was that backhand movement with a squeeze to her thigh.

"That's a nice offer, but I should get a room as I have quite a bit of writing and research to do."

"'Shoulds' won't give you much time in life for fun, you know."

Lishan just laughed. "I know. I've been told that before. You must know my ex-boyfriend."

"Which one?" They shared a hearty laugh before quieting into the remaining half-hour ride.

As they approached town, the same motel loomed. "I see a vacancy sign up ahead. Shall I drop you off there?"

It felt as though her stay in the motel was over a week ago, though it was only this morning. Much had happened in the past twenty-four hours. "Why not?"

"You're sure you don't want to stay on my couch? It's free."

Free, my tush, Lishan thought to herself. "It's a kind offer, but I'll just stay here and work."

"Need a ride in the morning?"

Lishan wasn't quite in the mood to further this dance. "No, but thank you. I'll just take tomorrow as it comes." Paying for both of the cabby's trips, Lishan bid her safe journey, with a none-too-soon sigh as the cabby drove off.

The motel lobby had a seventies feel to it, though it professed flapper fame. Lishan took in décor she hadn't noticed her first time. The placement of lamps and draperies suggested a former speakeasy, but the presence of plastics and linoleum detracted from the desired effect.

"Good evening." The clerk wore smugness in his voice. "We saved your room for you."

Lishan quickly replaced her wonder with a laugh. "Why should I be surprised?"

"Exactly! Customer service, you know." The clerk's beaming smile was straight out of the Twilight Zone. "You can thank the gentleman sitting over there." He nodded toward the couch, re-upholstered with a seventies faux fabric.

"More investigating to do?" Her tone was even as she addressed Beck.

"Yes, if you don't mind."

"I do mind. I have a report to write."

"I must apologize for last night."

"Why would you? What would happen to your precious 'getting what you want'?" Lishan had little interest in spending any time with him.

"You gave me quite a bit to think about last night."

"And what would that be?" Lishan's features were flat; she had little interest in giving up any ground.

"Can we at least have dinner and talk? In the short hour I've known you, you did me a favor. I can't continue being a self-centered ass. Pardon my French."

Lishan noticed the parallel assessment. "Go on."

"We can stop at any moment. Tell you what. I'm going to grab a booth and some comfort food. Come down if you like. If not, I will understand. Either way, please accept my apology, if you can. I hope to see you."

Beck gave a short nod with a meager smile and then walked into the restaurant.

Lishan headed up to her room, having no intention of meeting Beck. She changed into her pajamas, but something was wrong. She could remember when people had been there for her when she made mistakes and how it made a difference. She didn't owe anything to Beck. On the contrary. Still, perhaps some good would come from listening to him.

She changed again, putting on comfortable cotton sweatpants and a jersey that gave off a neutral, indifferent air.

When she showed up at the booth, she was not surprised by the wine and baguette already in place. Sitting down, Lishan picked up a distinct, familiar odor from the cheese.

"Boerenkaas, I see. The Dutch do make some of the best. The finest cheese shop I've had the pleasure of knowing is in Amsterdam." Lishan noticed the Merlot. *Clos du Bois. Good choice*, she thought. She sat back, taking in Beck's face.

Beck fidgeted with the cheese, then his wine glass. Then he put his hands down on the table and met Lishan's eyes.

"Thank you for coming down. I gave you every reason not to."

For a moment, there was just silence.

Lishan broke in, "Shall we order dinner?"

Relieved, Beck nodded. The waiter caught their body language—their eyes on the menus—following through from his years of experience.

"Last night, you would not accept me as I was."

"Correction. I could accept you, but I would not support you or your conduct, or choose to spend time with someone like you." Lishan was firm, but not unkind.

Beck hesitated, then said, "Yes, I understand. Last night, at home, I couldn't fall asleep, thinking about what I've become. Often it takes a catalyst—an event, a person—before change can be attempted. I felt if I could make amends, at least some, with you, it would be a step in the right direction."

Lishan just listened, a hint of compassion barely visible.

An older man, wearing an overcoat and a black leather fedora, came in and took the booth diagonal to where Lishan sat. He was on the other side of the muted yellow glass panel that separated the two rows of booths, lending privacy to both sides. Lishan caught a glimpse of him as he came in but thought little of it in this public place. The man came in to the rear of Beck, staying out of Beck's sight. Neither Lishan nor Beck could see the microphone he had rested on the ledge.

"I was spoiled as a child, as a teenager as well. I felt very little love growing up, though. It hardened me. About five years ago, I gathered the courage to sign up for a series of therapy sessions, but when my father found out he hit the roof. That was the end of that. I'm not too far from middle-age. You would think I would have overcome the obstacle, but I chose not to."

"Touching," Lishan said, a little too cold. She heard herself but then decided to recast her approach with a hint of warmth. "Look, Beck, I can appreciate that we are products of our up-bringing. But I'm not your therapist. If we're to continue this conversation, I would rather get back to business first. Then, if my agitation has quieted, perhaps we can talk about why I should suddenly see you differently. You can start by telling me more about who you work for."

"That could put me in jeopardy. They always seem to find out when loyalty is compromised. It may be as simple as a look they see in my face."

"Your choice. Then where do we go?"

Beck paused, long and hard. His eyes scanned the faraway walls. When he came back, his words were measured, cautious, at first, but they eased as time went by, as though he had history with many a confessional.

"The circles I travel in, they...trust me. I have an uncle who had some disgusting business dealings with Jack Conner."

"Why disgusting? It's not that I disagree with you. Just curious."

"The opulence in his family, especially Conner himself, gags me. Money is so obviously more important to him, to them, than the products they produce."

"Then why do you work in those circles?"

"Family. It's good money. Where else could I make eighty grand a year? My uncle was good to me growing up. As a kid, though—how was I to know he was a crook?"

"Is he?"

"Don't quote me. I still love him, just not what he does."

"I shouldn't ask what he does, should I?"

"No. At least not in reference to my 'crook' comment. Officially, he's an attorney. He presumably meant to do well, to be a reformer, to save the little guy. Perhaps most attorneys start out that way. Maybe they don't, come to think of it. Anyway, the money was good. Then my uncle Bill Conner..."

"Conner?"

Beck smiled. "Jack's brother. And, yes, Beck...Conner."

Lishan's eyes widened in disbelief. "You're a Conner?"

The grimace in his cheeks was evident. "Don't hold it against me, okay? I've felt the burden of it much of my adult life.

I was the product of an interracial marriage in the family—a marriage that Conner disapproved of."

"You're a Conner." Lishan felt the weight of the words. "You know I despise that man and all he stands for?"

"Yes. I can imagine."

Their dinners arrived, giving them a much needed break in the conversation. Minutes later, amid a discomfort that had lasted too long, Lishan broke the silence.

"Beck, you know I'm a reporter. I can keep your name out of anything I write, if that's your preference, but can you tell me something about Jack Conner, about the FDA, something you think the public should know?"

Beck's face tightened. "I don't know. That seems too risky. Why should...?"

The minute he said it, he knew he had made a mistake, but it was too late.

"Exactly," Lishan said. "Why should I consider that you are changing, wanting to make that difference people talk about? Same old Beck." Lishan caught the waiter's attention. "A to-go box, please. Thank you."

Turning back to Beck, Lishan said evenly. "Hold the line. Defend it and the crooks you work for. You'll make a difference, though not a positive one. Maybe just to your bank account."

As Lishan stood, the defeat in Beck's face was evident. "Ms. Amir, look, I made a mistake just now. I know. I'm only used to deceit, to keeping my walls up. I don't know how to do this. I should, but I don't. Please sit down. Talk to me."

"Give me a reason to."

Beck's sigh was evident. The road less traveled for him was new. He could only picture his security crashing down around him.

"Please, sit. I'll try."

Lishan just looked at him, evaluating. Some small point in her shifted. She sat down.

"I've witnessed food companies—don't quote me just yet, okay?—where someone of prominence in the industry essentially said, 'To hell with the public. We have stockholders to please.' So, yes, corruption—and not just from the men. The FDA is culpable as well. There's a faction of the Agency, including the current commissioner, that likes to run with the good ol' boys, people who put greed and self-interest above the well-being of the public. And don't forget the Senate."

"Go on."

"Senator Libby and Jack Conner have been in each other's pockets for years. Connulose would never have made it through the Senate and the FDA without Libby's arm-twisting. You know how much influence money wields. Remember Jerry Mande? He was an executive assistant to Kessler, the FDA commissioner at the time. Mande made a reference to a new labeling law, that it was a complete cave to the food industry. There was a fat substitute called olestra, made by Procter & Gamble. It was touted as a great dieting additive because it contained no fat or calories. The problem was that it caused cramps and diarrhea, and it interfered with vitamin absorption. When the FDA approved its use, it also required a warning stating the side effects. But the mega food companies strongly opposed any exposure to anything negative about their foods. Several years later, the FDA removed the warning label requirement—a blow to public health and a coup for the food companies."

"Yes, so I've heard."

Beck continued, "Do you remember a case about five years ago in which a young woman had died? It had been attributed to her daily consumption of a large diet drink."

"Yes. The FDA was implicated but only after a 'leak' suggesting the cola manufacturer and artificial sweeteners were complicit." Lishan's eyes lit abruptly. "Hey, that was Conner. Conner Foods!"

"Do you remember the outcome?"

"Let's see. I'm trying to recall if it ever went to court."

"No, it didn't. Do you know why?" Beck seemed steamy around the edges.

"I should. I think it..."

"No, you shouldn't. Sorry for cutting you off." Beck was getting worked up. "Everybody in-the-know knew it was on its way to court, or at least an FDA review, but then it disappeared from the media. Two reasons, assuming we're not talking philosophies and greed. One was a strong-arm threat to key individuals by Conner's henchmen. Two was that the key witness—a scientist working for Conner Foods—died in a mysterious car accident. The papers were never privy to these facts. If they were, Conner Cola's stock would have taken a nosedive, not to mention Conner would have faced a possible conviction for releasing a toxic substance. Jack Conner is always tinkering with sweeteners and fats that will increase his net worth."

After a short stay in the restaurant, the older man stood to leave. As he began walking away from Lishan's view, she noticed he took a glimpse of Beck and herself before departing. It seemed innocuous, but still it registered a flag in Lishan's mind.

"Lishan?"

She had drifted from the conversation.

"Oh, sorry. That man who sat down across from us, only about fifteen minutes ago, just took a long look at us as he was leaving."

Beck looked behind him, but no one was in sight. "Probably just curious," he said. "Where were we?"

"How did you know...about the court case that went flat?"

"I would rather not answer that one, if you don't mind."

"I can understand," Lishan said. Then she looked Beck straight on. "If you are coming to new terms with your values—if you are—how can you continue to work for the likes of the vice warden?"

Beck didn't like the question, but he knew why. It bothered him about himself.

"The problem is that the prison and the local officials have been a great source of income for me, and I...can't compromise..." His words trailed off.

"Can't compromise what? The loyalty to crooks? Your values?"

"Ouch." Standing, he walked a few feet, then back, like a caged mountain lion.

"You just accused me of not living by my values."

"You wouldn't be upset if I didn't strike a nerve. Perhaps you *are* compromising."

Beck stopped and turned. "Suppose I am. You don't know me well enough...." He stopped talking, then sat down. "I came here tonight to make amends, not to be judged." His features had hardened.

"Am I judging you, or are you judging yourself? If it's you yourself, it's not comfortable, is it? I know, I've been there. You didn't think it would happen at the flip of a switch, did you?" Lishan let her eyes soften.

Beck noticed. "It's.... It's me. Lishan, I..." He pursed his lips, his hands visibly shaking. "The restaurant is closing shortly. Could we continue this conversation? The lounge is open until two."

Aside from catching a train in the morning, she decided it wouldn't hurt her to stay up. Besides, she had enough compassion to not leave him stranded at this crossroads.

"Okay. For a while."

After settling the bill, they made their way to a quiet, dimly lit table in the lounge.

To help soften the tone, Lishan added a personal touch.

"I'm experimenting with an occasional mixed drink these days. I've always been a wine connoisseur, occasionally beer, but I managed to miss the boat for which tequila to buy, why rum, which gin. Maybe you have a few ideas."

"I have a few." Beck was clearly comforted by Lishan's decision.

Half an hour into their conversation, the waiter came over. "We're going to close early tonight, I'm afraid. I know it's only eleven thirty, but business is slow and the bartender's kid is sick. I hope you don't mind."

Beck looked dejected. Lishan looked pensive.

"Can we get the wine and cheese wrapped to go, please?" Lishan asked. "We understand."

Beck held a surprised look, but he said nothing.

"It's not an invitation," she said to Beck. "I just want to finish our conversation."

That was part of it for Lishan, but she felt hesitant about her well-being ever since the poisoning attempt. Having someone to talk to helped.

In Lishan's room, they settled in on the couch. Their conversation eased from deceit and corruption to family and travel.

As the last of the wine settled into their bloodstreams, they became more comfortable with one another. Beck no longer felt he was being judged, and Lishan was enjoying some distance from the recent threats and the tragedy of the poisoning. She tried to ignore it, but the wine had tempered her shell. Warmth encircled her loins.

Damn, I'm getting aroused, she thought to herself. *Is that okay? It's been quite a long time.*

They continued talking. He was sharing stories of his travels to India.

Damn, she thought again. *The Kama Sutra.*

She pushed him in a purely playful gesture.

Beck laughed, then pushed her back.

The next move was all Lishan's. She pushed him down on the couch, moving over him as she unbuttoned her blouse, unbridling her breasts. Half an hour later, they both lay there, a sweet exhaustion mixed with a sense of bewilderment. They looked at each other and just laughed.

Beck made no reference to staying. He wanted to, but felt it was best if he let her be.

Few words were spoken, but a certain levity filled the space.

They kissed goodnight—a sweet, simple kiss. Then he left his card with her and was gone.

Lishan snuggled into her bed for the balance of the night. It was the first time in days, perhaps weeks, that she felt at peace.

26

It was Monday, mid-morning, and time to take a break. Erik scanned a few channels on the television before coming to the conclusion he always arrived at: the canned applause and laughter, silly antics, and loud advertising insulted his intelligence. Feeling nauseated, he keyed in his favorite government channel.

"Good day, Chairman Bechtel and members of the subcommittee. I'm Dr. Fred Sendlen, Director of the Center for Food Safety and Applied Nutrition at the Food and Drug Administration, which is part of the Department of Health and Human Services.

As you are well aware, FDA is the federal agency that regulates virtually everything we eat, excluding meat, poultry, and processed egg products, which are covered by the USDA. I appreciate the opportunity to discuss the Agency's efforts to improve food safety, which is what we are here today to..."

Erik listened with relative detachment to the rhetoric that so often accompanied the opening, longwinded statements. He was about to doze off when a particular mention sparked him awake. Aspartame.

"There is increased evidence that the FDA needs to reevaluate a tradition in the United States. Recently, the producer of aspartame—Ajinomoto—has come before the FDA, requesting a rebranding of the sweetener under the new name AminoSweet. Yet, aspartame, also known as NutraSweet, has a reputation in certain science communities as a dangerous food additive. It's a reputation I believe the FDA needs to take under advisement again. Those communities state emphatically that aspartame can and does cause metabolic dysfunction, and that it increases appetite—counter to public belief—both of which far too often lead to obesity. Their arguments would have us look on our streets, in our schools, in our office buildings, noting that the incidence of obesity in the United States is appallingly high.

These scientists state that we are, in their words, 'yet again to be hoodwinked by an artificial sweetener, one whose marketers suggest trim waistlines when, in fact, quite the opposite—obesity—is the truth. Additionally, neurologic dysfunctions often accommodate this sweetener, resulting in headaches, seizures, vision problems, and more.'

Because of the high visibility and popularity of this controversial sweetener, one the American public is quite attached to, I thought it best to alert you..."

Again, the director droned on for several additional minutes before relinquishing his hold. A television camera panned the audience, settling for a few seconds on the FDA commissioner. He didn't look pleased, focusing his gaze on the director who, in Schuler's eyes, had said quite enough.

An immediate clamor arose as people vied for the microphone. The chair then recognized Senator Ellen Barbara, D-California. After her requisite introduction, she continued.

"I would like to address Dr. Sendlen's statements on the matter of aspartame. The science communities you reference are none other than those recognized through the highly respected National Institutes of Health. They have repeatedly upheld, with supportive studies, that the science exists—that is, aspartame is a threat to our public's health. They have posited categorically that it isn't the science that's lacking, but rather that political interests have blinded the FDA. As a result, a general mistrust of the FDA is growing out of the industry's deep pockets laden at the expense of the public's well-being.

Additionally, the FDA has acknowledged that well over ten thousand complaints have been registered wherein members of the public have suffered some form of illness from products containing aspartame or NutraSweet. It is believed, if not known, that this represents only a small fraction of the real complaints, since most go unreported. We expect this number ranges in the millions.

If the FDA is to promote the public's health and well-being as is mandated, and to ensure its highest standing in the public's eye, then it's time for the FDA to remove these dangerous substances, along with the misleading marketing, from our precious food supply."

Erik just sat there, feeling upset. Shutting off his HDTV, he pulled out his laptop and searched PubMed, the public's easiest window into the NIH database. Half an hour later, disgusted with all the evidence he'd found, he opened his cupboards and emptied them of anything containing artificial sweeteners.

He felt drained today, but he couldn't quite put his finger on the reason. He decided it would help if he took a short nap. Twenty minutes. He remembered his foxy science of sleep professor in college, how she stressed that these short, daily naps were important for brain health and reducing stress. As he laid his head on the pillow, on his nightstand he saw the small, framed photo of his favorite foster mother and father. Erik didn't think Lishan had ever seen it, given how he purposely oriented it away from view. It was a part of his life he didn't tell anyone about, including Lishan. He knew that being shuffled between six different foster homes was nothing to be ashamed of, but he was still embarrassed about it.

He had learned not to trust anyone's love, though the loving faces in the photo came the closest for him.

Go to hell, the woman yelled at him. *You are so unlovable.* He tried to run, but his legs were like rubber. Trying. Trying. *I knew I couldn't trust your love*, he screamed over his shoulder. Finally, Erik's alarm rescued him.

27

"Mr. Conner, Henry Krager from Krager Grocers is on hold for you." It was 11:30 Monday morning.

"Henry, good morning. How was your weekend? How's Maggie?" Conner's irritation was rising. Krager never called him until after his afternoon Scotch. He hoped the account wasn't going south.

"Maggie's fine, Jack. The board's not. Since the last meeting, they decided to do some investigating on their own, hoping to head off any potential downsides from an association with Conner Foods. Unfortunately, a quorum of members uncovered far more than I think you wish to hear about. It doesn't look good for you, Jack. They're beginning to seriously consider other suppliers. Someone leaked the news to the press, wanting to head off a stockholders uprising. I thought you should know."

Conner was practically speechless, thanking his previous friend for the heads-up. Within seconds of hanging up, all Charlotte could hear was the smashing of everything that wasn't nailed down.

"Mazzini, dammit," were the only intelligible words she could hear through the door as she saw his phone line go active.

- - -

Lishan made the 9:15 a.m. train back to D.C. Before losing cell signal, she received a call from Marie Elena.

"Hi, M."

"Hi, Lishy. Whatcha up to? Not coming in?" She knew Lishan quite well.

"Elizabeth Walker gave me the day off. Perhaps Jerry wasn't informed."

"Got it. I'll tell him. What are you bringing me?" She loved to tease Lishan.

"Chocolate. Imported."

"My favorite, as you know." Marie smiled. "Meet anyone sexy this weekend?"

"M!" They both laughed. "Are you keeping track?"

"As a matter of fact, writing a steamy novel. Okay, pretty woman. I've got work to do. See you…tomorrow?"

"Tomorrow. Don't forget to schmooze the boss for me. On second thought, don't bother."

"Ohh. He must be in trouble. Something to do with the therapist, as the rumor mill goes."

Lishan paused. "Beck."

"Beck, what?"

"Answering your unanswered question."

Marie Elena hesitated, then laughed out loud after hearing the smile in Lishan's voice.

Lishan settled into the train. M was always fun to jest with. She'd been there since the previous summer. She was a tough chick, having lasted this long with Hanson.

- - -

It was late afternoon as the train passed through Maryland's tenement housing bordering the tracks. Lishan knew it was time to call her aunt and tell her everything that had happened recently, including the attempted poisoning. She knew she should have before she left for the Cove, but she just didn't have the energy for one more in-depth exploration of her life. And, sometimes, she felt her aunt could be a bit too judgmental.

"What's my lovely niece up to today?" Niesha was warm and jovial as usual.

"Hi, Auntie. I'm coming into Union Station, from upstate New York. Albany. Do you have time to meet? Things have been a little challenging these past few days."

"I can get to the train station in about thirty minutes. How's that? Are you okay?"

"Am I okay? Mostly. Don't worry. Okay, thirty minutes?"

Niesha was knee-deep in writing a proposal for an essay she was presenting to a world affairs magazine. An editor had encouraged Niesha with a nod, but she said she needed the proposal before proceeding. The editor wanted it in the next three days so she could fit it into the editorial budget.

She could feel exasperation at her niece's request. "Kaka," she said in her native tongue. *I don't have the time for this.* Niesha stifled further frustration by acknowledging this was what family did for one another. That still didn't make it easy at times.

As Lishan entered the station and departed the train, she spotted her auntie. They walked to a local café, during which Lishan gave a brief picture of her trip to Albany.

After settling in a booth at the café, Lishan took a deep breath. Niesha couldn't help but notice.

"What's going on, Lishan?"

"Someone tried to poison me. I didn't handle it well, and now a child is in the hospital. A consequence of my actions." Lishan stalled, at a loss for words.

Niesha had so many questions, but she just said, "Go on," taking hold of her niece's hand.

"I received a box of cupcakes four days ago at the paper. They came in a box from the boulangerie I frequent. They were from someone I supposedly met at a county meeting. Just a thank you. I gave one to a coworker's daughter. They were poisoned. Now she's in the hospital."

"Is she going to be okay? And why didn't you tell..." Niesha stopped, not wanting her niece to feel admonished, but she was irritated that Lishan hadn't told her.

Lishan caught the shift and was thankful to just let it go. "It didn't look good the first twenty-four hours, but her vitals stabilized. The doctors are hopeful."

Lishan stopped talking. Niesha could sense the disarray in her niece's thinking, the emotional disturbance, so she took the lead.

"Why would someone want to poison you? Oh. Conner."

While Niesha listened, she sipped her coffee and made mental note of the trigger words—exposé, Conner, taxi driver, editor, poison.

"Okay, so you've pissed off somebody. Likely Conner, from what I know of him. He seems like the type who would step on any bug in his path. And the daughter? What's her name?"

"Jennifer."

"We don't know yet that he was trying to kill you. He definitely wants to frighten you so you'll cease and desist writing about him. Not to minimize the poisoning. Still, why would he care? Most men like that seem immune to public scrutiny."

"My friend JoJo, who works for the FDA and hears rumors, said it's likely that board members for some of the companies that buy Conner's products are upset with the publicity. It makes them look bad. JoJo thinks one of the large companies threatened to take their business elsewhere." Lishan paused. "You know, maybe you're right. He just wants to scare me.

That's bad enough. Maybe my life's not in danger." Lishan didn't believe her own words, but she wanted to.

"Still, you can't take any chances." Niesha had a questioning look on her face, then one of resolve. She just couldn't hold back a comment, try as she might. "Lishan, can you understand I'm hurt that this happened four days ago and you're just now telling me?"

"Yes, I'm sorry, Auntie."

"You don't need to be sorry. I just want to know you understand." Niesha paused, then continued. "Tell me more about your trip to upstate New York."

Lishan didn't have the emotional energy to tell all of it, but she expanded on the salient points as much as she could.

Niesha took it all in, letting her compassion shine through. "Okay. Can I give you a ride home?" Niesha said. "I have an assignment I need to get back to, if that's okay."

On the ride to her apartment, Lishan brought up the topic of her therapy.

"I didn't know you were in therapy." Niesha seemed disappointed to not have been told, again.

"I thought I should investigate the relationship side of my life, including Erik."

"I've often wondered how you do it, maintaining all those men."

"All those men? Auntie, I'm not at my best, so no lectures, okay? And there haven't been *that* many in recent years. I'm growing up, you know."

"Okay, I'll concede that to you, but lectures? You don't use that tone with me unless someone has gotten to you."

"I'm sorry, Auntie. That was disrespectful of me."

"Apology accepted. It did hurt a little. Okay, no lectures." She lightened her voice, giving it a loving, motherly tone. "Empathy, you know. Once, when I was dating three fellas at the same time..."

"Auntie?"

"Yes?"

"From the child's perspective, parents and aunties don't mess around. No sex. Okay?"

"I forgot." Two seconds of silence. "So, tell me what's troubling you."

"I'm not sure. Whenever I consider commitment, I can feel myself shying away. Auntie, you remember that bad patch when I was a teenager, don't you?"

135

"Yes, of course I do. It was a difficult time for you, but not an uncommon one for someone your age, then. Do you feel injured from it?" Niesha jumped back in. "I'm asking too many questions."

"It's okay. I think I'm holding Erik—anyone, really—at bay because of the...injuries...from the hurt, the losses."

"Quite likely. But that isn't necessarily bad. If those injuries keep you from fulfilling a loving relationship, one you would truly like to enjoy, then they're getting in your way. If you use those injuries merely as a measure to help you avoid disaster—for example, someone who is ultimately harmful for you—then you've learned lessons from your troubles and applied those lessons, which is part of the process of gaining wisdom in life. Did your juvenile history come up in therapy?"

"I stumbled when she asked me about my relationships and whether I had any fault in their failures."

Niesha sat fully upright, a stern look in her eyes. "She asked you that, in those words?"

"Not exactly, but close." Lishan shifted in her seat. "She was mildly inappropriate—the first words out of her mouth, recapping why I was there, did seem disparaging." Lishan paused, thinking. "I stumbled when I remembered Lucas. All I said was that I had a relationship when I was in juvenile hall, but I regretted mentioning it afterward. I know she told the editor, Jerry, because I got called into the HR director's office, asked about whether I had a felony I didn't list on my employment application."

Niesha's anger flashed to the surface, but Lishan pushed her way forward.

"The publisher, Elizabeth Walker, got involved. When it was apparent they had no proof, because there was no felony, and that Jerry and the therapist were in collusion, the publisher became quite furious with them. She gave me a day off. By that time, I had already called the therapist's office, saying I wouldn't be needing her 'help' anymore."

Niesha's anger subsided somewhat, but it was still in her veins. She decided to move past it, to the personal side, for Lishan's sake.

"Lishan?"

"Yes?"

"Do you want to be with Erik? I know—at least, I believe I know—that he's sweet on you, and he's a nice-enough guy. Also, if I recall correctly, you go a little wiggie at the mention of him."

"Wiggie?"

"Yes, wiggie. Deal. And?"

"We don't sleep together." The restrained exasperation in Lishan's voice was evident. "Yes, I know he likes me. And, no, well, yes, I do go a little *wiggie* about him, and I have hesitations as well. Goodness, Auntie. What else?"

Niesha smiled an understanding smile. "Backing up a step, do you have a gut feeling about being with Erik?"

"If I only knew. At times, I think so, that I would like it. But he gets so jealous, flying off the, what...handle."

As the conversation about Erik wound down, it turned to Lishan's safety.

"How safe do you feel it is to stay in your apartment?"

"I'm thinking I'm okay there. If that changes, I won't hesitate to leave."

As Niesha dropped Lishan off at the apartment complex, she insisted her niece keep her apprised of development. "Promise?"

"Yes, Auntie."

- - -

At last, Lishan said to herself as she entered her apartment. She was exhausted. Two voicemails had triggered her answering machine. She was one of a dwindling number of people who still liked having a landline and voicemail machine at home. Sometimes, she just didn't want to give out her cell phone number.

The first message was from Erik, just checking in, ensuring she was okay. Her face brightened, knowing how much he cared. She also felt a quiver of anxiety, wondering as to his jealousy. Rafael sleeping on her couch did seem to wrinkle Erik's brow.

The second brought fresh images. It was Beck.

"Lishan, hi. This is Beck. First of all, thank you for last night. You've gotten through to me where others did not, or didn't care to." He paused before continuing. "I'm conflicted about what to tell you, but I believe helping you is the right thing to do, my best next step in life." Beck paused. "I have two names for you. A Conner bouncer—Johnny Mazzini. Goes by Mazzini. He feels 'Johnny' is too, in his words, queer. And Fatima Habiba. Thought you should know. Before I began doing detective work for Conner, I was a production manager for one of Conner Foods factories for a while. Did I tell you that already?

In any case, Fatima, an employee, was injured due to Conner's testing one of his trans fatty additives in the factory's lunchroom. I hope your phone isn't tapped. Or mine. No, they wouldn't. Would they? Get in touch if and when you feel like it. Take care."

Lishan could hear Beck's uncertainty. She appreciated his attempts to make change in himself. As she had shared with him, it wasn't always easy.

The third. *Jerry, ah, Jerry. So predictable.* Lishan laughed as the message began, "Where in the hell are you this time, Princess Lishan? I'm deducting this from your pay. I hope you're not..." Pressing delete always felt good to Lishan, whether Jerry's message was finished or not. Especially when it was not. She'd deal with it tomorrow. *Soon enough.*

The hot shower felt lavish, washing off the remnants of travel. Flashbacks of Beck formed on her body as the water caressed her.

The top shelf of her closet bore a pile of neatly folded shorts. She contemplated a loose-fitting khaki pair but decided she was staying in. Pajama bottoms were in order. A dark pullover t-shirt, wide at the neck, finished the job. She never did like that tight feeling against her neck.

She decided to have that cup of coffee—an espresso from the small home system she purchased several years back. It had never failed to cheer her up or spur her on, whichever was in need. While making the espresso, she was reminded of two stories from her past. Six years ago, she'd talked her close friend, Robert, into getting an espresso. Robert was an Italian cowboy, raised on a Northern California ranch, riding rodeos before turning hairdresser. He loved coffee of his own making but had never tried an espresso. "This tastes like burnt coffee," Robert said after his first taste. The downturned expression of Robert's mouth made them both laugh. Then there was a sign Lishan had heard about from a hippie friend, a sign in an old coffee house in the seventies. Espresso was new to the area. On the chalkboard displaying the café's menu, below "Espresso," it read: "If you don't know what it is, you don't want any." She smiled at the memories.

"Erik, hi. This is..."

"I know. Did you get my message?" His voice had a distinct edge to it.

"If you mean the voice mail asking how I am, yes. If it was something else, no."

"You writers. So specific. Are you at home?"

"Yes. I arrived back several hours ago."

"Back?"

"From upstate New York. I didn't tell you?" It wasn't a question as much as a realization.

"No, you didn't. Are you okay? I've been worried about you for three days. You're in danger, and you just leave without letting me know?"

Lishan was quiet. She had no argument. "Yes. I, uh, can understand how you would feel. I'm truly sorry, Erik. No question."

Erik softened, to a point, but followed with more abrasion in his tone. "Did you go away with someone? Is he there?"

"No. No one is here. I didn't go away with anyone. I was following a lead on Conner." She knew she was avoiding the subject of Beck. "Look, can I come over. This is all done so much better in person."

"Sure. Come on by. But I don't know what you mean by 'this is all done so much better.'"

Lishan sighed to herself, knowing it could be a rough visit. She said she would be there in a few minutes.

After they attempted to settle in on his couch, he got straight to what was on his mind.

"Did you sleep with someone? I just need to know."

Lishan raised her voice. "Why do you always relate my life to having been with someone?"

"Let's see. As of late, there's the studly former work associate who stayed over the other night, then whoever you met this weekend. You did sleep with someone new, am I correct?"

She was silent at first, unsure of what to say. "Erik, I…"

"My point, exactly. James, Rafael, Miles from a year ago…"

"Got it, got it, got it. Look, I went to New York to follow a lead on an author who's in prison for writing about food and corruption. More specifically, about Jack Conner. I was being followed by this PI guy, Beck. I had to stay two nights in a motel. The second night he came by. I had no plans to sleep with him, or anyone for that matter. I guess I just got a little afraid to be alone, given the poisoning."

More silence.

"He's a private detective for the vice warden. Just checking me out." *Why the hell did I say that?* "I did get my interview, but the vice warden didn't make it easy. I had to stay an extra, unplanned night." She stopped. "Are you jealous?"

"Yes and no, all rolled into one messy concoction."

"Can we just start fresh, Erik? No, actually, I want to know. Do you think I was wrong to sleep with this guy? You and I aren't having sex. So I miss it. I'm not bad for it."

"No, I suppose not. I just felt...wounded." Erik's tone softened.

Lishan's breathing slowed a little, but she still needed to press a point. "Why do you get angry, then? You've done this before. Blue skies then wham, the tempest—usually unwarranted, in my opinion."

Erik stood, feeling caged. "Look, it's who I am."

"That's it? Your reason, your excuse, is that's who you are?"

Erik quieted, as though a switch had flipped. "You know, you're right. I should never treat you badly. I was just jealous."

Lishan felt the drawbridge lower, the tension ease. She wanted to please this guy she had feelings for. She cared, but she didn't want to lose herself in the process. Then she smiled—not too bright, but still a smile.

She pointed to a calendar on his wall. "Listen, do you see this day? It's today." She hesitated, finding her thoughts, her words. "The month is half over."

She turned the calendar to the next month, pointing to a Friday night. "It's the thirteenth. In olden times, thirteen was a lucky number, until the church cranked up the oppression against women. So, the thirteenth. It's a powerful day." Her voice was not loud, but it was strong, obdurate. "We now have a date for that day. Don't forget it." She drew something next to the date.

He looked at the calendar, the muscles in his face loosening. "A heart?"

Lishan managed a smile and then kissed him on the cheek. They both seemed to feel lost for a moment. Erik spoke up and broke the spell.

"Hungry?" Erik went to his kitchen, returning with chips and some guacamole he'd made earlier.

"Lishan, you—we—can no longer ignore that your life might be—no, is—in danger." He sat next to her on the couch, his knee pressing against her thigh. Taking both of her hands, the lover and caregiver in him came through. "Lishan, you know I love you...as a friend...all right, as a close friend. Considering who Conner is, your epitaph isn't far off, and I can't let that happen."

He stopped, asking, "What can I get you to drink?"

"You like cab, don't you? Got any?"

Erik smiled. He wanted to be in Lishan's good graces. "It's been in the fridge. I'll pour two glasses. While it breathes, I'll break out some Gouda if you like."

Their comfort level returned to what they had always known. Perhaps five minutes later, Erik continued.

"Okay. Should we seriously consider that Conner wants you muffled? Euphemism aside—dead or otherwise silenced."

Lishan told him what JoJo had said about Conner's clients pulling out.

"I can see that touching a nerve in someone of Conner's caliber. Say, where's that book I gave you...you know, the 'propaganda'?"

Lishan retrieved it from her bag. They spent the next hour under its hood, hoping to uncover anything additional that would help Lishan's case.

"What's this? Who's Johnny Mazzini?" Erik was pointing to a name that had notes penciled next to it.

"He handles tough customers for Conner."

"How do you know of him?"

Lishan swallowed. "For one, through the private detective."

"Oh."

"He also gave me info on a woman named Fatima Habiba, who I need to look up. She's an employee of Conner Foods, and she apparently has some dirt on him. Look Erik, the P.I. does work for the prison, but he took a shine to me because I stood up to his bullshit. I think his guilt has gotten to him, so he's playing counter-intelligence for me." Practically muttering, she added, "I wonder how they would react if they knew?"

"I'm glad he's helping. Just keep him out of your bedroom. I can only handle so much." Erik laughed, but it was stinted.

"Do you have any vacation or sick time to burn up?" Erik added.

Before she could answer, Erik continued with a plan. "This would give you the time to uncover your answers. Beginning in the morning, we can find out why this Mazzini is important. What has he done? What do you think?"

"Yes-s-s." She drew the answer out, persuading herself in the process. "I'll arrange for a couple of days, at least."

"Okay. I'll bet you would enjoy some sleep, some quiet." He gave her a hug and a brief kiss on the lips. "See you in the morning. Say, I should have your phone disconnected, don't you think? Privacy laws won't stop these guys."

The thought of her privacy being readily compromised gave Lishan pause. "Yes. Okay. What about my cell phone?"

"Get another one. A burner. Someone else's name. Easy enough." As he closed the door behind him, he whispered, "Oh, and don't use your car for now. You don't use it that often, if I remember correctly. I'll move it to a friend's house, nearby, if you don't mind. In fact, don't use it at all until this thing gets settled. Use well-lit public transportation, or I can rent a car for you. We have to do this right. Use the back entrance. Disguising your looks would be in order. Take this seriously. Good night, Lishan."

"Good night, Erik." Her answer was distracted as he left. Her life was truly in danger. *How could that be?* She was a reporter. *Did I ever hurt anyone?* That last thought was troubling. Maybe she did.

Sleep was laborious. After the first hour of restlessness, she took a three-milligram melatonin supplement. It always worked for those red-eye flights. Why not now? *Beck was calling to her for help. Pleading. Beck and Erik being subdued by Rafael—a jealous descendant of de Sade.*

Beck was finally home, settling in for the evening after a provocative weekend. It was Monday evening. The penthouse condo he purchased six months ago on State Street, in Albany's Center Square neighborhood, was perfect for him—comfortable, suited to his taste, his lifestyle. The blend of eclectic coffee houses and boutique shops nearby, amidst an array of taverns, felt like his former home in the Village.

Life is good, he said to himself.

He poured a glass of Saratoga Winery Cab, 2008.

"California's got nothing over us. New York rules," Beck would say when down at the local market. He had some cheese as well—Washington County Cheese, Camembert-style.

Beck felt smug when snubbing the popular establishment. This was his evening ritual—the wine, cheese, imported crackers, all before he took his evening shower. Beck felt extravagant, and he loved it. Then he remembered Lishan. Fear overtook him as he recalled the crack in his loyalty to Jack Conner. But Beck just shook it off, convincing himself it was nothing. The smile returned.

After the *hors d'oeuvres*—as he liked to refer to his snacks— he slightly opened the door to the balcony, enjoying the coolness in the air. He thought he heard his floor creak behind him, but turning quickly produced nothing. *Just jittery*, he thought. *Nothing to be concerned about. Jack won't find out. We just talked. It's not as though I jumped ship, or divulged anything I shouldn't have. Or, did I?*

He tried to shake the feeling. Pouring another few ounces of wine, he looked around his condominium. Everything was in order. Beck felt a sigh of relief and proceeded to finish the wine and head toward the shower.

Just in case, Beck thought, as he put his .38 and holster on the vanity. He knew Conner all too well.

With the warmth of the shower running down his body, a sweet waterfall from his elephant showerhead, he finally lost track of time and worry. After the final rinse of the Brazilian Citrus conditioner from his hair, he opened his eyes and thought he saw the flicker of a shadow on a living room wall.

Probably just the lights, he thought.

As he looked down, turning off the shower control, he heard something hit the inside of the shower, just above his head. Then he felt a squirming at his feet.

Beck looked down in horror, afraid of what unknown, unthinkable thing he would find.

There was a cobra at his feet.

Beck screamed, breaking the glass door out of its frame as he attempted to free himself from danger. But the cobra was too quick for Beck, protecting itself by inflicting its venom into Beck's left thigh. In the melee, Beck slipped and hit his head with full force on the bathroom floor. He stopped moving, though he still breathed.

Mazzini quietly stepped around in view of the bathroom. The cobra was on the floor next to Beck. Mazzini—with full combat boots, leggings, and a bulletproof vest on under his suit—reached in front of the snake with his gloved left hand, gently waving it slowly back and forth, flat palm facing the snake.

"Naja," he called to the snake. "Naja, Naja, Naja," he said over and over, soothing the snake. With his right hand, also gloved, he quickly grabbed it behind its head and put it in a sturdy, dark bag. "There, there, my pet. You're safe, now."

Mazzini looked one last time at Beck, whose breath was slowing.

"Not much longer, my friend," Mazzini said. Then he left as he had come—through the front door, with lock-picks stowed in his pocket and sixty-inch tongs in case Naja was unruly.

Elizabeth Walker sat in her office, slowly shaking her head when she recalled last week's HR meeting with her editor, the HR director, and Lishan Amir.

In front of her was a full file of Human Resources reports against Jerry. Keywords in the report continued to illuminate a pattern: mean, disrespectful, judgmental, harsh, inappropriate.

Picking up the phone, she sighed as one of the HR staff members answered. She was relieved that it was Camille, since her trust of the HR director was in serious question.

"Camille, do we know anything about Jerry Hanson's history? Anything offering insight into his anger, his inappropriate actions?"

Camille Hernandez sat back, gazing skyward for an answer. "We have very little on file," she offered. "Grapevine has it that he served a stint in juvenile hall for theft. He has been clean ever since—decades ago. I believe counseling is our only recourse, short of letting him go. Do you think he'll go for it?"

"I don't know. Most men who refuse therapy are the ones who need it the most. Reminds me somewhat of the Dunning-Kruger effect." Elizabeth paused. "Something tells me he would rather go down than exhibit anything approaching tenderness, of which there was likely very little in his childhood. Also, sources suggest he has a relationship with one of the Employee Assistance therapists. Let me think about the approach. Thanks, Camille."

- - -

"Is that it? You get off and leave me high and dry?" Stella was miffed.

Jerry looked at her from his anatomical position on the bed, his look faraway. "How can I get back at Lishan without getting fired?"

"I *thought* you were somewhere else." Stella lit a cigarette. She felt empowered when she rebelled against what everyone said was bad for her. "Why don't you set a trap?"

"Like what?"

"Like...I don't know. It could be an ethics issue, or..."

"No. She would see through it."

"Libel or slander?"

"Too smart."

Stella put on a robe and went to her bar, pouring two glasses of Glenfiddich. Up for her. Over for Jerry. She chose the twelve-year Reserve rather than her eighteen-year, which she wouldn't waste on a rascal like Jerry.

"Is there an issue—one where she's been known to, as they say, blow her cool?" Stella professed her dislike for clichés and idioms, yet she used them frequently. "I know!" She looked directly at Jerry. "You should reassign her—a position so utterly vapid and distasteful to her that she'll just quit."

Jerry's face lit up—clearly something he felt entirely at home with.

They both narrowed their eyes, then clinked glasses. "To evil," he said.

"Corruption," she said.

34

"Jerry Hanson?" The juvenile hall supervisor looked up at the youth standing in his office.

The boy simply nodded.

"I see you're here for robbery, Jerry," the supervisor said wearily, looking at the paperwork. "You're only sixteen. Why? What prompted you?"

It was a rhetorical question. He had already read an essay written by the boy who transferred to this facility earlier that day. Jerry Hanson had grown up in a family where his father had run off, and the mother repeatedly told her son it was his fault his father left, that she didn't love him and he was worthless. Jerry met her expectations at an early age, barely saved from a continued life of incarceration through a Job Corps program.

51

She smelled of sweat when she finally woke up the next morning. It was 7:00 a.m., Tuesday. Her sleep was interrupted by the scent of bacon and eggs. Erik had the tray in his hands as he let himself in. He had knocked lightly but chose not to wait.

"Hey, sleepy. A quick breakfast for you. I hope you don't mind. If I'm overbearing, don't let it slide. I've got to run. A full load today. Oh...your car is moved." He told her where it was, blew her a kiss, and was gone.

"Thank you!" She wasn't sure if he heard her or not. Lishan felt unsettled. Her life had encountered a detour.

After the surprise breakfast, she coerced an espresso through her sleepiness. Twenty minutes later, the full circles of her pupils were finally visible. She opened the book to find the references to Mazzini.

Lishan called Marie Elena, arranging for a few days off. She settled in, enjoying the bacon, eggs, and stout coffee.

Launching her Internet search—"Johnny Mazzini." *Go.* Several hundred hits.

Lishan knew, though, that a great deal of data was buried within websites and servers, not to be revealed to the average search. It would take drilling down. Government sites. Conner servers.

The initial hits all related to a few trials in which Mazzini was accused of strong-arming, abduction, and one known murder. Most articles hinted at a relationship with Conner Foods. Mazzini was acquitted of all charges. At a glance, there wasn't anything to go on.

But Lishan expected as much. Then she narrowed her search using the Boolean "and"—Mazzini "and" Conner. Mazzini "and" FDA. As she paged through the hits, one caught her attention. Who was that fellow, dressed to the nines with Mazzini? It struck her—Nathaniel Ferrali.

She made the pertinent notes, then decided to call Auntie, since she had a hacker friend who might help.

"Auntie, hi."

"Are you okay?" Niesha seemed unsettled.

"Yes. And you, Auntie?"

"I'm fine. Just concerned about my niece. Any new threats? Are you safe?"

"For now, I feel surprisingly okay. Auntie, can you give me the name of that hacker friend of yours, the Unix expert? I'm trying to break into the email of one of Conner's henchmen." Lishan gave a thumbnail sketch of what she found in Frazier's book.

A few minutes later, with the contact info in hand, Lishan hung up after they promised each other to be extra cautious.

"Joshua, hi. My name is Lishan. I'm Niesha's niece..."

After discussing the seriousness of what they were up against, ensuring that Joshua would be aware of the dangers if he agreed, he said he would call her as soon as there was news.

The coffee was especially warming this morning, given the increasing chill as winter approached. She contemplated going for a run when she recalled Erik's suggestion—no, command—that she disguise herself. Her hair was just below her shoulders. Perhaps a haircut was due, but someplace new. She decided against the running clothes, since the floppy river hat she chose for cover needed complimentary clothing. Long pants, cargo pockets, baggy sweatshirt. Boots.

Down the back stairs, using the service entrance, she headed toward downtown Georgetown. *Haircut first, then perhaps a stop at a bakery. One of those tasty butter croissants*, she thought.

Mustang Salon loomed. Catchy. It sounded a bit cowboy for the area, but perhaps that was the draw. Something unusual.

A walk-in with Sally, the owner. The particulars: something new and a need to not be quite so recognizable. Not short, though. Sally understood.

"Any relation to The Ranch?"

Sally gave her the long blink, as in "how original."

"Just making sure: which state is your reference?" Sally asked.

"Nevada. Is there another?"

"Depends on how worldly you are. Are you...worldly?"

"Depends on your reference." Lishan was already enjoying the banter. "But, yes, I suppose you could say I am. What is your measure?"

"By the way, don't perturb me. I *am* cutting your hair." She laughed. "My measure? Let's see. Do you prefer staying at the

Ritz? Ever been in a marginalized country? Do you speak any other languages?"

Grinning, Lishan listed her answers. "No, but I have stayed there. Yes. And yes."

Sally stood back a pace and took a long look at her new customer. "You're funny. You should let me cut your hair more often."

"Perhaps I will, if you answer my original question."

"Ah, yes." She was silent while a few additional wisps hit the floor. "You might say yes. I was a manager, along with three other women."

"Management. No men on that end, I see."

"We didn't particularly like men. We just wanted to see them get, uh, screwed." Sally laughed again, this time from deep in her belly.

They both continued to quip amidst seriousness over the next twenty minutes, culminating in a few ounces of hair on the ground, one hug, and a promise to do it again.

Glancing in a mirror as she left, Lishan decided she might still pass for Lishan, but it was a beginning.

Heading back toward her flat, a headline caught her attention from a *Mirror* newspaper rack. "Private Investigator Found Dead."

She felt her adrenals kick in. No, it couldn't be, she told herself. She paid six bits to the steel vendor, reading as she walked off. No name was offered, pending the usual, but the victim was indeed from upstate New York—Albany. Male.

Lishan's heart seemed to skip more than one beat. "No," she nearly said out loud. "It can't be." Her eyes moistened. Reading further...cause of death: snake bite. Further details pending autopsy. One additional item: a scribbled note on a pad near the body read, "One down, one to go."

Lishan stopped abruptly. Taking a seat at the nearest bench, she took in her surroundings. Her vigilance heightened. Was she being followed? Her entire nature felt grave; none of her normally jovial features were to be found. The phone call to her home, giving the names of Mazzini and Fatima, was this the final straw? Then she remembered the older man sitting behind Beck in the restaurant. Was that Mazzini? "One down, one to go" could only mean she was next.

She doubled back to the salon. Sally was lounging fully into a black leather couch, feet propped up on the coffee table full of magazines. She smiled at Lishan's approach.

"Hey, Sally. Can you take off another inch? I need to go underground for awhile."

"Sure, baby." She picked up on Lishan's distress. "What's wrong, Lishan? Anything I can help with?"

Lishan felt as though she was off the beaten path here with Sally, who seemed to be part of the underground as well.

"I didn't tell you before. We were newbies an hour ago, you know." Lishan braced a bare smile. "I write for *The Mirror*. I've apparently peeved the wrong person, or persons, once and for all—Senator Libby and CEO Jack Conner, in collusion with the FDA. Conner and Libby are the ones I don't trust."

"How bad can it be? You've written something someone doesn't like. That's not usually perilous in today's world. Or, is it?"

"You're right—not normally. But I've touched a nerve, a deep one. Here, look at this." Lishan put the article on Sally's lap. "I knew this investigator. Not well, or I should say, not long. We just met over the weekend. But he knows, or knew, this crowd and confided in me some information someone thought best kept private—so much so, that they murdered him. At least, that's how I see it. And I'm implicated by having attained some knowledge I'm not supposed to have." Lishan paused, pensive.

As she looked at the front page again, she saw a small article further down, one about Krager Grocers giving Conner Foods the boot. Now, any doubt was removed. She was next, and it wouldn't be just a warning.

"I need a different look. Maybe shorter still, something like what Halle Berry would wear."

Then she collapsed into tears. Sally quickly moved next to her, stroking Lishan's hair and holding her until the flow subsided.

"There, there," Sally whispered. After a moment, she said. "Okay, let's do what we can, but without ruining those good looks of yours...not that that's possible."

Thirty minutes later, with half of her hair length in a foxtail broom pan, Lishan walked out with the look of a groomed metrosexual, albeit with a barely suppressible female form and facial features to match. Again, it was the back streets on her way home.

- - -

151

As Lishan walked, she felt the need to be distracted, to talk with someone. On a whim, deciding she had some time and could use some encouraging words, she called JoJo on the off chance he was available.

Lishan pressed the call button next to JoJo's contact entry. "Of course I will," was the reply in the earpiece.

"Of course you will what?" Lishan asked, lightly perplexed.

"Meet you for coffee. You *were* going to ask me, weren't you?"

They agreed on an Ethiopian restaurant in Georgetown.

"JoJo, there's no longer any doubt. Did you see the front page today, about the P.I. being murdered? I met him over the weekend. Now he's dead. The note said, 'One down, one to go.' I'm next. It could be risky for you to meet with me."

"Count me in. I'll be right there," was all he said.

Twenty minutes later they were sitting with a large bowl of wonderfully spiced vegetables over injera.

"I thought it took you at least half an hour to get in the area?"

JoJo barely smiled. "I left early. Worked late last night. Overtime in check, you know." He looked at the bowl in front of them. "I suppose you just tear off pieces of..."

"Injera."

"...And scoop up the veggies?"

"Yes." Lishan said. Teach by example.

"I like your new look," JoJo said, as he reached over and felt Lishan's much shorter hair. Then the features of his face pulled inward. "Lishan, fill me in so I can know best how to help."

Lishan spent the next fifteen minutes telling JoJo the salient points, including talking with Beck in the restaurant and the man—probably a Conner hit-man named Mazzini—listening to their conversation. When she confirmed JoJo's earlier concerns about one of Conner Foods' clients bailing out by showing him the news piece, JoJo's face lost any hint of pleasantry.

"Okay. You must move out of the apartment building. I can scare up a couch for you. We can..."

Lishan was holding back tears, wanting to appear strong and unconcerned, but the moisture in her eyes gave her away. JoJo moved to her seat and held her, stroking her hair to soothe her. For a moment, neither one spoke.

"My life is falling apart, JoJo. *Falling apart.* I just wanted to call attention to some of the injustice in the world, get people to do the right thing. How misguided have I been?"

"Not misguided at all, Lishy. Where would the world be without King and Mandela, without their fortitude, their speaking up?"

"King and Mandela are dead," Lishan said, sniffling.

Shit, JoJo thought, admonishing himself.

"Yes, but you're not. And you won't be. We learn from these great leaders, as others will learn from you."

When Lishan's breathing had slowed, she sat up straight, wiping her eyes.

"Okay, you're right."

They spent the next half hour brainstorming, with Lishan coming away with a reasonably solid sense of what to do, what to avoid.

"Lishan, I have to go, unless you're not ready for me to leave. I can make a call and stay as long as you need me."

Lishan said she would be all right. Not to worry.

"Of course I'll worry. Okay, you have my number. Call me if you need anything, anything at all. Day or night. Doesn't matter. Promise?"

"I promise."

As he stood to leave, he said, "I just remembered, the other day I made a list of a few FDA items for your next exposé. I want you to have these."

Lishan looked up at the torn-out notebook page. "Thank you," adding, "My next exposé? Did I say I was writing one?"

"Perhaps. Perhaps not. But it's in your blood, or your genes. Take a look at this list when you get a chance. Wait until after this all blows over."

Lishan couldn't help but give it a once-over, holding the paper up to the sunlight bending through the window.

- Propulsid...heartburn medicine...subsidiary of Johnson & Johnson...eight children died...FDA didn't carry its own investigations far enough.

- Pharmaceutical Research and Manufacturers of America, the trade organization of Big Pharma, spends approximately $150M annually in lobbying, including the FDA.

- A Wyeth anti-nausea drug was deemed responsible (by a jury) for a Vermont musician having his arm amputated.

- In February of 2004, the Union of Concerned Scientists accused the Bush administration of interfering with scientific research by politicizing various issues, including asking National Institutes of Health nominees if they had voted for Bush.

- The Hatch-Waxman Act created a huge opening for generic drugs. It was found that certain companies got their generic drugs approved faster than other companies. Five FDA officials and numerous employees within certain generic drug companies were convicted of felonies. Greed and power are unfortunate aspects that thread their way through far too many of our species. Too bad.

- Check POTUS tweets for clues to Big Pharma favors

"A partial list?"

"There wasn't enough paper in the office," JoJo quipped.

As they stood, Lishan asked, "Have you heard of the author Alan Frazier, who's in prison for writing a book about Conner?"

"It created quite a stir in the office. I was a relative newbie at the FDA when it flared. Conner wanted this to be a lesson to anyone foolish enough to tarnish the name of Jack Conner. Nothing less than prison for Frazier. So an illegal surveillance charge was trumped up. Frazier received a four-year sentence, one that many knew was unwarranted." After a brief hug and kiss on the cheek, JoJo said, "Okay, gotta run. Remember the couch offer. Call me." JoJo's face was serious.

- - -

As Lishan approached the apartment building, she slowed. If this was a full-scale operation, all entrances might be covered. She took cover behind a few cherry trees and waited ten minutes. Finally, she opened the service entrance door.

She didn't know whether the stairs or the elevator was the safest route. This was new to her. She had been surreptitious in her time, tracking a few antagonists, or protagonists, depending, for a story. But never this—her own life at stake. Was she making this up, her situation? Instinct told her Beck's fate answered the question. The elevator it was. The solitude of the stairwells felt eerie.

Her apartment felt foreign when she entered. No telephone messages. Actually, no telephone. A familiar warmth emanated as she noticed a bouquet of fresh flowers in a vase on the coffee table. Aside it, the note from Erik brought comfort. "Hugs, *mon amie*. A new cell phone is on your dresser. Food in the fridge. Love. The Landlord :-) ."

Erik had always been there for her. At times she knew just what that meant to her, deep down in her heart. Attempting to hide the remnant of tears, Lishan thought she would distract herself with food.

Half an hour later, Joshua called back on her old cell phone. *I must remember to quit using this one.*

"It wasn't too difficult," he said. "I'm thinking he's a bit careless in the computer world of ones and zeroes, where otherwise he might wear gloves—from what you've told me."

Thanking him, she got to work. Joshua had given her Mazzini's ISP—a Conner Foods company website—username JMazzini, password Godfather.

Oh, brother, she thought. *How original.*

The logon would open a significant door for Lishan. She felt the adrenaline fill her bloodstream. Logging in through the mail menu item on the website, she downloaded any email that seemed pertinent. Lishan hoped no one would notice the intrusion.

Lishan spent the next two hours absorbed in text searches within the stolen mail. The first email to catch her breath was one received yesterday from Jacko@Connerfoods.com.

"He has betrayed us. As you know, the Mod X3 Connola Oil affair could be troublesome, especially with his handling of it. Still have your pet? J."

Lishan was nearly hyperventilating now; her eyes moistened. This was the most recent email. She knew it related to Beck. Did Mazzini have a pet snake? she wondered. Feeling lightheaded, she stood, steadying herself against the table. She found the stash Erik had left in the refrigerator. The turkey and avocado sandwich provided the carbohydrate and protein load she needed. She returned to her laptop.

Continuing, she keyed in 'Beck' as her search criteria. Seventeen items. When number ten appeared, Lishan slowed down, leaning into the display. Something had gone wrong involving Conner Foods and Beck. A mention of "two deaths" and "payouts" got her attention. An hour later, Lishan had developed a view into Conner Foods, a view the public was never meant to see. She was surprised at how candid these men were in their emailing. *Perhaps they think they're above the law.*

She decided on additional search criteria. What would she look for? After a handful of unsuccessful search choices, she tried "factory" on a whim. The third of four hits in the inbox caused Lishan to draw her breath.

"Johnny. Get in touch with Beck from Factory 17. We've been spiking the desserts in the employee cafeteria for a month, testing Mod X3 Connola Oil. Ran our own brand of testing of our improved X3, tested on our employees. It would have increased the shelf life for our baked goods line by over 50 percent, adding millions in sales. Two workers died. Others very sick. Do what you're good at to keep this under wraps. Jack."

Another. "Beck, X3 bailout. Fix this...now. Payout as necessary. Especially Fatima Habiba. She's a troublemaker. No more than $100,000 each family. For Haslak, $200,000 or a bullet. Your choice. Threaten them with their family's well-being if they say one word. Call me by day's end. Hush is vital. Mazzini, help if need be. His phone is 212-555-4355. Jack."

Email number fourteen: "Beck, good work keeping a lid on. Promotion. No more stressful managing at 17. New position. Own hours. Private Investigating for me. 30 percent pay increase. Again, good work; and not a word...to a wife, if you get married; to a girlfriend in heat. No one. Understand? Good. Jack." Lishan noticed that Mazzini had been cc'd for these emails sent to Beck. Otherwise, she would not have seen them.

Lishan printed out these two letters. Beck must have been trusted—highly trusted. But he was expendable, if he became a liability.

Lishan sat back, peering around the room with no particular focus. Now it was clear. Conner Foods had used the factory workers at Factory 17 as guinea pigs, an experiment that resulted in deaths and illness. Email dates placed this in March, seven months ago. Now here was a nosey reporter, digging up dirt—expensive, damaging dirt on an unscrupulous CEO.

She didn't know her chances of uncovering the grit behind Modification X3, but she did have a penchant for government cover-ups and buyouts. Lishan decided to take additional time and dig through PubMed, looking for all things relevant within the FDA.

A light knock on the front door brought Lishan back to her surroundings. Cautiously, now, she quietly approached the door, intending to not give away her being at home. The security peephole brought a distorted Erik into view.

As Erik came in, he said, "By the way, I could see shadows under the door as you approached...just in case you thought you were being clever." Then he stopped, looking at her new haircut. "Have you seen Lishan?"

"Funny! I hope it slows them down in finding me."

"It's a little shorter than I like, but, if you slick it back, you'll fit right in at the bank or among Washington's finest." Erik stepped back to give the haircut its due. "It's good, though. Your natural beauty is always the victor."

Lishan noted that this was the second time today she had been told this. It was good for her ego.

At the couch, Lishan could tell Erik seemed reserved. "Are you all right?"

Erik stood up, pacing in front of the coffee table.

"I received a phone call today. Someone posing as a Social Security official said he was updating his files, wanting to know if you still lived here. I told him no, that you'd abruptly moved out a couple of days ago. He asked for your forwarding address, but I said you told me you didn't know where you were moving to, or why. He seemed satisfied; at least that was the impression he wanted to leave me with."

Erik sat back down. Lishan could tell the trouble ran deep.

"I was able to download Mazzini's email to my laptop, using a hacker friend of Auntie's." Lishan continued. "It's already provided clues to the implication of a threat on my life."

"It's not an inference."

Lishan paused, thinking to move beyond the comment. He was right.

"It's not an inference, Lishan."

"Yes, I know." Lishan shifted in her seat, disquiet in her moves. "It's not."

After a pause, "Erik?"

He stopped and looked at her. "Why is that, recently, whenever you just say 'Erik' in that tone, I feel as though I'm in the batter's box and a hardball is aimed at my temple?"

"I just saw in the newspaper..." Lishan wavered slightly, not feeling too steady. "Beck—the upstate New York P.I.—was found

157

murdered. I believe it was because he shared information with me, information he was never to divulge to anyone."

The features in Erik's face hardened for a few seconds, but he could see the fear in his friend's face. "You know, if I were him, and I met you one night in the course of doing my work, I can see... Lishan, though I was prepared not to like this guy, I can understand both sides—his, and yours." Erik let the compassion show in his face. "I'm sorry he's dead."

Lishan's eyes moistened, but she decided they needed to move on. "Yes, he's dead because of me."

"I understand how you could feel guilt about this at first, but you have to know it's not your fault, not at all. It's Conner's greed."

"But there's more. It gets worse. A note left at the murder scene read, 'One down, one to go.' I'm almost certain Mazzini, the henchman, was sitting behind Beck and me in the restaurant that night. He certainly overheard our conversation, knowing then that Beck was betraying Conner. I'm next. I know it. And, if there was any doubt, there was another headline, smaller, again front page, where one of Conner's mega clients was dropping Conner Foods because of all the negative publicity. *That* is why Conner wants my head." Lishan looked dejected, without hope in that moment.

Lishan took a deep breath. "Okay, what if I share what I've found so far?"

Erik nodded, touching her hand.

"Conner Foods had created a modified trans fat that was fractionally different from the trans fat molecular structure currently on the market. It was supposed to increase shelf life of certain foods by another two to three times. No small gain, for them. It would appear they had been serving this in their cafeteria food for several months, during which two workers died and a host of others got violently sick. The employees didn't know they were the guinea pigs. Jack Conner contacted Johnny Mazzini with instructions to get a manager named Beck, who at one time managed the facility at Factory 17, to quiet the families with payoffs. I haven't dug through the layers as of yet, but the other name that Beck left, Fatima Habiba, appears to be a significant puzzle piece."

"And when did this all take place?"

"This past March. After these discoveries, I began delving into PubMed and the FDA. I need to understand trans fats a little better if I'm going to expose Conner further."

Erik stood up abruptly. "I'll be right back."

"Something I said?"

"Yes."

She couldn't tell if he was angry or not. It all happened so quickly. Before she could give it another thought, he returned from his apartment, a smile spilling from his face..

"I guess the smile means you're not angry with me?" Lishan said sheepishly.

Erik stopped, took in what she said, then laughed out loud. "Ohhh, I understand. When I left so quickly... Don't you know I couldn't ever be seriously upset with you?" For the next second, he had that faraway look, one tied to a flash of those memories when he had mistreated Lishan with his anger. Then he sat down next to her, thigh to thigh. "Take a look."

Lishan took in the stapled research project before her.

"It's a rough draft of a research paper one of my students wrote for another class. She enlisted my editing skills."

"When was this written? No, let me answer that." Lishan read the title on the cover page. "A little over a year ago. I didn't know about this. Where was I?"

"You're a tough chick to track down sometimes. I have no idea." He made a playful half-smile, then continued. "It was written as an entry to a cardiovascular journal. The student moved, and I never heard the result. Likely, I didn't mention it because it fell off the radar."

Lishan skimmed the pages. "This is perfect. Twenty-one pages. Quite a report. I suppose I can use the material to feed my inquisition?"

"Lishan, you know your situation is serious. While I would love to play it down, I can't. Even if you back off, I doubt he'll just forget about you. Disguising yourself is a good first step, but is it enough? You have to stay away from places where they would expect to find you. If they think you've moved, it helps, but we can't relax our guard. Not here, not anywhere, until Conner and his thugs are behind bars. One other thought is to not use the service entrance. It could look suspicious. Your disguise needs to make you look much older, maybe heavier, by, say, thirty pounds. Can you do that?"

"I'll try."

"Not good enough. Sorry to be so direct. Look, I know a makeup artist at the university. What if she comes over and helps?"

Lishan agreed, her breathing laborious.

Erik said he had some apartment issues to attend to and a class to teach. He said he'd be back later and asked if she would be okay until then. "Don't let anyone in. Don't answer the door. I'll call first. I have your new number."

After Erik left, Lishan sat back, taking in this male who had graced her life in so many beautiful ways ever since they met. Wondering where he fit in her life down the road, she found herself daydreaming. She pressed a fully-caffeinated Kenya AA coffee into the espresso maker and waited for the magic brew.

Coffee in hand, she adjusted a corner pillow on the couch and buried herself in the document before her. "If It Is On the Ingredients List, How Can It Be Called Zero, Mom?" *Clever*, she thought. She read on. The paper brought to light a host of questions suggesting conflict of interest within the Agency.

An hour later, she received a call from a woman at the university's performing arts department, asking if Lishan could come down to Nomadic Theatre on campus. Lishan knew it was the right thing to do, and it would please Erik. Two hours later, Lishan returned from the theatre with makeup that added some wrinkles, along with some special padding. Adding a wide-brimmed hat and sunglasses, as the woman recommended, she said to herself, *Good! I don't think anyone will recognize me.*

At half past seven, Erik called. "Want some company? I can bring a movie in about an hour, maybe an hour and a half. Might help to take the edge off, at least for a few hours."

He arrived shortly before nine with nachos and two non-alcoholic beers. When he saw Lishan in her disguise, he started with, "I'm sorry. I must have the wrong..." Then he recognized her and smiled. "She's good, isn't she?"

"Yes, she is. I decided not to wait, so I called and ended up meeting her at Nomadic Theatre shortly after you left. Thanks, Erik. And thank you for the treats." She took off the disguise so she'd be more comfortable.

As they settled in, they could both feel that a few hours without thinking about safety would do them some good.

"Some of these NA beers taste better than you might think," Erik said as he opened the beers.

"Hey, what did you bring? Nothing 'R' rated, I hope."

Erik grinned as he pressed play. *Soylent Green* took center stage.

"Have you seen this?"

"A very long time ago. I believe it's a seventies film about a society where food is a problem and a dying public becomes part of the food chain for humans."

"Yes. Now imagine Conner as an antagonist. Hey, this could be fun."

As the movie progressed, Erik eased just a little closer to her. The warmth and comfort were inviting. Friends.

Two hours later, as the movie ended, Erik was sound asleep on Lishan's shoulder. Lishan didn't want to move. But midnight wasn't far off, and she knew she didn't do well with less than eight hours sleep, especially less than seven. Tomorrow would have to be an early riser.

"Erik. Erik. Bedtime for you."

He was out for the night. She laid his back gently into the couch, tucking him in with a fluffed pillow and her grandmother's quilt. She left a night light on above the stove, in case he awoke to the discomfort of unexpected surroundings. She set the alarm for 6:30, ensuring she would have breakfast for him before he started his day.

Her sleep was fitful, full of dreams. Daylight woke her just before the alarm. She quietly showered before easing out into the kitchen. Erik didn't stir until she clanked one too many times with the skillet.

"Where...?" His question abruptly died as the surroundings became familiar. Then another start. "Did we...?"

"No."

"No, what?"

"Isn't 'Did we...,' you know, always the question when waking up in someone else's place? At least until your brain wakes up." Lishan tried on her best girlish grin.

"Maybe for *you* it is, Ms. Gallivanter, but *I* wanted to know if, uh...where *is* my shirt?"

"I have no idea. And, no, I didn't tuck you in that way. Maybe you got hot during the night." Lishan smiled. "Okay, how do you like your eggs?"

"Hard. No gush." Erik located his delinquent top, finagling it back into place. "What's your plan for the day?"

"Perfecting my disguise, for starters. Then seeing what I can garner from the Mazzini emails. I can't fritter away any of my time. None."

Lishan served breakfast at the coffee table, where they ate in relative quiet, unusual for them.

"Bye. Call if you need anything." Erik smiled and left, leaving Lishan to herself—a feeling she often craved.

Lishan made another espresso and set to work. She felt she had two tasks before her. Most important was to stay alive. But aside from staying out of sight, she didn't know yet what to do. She hoped those answers would unfold in the next few days. As she thought about it, Lishan sensed that gathering anything against Conner, anything that would hold up in court, was an important step. Maybe it would help to identify the pros and cons of the hydrogenated world, in case it would help her bring a case against Conner and the FDA. She didn't have much to go on, yet, but she knew she couldn't just sit idle, waiting for a .38 caliber slug.

弨

Trans fats: no acceptable level, from the scientists' perspective. Johns Hopkins Medicine confirmed it. This was back in the mid-nineties. Then why had the FDA allowed it to go so long? This was the question Lishan sought to answer. And there was the problem with Factory 17.

Lishan could imagine the FDA's response, including their document delineating the timeline. The tragedy was that years passed between the inception of evidence against trans fats to the ruling in 2006 that required trans fat labeling. Part of the problem, as Lishan saw it, resembled having a bad road for six years downtown, where the Public Works department put up signs for years warning of the bad road ahead without actually repairing the road until five years had passed. The difference, though, was that the bureaucratic delays cost people their health, *and* the life-threatening fats still were not banned.

Lishan couldn't help but speculate about Conner Foods' involvement. Perhaps it was time to seek out Fatima Habiba. She decided it was worth a quick search through Mazzini's email before resorting to the older tried-and-true methods that often took awhile. While pulling up Mazzini's mail, she was reminded of her own email that she hadn't checked in several days. Her talks with Erik about hackers being able to track her left her incommunicado. Could they truly track her to her apartment if she logged on? She knew the technology existed, but it was typically beyond the expertise at the average ISP, especially since the broadband circuit belonged to the building, not to her specific apartment. She decided to take the chance but to diminish the risk by using web mail, diffusing the path to her somewhat. She missed her Android phone with which she could check email without being tracked—at least that's what she imagined.

Twenty-seven new messages. Eighteen were pure hype from the marketing genius inherent in the web. Three from Niesha, questioning her whereabouts. Four from miscellaneous friends. True to form, she deleted the unnecessary ones without looking at them, read her aunt's worries, gave cursory attention to the next four, and put her focus on the two that tightened her chest.

One from Beck; one from Rafael. Lishan slumped back. She felt a true sadness at Beck's fate.

And what about Rafael? When she thought of Rafael and Erik in the same thread...too many men. If the conglomerate clans didn't kill her...

She opened Beck's. From the date and time, it appeared he wrote it several hours before the time of death reported by the coroner. From that alone, the email seemed as a treasure.

"Dear Lishan. I find you often in my thoughts today. I feel as though I would enjoy seeing you again. That hasn't happened for me in many years. Did you receive my voicemail about Mazzini and Habiba? Check out Factory 17. I can tell you more, but I'd rather do it in person. I hope I haven't put you in danger with my notes to you. Then there's my own life, though I don't think Conner would stoop to murder. Call when you can. Beck."

Lishan stood and walked over to the balcony, standing back slightly to avoid being too visible. Reading the hopes and dreams, ultimately dashed, of one so young brought sadness and deep despair. *Hasn't the human condition improved at all? Does human life continue to take a backseat to greed?* Lishan couldn't help but mull these thoughts into a steady stream of conflict, resolved in nothing. Finally, she had to move on. Rafael.

"Hi, cutie. It has been what feels like a week. I knocked on your door over the weekend. I'm a little worried about you, plus I could use some ravishing. Call me, okay? Love, Rafael."

Ravishing? Does he think I'll just fall into bed with him because he's cute? Lishan just shook her head. For now, she had to put them aside.

- - -

Kathy's daughter, Jennifer, crossed Lishan's mind. She decided to call.

"Hi, Kathy. This is Lishan."

"You changed your number. Are you okay?"

"Yes. I could tell you stories, but I'm calling to find out about Jennifer."

"I just brought her home this morning. She's okay. Listless and feeling afraid, but the doctor said she's out of immediate danger. They want to watch her kidneys over the weeks ahead. Her blood pressure is stabilizing. Lishan, thank you for calling. I know this weighs heavily on you. Are you sure you're okay? Are you in danger?"

"I'm getting excellent counsel from my friends and my auntie. I just have to play my cards right to stay out of Conner's sight. Part of my work, now, is to find out everything I can about him—anything that will help put him away." Lishan decided not to mention the murder of the P.I. They agreed to call if any news, either about Jennifer or Conner, came up.

Feeling cooped up, she donned her disguise and went for a two-hour walk. The cold air was refreshing. She could feel the significance of having her life, of being able to experience the wonders that appeared each day. Yes, she would have to be careful so this didn't change.

Back at her apartment, she opened *CEOs & Senators*. There she found her bookmark—the business card Howard Perkins had given her at the gala. She set it aside while she read through the most pertinent chapters over the next few hours.

When she replaced the bookmark, she thought, *Yes, why not.*

"May I speak with Howard Perkins, please?"

"This is he." The voice was garbled, as though his throat needed clearing. Though the three words weren't much to go on, Lishan detected hesitation.

"Mr. Perkins, this is Lishan Amir. Do you have a minute or two?"

"How many millimeters in a meter, Ms. Amir?" His voice turned jovial after hearing her name.

Lishan blinked, catching the quip. "I would enjoy your wisdom regarding an exposé I'm planning, in part because I appear to be following in Alan Frazier's footsteps."

The pause was audible. "Not all of them, I hope. Am I drifting your way?"

Lishan smiled. A poet in this man's demeanor. "Yes. I know Alan Frazier's whereabouts. I spoke with him recently, face-to-face."

"You know, then, that my phone might be tapped. By the way, I enjoyed our interchange at the media roast."

"I was delighted, as you could no doubt tell."

"The pleasure was mine. How can I help you?"

"Can we meet for coffee, or something of your choosing?" Lishan said.

"Of course." A cough broke through. "Pardon me. My health has deteriorated since I quit spiriting my many causes. This will be good for me."

"I have another reason for wanting to meet with you, Mr. Perkins."

"Howard."

"Howard. I have managed to, shall we say, anger Jack Conner to the point where my life is in danger. I'm looking for ideas on how to mitigate his threats, and I thought you might have some. I should tell you, though, if he finds out it could be dangerous for you."

"Oh, bring it on," Howard said with an air of playfulness. "He and I have had many a go-round over the years. Why not spice it up?" Howard paused. "Are you familiar with the American Indians and Ginsberg? The architect had a significant presence here in D.C. as well. I'll meet you next door, at a venue of similar style to the original, if I haven't lost you. Today?"

Lishan thought for a few seconds, tracing thread after thread. Then she lit up. "Yes! At..." She caught herself, the possibility of a tap now all too real. "Yes. I know the place. Half an hour? 4:30?"

"Ah, the brash and the young. Give me an hour."

Lishan was pleased with her knowledge of where Alan Ginsberg hung out in Manhattan, which answered the American Indian question. The Algonquin Hotel—not quite Algonkian, but it would do. Goldwin Starrett was the architect, and Starrett was an architect for the former Garfinckel's, now Hamilton Square in D.C. Lishan knew of an aesthetic hotel on the next block that journalists lovingly referred to as the Gonk, in memory of the Algonquin.

As she wound down the stairs to the rear exit, she realized she had no disguise. Returning briefly to her apartment, she changed into the new character Erik's theater friend had created for her.

Catching a Diamond Cab, she arrived at the hotel fifteen minutes early. None of her journalist buddies called it by its real name. The Gonk would do perfectly. Besides, it was a remote reference few outside of newspaperdom would recognize. Ten minutes later, Howard entered.

He didn't recognize her, which Lishan felt was an important test to pass.

"Howard," she said quietly as she approached him.

He looked at her for a few seconds and then smiled. "Very nice," he said with kind eyes, taking in her hair. "You've put on a few pizza pounds since I saw you last. The disguise works. I didn't recognize you."

166

Without hesitation, he suggested, "Shall we find a booth?" nodding in the direction of the Whitman Lounge.

Both took in the aesthetics of the eighty-year-old brick building. It had a certain charm. Lishan thought it an ideal lounging area for those San Francisco hippies.

Leaves of Grass poetry graced the walls above the booths. The lighting was dim, perfect for their situation. Settling in, Lishan with her latte and Howard's coffee black as they come, Lishan took out her notebook.

"I admire you for taking this on. You do know how dangerous it is—what you're doing."

Lishan nodded, at first overcome by the sincerity that couched Howard's tone.

"Only too clearly. I hadn't planned it this way. I was doing my activist journalism thing, pushing the envelope, when I came across Alan's story. I had to visit him. Then I ran into Conner's private investigator."

"The P.I. recently murdered?"

"Yes. Within two days of his conscience getting the better of him, after which he shared Conner stories with me, he wound up dead."

They sat back, sipping their caffeine, contemplating the gravity of their respective situations.

"How can I best help you?"

"I've been fortunate—if that's truly what I am—to have gathered what appears to be enough information to annoy Conner, and the FDA, but my life has now been threatened, and I've never been in this situation before. Anything you know about Conner, about what you think I should do, would be greatly appreciated."

"Conner and I go back to my days as an investigative reporter. He was the bad guy. I was the hero, at least in principle. Once I wrote an exposé, much like yours, that put him and his food business in a bad light. Two days after it hit the streets, my front window was shattered by some drive-by character wielding a fist-sized rock. An attached note found in the glass shards said 'Curiosity killed the cat. We know where your sister lives.' The next day, I lost my brakes. A brake line was cut, leaving just enough fluid for the brakes to just barely work when I first drove off. I ran off the road, into a fire hydrant." Howard took a sip of his coffee. "I pretend to be a tough guy, gruff, you know, but the truth was it scared me."

"How did you resolve it?"

Howard hesitated. "You know, I'm ashamed of what I did next. I was in my early forties, feeling invincible and out for justice, but the inference was clear. Someone I knew, someone I cared about, would be drawn into the picture. I called Conner. Said I wanted to make amends. I wrote a retraction in brush strokes that painted Conner as not such a bad guy. My editor didn't want to give in to Conner, but she was concerned for me, so she agreed. I left that newspaper shortly thereafter, my tail between my legs."

"That must have been hard for you."

"Yeah. It was. Deflating. I lost faith in myself for a couple of years. When I quit doing menial jobs and went back to journalism, I took a job reporting in Lifestyles. You know—feature stories without any reference to the darker side of life. Nice and safe. Then I retired."

Lishan touched Howard's hand, letting him know she felt compassion for him. Then she drew in a deep breath, exhaled, and said, "Fear is a powerful tool. It can cause any one of us to question our mortality, our morals, our actions. But, you know, Howard, don't discount your wisdom."

Howard gave the faintest smile.

"So, what should I do about Conner?"

Howard sat up straight, as though coming to. He could see he was needed.

"You need to gather evidence—hard and fast evidence—against Conner. And you need to do it now. Not a week from now. If you can make a case against him, one that shows your life is in danger, or the lives of others, including his part in any murderous activity, you might get some judge to issue a warrant for his arrest. Is there someone you know who could press this matter?"

"I'll call my auntie. She will know. Would it help to draw in the FDA, since I'm certain the commissioner has a hand in allowing some of Conner's misdeeds, though probably not the threats against me?"

Howard leaned in, putting both elbows on the table. "Yes, it would. If you need it, I have a library of information, some specifically supporting Frazier's book and references to Conner, and some pointing out failings within the FDA."

Lishan copied Howard's posture, both giving the appearance of an illicit deal in the making as their faces leaned into one another. "The FDA. My concern is when they intentionally look the other way and support a product that patently shouldn't be on the market."

"When there's a trawler full of money to be made, you would be astounded at the excuses our species can make up in favor of their bank accounts. Have you ever heard of a Dr. Graham? He was the Associate Director for Science and Medicine in the Office of Drug Safety for the FDA. He spoke up, sharing problems in the FDA."

Lishan broke in. "I know a little of him. Didn't he make some public statement about Vioxx and the hundreds of thousands of heart attacks and deaths associated with the drug? Go on."

"Yes. And, as you might imagine, the FDA took a dim view of Dr. Graham's public airing. There are substantiated documents showing how senior officials attempted to discredit Graham—through *The Lancet*. They also tried to null Dr. Graham's senate testimony by attempting to disarm Iowa's Senator Grassley, a strong voice calling for the FDA to do its job. Then there was the pseudo Peter Principle job offer where Graham was offered a position in the commissioner's office. It all backfired. I haven't followed the most recent status of Vioxx, but I believe Merck, the manufacturer, issued a voluntary recall whereas the FDA had not—conceivably it would appear as an admission of error within the Agency."

Howard took a sip of his coffee. "Ah, I love this elixir. I hope the FDA never bans it." They both smiled at the thought—the public rising up in arms.

Lishan took the edgewise opportunity: "Wasn't the FDA's standard response that their initial studies showed no dangerous side-effects?"

"Ah, their caveat. Yes, this is nearly always their claim. But, remember that senior officials—hell, it's likely written in the creed—quote that 'Industry is the client,' with an inference that the public is not. The client gets the attention. The client wants their drugs on the market. Whatever it takes."

Lishan took a reflective pose, causing Howard to sit back, questioning Lishan. "Yes?"

"Okay. Graham, Vioxx. Now, how do we tie this to Conner, or Senator Libby, or do we even need to? And, don't let me forget Frazier. Prison, or a coffin, doesn't fit anywhere in my life's plans."

Howard replied. "Ah. Yes, let's tie it together. Are you hungry?"

"Yes, a little. Toast and coffee should do it."

"Remember the toasted chicken salad sandwich without the chicken? That was a scene to go down, somewhat, in our idiomatic halls. Nicholson was perfect."

Shared mirth and their love of film and writing brought Lishan and Howard a little bit closer. It was apparent in their body language. With food ordered, they returned to their task.

"The question is," Howard said, "does including the FDA in the case against Conner further the case at all? Or is there any chance it would muddy the water, giving Conner a loophole to squeeze through? Perhaps we don't need to concern ourselves with that decision, at least for the time being. It would seem we dig up all we can, then turn it over to the courts, if we can find one we trust. If the FDA layer becomes a separate issue, then so be it. For now, Conner must be convinced he needs to put the well-being of the public in front of profits. Everything of substance you uncover must become public...yesterday."

Howard's corned beef on rye arrived, with Lishan's toast in tow. The waitress, with whom they kidded about the chicken, rolled her eyes as she put the toast in front of Lishan. "One chicken san, sans chicken." Literary establishment that it was, she decidedly had her fill of those hackneyed references.

"Narrow escape." Howard laughed, audibly. "Okay, what do you know about Conner's additive?"

"Conner wanted to exponentially increase the shelf life of the oils in his products. Nothing wrong with the concept, except that the structure of the oil took on a nasty characteristic, a likeness to formaldehyde. I...we...have emails to prove that Conner knew about this in advance of including the experimental fat in the cafeteria at Factory 17."

"Factory 17?"

"Oh, sorry. It's one of Conner Foods' factories. Conner decided to do a test by using his employees as test subjects, without their knowledge."

"Why didn't he just go through the FDA channels?" Howard caught himself. "Puerile question. Conner wanted to fast-track the substance with some of his own test figures."

"Yes. In any case, two employees died. Others were hospitalized with severe complications. One of the surviving employees is a woman named Fatima."

"Had it gone through the requisite channels of testing?"

Lishan hesitated. "I'm not completely sure. Also, I don't know if it would have made a difference, unless the health hazard was too blatant for even the FDA to overlook. Remember that Conner Foods has a powerful lobby, undeniably more so than we would hope. Senator Libby, for one. We just can't forget that the FDA relies heavily on the testing by the client, and the client is industry—Conner Foods, in this case."

"Yes," Howard added, gaining a placeholder in the conversation. He took a brief sip of his dark brew and said, "Lishan, you doubtless know that the FDA does do a service for the American public. It's just that it falls short. They put entirely too much emphasis on whether a product works and not enough on its downside. If an industrial giant states that its new drug reduces blood pressure, and it does, then it has satisfied at least the primary entry requirement onto the list of approved drugs. Side effects get much less press. At a minimum, the side effects should be, in my opinion, at least on par with the other entry requirements—does it work, and is it safe, or at least safe enough. I'm making up these numbers, somewhat, but, for example, a drug's side effects cause fifty thousand heart attacks but the drug improves the lives of four hundred thousand people. It isn't a proper tradeoff. Perhaps a few heart attacks out of four hundred thousand might pass muster. But, again, who is the FDA's client? Industry."

"So how *did* Frazier end up in prison? He couldn't tell me much. And you? Your name is in the book. Any effect? Were you ever threatened?"

"That's a mouthful. You *are* a journalist, aren't you? Got to get all your questions in while you can." Howard smiled. "Frazier just pushed too many buttons, especially Conner's. Then again, you really aren't any different, except that Frazier ended up in prison, and Conner wants you quiet, however he can accomplish it—troublemaker that you are." Howard winked. "You see, he knows how smart you are, your perseverance. He can't afford to have you digging, talking. I wish I could tell you otherwise."

Howard gave a hearty smile after eating more of his corned beef. "I sure do enjoy this place." Then he continued.

"You've already put yourself in Conner's firing line. You need to be smarter than Frazier, who no doubt thought he wouldn't end up in jail. His mistake. You can profit from these errors, but you know you'll end up compromised if you don't get Conner in jail, or at least in court, before he gets to you. Incognito—for you, your friends, and your family. Perhaps a vacation for everyone. A cabin in the woods."

"It's becoming clear what I need to do. I just wish I didn't endanger everyone who helps me."

"A commendable attribute of yours, Lishan. Not everyone is as unselfishly caring as you are. Just know that those who care for you, believe in you, won't hold back. That's what true humanity is all about."

Lishan nodded, thinking.

For the time it took for them to order and share a cheesecake, their conversation eased into journalism, how they each got started in the field. Lishan liked this new friend. Perhaps there would be room for future coffees together.

Howard stood to leave, his face serious, "Don't do anything unwise—not the slightest hint."

After the goodbyes, Lishan took a close look out the window before she headed outside. She started as a Yellow Cab pulled up in front of the hotel. The driver looked directly at her. But she finally exhaled as two passengers embarked.

- - -

She was home. Seven o'clock. Now Lishan just wanted to be left alone. She would, as a rule, arrange for downtime or alone time, but it was usually at her whim. Recent developments seemed to have wrested control away from her. She closed her eyes on the couch. *Just for a moment,* she thought.

A knock on her door startled her from sound sleep. She awoke from the disappearing dreamy image of having three husbands at the same time, each hating the others.

Her body was sweaty, but, given the dream's content, the dream was surprisingly devoid of emotions—characteristic of her non-REM dreams. Lishan's inclination was to nonchalantly ask who was there. But recent events flooded in as the fog cleared. Another knock, then quiet. What if it were Erik? She doubted it, as he would announce himself or just let himself in. He had donned the role of bodyguard, being none too careful with her every move.

Now she was unnerved. How long should she remain quiet? Tip-toeing to the door, she was careful to avoid any change in the shadowing under the door this time.

She heard the doorknob being tried. This stopped Lishan in her tracks, thinking about what weapons she had and how quickly she could get to them. The doorknob quit moving when she heard the couple from across the hall walking past her door to their apartment. Waiting another minute, hearing nothing more, she peered through the security peephole in the door. She could see nothing. She decided to call and ask Erik if they could take a look at the security camera recording.

Moments later, they were both sitting on her couch, logging in to the security system via Lishan's laptop. Viewing the digital recordings over the past hour turned up an individual they didn't think they recognized—an older man, medium-heavy build.

"It appears he came into the building thirty minutes ago and left just five minutes ago." Erik called his voicemail to see if any other residents had registered a concern. "I hate to say it, but maybe he saw you at night, or someone he thought looked like you through the flimsy curtains, as he scanned the windows from outside."

"Or maybe he knows where I live. It couldn't be that hard to obtain my address in today's world." Lishan suddenly sat up straight, her pupils dilated, her hands beginning to sweat. "I...I think I've seen him before. Remember the man I spoke of, the one sitting behind Beck in the restaurant? I think it's the same person." Lishan's face was harrowed, looking like an acquaintance from Georgetown U who had failed both the Multistate Bar Exam and the Multistate Essay Exam—life appeared hopeless. *I have to move.*

Any mention of Beck was, at least, a minor challenge for Erik, but he saw the value in just letting go of it.

"I don't know just what you and Beck talked about, but if he divulged anything that Conner wouldn't like, then his death and the threats to you make even more sense now." Erik gathered his thoughts over the next few seconds.

"Lishan, you can't stay in this apartment."

"I am so worn down." Lishan's face was as drawn as Erik ever remembered seeing it.

"Is there anything in your email search that would help us bring Conner to justice?"

Lishan replied with reluctance, wanting to do nothing more than curl up and forget it all. She suggested they continue their search through Mazzini's email for any reference to Factory 17 or Fatima. One email, from Conner to Mazzini, struck pay dirt.

It read: "Mazzini. Fatima Habiba is causing additional trouble. Threaten her. Jack."

Lishan turned to face Erik. "I believe my next step is to find Fatima. It could be trouble. I can't just let the whole thing go, can I?" She wasn't really asking. She knew she couldn't. Lishan needed a rock to lean on. She knew Erik would be there.

"No, you can't. I wish you could. I'm worried about you."

Lishan took a deep breath, giving Erik a brief yet knowing half-smile. She continued her search for information on Fatima Habiba. Only one result, a newspaper article, shed any light. Fatima's residence as of one year ago was a small city just south of Baltimore. A generic, free people search proved fruitless. Lishan decided to opt for her peer at the Baltimore Sun, with his database access. Lishan felt it was safe enough, given that she and her journalist buddy hadn't been in touch for six months and might therefore not be monitored. Ten minutes later, and a promise to have coffee with him soon, Lishan had an address and phone number.

"Do you think they'll be watching her phone line?" Lishan expressed her concern as she reached for the new cell phone.

"Hmm. Though they might not be able to trace the call back to you here, since I registered the phone under a bogus name and address, they could monitor your phone conversation, including any meeting place you might both agree upon."

"I'll just have to go out there." She paused. "Why not tonight?"

"I should go with you. There might be a greater chance of your gaining an audience if we appear as a couple."

Lishan gave Erik a long, hard look. She could see there was little to be gained by arguing with him as his point was well made. She told him as such with a slow but poignant sigh.

"Good," was all he punctuated. "If we leave soon, it won't be too unfashionably late to knock on her door, given the circumstances."

33

They took Erik's car. With minimal traffic—an unusual occurrence between D.C. and Baltimore—they arrived on Fatima's street by 8:45 p.m. They drove down the street once, looking for signs of surveillance. Then, parking several blocks away, they made the same check on foot, as a couple going for a stroll. Lishan's disguise was in place, but the hat was inappropriate for the meeting they were hoping to have. She left it in the car, but did put on a pair of thick, black-rimmed prescription glasses she had worn a few times. They had been relegated to a shoebox of miscellaneous items since, ultimately, they didn't suit her. Tonight, though, they would do nicely.

Finally, with a sense of satisfaction as to their safety, they approached Fatima's door. Erik and Lishan had rehearsed their lines to keep from alarming Fatima.

They could hear the inhabitant behind the door, checking them out through the tiny lens. Finally, she opened the door against the short chain. "Yes, who are you?" Fatima said with a sense of caution.

"Hi. My name is Lishan Amir. I'm in trouble because of a run-in with Jack Conner. My closest friend, Erik, is with me. We need your help, if you can. Are you Fatima?"

"Tell me more." Fatima didn't budge.

"I'm possibly the next target of Conner's henchmen unless I can tag them first. I'm a reporter for a newspaper in D.C., *The Mirror*. I'm outspoken against government officials and companies that cheat the public. I've uncovered some evidence that references the deaths and illnesses at Factory 17."

Lishan opened her wallet. "Here's my driver's license, for starters, and my employee ID from the paper. I look a bit different since I've gone into hiding, somewhat, with this disguise." Lishan grabbed the extra thirty pounds and moved it, for effect. "I also have a copy of the exposé I wrote that got me this deep into trouble." She reached into her tote bag and gave the front-page article to Fatima.

"I'm her support system," Erik added, wishing to appeal to the compassionate side of this woman before them. "I've known

Lishan for many years. She just wants the government to toe the public line."

"How can I help?" Fatima said, clearly not yet buying into the situation. "I'm already in enough trouble with these...people. I'm lucky to be alive. If I hadn't become so visible to the public, I wouldn't be. And, yes, I'm Fatima."

Lishan nodded in understanding.

"Ms. Habiba, I can't expect you to help. I can only hope that you will. The only harm I wish to see is to those people who don't give a...darn...about how their actions negatively affect the health of the public. If you're not in a position to speak out, just tell us, and we'll let you be. I promise."

Fatima hesitated—a measured pause—looking once more at the driver's license in her hand before handing it back.

"You know, where I come from, cheats and liars are dealt with by the locals. Give me your cell phones. If you're clean, you won't mind. I'll take them to my CIA neighbor, who will hang on to them until you leave. I won't budge on this."

Lishan and Erik looked at one another, feeling hesitant because of all the personal data their phones contained. They gave each other a cautious nod then passed the phones to Fatima, who took a photo of the two visitors with one of the phones. "I'll be right back." She closed the door.

Perhaps five minutes passed before Fatima returned, removed the door chain, and invited her guests in. "Remember what I said. It's no BS where I come from."

They sat in the living room—Fatima facing Lishan and Erik, who sat on a weathered, yet quite comfortable, dark green couch, the kind with tuxedo arms. Lishan removed the padding, wanting Fatima to know the woman before her.

Fatima fingered the padding, giving her blessing with a lift of her eyebrows and a brief "hmm."

"I don't wish you to find me unfriendly. But I believe you understand my precautions, at least until I get the feeling I can trust you. I have solid instincts." Fatima took a full moment to search the eyes of her unexpected guests.

Lishan gave Fatima the briefest of stories, including the gestalt of her exposé and the very real threats that ensued. She didn't want to overwhelm Fatima, yet she did want to give her enough reason to trust these new visitors. Fatima registered each point, filling in her puzzle with the information before her and the feelings she had, until she finally painted a picture of her visitors that satisfied her.

"I have some documents I'd like to show you. I saw to it that the Feds and the local police didn't see these, or know that I have them. I kept quiet about them because I didn't know who I could trust. But I have to take the leap sometime." She looked at her visitors again closely, eyes unblinking. "My intuition tells me I can trust you. Don't fail me." Fatima disappeared once more, returning with a folder containing a handful of papers. Among them were a couple of molecular diagrams showing carbon and hydrogen atoms in various configurations.

"These didn't mean anything to me when I first saw them. But I was determined to understand the full implications of the placements of these molecules. My schooling hadn't gone beyond high school, which is why I was at the factory. But after the illness, due to Conner's greed and disregard for the well-being of others, I felt it was my obligation to step up my education a bit. Several months ago, I enrolled in our local community college, learning about science and food as my goal."

Lishan didn't know the significance of the bonds and atom placements, but Fatima did, and Erik wasn't far behind. Fatima's excitement overtook them. "You see those double bonds, indicated by that symbol that looks like an equal sign? And notice the hydrogen atoms, each having its placement across from its partner, hence 'trans,' or 'across,' as they say in Latin."

"But this looks different than the trans fat configuration I have seen," Erik said.

Fatima looked steadily into his eyes, assessing. "Yes, you are correct. Conner wasn't satisfied with the increased shelf life from the oils we have come to know. No, he wanted to provide a shelf life that doubled, or quadrupled, the already extended life. But Jack Conner is an impatient man. He decided to use the empirical method, incorporating the test trans fat in Factory 17's cafeteria's baked goods. Then the illnesses set in, followed by the deaths. We didn't know what had happened. But Conner did."

Fatima stood and headed toward the kitchen. "Would you like some tea?"

It was more than Lishan and Erik had hoped for. An offering of tea was an invitation to stay awhile. They looked at one another for guidance, both piping up simultaneously with a "Yes, please."

"Black? Herbal?"

Again, together, "Black."

"Are you two twins?" Fatima boomed from the kitchen.

All three laughed. The tension diminished, though an underlying edge of Conner's threats persisted.

With tea in hand, and a pot on the table, Fatima continued, focusing on two other documents. "Conner's concoction was poison. It was a nonessential fatty acid—devised in Conner's labs—made to mimic one of the fatty acids that our bodies produce. This fatty acid apparently could sit in a product, on the shelf, for two to four times longer than today's trans fats. Aside from his distribution in the U.S., Conner planned to market this to the far reaches of the planet, where refrigeration was costly or nonexistent. Admirable on one hand, but he was not a philanthropist. His products would reap maximum profits. He would see to it.

"The problem was this fatty acid didn't perform like the body's fatty acid. Instead, it interfered with the body's metabolism, causing failure in the central nervous system. When one of his scientists, working on this project, purported concern that this might occur—bear in mind that the trials to-date had only been animal trials, where this particular failure might not appear—Conner fired him. Conner had read the scientist's report that suggested there might be a failure in humans, but Conner hoped it would not be much of a problem, likely not traceable for a year or longer, well after he had recouped his investment and profits."

"How did you find this out? That is, how did anyone know it was Conner's doing? And the poison—where did you get this information?" The reporter in Lishan would not miss a single syllable and its meaning. She leaned forward, in Fatima's direction, the tea cupped between her hands.

"I was working late one night. This rough-looking character, perhaps five foot ten, two-hundred-plus pounds, was talking with the factory manager, Beck."

Both Lishan and Erik flinched.

"What? What did I say?"

Erik broke the hold. "It's okay. Lishan met Beck when she took a trip to upstate New York to see a writer who had been imprisoned for speaking out against the FDA and Conner. Beck shared some inside knowledge with Lishan. Within a day, he was murdered."

As he finished his last sentence, Erik had the sinking feeling he'd undone the progress made in the past half hour. With this news, perhaps Fatima wouldn't want to divulge anything further.

To the contrary, Fatima was more emphatic than before.

"I read about Beck in the paper. Too bad. I liked him," Fatima said. After a pause, thinking about Beck, she said, "I know there's a risk, but someone's got to bring these crooks down. As I said, I'm fortunate to be alive, given all I've told the press. I was, by then, known well enough in the media and in the public's eye. He must have thought it best not to off me just yet. Instead, Conner just passed me off publicly as some crackpot Muslim."

Sipping the still-steaming brew from the polished white mug, she continued. "They of course didn't know I was sitting in a chair nearby, quietly reading my novel while on a break. I heard this guy—Mazzini—talking with Beck. He was being heavy-handed in his delivery, not mincing a single word. He wasn't blaming Beck for any of this, but he made it clear that their responsibility was to keep this from hitting the streets, keep it from smearing Conner's name. Conner entrusted Beck, and Mazzini—one of his henchmen—with one million to pay off the families and anyone else who might squawk. They continued like this for another ten minutes, then turned out the lights and headed out." Fatima stopped to sip her tea. "Is this all making sense?"

Receiving a pair of nods, Fatima continued. "I entered the office they had just vacated. They were sloppy—narcissistic more like it. The trashcan held the diagrams you just saw."

The next minute, seeming like an hour, found the trio engrossed in thought, edging toward disbelief. It wasn't that the extent to which members of the species would generally stoop was in question. This was in blatant disregard for the well-being of an entire factory of workers.

"In discussing these diagrams with my bio-chem friend, who was fired several months ago for questioning the Mod X's safety, he pointed out a resemblance between Conner's Mod X3 Connola Oil and formaldehyde, both effecting a preservative response." Fatima removed her glasses and looked at her two guests. "He stressed it was only a resemblance, since Conner is saturating the available slots in the molecular chain with hydrogen so oxygen can't get in and oxidize the oil—which would cause it to go rancid—while formaldehyde functions differently. He didn't explain the difference, but he did add, 'Suffice to say it's highly toxic. While I was still employed, we ran experiments with pinkies...'"

"Pinkies?" Lishan was never one to let references to the arcane slip past her.

"Sorry. Baby mice used to test foods and drugs. The end result was that the...pinkies...developed severe cardiac and respiratory problems. Most died."

"In a sense, then, we could view this as willful negligence, couldn't we? Conner was aware of this." Erik's conclusion drew agreement from the others.

Lishan added, "With testimony from a knowledgeable chemist—like your friend—a jury would find Conner guilty of third-degree murder. No, he wouldn't want that information to get out." Lishan paused, sipping her tea. "Can you fill us in on why Conner didn't get prosecuted, and, as you so aptly mentioned, why you're still alive—not wearing cement shoes?"

"Cement shoes?" Fatima searched her knowledge of English idioms.

"It's a bygone phrase." Lishan explained it.

The shutting of a car door and the creaking sound of footsteps on the front porch steps interrupted their conversation. Fatima motioned her two visitors to move into the kitchen, out of sight of the front door.

While Lishan respected privacy, she'd also learned to keep an ear tuned to conversations she wasn't invited to, if it was pertinent to her work—in this case, her well-being. She eased back to the doorway separating the living room from the kitchen. Erik somewhat alarmingly motioned her back away from the door. Lishan just gave him the *shhhh* sign and continued her eavesdropping. Through a reflection in the glass covering a framed art piece, she caught a glimpse of the visitor. He fit the description of the thug Fatima had mentioned. As the conversation at the front door ended, Lishan edged back into the kitchen's center.

Fatima returned, her eyes showing mild distress. She led them back to the couch.

"Are you alright?" Erik posed the question that he and Lishan both shared.

Lishan stepped in. "I should stay out of your business. Yet it appears that some of yours and mine have mingled. I didn't tune in to your conversation at the door, but several words were loud enough to catch my attention. Did I hear you say 'Mazzini' and 'that's all I have'?"

Fatima had a far-away look. She stood again, pacing. Pinching the blinds at the window to the right of the front door, she peered out to see if the intruder had left. Satisfied that they were alone, she sat down again.

Looking once again at Lishan with no malice or judgment, but rather searching—deciding on her level of trust with these two relative strangers—Fatima proceeded.

"Yes. That was Mazzini. I don't know his first name. He always insists on 'Mister.' Extortion was the reason for his visit."

"Is this why you are still breathing?" Lishan's direct comment gave Erik a start, but he gave the nod of understanding to her straightforward approach. This was, after all, serious business.

Fatima, too, understood. "In part. Beck, the Manager as we called him, paid off everyone to keep quiet. I myself was deathly ill for two weeks. Conner, through Mazzini and Beck, paid us handsomely, if you consider being paid to keep quiet any satisfaction. But then Mazzini came around to a few of us—I don't know, maybe all of us—and said he would see to it that our families would suffer consequences, perhaps deportation, whatever hit us the hardest, if we didn't pay him a monthly fee. He called it insurance. Whose, I don't know."

"I know a little about Mazzini from some emails I've uncovered. What else did he say just now? How much do you pay him, if I may?"

Fatima seemed reluctant, if not embarrassed. She was used to her own unabashed demeanor, her strength. She had stature among the workers. She was gutsy. But the strong-arm tactics of Conner's lead bodyguard were unnerving.

"How much? I was given a settlement in the amount of $50,000. Then, two days later, Mr.—sorry—Mazzini shows up, telling me I'm in deep trouble. And if I want to keep my health up, and the health of my loved ones, I had to start paying him $500 a month. $500! I said I could only afford $300. He took out a folder containing a copy of the $50,000 check, waved it at me, and said '$500. Pay, or you will regret it. By the way, how's your mother, and your sister Kassa, and her children, Desta and Negasi?' What was I to do? He comes by each month, like clockwork. And the $50,000, it's not like it's all just sitting in the bank. Conner's healthcare coverage stinks. I had to pay out nearly $12,000 in medical bills because of the illness, and, at this rate of extortion, Mazzini, and Conner, I presume, will have most of their money back."

Lishan braved the question, "Are your children safe?"

"Yes, they are. They're with friends, for now. Not easily found, even by someone with Conner's connections. Our family ties run deep in that neck of the woods. Even Mazzini wouldn't dare set foot there. I don't tell anyone where they are. I know you understand." Fatima took a sip of her tea. "I look forward to the day they can live here again, without having any fear. I couldn't risk their lives. They are fifteen and seventeen. They understand."

Fatima caught her own reflection in her teacup, the grave look on her face. "I think it's time for something stronger. I have a Merlot—it's from a California vintner, Napa Valley, one that was taken to court for advertising Napa Valley grapes when in fact most of their grapes were from south of San Francisco. I was given a case, gratis. It still has a nice flavor. In my home country, my family didn't drink alcohol. Here, though, I will have some wine on special occasions."

"What do you think?" Erik posed to Lishan.

"I'm thinking we could use it. What if I go to the store and pick up some sandwiches?"

"I should tell you. Mazzini asked if I had company this evening. I said no. He noticed a newer car on the street, a car he hadn't seen before. He's the suspicious type. I just don't know if he's watching the front door. It would be best if you didn't leave just yet. I have some Digaag Duban left over from dinner. I'll be right back." Noticing the perplexed faces, she added. "It's a popular Somalian dish—spicy baked chicken."

Lishan and Erik brightened with anticipation.

A few minutes later, with the most delicious chicken and a glass each of Merlot in front of them, they resumed their serious discussion. "What else did you ask? Ah, yes. How did Conner escape prosecution? I don't know the entire story, but I'm certain his impunity is because of friends in high places—perhaps including Washington's U.S. Attorney as well. Star witnesses were all bought off, yes, but mostly intimidated. I'm sure everyone was threatened. Conner and Mazzini wouldn't take chances. Besides, I think Mazzini gets a kick out of playing Mafia Boy. If we were home in my country, my brothers and cousins would see to it that Mazzini wouldn't show up at my door, ever again."

A few tears moistened Fatima's cheeks. She quickly shrugged them off, moving on.

Over the next half an hour, Lishan took notes as Fatima spelled out all she knew of the judicial proceedings, other workers from the factory, and what she saw of the future, both for her and her coworkers, and Conner's business.

Then Fatima raised one finger, a signal to pause. "I'll be right back." She returned with a *New York Times* article, two months old. "Why don't you both read this, if you would? It's talking about the FDA, yes, but I see parallels between the Menaflex CEO and Conner."

Erik was immediately engrossed by the title: *F.D.A. Reveals It Fell to a Push by Lawmakers.* "Do you know the authors, Gardiner Harris and David Halbfinger?"

"Yes. I don't *know* them, but I heard them speak a few days after their article was published," Lishan said. "It was quite a blow to the FDA."

After a few paragraphs, Lishan continued. "ReGen Biologics was not pleased by this report, which revealed how the FDA's scientific reviewers unanimously found that ReGen's device—Menaflex, a knee implant—failed. As you can see here, the patients who tried Menaflex had to get another operation. Where the FDA came under fire was when its management overruled its own scientists and approved Menaflex. It was quite an embarrassment for all concerned, including the New Jersey senators and representatives—who received campaign contributions from ReGen—who pressed the FDA to approve the device. And the commissioner at that time—Dr. Andrew C. von Eschenbach—said he had acted 'properly.' It's no wonder the FDA's reputation has significant blemishes."

The article continued, but Lishan had seen quite enough.

"Greed at its finest." Erik concurred.

As the wine lightened their moods, they managed a few segues into more personal subjects. The conversation was enjoyable, with each giving views from the perspective of their upbringing: Lishan—Ethiopia and the East Coast; Erik—Scandinavia and New York; Fatima—from Somalia, with the past ten years being a cultural struggle here in Maryland.

When that imaginary timeline struck, they all rose as though on cue. As they headed toward the door, Fatima held back, a trepidation holding her feet steadfast.

"Maybe you shouldn't use the front door. Could be trouble for both of you. I know it would be for me, if Mazzini is watching. Oh, and hold on a moment while I retrieve your cell phones."

A few minutes later, Fatima returned with the cell phones, but she also had copies of the documents she had recovered, and a copy of a signed letter she had written about her dealings with Conner. Penciled in was the phone number of the chemist she said would testify if need be.

"I hadn't mentioned my letter before because I had forgotten about it. I wanted to write down all that I know about Conner, Mazzini, the Factory 17 problems, the strong-arm tactics. I remembered it when I grabbed these other copies for you. These should help." Fatima looked hopeful. She paused, something apparently on her mind.

"I don't know if this helps, but a couple of times when Mazzini came by he seemed sad to be taking the money from me. He of course didn't say so, but it showed in his face. A weariness, you might say. One of those times I didn't have the money here. I anticipated him shooting me, but all he did was stop, look off in the distance, and then tell me 'not to worry about it this time'. It kind of shocked me. I tell you in case someday his conscience might get the better of him."

Lishan and Erik took note and thanked Fatima profusely for her help. They left their phone numbers in case she needed to call them.

Moments later, Lishan and Erik headed toward the back door. There was the feeling of camaraderie, brothers and sisters in the underground, as they said their goodbyes.

Once the revealing outside lights were turned off, Lishan and Erik exited and navigated the alley behind the house.

Lishan didn't feel especially safe in this dark alley. Every backyard had a chain link fence. Most had a dog weighing upwards of one hundred pounds. They finally made their way to the lit street where they began walking, heightened surveillance with every step.

Driving back to D.C., Lishan broke the silence. "Tell me what you're thinking about what Fatima shared with us, and Mazzini showing up at her door."

"Let me focus for a moment. First, I want to get us out of this neighborhood safe and sound." It was apparent Erik was wary of relaxing his diligence, his attention to every nuance in their surroundings. Lishan just let him be. When they arrived at Highway 50, he let out a long-held sigh and touched her knee.

"You're in extreme danger, Lishan. These guys aren't just covering up some misalignment in a food property or a stretch in their marketing. They've caused death and illness and attempted a cover-up with cash and threats. They're playing for keeps, and some reporter from D.C. is *not* going to get in their way if they have any say in the matter. And they seem to feel that they have a say in whatever they want. It's already clear people can go to prison at their whim. Who knows, they may have the police in their pocket. Unless you move out of state, out of the country, and change your identity, you're in it deep enough that you can't even drop it and think they'll leave you alone. No, you know too much."

Lishan listened intently. She trusted Erik's opinion. "You know, my main concern now is that I've dragged you into this."

"I'd love to tell you I know I'll be okay. I *will* be okay. I just don't want to give you a canned answer that lacked thought. But we do have to play it smart." Erik shot a reassuring smile at Lishan, a brief one given the ninety feet of roadway flying by each second.

"Back to our next step. I could say *my* next step, but I know you won't stand for it. So, *our* next step?"

"We need the information that will put Conner behind bars. The copies of those diagrams Fatima gave us will help, along with her testimony and that of her bio-chem friend when the time is right." Erik paused, glancing at Lishan with a loving but serious look. "You don't hold back when you get into things, do you?" He laughed. "Taking on the big boys."

A long pause ensued before Lishan said, "We should form a non-profit. The D.C. Vigilantes." They lapsed into silence until the apartment complex loomed.

Erik broke the silence as they pulled into his parking spot. "You need to find an alternate place to stay for awhile. I prefer you nearby, but we can't take the chance. That Mazzini character, for one. I don't want him showing up at your apartment again, or mine. He may have already traced my license plate."

"They are dedicated to their task, aren't they." She wasn't asking.

Erik walked her to her door, doing a cursory check inside before he bid goodnight. The warmth in their goodnight hug transferred quickly, neither wishing to let go. Finally, Erik spoke up.

'You can't stay here, Lishan. You just can't. Come stay on my couch."

She grabbed a few items, including her laptop, after which they headed to Erik's apartment.

"Erik, I'm frightened by all of this. Conner means business. Could we open up your couch, both of us sleeping here in our clothes?"

185

"I think it's a good idea." Erik retrieved the necessary blankets and pillows.

Erik said, "I know we're alone here. I know all the entry points are locked. It is likely—somewhere between possible and plausible—that no one knows about me or where I live. No guarantees, but I feel comfortable enough—your staying here tonight. Tomorrow, we can re-evaluate. What do you think?"

Lishan agreed. "Do you mind if I stay up and study the information we received this evening?"

Erik nodded. He sat up against the back of the couch, delving into a newly arrived *New Yorker*, reading the cartoons first. Lishan sat near him, laptop unfolded on her lap.

She opened the folder containing Mazzini's email, this time with a search for anything to do with Fatima and the factory. The pickings were slim, requiring that she modify her search to account for Mazzini's slang. Lishan's perseverance paid off, since a few of the emails made no mention of Fatima or the factory, yet they contained clues supporting Fatima's disclosure. Many of the emails were at least two months old, but that didn't change their importance in establishing Conner's path to jail.

July 19th, 11:30 p.m. From Mazzini to Conner. "That Fatima woman's causing trouble. Go for the jugular? M."

The reply came at three in the morning. From what Lishan could see, Conner practically never slept. This seemed to be a pattern among crooks, she thought. There was clear science that showed a lack of sleep interfered with moral judgment. Yes...Conner.

"Too visible. Put pressure, but just shy of the artery you seem fond of severing. She should be an example, but a live one. Three steps. Pay her off. Period. Threaten her, strong-arm, with references to family. Extort her for your protection. Got it? Jack."

Lishan printed these as PDFs then emailed them to herself and Erik for safekeeping. She began thinking that searching for specific criteria was not the way to go. She should just skim through each email. *Who knows what may lurk,* she thought. With 1,250 of them to look through, the words "may as well get started" formed on her lips. *Didn't he ever do a little file housekeeping,* she mused to herself.

An hour later, she perked up to an unfamiliar sound. It was the faintest snore from Erik. Lishan smiled, experiencing the intimacy.

He opened his eyes, finding her looking straight at him. "What?" he complained.

Lishan just grinned as he fell back asleep. She spread out a blanket over him and continued her research. An hour later, she shut down her laptop.

Throughout the night, Lishan was aware of the occasional spooning. She wondered if he was, as well. *No doubt,* she thought. When dawn broke through the curtains, Lishan found herself wide-awake. It was seven o'clock. As the alarm sprung into their consciousness, they managed an awkward kiss on the lips, and then arose.

Lishan noticed the fullness in Erik's pants, but she buried her hormones beneath an audible sigh.

"And what was that?" Erik decried playfully, hands on his hips.

"Pheromone induced. Don't be afraid." She laughed. "Okay, a plan for the day?"

They agreed to get in touch in the hours ahead.

Left alone with a jumble of thoughts and emotions, she set about reviewing the day before her, knowing she should replace the feelings of the past eight hours with more useful ones if she was going to make any progress. Erik lingered in every corner of her being. A shower should have helped provide the separation, but washing her body brought him closer. She dallied at thigh level until the feelings jumped the fence. Now she could regain her focus.

五四

The hands were rough-hewn. His facial features reminded people of someone to be feared, someone who led a challenging life. The apron he wore, covered with bright images of olive trees and expeller-pressed oil cans, didn't fit the impression he generally bestowed upon those he met or those who knew him. He was generally not affable. But in the kitchen...

He whistled as he created and mixed the batter from scratch. Cake mixes from the store were not in his repertoire. His grandmother would be proud.

This will be my finest sheet cake ever, he told himself, smiling at the thought. *Twelve by eighteen. Plenty of servings. Yes, plenty.* A spice cake with cream cheese frosting. He enjoyed sampling the batter as he mixed it by hand. *I'd better back off,* he told himself as he tasted it. *There won't be any left,* he thought, as he ate another spoonful.

As he baked, the features on his face relaxed, giving him the look of someone's grandfather, the kind everybody loved.

An hour after the cake had baked and cooled, he was ready to add his secret ingredient—*A bit more than last time,* he said to himself. He found it was best disguised when added to the cooled cake, then topped with an abundance of frosting.

He continued whistling while he scraped the bowls of delicious remnants of batter and frosting. Lowering the cake into the boulangerie box, he smiled. *Yes, this will be a memorable cake.*

55

Lishan perused the small stack of papers from Fatima, curious how she could best use the information. There was the public's health, and her own life to worry about. She sat back, contemplating whether leaking any of it to the media would help.

"Howard, hi. This is Lishan."

"Lishan! How very nice to hear from you. I'm glad to hear you're still alive." Howard chuckled.

"Yes, I am, too. I'm lying quite low."

"A proper maneuver," he said in an upper-crust voice he often employed. "By the way, I quite savored our rendezvous the other night."

"So did I. I felt honored. Thank you, too." Lishan paused to separate the somewhat disparate subjects. "The reason I called is that I've been thinking about another exposé, giving more exposure to the ties between Conner and the FDA commissioner. But I can't write it, at least not now. If I remember correctly, you have ties with *The People's Advocate*. Could your write it? I can't just sit by and watch the shenanigans. What do you think?"

Howard paused, considering the weight of it. "You know, I would enjoy it. I'll get in touch with them and see if we can rattle Conner soon. What'd you have in mind?"

Lishan shared her thoughts. Howard said he liked her ideas, added a few of his own, and then wove in a comment about "great minds."

After talking with Howard, Lishan revisited Fatima's papers and the Mazzini emails from the night before.

The payoffs, and the Conner-Mazzini willingness to include death as a substitute for good will and responsibility, corroborated with Lishan's earlier findings. And now she had it in writing, at least to the extent that the courts would accept email and a signed letter as uncompromised evidence. The revelations also clarified why Fatima was still alive. *I nearly forgot—Fatima said her chemist friend would testify.*

Lishan stopped, sitting still. She wasn't sure of her next step. She wasn't likely to have any grandchildren unless she had the right kind of dirt on Conner and found an authority who would listen. After all, she was just a reporter, and Conner spoke to the dreams and aspirations of many upward-seeking officials. Lishan couldn't afford to mistakenly enlist a Conner advocate. No, that would be her last mistake.

Contemplating her options included making a detailed list—a list of possible next steps and contacts. Initially, though, she needed to finally put in an appearance at the paper. She assumed her disguise, which took her nearly fifteen minutes. *I'll just change back to normal before going into the paper. Let's see, what will I do with all the garb and the makeup kit?* Finding a suitable cloth bag to put her disguise gear in, she headed out into the daylight to catch a taxi.

Arriving at her desk, undisguised, she was rewarded with a sinking in her gut. Her desk had been cleared. Her previous neighbors were all on the phone, so she turned toward Jerry's office. He motioned her to come in. He had been watching her entrance.

"What is it, Jerry? You can't just let me be?"

Jerry offered the pretense of not understanding, finally saying, "Ah. Your desk."

"Yes, Jerry, my desk. I feel like we're two students in junior high, don't you?"

Jerry replaced his smile with a smirk, making no attempt to hide it. "Ms. Amir. I have needed to do some reorganization. Starting with you. It was convenient that you were out for a couple of days. You see, I intend to improve upon the newsroom's throughput, and you are a star candidate."

"Meaning?"

"You know how much I value your work." Jerry barely managed to suppress the extremities of his grin. "Lifestyles needs you. They have a long-term engagement writing features about the National Zoo. If you are lucky, you can write about your favorite orangutan and your favorite bunny 'til your heart's content."

"Jerry, you know damn well it's of no interest to me. The monotony would kill me. Or is that your intention—to drive me out of here?" Lishan's voice began to carry deeper into the newsroom. "Dammit, Jerry."

Jerry stood up. Lishan was playing into his game better than expected. "Are you questioning my authority, Ms. Amir?"

"You know I *never* question your authority. But I can and do disagree with you at times." Lishan chose her word and her tone carefully, getting a sense of where the editor would love to go with this. "Isn't that part of the newsroom creed?"

Beads of sweat formed on Jerry's forehead. "You, young lady, have missed the point. The creed—authoritative or otherwise—does not support insubordination. Now find your new home, settle in, and spend the afternoon at the zoo with your relatives."

"My relatives. My relatives, Jerry? Speaking of disparaging remarks, and coming from a supervisor, too. As a matter of fact, I would much prefer to align myself with *my relatives* than... Skip it. A waste of my breath."

"You, Ms. Amir, are on report. Strike two. You should know better than to trifle with me. Now, get out. You're done for the day. Maybe more."

Lishan felt the storm within her, but decided to present a calm exterior. She knew this would undermine his confidence. Heading toward her new location—not surprisingly in a corner near the library, one with no view out a window—she promptly fired off an email to Elizabeth Walker, detailing the interaction with the editor. She wouldn't color it one way or another, letting the publisher draw her own conclusions. Lishan said as much in the email. Afterward, Lishan headed home.

In a nearby restaurant restroom, she reapplied the disguise. Looking much older and thirty pounds heavier took some doing. Tired of sitting, she finished her latte then proceeded to take a bus to where she thought Niesha might be. A consultation was in order.

Over the next hour, she replayed, time and time again, the sequence of events and the situation she was in. She thought back to one month ago, when life seemed carefree. Realizing this line of thinking was not productive, she finally let go and came back to the moment at hand.

Lishan got off the bus, thinking she might catch Niesha at the non-profit where she volunteered part-time each week. She asked for her auntie, and she was in luck.

"Do I know you?" Niesha said with an air of caution when she arrived at the front counter. Then her face softened with recognition. "Aw, you didn't have to get all dressed up just for me. I still prefer men, you know."

"Funny, Auntie. Can we go somewhere? Lunch, maybe? I need to run a few things by you."

"Sure, cute girl."

191

Lishan frowned, but Niesha knew it was fake. Ten minutes later, they were seated in an old diner neither of them frequented.

"I'm just being a bit paranoid," Lishan said, nearly in a whisper.

Niesha leaned in across the table, toward her beautiful niece.

"I've stumbled, more or less, across some information about Conner Foods that could help to put him away. And something else, though that isn't why I wanted to talk with you. Jerry, the editor, is trying to bump me out again. But he's losing ground, I believe. He just can't see it. But, about Conner..." Lishan paused, feeling a slight ache in her temples.

Niesha didn't waste time with hyperbole or motherly advice. She knew this was serious. And she knew the editor issue would resolve in Lishan's favor. "Okay. Talk to me."

"You've always had the right answers when I was growing up." Lishan ordered coffee and sourdough toast when the waitress returned with her pad in hand.

"And you, miss?" The waitress looked at Niesha, who was clearly somewhere else.

"I'll have some apple pie, if you have any. Thank you."

Niesha returned her focus. "Conner. Has something else happened?"

Lishan sat back, taking a sip of her coffee, taking in the sum of Auntie as she knew her. Her intuition was always right-on. Well, mostly.

"Okay, number one. I met a man when I was in Albany. He was a P.I. He shared some information with me about Conner. Now's he dead. Murdered."

Lishan stopped, for she could see the pain in her auntie's face. She palmed Niesha's hands. "You probably heard about his case. Upstate New York."

She had read about it. "I'm sorry, Lishan. Truly. Had you gotten to know him a little?"

Lishan hesitated, then said, "Well, yes. He was a nice guy."

Niesha filtered out any questions about sex. It just wasn't appropriate.

Lishan spent the next half an hour outlining the events that her auntie didn't already know about. Niesha took copious notes, including how to access Mazzini's email. Her notebook was never far from reach.

"Would it help if I get into Conner's email as well? Our hacker friend should be able to help."

"Yes, please."

"Lishan, I'm sorry about your friend's death. What was his name?"

"Beck."

"Last name?"

"Conner."

"Hmm. All in the family." Niesha looked up at Lishan to see how her niece was doing. "You know, I bristle at the thought of you getting hurt."

"Auntie, I'm mostly concerned about you. They won't care that you're a woman, an auntie—not in this part of the world."

"Elders aren't respected in the U.S. like they are in most other countries." Niesha stood. "I'll call Joshua. I hope to have something of substance to you within twenty-four hours, if not before."

Niesha gave Lishan a kiss on the cheek. "Lishan, be careful. Really careful. You are important to me, and to many others as well."

"Thanks, Auntie. You, too. Love you."

弱固

A black Ford Crown Victoria pulled up in front of the apartment complex where Lishan lived. Double-parking for just a few minutes, the driver opened the trunk and removed a bright boulangerie box. Taking it inside the lobby, he set it on a table near an array of couches. He neatly put a stack of small plates—not plastic, but simple china—along with stainless forks and folded cotton napkins next to the box. Opening it to reveal the cake, he ensured that the note on the inside of the cover was readily visible. It read, "From Lishan. Just because. Have fun, everyone!"

Smiling to a few of the students who came to investigate, he left the way he came. As he pulled away, Mazzini knew Conner would be pleased.

- - -

Erik was busy in his office on the other side of the lobby. He looked up to see students gathered around the coffee table. He just smiled, happy for them.

A couple of hours later, a young woman came into his office, carrying her piece of cake and one for Erik.

"Hey, Erik. Some nice man brought in a cake. A note says it's from Lishan."

Erik started to make a pleasant remark as to people's kindness when his eyes suddenly grew enormous with fear. He jumped up and ran toward the cake, purposely knocking both pieces from the student's hand as he passed by her.

"Stop. Don't eat that cake. Stop," he yelled at everyone. "How long has it been here?"

One of the students, with a half-eaten piece, said, "I don't know. Maybe two hours ago?"

"This cake might be poisoned," Erik shouted. He looked around at the handful of students hovering. "Is there anyone who ate some cake, or took some, who isn't here now? Hurry, this is important."

"Mannie took one to her room."

"Someone who hasn't had cake, go get her. Now! Everyone else, stay here."

Erik called 911, saying they would need ambulances for possibly six poison victims.

All hope of an error on his part vanished as one of the students vomited and had a seizure. A second student followed suit a few minutes later.

Sirens blared in the distance. It sounded like a fleet.

37

As Niesha walked the four blocks back to the nonprofit and thought about Lishan's well-being, she found herself reviewing their years together. She wondered if she could, or should, have done anything differently. Should she have guided Lishan in a manner that was less provocative toward the world?

The answer came easily. She knew that sheltering her, the family, from the world's problems wouldn't solve anything. She couldn't perpetuate the lesser role of women that most cultures had dictated for so many centuries. And in order to combat that lesser standing, Lishan needed to be strong in the world's face. Her charge—her niece—had picked up on this. In truth, Niesha knew she wouldn't have changed a thing.

As she walked, several times she quickly turned around as though she had forgotten something. There was no obvious tail, but criminals could be smart, and they played their hunches, including having photos of parents, aunties, siblings.

After finishing at the non-profit, she headed home and immediately got to work on what she and Lishan had talked about. Fortunately, her home Internet connection was still deftly buried under so many layers of incorporation and DBAs as to render it undetectable by most anyone, including those of criminal intent. Then again, if someone were to use a data sniffer to monitor her connection, her privacy would be compromised.

Settling in at her desk, she had to wait too long for her computer's operating system to come alive. She decided it was finally time to buy that Mac. Time was precious.

Niesha pondered the situation—her good life, good health, wonderful relationships. Was she putting it all on the line? But the question was rhetorical. It didn't matter. Her niece mattered.

Spreading her notes out on her desk, she planned her approach. Number one was digging through Mazzini's email, for this would give her some insight into character. She did this for the first hour, making a few scribbled notes on scratch paper.

Next was Conner's email. She called Joshua. He answered on the first ring, as he always seemed to, causing Niesha to poke fun about his being a nerd without a life. They both laughed. Two hours elapsed before she heard from him. Because of his earlier success with Mazzini's email, it cut the time a little for getting into Conner's.

Over the next two hours, Niesha amassed a list of mail related to her niece's investigation and plight. One of the emails caused her to nearly choke on confirmation of her fear: Conner had contacted Rudy—Rudy Conner, a hit man separate from Mazzini—and her niece was the target.

It was no surprise, but it did validate her fear. At least now she knew what she was up against. Then, halfway into this particular email, she was hit with an eye-opener. Conner had written to Rudy: "And Mazzini. It's time to take him out as well. He let that Fatima woman and two others off the hook for not making their payments on time. His conscience is getting to him. He has served his purpose but he's weakening and is no longer reliable. No hurry on Mazzini, but the reporter can't wait. J"

The email was written this morning at 3:30 a.m. She printed out the email, along with Rudy's email address, curious why a hit man would be so imprudent as to transact business via electronic communications. Perhaps Rudy was enthralled by the latest technologies, wanting to appear modern. Perhaps he just didn't have any savvy when it came to confidentiality. Niesha had read of old-time mafia members who still lived in the pre-World War II style of the twenties.

Then it struck her. Mazzini could become an ally if he knew of the double-cross. She had to get to him as soon as she could. She also had to slow down this Rudy fellow. If she could track him down, a well-placed phone call might just do the trick. Perhaps she could pit Mazzini and Rudy against one another. No, she needed Mazzini. He would be a star witness, if they got that far. Not if. They had to.

R.C.@goon.biz. This guy was ego, all the way. A domain search through Network Solutions uncovered the domain's owner and webmaster Paul Rollins, including Rollins' contact info. Using a calling card, providing a barrier behind her real number, she placed the call.

"Mr. Rollins. This is the Internal Revenue Service. I'm agent number 743552. I need a minute of your time." Intimidation was the root of Niesha's usual success with this line.

"Ye-e-s. How can I help you? Am I in trouble?"

Paul Rollins was a recluse, hidden behind his computers in a small, damp apartment. The recently delivered groceries were still on the counter. Rollins' fear of the world kept him inside. What he feared most, though, was the government.

"Not yet, Mr. Rollins. But there's a client of yours whose contact number I need from you. His evasiveness will only prove judicially disastrous for him. We know you have means of contacting him. Rudy Conner. I need his email address and phone numbers. And, Mr. Rollins, you must not divulge our conversation. By the way, we haven't audited you in a few years. We do hope you are staying on track this time. About that information..."

"Just a minute, Miss...? That information is private, you must know. I can't..."

"You have my agent number," Niesha interrupted. "Feel free to use it. File a complaint if you must. On a side note, do you have all your records in order toward your declared expenses for your two past tax seasons? It shows here that if we need to, we can..."

"I have it right here," Rollins blurted out. "It's Rudy Conner. 525 Bishop Place, D.C."

"And?"

"Uh, yes. Email is r.c@goon.biz."

"One more."

Niesha could hear the hesitation. "Mr. Rollins?"

"Yes. Okay." The breathing was audible. "202-555-7447." With no response from his caller, he quickly added, "and this is his cell phone—202-555-7138."

"Thank you, Mr. Rollins. We'll be in touch. Good day." Niesha hung up, satisfaction in her eyes.

Niesha brewed up some French roast decaf, busying herself with a couple of brief chores while it dripped to perfection. Sitting down, she drafted what she would say to Rudy Conner. Before she did, she wanted to understand the connection between Jack and Rudy. It might come in handy. A quick search through her lineage software drew the necessary data: they were cousins. The blood relation between the Conners—though, for some reason, not including Beck—would historically stand the test of time, a test that the crooked relationship between Conner and Mazzini would invariably not. Honor among thieves was tenuous at best.

Sipping her coffee, she gathered the wisdom of her years to put her best foot forward with this thug. She only had one shot. She had to establish that her bite, and that of the organization she stood for, was indeed dangerous. Just enough to throw him off track, to slow him down. She wrote down a few key words and practiced a delivery. She knew that reading from a script sounded stilted, and too much rehearsing just got in the way of her poise on the fly. Understanding the importance of the call, she closed her eyes, found her breath, and practiced a mediation she knew from Jack Kornfield, one of her favorite Buddhist guides.

She called his home number, the private one. Her preference was to leave a message this time. She was in luck. "This is Rudy. You know what to do." *Beep.*

"Rudy Conner. We know who you are and what you do. If you harm one more person, it will be your last. My organization and I promise you. Our track record is lengthy and unblemished. Find another line of work. Now." She hung up.

Next, she called his cell phone. This time he answered, but she was prepared. "Rudy Benito Conner. There is an important message waiting for you on your private home number. Goodbye." She had already uncovered his middle name from the lineage database, a name not appearing anywhere else that she saw. Using it here punctuated that she knew a great deal about him, giving him cause to take the threat seriously.

Not wishing to overlook any detail, Niesha put down her thoughts in her notebook. *Call Lishan. Advise on findings / Move Lishan to safe location / Exhaust findings in Conner's and Mazzini's email / Determine best fit for contacting Mazzini, getting him to turn himself in / Send follow-up threat to Rudy Conner / Heighten security at home / Formulate plan to incarcerate Conner.*

The afternoon was disappearing. Lishan felt better since her meeting with Niesha. Her auntie's wisdom never failed Lishan. She'd hoped to hear from her by now, but Lishan knew Niesha wouldn't waste time and words, so a call wouldn't take place until she had substantive information and a plan in place.

Before calling her, Lishan decided to check in with Erik. She thought they would have touched base by now. She understood that life had become more complex for her auntie, for her friends.

"Erik, hi. I..." She stopped, hearing sirens in the background.

"Lishan, someone dropped off a cake at the apartment building." His voice was shaking, barely intelligible. "It was poisoned, just like the cupcakes, I think, since it came in a boulangerie box. Six of the students ate the cake. Oh my God, Lishan."

Lishan held off breaking down, though it's what she wanted to do. She knew it wouldn't help the situation.

"What can I do, Erik? Can I help?"

"I don't know. I don't know. Maybe call the hospital and tell them this is likely what happened to the young girl in your office. Don't come here just yet, okay? I gotta go. Will you be alright?"

"Yes, I'll be alright."

Within the next few minutes, Lishan called the hospital, telling them about the likely relationship with the poisoning—the ricin.

When her phone rang, displaying her auntie's name, Lishan couldn't hold it back.

"Auntie, auntie." The distress in her voice told of a tragedy. "There's been another poisoning. A cake left at the apartment building...down in the lobby...for the students." Lishan was sobbing by this time.

Niesha did her best to console her niece but pressed forward. "I called to bring you up to date on my findings. We have to talk. We can't delay getting Conner arrested. I was just about to go into Friar's. Meet me here, now. It's close to you. Take a taxi. Not a Yellow." Niesha was firm, demanding, in control.

As Lishan approached the restaurant, she saw Niesha pacing out front. They decided it would be best to walk.

"I know you want to go to the hospital," Niesha said, "but leave the students to the ER. They'll do everything they need to. They're good at what they do. Right now, you need to stay out of sight. We need to speed up our plans."

They walked for perhaps half an hour until Lishan finally felt she could go inside. Niesha was clear that keeping their strength up was vital.

The *maître d'* took them to an out-of-the-way table, at Niesha's request. As they sat down, they both carefully scanned the clientele.

Niesha didn't ask her niece about the menu options. She just ordered a substantial fondue—the restaurant's signature item—and two salads.

Niesha was pointed in her pressing to discuss how to get Conner. "Look at this email from Conner to, uh, Conner. Rudy and Jack are cousins. Conner wants Rudy to eliminate Mazzini, and you." She continued: "Here's what I've done this afternoon after I found this email." She told Lishan about her calls to Rudy.

"My hope is that Rudy Conner will have second thoughts about going after you, buying us additional time to pull this puzzle together. And, where Mazzini is concerned, if he believes that Jack Conner wants to deep six him, he just might play ball with us. Of course, if he thinks he'll go to prison, he might clam. But we'll work on that angle."

"Where do we go from here?" Lishan was doing all she could to pull it together.

"My next step is to call Mazzini. I saw his phone number on one of Conner's emails. We need him on our side. It's like a flowchart. He is either a 'yes' and proceeds to help us, or an 'up yours,' in which case we get heavy-handed. As far as Rudy is concerned, he may not be too worried about threats—no doubt lived with them all his life. But it could slow him."

Feeling the pressures of time, they didn't linger in Friar's as they normally did.

Niesha suggested they go to a family restaurant she liked well enough. It was large, with enough seating to accommodate sitting in the back, out of the way. Niesha had her notes and the email printouts with her in her bag.

With coffees ordered, Niesha got out her phone.

54

Mazzini was a descendant of Ellis Island Italian immigrants. He grew up in the Bronx—a street kid. Rough and tumble was his means of survival, and he had little compassion for anyone beyond his mother and sister. His father's cruelties defined Mazzini. At 140 pounds, five foot eleven, in his freshman year at South East High, the skinny kid took a beating from most of the other boys.

But in his senior year, he began to buff out. He was tired of being the underling. It was steak and potatoes, when the family could afford it, and extra hours at the dilapidated school gym. He weighed in at 210 in the middle of his senior year. The day after he graduated, he took his last slap from his father. With one solid uppercut, Mazzini laid the old man out on the floor. An hour later, Mazzini moved out, unsure of his next step. But he knew he wouldn't be with the father he hated. Where he went didn't matter.

His line of work bothered him at times. Mazzini was an underground bully, wearing a suit and tie much of the time. It added respectability to how he saw himself. It was a falsehood, but if he didn't think about it, he could live the lie without his conscience coming to the surface.

Many years ago, his mother gave up trying to set him along a straight path. It wasn't that Mazzini didn't love or listen to his mother. Anger and a raised fist were all he knew, all he carried with him. His mother's lessons fell just enough out of reach that murder entered Mazzini's list of notches. He procured a gun, took out his father, and served the next ten years in the penitentiary near Albany. There he met Jack Conner's cousin—Johnson. They had an immediate dislike for each other, but a high respect accompanied the dislike. When Mazzini got out, the vice warden recommended him to Jack. That was fifteen years ago.

Jack Conner needed someone to do his back-alley work. Mazzini fit the bill. Mazzini knew, as did Conner, that as an ex-con, Mazzini would be beholden and loyal to Conner. This fit with Conner's needs, since they included some heavy handling of the ever-increasing list of troublemakers.

In the early stages, Conner's list included mostly other crooks, and an occasional potential whistle-blower. These Mazzini could readily balance in his skewed values. But ever since the Factory #17 affair, his conscience was taking increased hits. Bullying disadvantaged men and women left an increasingly bitter taste on his palate. If he tried talking Conner into a lighter sentencing of these victims, Conner wouldn't hear of it.

The ringing phone gave him a start. He answered as always—gruffly. "Mazzini."

The female voice was clearly no-nonsense. "Mr. Mazzini, listen carefully. I won't repeat myself. Jack Conner has a contract out on you. Check your email. Our organization has a hollow-point and a headstone, both reserved for you if you harm one more factory girl, one more reporter. This is no idle threat. We know where you live, where you drink your coffee, and each of your previous victims. We want Conner. We'll be in touch." The line went blank.

Mazzini sat back, searching his mind for a fit for this voice. Nothing came. He went over to his laptop and checked. The email was there. He had no doubt it would be. His years in the business helped him easily separate the novice from the pro. This woman was a pro. As he read the email the caller had sent, especially the part in Conner's hand, he became angry, and just a little concerned. It wasn't a complete surprise to receive a message that Conner had put him on the contract list. He was expendable; of that there was never a question. What bothered him, though, was the ease with which Jack Conner wiped out a human life, especially now that it was his.

This struck a nerve in Mazzini. "I'm no better than Jacko," he said out loud. He lived alone. No one could hear him. But *he* could.

Mazzini looked at his mother's photo in a frame on the end table. Sometimes it was hard for him to look at her; he was always deceiving her into thinking he sold insurance. *Not a complete lie,* he thought to himself.

He put together that if Conner wanted him rubbed out, Conner had to have seen him as a liability, of no further value. Knowing that his life could end soon seemed such a waste. What had he contributed?

Before he could berate himself any further, there was a loud knock at the front door. Mazzini stiffened, reaching for the .38 he had in his briefcase. He had few unannounced visitors. And with today's news, his next might just be the makings of a painful day.

The knock came again, more insistent this time. No voice called his name. He could hear the doorknob being tried. These were bad signs. No doubt, the would-be intruder knew he was home. Lights at the window. Light under the door. Mazzini eased over to the side of the front door hinges. He would have just one chance, if Conner's style of thug was any indication.

The pins in the door lock tumbler were falling into place, the lock-picker's success apparent as the knob twisted all the way. But the deadbolt was more difficult. The intruder couldn't easily pick it, or at least patience ran out before 225 pounds of body busted open the door like a linebacker. Mazzini responded by kicking the door back into the assailant, hoping to knock him down. But the opponent was sturdier than he had counted on. Mazzini fired one round through the door, not certain of his target's exact position, but he had to take the offensive. A groan followed by two gunshots from the intruder were all Mazzini heard before the assailant ran off down the hall. He considered looking out the door and taking another shot, but he couldn't be sure if he might take a bullet in the head. Instead, he closed the door as well as it would shut after the three bullets and splintering took their toll. A few drops of blood, indicative of a hit, though insubstantial, lay within a foot of the doorframe. Mazzini escaped harm, but he was visibly shaken for the first time in many a year. He knew the guy would return; he just didn't know how soon.

Mazzini sat down, taking deep breaths. Now he knew what his victims felt, whether at the point of a gun or just his heavy threats. All he could hear was his own breathing. No wonder no one in the building made any noise. In this neighborhood, it was best to stay inside.

What now? He wanted to thank the earlier caller—the warning had heightened his vigilance. He recalled taking walks with his mother, her talking about how life could change in a few heartbeats. He could run, face Conner and his hired bodyguard in the style he was accustomed to, or come clean and help put Conner behind bars.

Funny, he thought—thinking about turning the leaf, about putting a crook behind bars. *Perhaps it's time.*

Could he trace the email? He was good and had ways. But he didn't underestimate the woman who had called him. *Ballsy,* he thought.

As to his immediate dilemma, he knew he had to leave. The would-be killer wouldn't be far away—injured, but probably not seriously. Mazzini wondered whether there was any comparison between an injured crook and an injured lion when it came to ferocity. He just didn't want to find out. Picking up the small suitcase he kept packed, he checked the hallway, where he noticed a few footprint tracks with smeared drops of blood.

Better to wipe the tracks so the neighbors don't get too fed up and call the cops, Mazzini thought. He stepped back inside, grabbed a handful of paper towels, and wiped the hallway as clean as time permitted.

And now? His front door was splintered. He put down the suitcase and fabricated a hole in which the deadbolt could give the appearance of holding. A few minutes later, he left.

Mazzini was no fool. He expected the same of any other above-average thug. Should he use the front door or the rear? His end-result should be the garage, but it didn't feel safe enough. Too confining. Besides, he would want to check for a bomb before entering or starting his car. He decided on a side entrance, with due caution. A taxi from there to a motel.

From the backseat of a Diamond Cab, he contemplated the life changes he was experiencing. How quickly they appeared. He found comparisons between the images flitting by, as the taxi driver wove the streets, and the more memorable episodes from his life. Something had to change. He now knew what it was.

Secure, or so it seemed, inside Motel Indigo on the outskirts of town, he set his handgun by the nightstand—not on it, in case he had a reputable visitor for some reason. He didn't want to upset anyone or cause undue interaction with the police. But it would be leaning against the stand.

He just settled in on the bed, TV clicker in hand, when his cell phone triggered. "Damn," he objected. Should he answer? "Mazzini."

"Yes, I know." The female voice of earlier paused, giving her offense time to do its work "Time can be our enemy, if we abuse it. Have you made up your mind?"

Mazzini drew a long, slow breath. "Yes. Before we go further, I need to know who you are."

"Femme fatale will do. What is your decision? You have only one, you know."

"Yes. Only one. Forgive me, but I don't like divulging my life and my plans to a stranger."

"We can arrange a meeting. You won't tell me where you are, but you *will* tell me where we can meet."

"Pushy, aren't you? What part..."

"Pushy? You prick. You accuse me of being pushy? You, who threatens single mothers, who kills undeserving men and women who just happen to be speaking up against moral depravity. I should just put a 30-06 between your eyes; save the court's time and wasted energy." The caller was hot and angry.

A few breaths were the only sounds breaking the silence.

"Fuck off." Mazzini hung up.

"Fucking imbecile," Niesha said out loud. She had quite a mouth when need be. Her girlfriends knew this. But Niesha had made a pact with herself many years ago to never let Lishan hear her talk this way.

Lishan's eyes drifted skyward as her aunt cussed. She thought it best to just let it go.

She dialed again. No answer. This time she sent a text. "Do you really want your mother to know what you do? Do you? I know the rest home. Don't push me, Mazzini. You've got ten minutes."

Niesha had uncovered Mazzini's family data—not an easy task. She hoped not to play that card, the threat, but he left her no choice.

Six minutes passed before he called back. He knew the caller wouldn't fall prey to any of his angling. He wouldn't call her bluff, nor would he delay. His mother's happiness was where he drew the line, even if it meant his own demise.

"You're right," was all that Mazzini could muster. In the past, he would have exploded, but he had begun to feel the person he had become.

In fact, he thought, *I've become my father.*

The change in Mazzini's voice was apparent. He knew it; it didn't matter. Lightness enveloped him—the relief, the confession. He heard a familiar click, the sign that his caller was now recording.

"You know I'm recording this."

"Yes."

"Have you been Jack Conner's hired gun for the past fifteen years?"

"Give or take."

"I need you to be more specific. What did you do for him? Include Factory 17."

"I bullied for him. If someone got in his way, I took care of it." Mazzini's hands began to sweat. He knew this was as good as being in front of a judge and jury. "I killed a few people along the way."

"What about the P.I.—Beck—in upstate New York?"

Again, a pause as Mazzini took in just how much his caller knew. "Yeah, I was the hit man."

"And Jack Conner told you to kill him?"

Another breath while he gathered his wits. "Yes," Mazzini wiped his brow. "You asked about Factory 17. I..."

Mazzini stopped, tears in his throat clogging his words. He didn't want the caller to hear any weakness in him. "I..."

He stopped again, gathering his strength. Niesha could tell what was happening, but she kept quiet.

"I've been harassing workers from Factory 17, extorting them, threatening. Just yesterday..."

"Fatima," the caller broke in.

"Yes. Fatima." Again, the depth of the caller's information.

"All of this at Conner's hand?"

Mazzini could feel the anger toward Conner welling up inside his skin. Take Conner down—his mantra.

"Yes. Jack Conner is a ruthless man. He has bought out FDA officials and senators all his life. I threatened a couple of them for him, bringing family names into the threats so they knew we meant business."

"You're telling me that Jack Conner was responsible for these threats?"

"Yes."

"I need documents," the caller pressed, though more gently than before. "Can you help secure them for me?"

"I'll do what I can. How soon..."

The caller broke in again. "Yesterday. You know Conner has put a price on your head? His cousin Rudy Conner is looking for you. You might be dead later today."

"He already tried. An hour ago." Mazzini felt latent tears and anger heave in his chest. Yes, he was supposed to be dead by now.

Niesha continued, taking note of Rudy's persistence. "Not to undervalue your life, but if you want to begin making a difference—a positive difference for humanity—then we need a deposition from you as soon as possible. If you want protection—physical protection—I'll do what I can. We can determine that course later. Are you safe where you are?"

Mazzini peered around the room. "Yes. I have changed locations for the night. I don't think I was followed."

"And coordinates for your cell phone calls?"

"True. They could track me that way, but I don't think they've felt a need to go that far just yet." As he said it, Mazzini knew he didn't believe it.

"What can you provide tonight—you know, documents that could be used against Conner?"

"I can give you my email access."

"We already have that."

Mazzini smiled—again, appreciation for the true professional. "Yes," he continued, "but I have another account." He waited for the second declaration of having already gained access. Hearing none, he allowed a quiet smirk, a small notch in his belt. At least he knew his veil was somewhat intact. "It's mazzman@CH2O.com. I have some important documents there, in case of my demise."

"Password?"

Another hesitation. Mazzini was truly handing it all over, wasn't he, he thought. "Hench-hell. I think you'll find everything there you need. I'm tired. It's not every day my life comes to within a centimeter of death."

"Centimeter?"

"I'm of European blood. Inches and feet are for imperialists. Good night, Cleopatra." In his exhaustion, he just hung up.

44

Cleopatra, imperialists. Niesha mouthed the words. The former stirred her; the latter a downright insult if directed at her. She shook the sensations, returning to her task.

Lishan had heard Mazzini's comments, his confessions, through the other half of her aunt's phone earbud. She blinked at the Cleopatra line but let it go. Another time and it would have been the source of some ribbing between them.

"I have a stack of emails to consider, to sort. Let's go back to my place. It's quite secure, but I'll call the owner/manager first and ask him to check the security tapes before we get there."

Within half an hour, they approached Niesha's home, a conversion into high-end condos on 21st Street NW.

Lishan said if her auntie didn't need her help for a few minutes, she would call the hospital. The call proved fruitless, since HIPAA regulations preserved patient privacy. She decided to call Erik.

"Lishan, where are you? Are you okay?"

Lishan said she was with "N." Erik understood the secrecy.

"The students aren't yet in good shape, but the doctors are optimistic given the information they worked with when the girl from your office was there. It sped things up, at least somewhat." Erik paused to breathe. "The police have the cake and the box. They dusted for fingerprints. I just found out a few minutes ago that they matched with Mazzini. We've got him cold."

"Should I come down? We're working on... on putting together the coffin nails for Conner."

"No. Stay where you are. Be productive. The other students know why your name was on a note on the cake box. They're all hoping you get the bastards."

"Thanks, Erik. I hope the building has police protection. You don't take any chances, okay? You're important to me."

This last comment meant something to both of them. They could tell.

One hour later, Niesha and Lishan stopped for a moment, noticing the tally of processed emails before them—sixty-five emails of substance, which they copied to both Lishan's and

Niesha's email accounts. They packaged these up in a new Mazzman folder under each inbox, just below the recently born Mazzini folder. Niesha was meticulous about order. She declared at an early age that order would minimize her efforts when it came to locating documents and other paraphernalia. This left, she preached, more time to be at the beach.

For additional backup, they created and deftly concealed two CDs with copies of all of "Exhibit A" emails. They both knew there was no guarantee about the safety of their homes.

This caused them to discuss Mazzini and Rudy. Mazzini was seemingly no longer a threat. In fact, Niesha, who had spoken with Mazzini and heard his tears, knew he wasn't. She could feel the change in this man. But Rudy—she had possibly instilled a hesitation in this bullet-for-hire, but he would only break stride for a few yards before continuing his assignment.

Mazzini was at considerable risk. Niesha wanted him alive— in part for humanitarian reasons; in part for the well-being of her niece. She couldn't lose sight of the plight Lishan had become embroiled in with Jack Conner's vision of her future.

Resetting focus, they set about assembling the data found in the Mazzman folder, creating three subfolders—labeled Foundation, Incriminating, and Substantive. In Foundation, they placed forty-six—those giving rise to Conner's intent but containing nothing that would hold in court. They housed fourteen in Incriminating. These would give a judge and jury cause to fabricate a noose but not use it. In Substantive, they held the last five. Here was where they devoted the next hour, for the other sixty laid a foundation that had already been poured.

#61—"Arrange for baked goods in Factory #17 cafeteria to use Mod X3 Connola Oil. Keep the employees in the dark. Monitor any significant results."

#62—"Shit, Mazzini. Do I have to do everything? We have two dead workers and a host of very sick ones. Can you handle this, or do I have to?"

#63—"Take that jackass out. He has spoken up once too often. $50k in your wallet."

Niesha didn't know who the jackass was, but the email still incriminated Conner as someone who would resort to strong-arm tactics with little hesitation.

#64—"Pay the FDA manager $200K. We need this trans fat mod on the market—period! Get the approval fast-tracked. Cannot wait long for approval."

#65—"Fatima. Too visible now. The media. Don't touch, but bi-monthly harassment, face-to-face. Collect protection money. We'll get our money back from that troublemaker."

"My darling niece, I believe we've got him." Niesha paused. Lishan's questioning look prompted her auntie to continue. "Just thinking. I need to decide who we can trust with this evidence." Niesha paced for a moment. "I know! Maya Rosenstein. She's a chief U.S. Attorney for the District of Columbia, the head of the Criminal Division. She's an old friend of mine, though I haven't seen her in months. I'll find out how soon she can meet with us. You should stay the night."

$$41$$

"I'm here for my nine o'clock meeting with the director," Jerry said condescendingly to the HR assistant. "Any coffee?"

The coffee comment was ignored. "They are expecting you—in Ms. Walker's office."

They? And the publisher? Jerry thought to himself.

As Jerry took a seat at the conference table, Elizabeth began. "Given previous employee relation problems between you—Jerry—and Ms. Amir, I advised that any meetings regarding continuing issues, including accusations of insubordination, be brought to my attention. Jerry, tell us—exactly—what happened. The absolute truth."

"Dammit, Elizabeth. I always tell..."

"Ross, make note of the language. Go on, Jerry."

Jerry Hanson told his version.

"Now, Ross, play the recorded interview you had with Ms. Amir—recorded, of course, with her permission."

The recording—in Lishan's voice—held back nothing. She recited back everything she said, everything he said. Jerry noticed she made no attempt to cover up her self-incriminating comments.

After the recording, Jerry slammed his fist on the table. "You see! Insubordination at its worst. She must go."

"Describe to me the insubordination, Jerry." Elizabeth was cool and calm, of obvious concern to Jerry.

"She said, 'Damnit Jerry,' and made reference—a comparison—between myself and the animals at the zoo."

"A comparison you initiated. And why is it insubordination?"

"Isn't it obvious? I'm her boss."

"And, when you express those same words to me, and in meetings?"

Jerry stammered. "That's different." Jerry wiped his cheeks where the sweat was beginning to drip.

"Because?"

"Damnit...I mean...we're management."

"And we play by different rules, allowing you to speak to me, and others, disrespectfully?"

Jerry was quiet.

"Exactly, Mr. Hanson. We are governed by the same rules. I believe Ms. Amir treats you with disrespect because you treat her, and many others in the newsroom, disparagingly. Jerry, we have a very long list of indiscretions on your part. We've tried to overlook them. I'm afraid that you're the one being put on report. Mr. O'Brannigan will outline the terms, you will sign the papers, and, hopefully, you will change. Ms. Amir has been reinstated to her position as a reporter for the city desk. Ross, see to it that Ms. Amir is apprised of this, today. It can't wait. I don't wish to lose a key employee. That might include you, Jerry. Think about it. The choice is yours. In fact, the choice has been yours all along. Good day."

The two men left her office. Elizabeth Walker shook her head and returned to the pile of papers in front of her.

The next morning, after breakfast with Niesha, Lishan decided to take a little time for herself and went for a walk in the neighborhoods northwest of D.C. This was all getting to be a little too much, including her Lifestyles assignment, if she still had a job. For some reason, she thought of Rafael. She wanted, once and for all, to decide whether he could be a friend, or not, where he stood in her life. Did she trust him? If he weren't a journalist, she had decided she would just forget about him, but she knew it didn't pay to have unresolved issues within the local sphere of one's career path.

After walking for a couple of hours, her phone rang.

"Ms. Amir. This is Ross O'Brannigan. We had a meeting this morning—the publisher, myself, and Jerry Hanson. Your position has been reinstated. We're hopeful there will be no further problems between you and Mr. Hanson."

Lishan brightened, then her face dropped. "My worry, of course, is that he'll retaliate."

"Ms. Amir, I'm not at liberty to discuss specifics, but I believe you will be pleased with the outcome. Rest assured." That was it.

Lishan could feel her shoulders lifting. Just a little. *Perhaps there will be justice. Where was P. Ah, Rafael.* Her temporary cell phone wouldn't have his number, but she was always good with numbers—her mother always said. She decided to call, pausing the tragedy of her life for at least a few more minutes.

"Hi. Is this Rafael?"

"Lishan! I've missed you. Did you move? Are you okay?" He stopped short, sounding worried. "Are you calling me to tell me you have a boyfriend, or you're getting married?"

"No. No boyfriend. Not getting married."

"Can you come over?"

His enthusiasm seemed a little too fake, but she decided to ignore it.

"I can. But I can only stay a short time."

"It's not my preference. You know that. But I'll take it. Am I sounding desperate? Sorry."

"No, not desperate. Where do you live? I'm on foot."

215

"925 L St. NW. Where are you?"

Looking around for the street signs, she spotted a crisscross of signs on the far corner. "I'm in luck, I think. I'm on 11th Street, in front of Samuel Gompers Memorial Park."

"No! Just a minute. I'll call you right back. Oh, I don't have your number. It's listed as private. Don't explain now. But if we don't connect in five minutes, call me right back. Promise?"

"Promise." The line disconnected. Lishan felt a continued twinge of unease about Rafael as she browsed the neighborhood for the next couple of minutes. She hoped she was wrong.

Then she saw Rafael walking out into the intersection. Traffic was light to non-existent. She started to say hi to him when she noticed he seemed to look right past her. Then she remembered her disguised appearance.

When Rafael was within two meters, she said, "Rafael."

Startled, he stopped abruptly, recognizing her voice. "Lishan?" Then his face tightened. "Don't *ever* scare me like that, do you hear?"

Lishan recoiled, thinking about leaving.

Rafael realized his mistake. "Look, I'm sorry. I just felt like I lost control of my surroundings. That scares me."

"Giving you the right to mistreat me?"

Rafael heaved a breath. "No." He hesitated. "Can we start over?" He paused to take a closer look. "Hey, why the disguise?"

If he asked her that, he wasn't aware of recent threats, or he didn't care. She felt her mistrust growing. "Listen, I really have only a few minutes. We can just talk here."

"No. Come up. I have something for you," he lied.

Lishan felt confusion. *Just for a few minutes.*

As they walked to his apartment, Lishan parsed out the pieces she felt she would share—just enough to explain her camouflage, but no names or places. If he pressed for these, she would find a way to downplay it.

Inside, Rafael attempted to make Lishan comfortable. "Have a seat. Beer, wine, water?"

Before she could decline the alcohol, her phone rang. Lishan decided to see who it was, in case it was Niesha. "Ring, ring," it rang again, a cute verbal ring tone she had created.

"Who's that?" Rafael stole a glance at her phone. His eyes narrowed when he saw a photo of Erik on the phone. "Oh, it's that white boy from the apartment where you live."

"His name is Erik," Lishan said haughtily.

"Whatever. You like him don't..."

"It's not 'whatever.' He's a good friend."

"Like I said...Isn't he a bit white for you?"

Lishan stood abruptly to her full height. "White for me? You can't honor a name that's not from your own culture, can you? And *you* complain about racism in others. What in the hell am I doing here?" She began gathering her things, the cell phone insisting with its reminder ritual.

Rafael's face revealed the intensity he was feeling. He wasn't one to lose the game.

Lishan's rant filled the room. "You can't begin to recognize the apologies that are in order because you're such a xenophobe. If it's not your culture, you can't be bothered. Your kind of thinking—or lack of it—is what's wrong in our world." As she opened the door, she looked back. "I'm sorry for you, Rafael. You haven't got a clue, have...?"

Seeing her Frazier book on a kitchen counter stopped her. She literally screamed at him. "It *was* you! Damn you. Damn. You are filth."

She grabbed the book and was gone.

Lishan's rage consumed her as she briskly walked into the business district. Passing the library, she saw it as an opportunity to return the book. Keeping a low profile—which she knew the reference librarian would want—she merely handed it to him, saying it was a delightful read, and thank you for the recommendation.

Outside, she felt a need for coffee, maybe something stronger. In the first pub she eyed, she took a barstool at the far end of the quiet bar. The bar was all but empty.

"One Irish coffee, please."

While the bartender tended to his craft, a fellow from a nearby table approached her.

Lishan turned to face him straight on, firmly implanting her message with a loud voice. "Don't you dare disturb me. I haven't been here two minutes and you predators think nothing of harassing people, like it's your right. In fact, I think I'll just go ahead and call my brother and his friends." She reached for her phone. The aberrant male, wide-eyed, left abruptly.

A few minutes later, Lishan began to quiet. Then she remembered Erik had called, and she wanted Erik to know about her finding the book.

Her face turned somber. *He'll know I went to Rafael's. I can't lie to him. And what about the thirteenth?* Lishan put her face in her hands, elbows on the bar. Her eyes moistened. *Now what?*

She knew she had to tell him. It's just that she was worried his jealousy would create a scene. With the thirteenth in view, at least she knew, she thought, that she had the presence of mind to keep sex out of her intentions with Rafael.

43

"Erik, hi. I wanted to see if you have some time today. First, though, tell me how the students are."

"One is still in intensive care. She has another health problem, which made it harder for her body to deal with the poison. The other five are under observation. For now, they can't leave. Too unstable." Remembering Lishan's request, he said, "Why don't you come to my apartment? Likely a safer bet than yours these days. Don't go back to your apartment. By the way, where were you last night, if you don't mind my asking?"

"Auntie's. I'll tell you later." Lishan agreed to come by. Thirty minutes later, she knocked on his door.

"Hungry?" he asked, as she settled in. A nod sent Erik to the kitchen, returning to the couch with sushi from the deli and a Sierra Nevada Pale Ale. As he ate, he looked at her as though he were waiting for something.

She picked up on the hint. "Oh, yes. Auntie. We worked on Mazzini emails until late. Then she took me to breakfast this morning." Reaching its end, she knew she couldn't contain her thoughts any longer about where she would live, and Rafael, both of which were stressful baggage for her. "Erik?"

Her tone must have alerted his instincts. "You want to talk about where you should live, right?"

"Yes," she said, though inside, she was screaming to get the confrontation with Rafael out in the open.

Finally, Erik spoke, relieved that Lishan didn't want to talk about men, Rafael in particular. "I asked my friend Jean-Antoine if he had a place for you to stay, just in case. He's an artist who owns an apartment building two blocks from here. He has a room being renovated, mostly done, that you can use. If you help with the work, or do the remaining work yourself, he'll cut you a freebie deal. I doubt he'll charge you, in any case, but I thought you would like to help out."

"That's good news. Artist that he is, can I call him Watteau?" Lishan gave a weak smile at her quip and added, "You know how much I love it here. It's difficult, thinking about leaving."

"I'm hoping it's just a temporary move, until you're safe again. I had already talked with Antoine yesterday about the possibility. By the way, have you ever had a broken arm—in a sling—annoyed by the incessant question? What I mean is, don't call him Watteau."

"He'll break my arm?"

"No. Well, maybe. That's not what I meant, though."

"Then..." Lishan interrupted herself, thinking best to just move along since she was merely jousting, attempting to lighten the mood.

"I should tell you, he can be a bit narcissistic. He prefers to be called Antoine—something to do with his ego, and women."

"Wonderful," Lishan said dryly. "And when am I supposed to move to the Louvre?"

"Cute. Tomorrow. Tonight is up for grabs." Erik looked at the time on his cell phone. "I have to get back to the office. Settle in here. I'll be back this evening, okay?"

Lishan felt her breath stiffen. She still carried the Rafael burden with her.

- - -

The afternoon slid by, one slow minute after another. Lishan intended to be productive, but residual fatigue and depression caught up. Thoughts of Rafael and Erik knotted her gut. She napped on the couch instead. A ring-ring on her phone woke her as 5:00 p.m. approached.

"Hi. It's Auntie. I've got the details for meeting with Maya. Monday, ten in the morning." She paused. "Were you asleep?"

"Yes. Tired. Where do we meet?"

With the details written, Lishan thanked Niesha and begged for a shorter conversation, if she didn't mind. She put on a Kenyan decaf to brew, wondering if Erik would call. She dug into FDA.gov and continued her search.

At 8:00 p.m., she could hear the key in the door. It was Erik.

"Progress today?" he asked.

They exchanged the essence of the afternoon. By 9:00, both of them were haggard.

Lishan picked up *The Economist* from the coffee table.

Erik nibbled on a few nuts from the bowl on the coffee table. "Tell me an *Economist* story."

"Here's one. I'll paraphrase. The FDA's Nanotechnology Task Force is evaluating the ramifications of using nanotechnology in food production. When asked how small a nano-particle is, they said that to compare it with a meter is like comparing the diameter of a dime with that of the world. Damn, that's tiny."

Lishan continued. "The food industry is looking at this to improve shelf-life, especially for those foods with oils in them." Lishan turned to face her companion. "Unfortunately, many in management will pursue ways to improve their profits without being absolutely certain of the effects on the human body and mind. The FDA, when pressed, tells the public that its GRAS—Generally Recognized As Safe—classification is awarded after an appropriate amount of time and testing has taken place. 'Generally'—can you believe? The problem is, industry and its lobbyists have strong connections and pull. Last year, industry alone contributed more than thirty billion dollars to further their own political stratagem. The politicians don't like to ignore those folks. Shall I continue?"

Erik leaned in a little closer, chin now resting in his palm, clearly engaged.

"Conner Foods was responsible for nearly one-quarter of those—shall we call them—donations. Bribery is more like it. The additive that killed those people at Factory 17 is similar to an earlier rendition that was initially given a GRAS classification, before it was revoked. It never hit the market in that deadly form. But that isn't the point."

Lishan stopped for a breath, measuring the pulse of her confidante.

"The article states that an investigation of the nanotechnology in use at Conner Foods was terminated after the GRAS announcement, but it's now under review due to some *problems* at Conner. Quoting: 'Jack Conner, CEO of Conner Foods, announced yesterday that the nanotechnology being developed at Conner Foods is cutting-edge, a boon to the food industry.' B.S. He is such an egoist."

Erik added, "Will the data Niesha—you and Niesha—collected help bring this guy down?"

"It would seem. No, that's not good enough. Yes is the answer. Yes, we will bring him down."

Lishan reached for her laptop, thinking she would examine the Conner emails further, but then she remembered the move tomorrow. "What do you think about tomorrow's move?"

Erik looked at her, conflicted. "I know it's best," is all he said.

"Yes." Lishan glanced around the room. "I guess the idea of my moving sounds better than the reality of it. I'm thinking we both agree it's the right thing to do."

Lishan knew it was time.

"Erik?" Her tone was somber.

He felt paralyzed. Erik held his breath, feeling trapped though he didn't know what followed.

"I saw Rafael yesterday. I called him because I, once and for all, wanted to know if I should consider him a friend or not. I stopped by his apartment, but just for a few minutes."

"You slept with him." Erik could feel his love taking wings out the window.

Lishan's "NO" came out a little more forcefully than she intended. "What I finally understood was that I just wanted to know whether to write him off my list of friends, my list of associates in the newspaper world, or not. Then he made a snide, racist remark about you, one I couldn't stand, so I left. On my way out the door, I saw my missing Frazier book on his kitchen counter. I screamed at him, took my book, and left for good."

Erik stood. "Did you consider fucking him?" He took note of her defense of him, but he felt her loyalty was thin, given their commitment. "You haven't forgotten the thirteenth?"

"No to your first question," Lishan said with some force. "And I haven't forgotten the thirteenth."

"Should we?"

"Dammit, Erik. You've got it all wr...."

"Hold on, Lishan. Let's get it straight who is hurt here." Hostility controlled the small muscles in Erik's face as they became well defined and visible. All manner of softness had disappeared.

Silence, the color of dread, filled the space.

Lishan gently grasped Erik's hands, attempting to lower him back onto the couch. But he resisted, standing back.

The air between them was thick—a barrier, palpable.

"I think it's best if I call Antoine. He'll get in touch with you later," Erik said.

It was clearly time for Lishan to leave. She heaved a sigh before departing. No kiss. No hug. Devastation. Tears.

Entering her apartment, Lishan knew hypervigilance was key. *I shouldn't be here. But where?* Turning on every light as soon as she could, she scrutinized every corner, every hiding place, from a distance. Finally, convinced she was alone, she set the dead bolt, wedged a chair under the doorknob, checked the windows, and put a kitchen knife on her nightstand. But she couldn't think about sleep.

For the second time in a week, she thought of the cove—the quiet, the safety. Staying in the apartment had become just too fraught with darkness. Yes, she would go. Packing an overnight bag, enough for the weekend, she left. Her senses were heightened as she left for the closed garage where Erik had moved her car. *Damn, I forgot my disguise.*

As she approached the garage, around the edges of the garage door she saw a dim, erratic light coming from inside the garage, as though a flashlight was on. Her heart sped up, the adrenalin doing its job. When the sudden, muffled sound of breaking glass stopped her, she panicked, yelling out "*No.*" Before she could think about her error, the side garage door opened and out stepped a man she had not seen before. He was about the same size and age as the man who sat behind Beck at the restaurant, but he was clearly someone else. An overcoat with upturned collars made him look menacing.

Lishan's eyes grew round and frightened as he ran straight for her. Just before he got to her, Lishan finally broke her own spell and ran. And ran. She did not look back until she just couldn't run anymore. *I've outrun him. Thank God* was all she could say to herself. Her overnight bag was a small one, meant for easy foot travel, so it hadn't slowed her down much at all. She was glad she hung onto it, almost like a homeless man's shopping cart is full of his life, his security. She found herself in a neighborhood whose streets she hadn't been on before.

I just want out of this darkness. Let me find a place to stay where nobody knows I'm there. Nobody. Finally, she found her way to a main thoroughfare. There she grabbed the first bus to come along, not caring where it was headed. Perhaps an hour had gone by before it had taken her to the other side of D.C., an area she didn't know. Seeing a small motel with a Mexican restaurant and an Indian restaurant nearby, she got off the bus. This was where she would stay, for now, maybe forever.

44

Monday morning found Lishan tired and alone, not quite sure where she was. She called M to say she wouldn't be in. She retrieved a voice mail message from an unknown caller. It turned out to be Antoine, wondering what happened to her. She decided to let it go, for now. She just didn't want to deal. Then she called Niesha.

"I'm okay, but I should tell you some hoodlum found my car Friday night. An older guy. The style of his overcoat made me think of the Mafia, likely on Conner's payroll. I was going to go to the cove when I interrupted him breaking into it. He came after me. I barely got away, running until I couldn't run anymore. I took a bus to the other side of D.C."

Niesha didn't say anything at first, letting her niece get it all out. "What can I do for you, dear? If I get within five meters of this guy, he's toast. I'll hang him by his fuc...." Niesha caught herself.

"Auntie!"

"I'm sorry, Lishan. It's the temper side of me you don't get to see—and you don't want to."

Her auntie cussing suddenly made Lishan feel a little less safe, if that was possible. Lishan needed to be able to abandon all worries when her auntie had her under her wing.

Niesha tried recovering.

"My anger really isn't that bad. It just comes out when someone I care about is threatened." She continued. "You'll be okay. I know it. We'll talk some more when I see you, okay?"

"Yes, okay." Wanting to move past the chaos, she changed the subject. "Are we still meeting with your prosecutor friend?"

"Yes. At ten. She's not far from here. We've arranged to meet her there." Niesha paused, sensing her niece might be holding something back. "Is there anything else, dear?"

A hesitation as Lishan remembered. "Yes. Erik's jealousy is driving a wedge. It's all feeling like just too much."

"Will you be all right until I see you?"

"Yes...Yes."

They agreed to meet at nine at the same café where they met the previous week. This gave Lishan a little over an hour to find her way.

Arriving a few minutes early, Lishan noticed a *People's Advocate* rack with a front-page headline that caught her eye. Front and center was a cartoon with the FDA commissioner eating hydrogenated oils while some Food & Drug CEO put a fistful of dollars in the commissioner's pocket. The headlined story read, "FDA Turns Blind Eye to CEO's Toxic New Trans Fat?" Lishan read the first couple of paragraphs, all she had time for at the moment.

> There's news on the street that some uppity Food & Drug CEO has arm-twisted—or otherwise influenced—the FDA commissioner, hoping to get FDA approval soon enough to have it in the stores by Christmas. If you thought the current trans fat clogs arteries at an alarming rate (what's a mere twenty years cut off your lifespan?), wait until you try the new and "improved" version—if you survive it. Word has it that certain employees were used as test subjects, unbeknownst to them. They didn't fare so well, unless you disregard death and illness. How will this get approved in the FDA? I saw the commissioner and said CEO laughing it up the other day at a swanky restaurant. Guess who picked up the tab? We heard that Jack Conner was in the restaurant. Of course, there's no connection.

Yes, it was Howard's byline.

Lishan found Niesha sitting comfortably in a booth, coffee in hand, a *USA Today* laid out.

"Hi, Auntie. I thought you didn't like mainstream newspapers?"

"I don't, as a rule. But I do like to keep tabs on the Republicans. You know, they manipulate the news to drive their agenda. I don't want to be blindsided."

Lishan nodded. "Did you see this?" She put the *Advocate* over the *USA Today*.

"No, I haven't."

Lishan told her about the conversation with Howard Perkins.

"You do get around, don't you? I mean that as a compliment."

Both women were pleased.

A few seconds later, the breakfast arrived along with an additional cup of coffee. Lishan looked up at her aunt, a questioning look on her face.

"As long as I'm coordinating your life, sweet niece of mine— yes, I already ordered." They managed a lean smile.

"Tell me what you can, Lishan." She reached out and touched her niece's hand.

Lishan added in a few remaining details about the garage incident, then explained her visit to Rafael's apartment and the evening at Erik's, prompting her to head to the cove.

"I'm tempted to offer advice about Erik, but I'm thinking you already know what you need to know. About your car, at least you're safe. I'll call the police. Just give me the address."

Lishan nodded, thinking about her life. She wrote down the address and continued. "I need to give him some time. The body latches onto these emotional hits, only slowly releasing them over time. I need to forgive him for being jealous. I wonder if something happened to him years ago."

Niesha nodded, sipping her coffee. "It sounds like it." Niesha paused. "I know the relationship issue with Erik is important, but we need to focus on what happened to you at the garage. When can you move? I know you've been thinking about it."

"Yes, Auntie. I know." Lishan stopped, thinking. "I'll bet that guy was Rudy."

Niesha thought about the implications. "Maybe so. We'll stop him, in any case. At Maya's, we'll come up with whatever plans are necessary to keep you safe, okay?"

"Okay, Auntie." Defeat had lodged in Lishan's voice.

Her head was swimming. Then she remembered the students. She relayed their current status, as Erik had told her. As she was finishing telling Niesha of Erik's call, her phone rang. It was Erik.

"She died, Lishan. The young college student died." The grief in Erik's voice was beyond Lishan's comprehension.

"Oh, no," Lishan cried out, looking at her auntie. "The student in ICU just died. Erik, I'm so sorry. What can I do? I'm sitting here with Auntie. Oh, Erik."

"Just put those sons-of-bitches behind bars. Every last one of them. You two talk. Figure it out. I can't stay on the phone." As his eyes flooded with tears, he hung up.

Niesha moved to her niece's side of the booth, holding and consoling her until the sobbing had slowed. They spoke of the tragedy of the loss of such a young life until they just couldn't discuss it anymore. Niesha's wisdom then suggested it was time to move along. Lishan agreed. Besides, the tone in Erik's voice left her with the impression that he was still angry with her. *Yes, it's time to move along.*

Lishan dried her eyes, listening.

"I have copies of every pertinent Mazzini and Conner email, including what you and I already shared. Also, the documents Fatima gave us, and her written, signed statement. Do you think you can look these over?"

"I have to, Auntie. I have to." Lishan skimmed the emails, sharing her thoughts with Niesha as best she could.

"Look at this," Niesha began. Her notations in the side margins were standard fare, as was the pink highlighting. "I made quadruplicate copies before making any marks; one is for Maya." Sipping her coffee, Niesha continued. "Each email is numbered, a number you will find on the spreadsheet that was on top of the stack." She sat back, taking a bite of her omelet while Lishan perused the rows and columns Niesha provided.

"You'll see there are five columns. Each email's relevancy is indicated: Factory 17, Jack Conner, the FDA, Senator Libby, or miscellaneous. We can further break it down if need be."

Lishan noted the differentiated rows, each referencing a different email, each with one or more columns ticked. "This is excellent. It looks like most of these have the Jack Conner column checked."

Lishan read the first three, taking in the implications before her. In the first, Mazzini had responded to an email from Jack Conner, whose words read, "It's too late to back out now. So a couple of workers died. They were sickly, anyway, I would wager. This modified, incognito trans fat *has* to be approved. It's the only way I can get the shareholders off my back. Call your buddy at the FDA, the one you have your thumb on. We want that application pushed through—tomorrow. Double bonus."

"See what I mean," Niesha said. "We've got him. Read on. Remember, these are in order of importance, not by date." Lishan picked up the second email. Within a few seconds, she felt tears.

Niesha reached across and took her hand. "Beck was your friend, wasn't he?"

Lishan just nodded. Mazzini had responded back to Conner's command to compromise him, that he had outlived his usefulness and trust. Mazzini wrote, "It's done. Swift and not quite as painful as you suggested, but he's no longer a threat. Nice fella. Too bad."

Lishan looked out the window. She took note of Mazzini's "nice fella" and "too bad" comments, thinking they further compromised his standing with someone like Conner.

Niesha gently squeezed her niece's hand. "Go on," she urged.

Lishan picked up the third email. Mazzini to Conner. "Our FDA insider responded to the prod. Additional $125k. Shareholders should be happy. GRAS before too long. M."

"Auntie, you inspire me. Next step the U.S. Attorney's Office?"

Niesha just nodded.

.

45

Maya's office was in the United States Attorney's Office building—it had an angular design with abrupt edges, uncharacteristic of the neoclassical, federal, and Beaux-Arts architectures that graced much of Washington, D.C. Below her stenciled name appeared Criminal Division Chief. Niesha had always referred to Maya as her DA friend, partially for brevity's sake, but mostly because Niesha always felt Maya would have someday moved up to the Principal Assistant U.S. Attorney position, then a top DA slot in some East Coast division, were it not for her racist boss.

"Niesha! So good to see you. And Lishan, of course. A true pleasure." Maya and Niesha embraced one another like very old friends. Lishan was surprised she had never met Maya before, but she smiled to herself, taking in that her aunt had a life beyond her.

Lishan took note of the trim Donna Karan outfit Maya wore. Finely tailored black flared pants and a matching lightweight cardigan. Maya's slender form contrasted with Niesha's generous body, yet each complemented the other, exceptional beauties in their individual ways.

Pleasantries exchanged, they settled into ergonomically designed chairs at a round conference table in Maya's office. Before they plunged into how to proceed, Niesha told Maya about Lishan being accosted Friday night, adding to the urgency of whatever steps they took.

Maya saw no need to make any soothing remarks. She knew where they stood. The compassion in her eyes told the story.

Niesha saw a faraway look on Lishan's face.

Lishan saw the question on her auntie's face. She decided to elaborate.

"Nothing I need to know. My mind had wandered to...how far back do your two families go?"

"Are you asking how we know one another, or perhaps how Maya and I—given that she's Jewish and I'm Sunni Muslim—dealt with the Israeli-Palestine conflict?"

Maya and Niesha exchanged glances. Maya took the lead.

"My parents, and extending back to my grandparents, had staunch ideas of their rights to the land. I carried those feelings with me when I immigrated here as a youth." Maya looked at Niesha, who nodded.

"But as a youth, after awhile I questioned how I wanted to move forward in the world. Did I want to keep hating? When Niesha and I met a number of years ago, while attending political gatherings, we began to talk about these feelings. We decided to let go of the anger we experienced growing up, wanting to see if we could make a difference. To this day, we present peace as the best approach. Not everyone agrees."

Lishan just nodded. There was no need to pursue any of it further.

Niesha asked Maya if she had heard about the poisoning of the students. She had, noting the newspaper article quoted the note with Lishan's name on it.

"I'm so very sorry, Lishan." Maya thought to tell Lishan not to feel responsible, but she decided it was best to just not open that door, at least not now.

They moved ahead, with Niesha spreading out the initial pages of each of the two stacks of emails. Maya already had conceptions of the situation, given phone conversations with Niesha. She spent the next twenty minutes fairly quiet, poring over each email, one stack then the other, as Niesha suggested, followed by the documents from Fatima—which drew nods from Maya. Occasional questions or comments were conveyed, but mostly it was silence.

"Hmm. Jack Conner's not going to be pleased with this, is he?"

Niesha jumped in. "Maya, my primary concerns have to do with the safety of Lishan and everyone who has aided her. Beck, the P.I., has already been murdered for his complicity in what he shared with her. Now a dead student from Lishan's apartment building. How would you suggest we protect my niece—all of us, really? I don't know...restraining order or some form of court injunction?"

Maya walked over to her expansive window.

"Jack Conner is a powerful figure in Washington. I've had the pleasure, shall we say, of running up against his fleet of attorneys on more than one occasion." Speaking quietly, Maya continued. "Niesha, you and I are old friends. I can tell you and Lishan something I don't often discuss. I believe part of the roadblock for my last two attempts for the Principal Assistant

U.S. Attorney position came from interference by Conner and, I suspect, his association with Ferrali. Conner knows I wouldn't side with him in court."

Maya sat back, continuing in her earlier tone. "Yes, there are immediate actions we will take. I can see...it's time. I just need to take the steps without checking in with Ferrali. He'll be furious, but if we win, he won't have any easy recourse. If we don't..." Another notable pause. "Okay, here's what we're going to do." Maya called in her assistant, Leana, for whom she had complete trust.

"Leana, please shut the door." Maya paused, directing her initial comments toward Lishan and Niesha. "Earlier, in anticipation of the evidence before us, I drew up a document called an *information*, a document that alleges wrongdoing, allowing us to issue a warrant for Jack Conner's arrest. It includes murder—third degree for the Factory 17 employees—and first degree for his engineering of Beck's murder. Oh, and one more—the poisonings. Six students were poisoned, with one death, and the young girl at the newspaper. Leana, I need you to finalize it. This is of an extremely sensitive nature, so you must be absolutely discreet and not share this with anyone, not even my associates. Especially Ferrali."

Leana's eyes widened, then narrowed, indicating she registered the import.

"Additionally, I need you to obtain a restraining order prohibiting Conner and his charge—including Mazzini and Rudy Conner—from any contact with Lishan and her affiliates. People's lives are at stake, and I can't afford any friendships or other cohesions to stand in the way. Also, get in touch with the U.S. Marshals office—specifically Juan Jalasca, who can be completely trusted—and give him advance notice of our need for his services this afternoon. Request two U.S. Marshal vehicles—a little extra pressure upfront decreases the likelihood of someone like Conner bending the truth. Do you have any questions? The signatures you will need?"

"I know just what to do," said Leana.

Maya stood and walked over to her. "Leana, pardon my being so abrupt. It's nothing personal. This just stands the probability of being the stickiest and most litigious case before us. Conner won't come willingly, and he has friends in most influential departments, likely including Justice." Maya gave a meaningful glance toward Nathaniel Ferrali's office.

Maya and Leana conferred quietly as Maya walked her to the door, her arm around Leana's shoulder. Leana departed quickly, a mission in her sights.

Coming back to the conference table, Maya let out a rather grand sigh. "Whew. Either we'll all be at Conner's sentencing, or we'll be pushing hot dog carts. Any questions?"

"How long will it take for these processes to take effect?" Lishan asked. "In my experience, it takes months for any real movement where the elite are concerned."

"Correct assessment, Lishan, regarding the usual. But we can expedite when warranted. I should add that we've known all along, or at least had strong suspicions, about Conner. It looks like we have the firepower to put him away this time—but, again, not easily."

Niesha managed a smile, a genuine look of relief shared by all three. "What do you two think about leaking a story to the media?" Niesha looked directly at Lishan, then at Maya, since Maya's input was key.

"It would be helpful to make this as public as possible, making it more difficult for Conner to squirm out of, and more difficult for his cronies to assist," Maya said. "But which media will do this?"

Both the women looked at Lishan, waiting.

"I could play one last card at the paper," Lishan said, somewhat thinking out loud, "but I don't know that I should put anyone at the paper on the spot, since a job—not just mine— would most certainly be at stake. But, you know, I would like to believe the publisher would back me up. She always does, as long as I don't put her in a bind. It would be quite a scoop for them. Maya, how soon could, or should, a newsflash hit the streets?"

"Today isn't soon enough. We have to hit them hard and fast, like being in a street fight," Maya said.

"I'd forgotten your roots, my dear." Niesha smiled. "I'll fill Lishan in on your street smarts later."

Lishan took it all in, raising her eyebrows along with a purposeful smile. "Can we take a few minutes and compose the gist of this front-page exposé?"

Maya took the floor while Lishan wrote. "Let's, as I said, hit it forcibly. Sentences like—and be careful to use these words specifically, given libel—'Jack Conner indicted on counts of purposeful negligence for public health and complicity in first and third degree murder cases.' Those are strong words, but a mainstream paper can do it, and it gets the message out to the public."

They spent the next twenty minutes deliberating and finalizing a quick, poignant story.

"I like it. Does it fit for your timing if I make the call here and now?"

"Lishan," Maya said warmly, "when I heard from Niesha what you were undertaking and who the antagonist was, I canceled my appointments from ten until two. My staff will wonder what has overtaken me. They'll find out soon. By all means, make the call."

Nodding, Lishan walked to the window, calling Elizabeth Walker.

"Ms. Walker, I have a scoop for you. It could be a dangerous one, but I'm hoping you'll take it for tomorrow's edition. It's about a probable indictment on Jack Conner."

"Conner? I'm all ears."

Before Lishan proceeded with the text of the story, she told the publisher about the Criminal Division chief's involvement and stance. Then she asked if Hanson would be a problem.

Elizabeth laughed. "Not these days. He just hides out in his office, afraid of offending anyone, afraid of getting fired." The publisher's tone made it clear she was pleased. It would be on the streets tomorrow afternoon. She added one last check. "Lishan, any doubts before we proceed?"

Lishan thought for a moment. "No. None."

"Good," was her confident reply.

With the three of them back at the conference table, a sense of anticipation gathered. Now they had to take their refuge into account, including Maya's. They decided to have sandwiches brought in while they further discussed their options. Lishan bowed out to call Erik, but she stopped abruptly, remembering. She didn't know if she had the wherewithal to talk with him if he was in a foul mood.

Maya spent the last half an hour sharing highlights of the vast body of information she had garnered on Conner. Past attempts at sending him to jail had engendered quite a portfolio. Lishan and Niesha were both pleasantly surprised by the thick file she had already amassed. They were beginning to feel like the game had shifted in their favor—but they knew not to get comfortable.

As two o'clock approached, Maya reminded the group of her impending departure. She had just fifteen minutes to wrap it up.

Leana reappeared, again closing the door. "I spoke with the U.S. Marshals office, and the necessary signatures and a Probable Cause affidavit are forthcoming. Too many people in this department hate the likes of Jack Conner, who has skated out from under his penalties at least twice too often."

Maya just nodded. "Good...and good." She looked up at the trio. "Fluent, aren't I?"

Maya smiled as she returned her attention to Niesha and Lishan after Leana left. She took a deliberate breath. "The warrant will be served this afternoon, if Conner can be found. There will be no turning back."

Maya stood, grabbing her attaché case. "It's quite courageous what you two are undertaking. Jack Conner is a menace. You're welcome to stay here in my office. It might be safer than your alternatives—at least for today. Do you think you'll stay? I don't need to know. Just looking forward."

Niesha and Lishan looked at one another. Lishan spoke first. "The question is, where can we make the most effective use of our time, or how can we help further?"

Maya looked at them both, as seriously as she could. "You've both given the judicial system what it needs to put away a criminal. While he doesn't appear as a cold-blooded killer where the public is concerned...believe me, he's no different. The best way for you to help is by keeping yourselves safe. Aside from the obvious difficulty to the case if you—either of you—are murdered, I can't imagine losing you, for so many other reasons. Besides, the public needs this case. Can you locate Mazzini? We need to protect him."

It was Niesha's turn. "I may be able to. I spoke with him about it last night. It appears that Conner's other hit man, Rudy Conner, already tried to take Mazzini out. I'll see what I can do."

"Good. Can you two stay somewhere safe tonight? No relation to anything in your past, perhaps some hotel or motel no one would expect to find you in. And stay off email. Read a book—perhaps one of those Lescroart suspense novels to heighten your vigilance. I've learned some of my best moves from him and his judicial insider, Al."

Lishan turned toward Niesha. "Why don't we work from here for a couple of hours? See what you turn up with Mazzini. Then we'll find a place to stay. Maya, do you want to know where we'll be?"

"Leave your possibilities with Leana. Don't use your credit cards. Here"—she reached into her bag—"use this card. It's my alter ego—Cleo Steinway."

Niesha blinked at the mention of "Cleo," then turned to her niece. "You have a cell phone that no one knows about—supposedly—don't you?" Niesha kept her gaze on the papers, the Mazzini emails, as she spoke. "I should call Mazzini."

Lishan handed the phone to her. She was too immersed in her own emotions to listen, thinking about the next phone call she might make—Erik, who never completely faded from her emotional view.

"Auntie, while it's daylight, I should go to my apartment to gather some clothes and incidentals. I could be back here in an hour. Maybe I'll see Erik—see where things stand. What do you think?"

Maya jumped in. "Not a good idea, Lishan, to go by yourself." Maya turned back from the door, where she was about to leave. "I have a couple of staff members who carry guns. If one of them takes you, I'm okay with it. Who's Erik?"

"Her putative boyfriend." Niesha shifted her gaze to Lishan. "I don't mind if you go. Maya's right, though. By the way, where's your disguise?"

"I left it in my apartment Friday night. I was upset."

Niesha just nodded. Nothing needed to be said.

As they each focused on their individual tasks ahead, an alternate plan was being put in place down the hall.

"Nathan. This is Leana. There's something you should know."

牛伍

A knock on the door preceded Etta's entrance into Erik's office at the university. Startled, Erik stood to shake hands with this provocative young woman. Her olive complexion and lissome form readily reminded him of their interlude one year prior.

Etta bypassed the handshake. She promptly headed toward the hug she meant as a delicious invitation to continue where they had left off. She kicked back with her right foot, shutting the door. Erik was hesitant, well aware of the predicament this might get him into, but the recent cheat—as he perceived it—by Lishan left him feeling a little reckless. He reciprocated.

Within a few seconds they heard another knock. Etta was slower to withdraw than Erik.

"Oh, pardon me." It was the Dean of Instruction, taking in that, while there was no immediate embrace, her professor had unequivocally crossed a line.

"And Etta...how nice to see you." She narrowed her gaze, locking eyes with Erik. "Mr. Andersson, I wanted to congratulate you on your committee work regarding HR violations. Well done." The question, *was I remiss?* lingered on her face. She nodded toward each, "Erik, Etta," as she closed the door, leaving them alone.

"That was exciting," Etta proclaimed.

"Your words. Potentially devastating on my end. But..." Erik paused. "Do you have dinner plans?"

Etta's eyes opened fully. "I *am*...hungry."

"Do you know where I live?"

"Any self-respecting...female...Yes, I know where you live. Near the Potomac, by Georgetown."

"Yes. In an hour?"

The date set, Etta swiveled her hips on her way out, cinching the affair.

On his way home, Erik felt conflicted. He did his best not to think beyond the eve ahead and Lishan all in the same breath. Organic spinach and field greens, olive oil and vinegar, a six-year-old Cabernet. Follow with wholegrain pasta, select herbs, roasted red peppers, and grated Parmigiano-Reggiano, finished with a fine chocolate mini-cake in a pool of raspberry sauce. Then....

Etta wore a loose-fitting white silk top with nothing underneath. Her drawstring pale green silk pants rode low on her hips.

It was all too much for Erik to contain. Twenty minutes later, the room was filled with the scent of sweat.

As they wound their way back into the living room, Etta did a quick scan of various photos in the apartment. "Who's that babe?"

"Lishan. She was a student of mine." He turned to face Etta. "She lives in the building. We are friends."

"Good friends?"

"Yes, I suppose so."

"Suppose? Hmm." Then she dropped it, or had at least intended to. "Why the red heart on the thirteenth?"

Erik's glanced at the kitchen wall calendar. "It's..."

"It's what?" She wasn't going to let it go.

"Just a date."

"Just? With a red heart?"

Erik wasn't fast enough with an alibi.

"Let's try ten questions. Does it regard Lishan?"

"Why ten questions?"

"It's my way of getting to the heart of the matter. Lishan?"

"Yes."

"Birthday?" she said.

"Do you want some pasta?" Erik attempted to contain his anger. "Listen. Yes, she's special to me."

"Then why am I here?"

"To get an 'A.' That's why you're here."

Etta smiled, thinking of a reply. "Yes, that's true. What's wrong with that? Besides, I like the illicit side of this affair, holding something over you."

"I think you should go."

Etta stood, glaring at Erik. In her best haughty voice, she said, "Now that you've had your rocks—if that's how you Americans say it. I see." Etta gathered her things, heading to the door. With a contemptuous grin, she added, "Don't forget that 'A.'"

Not ten feet from Erik's door, Lishan halted as she saw his door open. Chris had agreed to wait at the end of the hall, with the odds and ends and the disguise Lishan had gathered. He knew Lishan needed a moment with this fella. Lishan pretended to fumble with a key at another door as the tall, hot, olive-skinned woman flew past her, pausing just long enough with an inquisitive look at Lishan, then a glare.

Erik thought he heard Etta say 'tramp' as she headed down the hall.

47

Niesha put the phone's ear bud in place, then decided against it, opting instead for the speakerphone.

"Mazzini," the voice was now familiar to Niesha.

"I'm glad you've made it this far," she offered.

There was a moment's pause. Niesha imagined him finishing genuflecting to his God. "That's kind of you," he offered, allowing himself to be touched by her generosity. "You, too, apparently."

He paused, but continued. "I'm assuming you would like to meet today. Is that correct?" Mazzini sounded even, though tired. "There's a café within walking distance of my room. I believe it's safe enough to meet there."

Niesha held the air for a moment before speaking. "Mazzini, though I know this might not sound the best to you, I believe you would be safest if taken into custody. I have a great deal of pull within the system, so I won't let anyone mistreat you. I suggest you agree." Niesha had to use all of her restraint to keep from lashing out about the poisonings. *There will be time,* she thought to herself.

His silence was palpable, though not unexpected. The idea of being behind bars was nearly unimaginable to him, given the experiences that brought him in contact with convicts, lockdowns, bailiffs, the clank of solid boundaries between freedom and the lack of it.

Niesha imagined the thoughts that had to be streaming through Mazzini's mind; the time had come to face the karma he knew one day would catch up with him.

"Yes." Silence again.

When Lishan opened the door to Maya's office, Niesha just issued the *shhh* finger sign. There was an unspoken agreement that Niesha would appear solo in this call, not wanting Mazzini to feel ganged-up on.

Lishan tried to feel compassion for Mazzini in that moment, wishing to be completely respectful of the pain this man was no doubt undergoing—the prospect, the likelihood, of prison. But she was losing. Thoughts of the young student's family and the life cut short obliterated any kindness she tried to muster.

"How can you ensure that I won't end up in the jurisdiction of a corrupt cop, one on Conner's payroll? I could easily be shot under the guise of attempting escape."

Niesha spoke up: "We have an adjunct witness protection program comprised of hand-picked, trusted men and women. In fact, the lodging is quite nice—better than the digs I lived in in my early twenties." She glanced at Lishan, who had given her an odd look when she used the word "digs." Niesha just shrugged.

She continued. "I'll do all I can. Truly." She took a breath, giving her thoughts a chance to gather. "I should meet with you and have an unmarked police car take you in. I'll be with you to ensure you get proper treatment. If you don't mind, my niece Lishan will be with us."

Again, "Yes...it's...it's all just fine." Then, in a timid voice Niesha hadn't yet heard in him, he asked, "Is it safe to tell you where I am? Not *you*, but rather, now, over the phone."

"Is this your first call from this location?"

"Yes."

"So, if they're tracking your calls, they're just now learning your whereabouts."

"Likely."

"Then change locations now. We will be in your vicinity in half an hour."

"Make it an hour and a half. I have an errand. I'll meet you out on Highway 97."

Niesha decided against arguing. "If you must. I'm hoping you can stay relatively unnoticed during your errand."

"No concern of yours."

"Then call us from wherever you land—preferably a public place, somewhere close to where you are now. And don't delay leaving where you are. Be gone within one to two minutes. Can you do that?"

"*Va bene,*" Mazzini said in his native Italian tongue.

Niesha used Lishan's cell phone to call the witness protection office. Within twenty minutes, an undercover agent picked up Niesha and Lishan, and then they waited for Mazzini's call.

Mazzini called a taxi. As he waited outside, he could tell he just didn't want to think anymore—about anything. His life, his income, his future. He decided to take the taxi to where his car was parked in the garage. He wanted to drive to his next destination. *None of it matters* were the only words in his head.

- - -

240

"Mr. Mazzini, how are you this lovely day?" The reception nurse was pleasant, always happy to see this reliable visitor. Mazzini hadn't missed a day in the three years she knew him.

"Just fine, Mrs. Maxwell. And you?"

"How could I not be doing well with elders like your mother? Such joys to watch over."

Ridgeview Heights was the finest rest home Mazzini could find for his mother. At ninety-three, perky and alive, she just needed company, with only occasional assistance—medications, mostly. This was nothing like the homes where the ratio of staff to residents was pitifully low, where these stately seniors had been reduced to chores in the minds of many of the underpaid help. Mazzini had made that mistake only once—a previous home where he was given the kind of promises he needed for his mother, but, sadly, promises that were only lip service. That home was no longer in business. Mazzini didn't take kindly to falsehoods.

He knew the staff, the spacious rooms, and all of the residents of Ridgeview well. His mother was not going to be stuck anywhere with anyone where he perceived the slightest risk to her emotional and physical well-being.

"Hi, Mother." Mazzini hung his hat on a bedpost. Then he sat down on the single bed after giving her a kiss on her forehead.

"Hello, son. You should have seen what happened to that pretty, young pregnant girl on *Lost* today. If I were on that island—it's an island, isn't it?—I would have seen to her welfare." She looked up. "How are you? You look weary."

Mazzini did his utmost to keep the strains on his life from his mother's view.

"I just didn't sleep well." A truth blended with omission. "Mother?"

She sat up straight. "Something *is* wrong, isn't it?"

"No, truly." He delivered the lie he had practiced on the drive over. "I've been sleeping poorly. I've enrolled in a sleep clinic for the next few days, and I'm afraid I may not be able to visit. That's all."

"Oh, I'm so relieved." Her held breath expelled, allowing her to lean back into her comfort. "That's okay, son. No other resident has a daily visitor. I'm fortunate."

They spent the next half an hour talking about nothing in particular—a routine they had settled into, one in which she seemed to find the most comfort.

As he was leaving, Mrs. Maxwell also asked if he was all right. She could see a twinge of moisture in his eyes, something she had yet to experience with this apparently mild-mannered, loving man.

"Yes, Mrs. Maxwell. I'm just tired today." He stopped, thinking he should alert her of his likely absence. "I have been having trouble sleeping and have checked into a program for the next few days, one that will help me sleep. I doubt I can visit. I'm sorry."

"Now, don't you worry. We'll take good care of your mother. You know we will."

Mazzini nodded, delivering a weak smile on his way through the double doors as he headed back toward the Highway 97 Motel to meet his fate.

48

"Tom, you've got a problem." Ferrali didn't waste any time calling Conner's top counsel, Tom Danforth, after the call from Maya's assistant.

"I'm listening." Tom said curtly, mimicking his boss' nastiness whenever he could.

"I just got a call from a trustworthy employee who said she was instructed to send out a U.S. marshal with a warrant for Jack Conner's arrest—apparently for murders he has ordered, for starters." Ferrali chose his language carefully, covering any tracks that might implicate himself as interfering with justice.

"You've got to be kidding. And you can't stop it? Why are you calling me?"

"You know best how to advise Jack. *You* call him, if you feel that's the right thing to do."

"Dammit, Nathan. You're putting me in a bind. And, you didn't answer my first question."

"I'm working on it, but the Criminal Division Chief is no slouch. Her assistant, Leana, could only delay the order for a short time. We are fortunate that Leana is loyal to me—we have some, shall we say, history. Listen, Tom, this is serious. I wanted you to know ASAP."

Silence filled the conversation. They both knew Jack Conner was not accustomed to real threats. He had been subpoenaed before, but never faced an outright arrest warrant.

"Let me know how I can help." *Or not.* "I've gotta run, Tom." Ferrali hung up.

He did a slow blink, after which his thoughts turned to Maya.

Maya saw the incoming phone call from her boss, but she knew her next conversation with him would be about the warrant for Conner's arrest. *He can wait,* she thought. *Tomorrow is soon enough.*

44

As the evening advanced, Niesha felt it was time to call Mazzini. No answer. She tried again, with the same result.

"I'm worried," she said.

Lishan, from the backseat, and Jason, the driver, just nodded. They knew the possibilities.

Niesha tried several times over the next five minutes. Niesha tried calling Mazzini again.

"Mazzini here."

Niesha sighed. "I thought something had happened to you. Where are you?"

"I'm pulling into a BP gas station a few miles south of the Highway 97 Motel, where I thought I would meet you."

Jason heard just enough of the call to put the car in gear and gun it. They were on 97, near the motel, thinking that is where he may have spent the night.

"Why didn't you answer my earlier calls?" Niesha let her irritation ring through.

Unperturbed, Mazzini responded evenly. "I went to visit my mother. I wanted her to know I love her—especially if she never sees me again."

Niesha softened. "At least those are points in your favor. Are you there yet?"

"Yes. I'm getting out of my car, to get a soda." There was no sound for a couple of seconds.

"I knew you'd find me," was all she heard.

Then she gasped as two rapid gunshots followed. "No! Mazzini. Mazzini!" Then a strange voice came on the line.

"Go to hell."

The line went flat. The blood drained from Niesha's cheeks.

Minutes later, as the gas station came into view, Jason patted the firearm under his jacket. Niesha and Lishan were diligently watching every speck of the well-lit station. As Jason put the mobile flashing light up, coming to a halt ten yards from what was suspected as Mazzini's car, the station attendant came rushing out.

He was flushed, nearly unintelligible. "This guy...this guy, he just came right over to this dude—this dead guy." He pointed at Mazzini lying in the driver's seat. "I was watching close, like we always do after dark. Then, this guy, he just pulls a gun and shoots him. He looked up to see if anyone saw him, but I ducked. Then he drove off."

"Which way? Make and model of his car?" Jason wasted no time.

"That way." The attendant pointed north. "It was a Yellow Cab."

"Just fine. That narrows it down." Jason's sarcasm hung in the air.

A call to the taxi dispatcher proved worthless—their computer system was down.

🜄🜃

Niesha and Lishan considered one another, an unspoken *what to do next* on their collective minds.

"What about his testimony?" Lishan looked defeated. "Wasn't it key?"

Niesha put her hand on Lishan's shoulder. "Yes and no. It would have helped, but I have recordings of his confessions, a stack of email that incriminates Conner, and Fatima's documents and bio-chem friend's testimony. The Internet service provider will corroborate the validity of those emails, showing that they were the originals."

Lishan looked down at Mazzini. A mixture of relief and fear crossed the face of the young reporter. She knew that with the faction she was dealing with, the body on the ground could just as easily have been her own.

"We need to establish our hiding place." Niesha said.

Lishan raised her head, taking in the beautiful sage before her. She wanted to sequester herself away with this woman she so admired, but she couldn't.

"I can't just disappear. I have too much work to do."

Niesha took in Lishan's tone. She knew there was no point in countering her on this issue.

"I have a place to stay," Lishan said in a whisper. They had no reason to mistrust Jason, but he was new to them. "No one knows about it. He's a friend of Erik's. But what about you? I can't just leave you by yourself. You could stay there, too, but you're safer far away from me."

"What do you mean—safer?" Niesha's eyes gave away her concern.

Lishan took in her error. "It's just that it's not that far from where I lived. But I'll remain as obscure as possible—don't you worry."

"I will."

"I know. But what about you?"

Niesha smiled. "I'll stay at the Gonk for a day or two—longer if need be. Are you comfortable with that?"

Lishan nodded.

After a policewoman and an ambulance arrived, Jason took Niesha and Lishan back to town.

"Back to the office?" he questioned.

"Yes, that's fine," Niesha answered.

They were mostly silent during the return trip. "I feel disillusioned when someone like Mazzini turns the leaf, then the opportunity to realize it is taken from him." Niesha had a far-away look.

As Maya's building came into view, Lishan and Niesha made their last-minute arrangements. "Thanks," they chimed to Jason.

The two women had agreed to walk a block or two from Maya's office, then taxi it from there.

"Niesha, can you get a new phone? No link to your name and addresses. Promise me."

"Promise."

"Then call me on my temporary cell when you know your next step. I love you, Auntie. Let's talk in the morning. On second thought, call me when you get settled in tonight, after you have a new phone to use until we're all safe."

51

Lishan grabbed the next non-Yellow taxi after Niesha was safely whisked away. She straightened her stance and collected her thoughts, then pulled out her cell phone.

"Antoine, hi. This is Lishan—Erik's friend."

"Hi. Oh, I know who you are. I know all about you." His tone was playful. "I was a little concerned when you didn't show up yesterday. Are you all right?"

"Yes. Can I tell you in a few minutes? I'm en route."

Before ten minutes had passed, Lishan had navigated a careful route, arriving at Antoine's door.

"*Entre.*" Antoine was friendly, quick, and all smiles. He gave Lishan an immediate hug. "Some of your goods—stuff, as you Americans like to say—are here." He gave her the once-over and said, "I didn't recognize you. Erik showed me a photo of you. You seem different."

Lishan laughed. "I'm disguised, for my safety. Makeup and thirty pounds," she said, as she poked the padding. It bothered her when Antoine reached over and squeezed the padding, right below her breasts. She tucked away a reminder to be careful around him.

She sat on the couch. Antoine sat fairly close to her. She recounted a few of the day's details, but she didn't know just how far she could trust Antoine. She felt pulled in, tightening her guard.

Fifteen minutes after Lishan's arrival, she said that as much as she enjoyed his company, she must get to work. She added that her aunt's safekeeping was also at stake.

Lishan spied her messenger bag in the corner, the bag that held her primary notes. Erik had moved her essentials there during the day. Lishan felt hope that he hadn't written her off completely.

Antoine implored her to join him for a dinner he had cooked for the two of them. In her hesitation, he added, "I'm going to take a shower. Just let me know if you need anything, anything at all. Your bedroom is there. Mine's to the left." He patted her leg and left.

Lishan nodded and smiled, taking in the forward gestures from her new acquaintance. She felt uneasy, tracing the cause to Niesha staying alone at the motel. She hadn't heard from her yet. Lishan decided a brief walk would clear her head.

Lishan stood next to the opening of Antoine's bedroom. She could hear the shower just stopping.

"Antoine, I'm going for a walk. Be back shor..."

She stopped as Antoine stepped into full view, dripping wet, a luxurious Lauren towel intermittently exposing his developed pecs down to his knees as he dried off.

He smiled. "Oh, I was hoping you would cozy in. When will you be back?"

Lishan avoided a stammer. "It's, what, eight now? Won't be long. I'll be calling my aunt. If she's not okay, I might stay the night with her."

"Must you?" Antoine was just too casual with the towel cover-up. "I hope you're back soon."

Lishan nodded a noncommittal yes. Grabbing her messenger bag and all her notes, she left the apartment. She didn't want to get wrapped up with Antoine.

Catching a stray Diamond Cab, she headed straight to Niesha's hotel.

Erik tried calling Antoine. There was no answer. Thinking a short walk would do him good, he proceeded to his friend's place. He hadn't completely forgiven Lishan, but he was trying. He was about to knock when he heard soft music coming from inside. He hesitated—not wanting to interrupt Antoine's evening, especially if Antoine was entertaining another guest. But he decided it might be an odd night for such an occurrence, since Lishan was supposedly there. He knocked.

The door opened. Antoine stood there in sexy, clingy pajamas, unbuttoned down a little too far.

"Lishan, I'm glad you changed..." He stopped when he realized his error.

Erik pushed his way into the room.

"Candles? Music? Bare chest? Is this all for Lishan?"

"It's not..."

"Not what?" Erik was fuming. He pushed Antoine hard against the wall, then left. Without thinking, he called Lishan.

"Hi," he said gruffly, when she answered. "I was just at Antoine's. Is there anyone you *haven't* fucked?"

The line went dead.

He called again. "I'm furious. Do you know why?"

"I have an idea, but I doubt you care to hear it."

"Try me."

"Why should I? If all you care to do is cuss and accuse...your ignorance doesn't excuse you."

His breathing slowed, anger and fear competing with his sanity. "Okay, I'm listening."

Silence. Erik couldn't stand it. As he elevated his voice, "Would you just tell me...what the fu...yes, what the *fuck* happened?"

Lishan waited a few seconds before replying. Her tone was even, as though she were conducting a business meeting. The feeling that they were in a feud was difficult enough, but the extent and abrupt rise of his anger concerned her most.

"Listen, Erik. He came on me rather strong just before I left this evening. I wasn't there more than an hour. He clearly let me know he was feeling sexy—dripping straight out of the shower with only a marginal attempt to cover himself. I'm staying in town tonight. What happened between you and Antoine?" She paused. "No, I don't want to know. I don't care. I can guess. But, I'm curious about the babe that left your apartment earlier, calling me a tramp on the way out."

Confusion spun through him. What was Lishan doing in the hallway? More to the point, what was he doing with Etta that was any different from Lishan and Rafael? Retaliation somehow became his default when he felt lost, out of control.

"Given your sexual proclivities, I'm not so sure about the thirteenth. I think..."

Before he could finish, Lishan delivered the closing dictum. "*My* sexual proclivities? *Mine?* We're adults, Erik. We talk. We're civil. We work these things out, if it matters. None of this duplicity about sex, this ultimatum and junior high haughtiness. I'm staying with my aunt, Erik. Don't call. I need to think. Good night."

Half an hour later, Lishan appeared at Niesha's Gonk hotel room. "Lishan, what are you doing here?" Niesha was pleased—and concerned.

Lishan felt tears tugging to be seen, but she wouldn't hear of it this time.

52

Jack Conner opened his eyes to check the time. 5:13 a.m. His Jaeger Lecoultre watch never lied. Without moving from the comfort of his Ritz-Carlton bed, he picked up the phone and ordered room service. Eggs Florentine, a side order of strawberries and cream, and a pot of their best coffee. It was going to be a long morning—a long week, in fact. Yesterday's call, warning of the impending arrest warrant, got his attention. The lack of a decent response from his supposed top judicial bodyguard didn't help. *Why in the hell do I pay top dollar to that Ferrali if he can't pass muster?*

When his lead counsel called yesterday, late afternoon, Conner was already well into his fourth Scotch at the Ritz-Carlton bar. Tom could tell his boss would likely make a grave error if they tried to meet in his three sheets condition. Tom managed to convince Conner to get a room there for the night, not to call *anyone*, not to leave, and to be ready to tackle this first thing in the morning. Tom assured Conner he would assemble the necessary players and have a game plan. Fortunately, for Tom's sake, and his boss', Conner passed out in his room an hour later, a mostly empty bottle of Spottswoode Cabernet on its side on the floor. The silk Persian rug would likely never recover.

This morning, Jack Conner had the worst splitting headache he could remember. He couldn't stand the thought of talking to another soul until after a hot shower and breakfast.

55

At 8:00 a.m. sharp, Lishan was on the phone with Maya, who had been informed of Mazzini's murder the evening before. Niesha had left for the non-profit to put in some time. Maya reassured Lishan that they would still be in good shape, given the emails, recordings, and documents.

"And," Maya added, "we have the addition of another first-degree murder, which I believe we can press. We have a warrant out for Rudy Conner's arrest, given the data you've given us. Your auntie also told me she reported the garage incident to the police. We haven't heard if they found anything. Likely they won't, but we'll all try. I know you consider Rudy Conner to be a top suspect. We are also working on how to best tie the poisonings in with Conner."

Maya continued. "The warrant for Jack Conner's arrest and the restraining order were supposed to be delivered by the U.S. Marshals Service to Conner's head office yesterday afternoon, where he was expected to be. But the Service didn't get an approved arrest warrant until after seven in the evening. No one was in Conner's office by that time. He was not at home, either. Someone may have tipped him off, though I don't know who else could have known. I called Leana, but she said she wasn't feeling well later and had to leave early. She said she thought it would all be handled on time. She apologized."

Maya hesitated while she imagined the possibilities.

"However, we are certain he has the news since, this morning, his top attorney was in the office when Juan Jalasca, along with two other officers, arrived. The warrant now becomes an outstanding arrest warrant. Conner has advanced to fugitive status. He won't be easy to find, since he'll want to buy all the time he can, but we're persistent...and very capable."

"Lishan, Conner knows what he's up against and the game before him. Of course, you know that makes you doubly vulnerable. My apologies that I must be blunt—but don't take any chances. Same with your aunt. Conner will pull every string he can, but he isn't the only one with connections. It's vital that this story becomes public ASAP. Is the story still planned for publication today? Public visibility will improve your personal safety, now and later."

"Yes. By noon or so." Lishan paused. "Maya, is there any chance this will backfire?"

"Lishan, I've seen some cases previously sewn tight that came undone. But I would bet my reputation on this one. In fact, I believe I already have. Can you let me know the moment the story hits the newsstands? And one more thing—no, two: is your aunt safe, and can you get a copy of the newspaper to her?"

"Yes on both counts. As to where we will stay for the nights ahead, we're considering our options. I'll call my publisher about today's edition."

"Okay. Lie low." Maya's instructions were clear. Nothing to be toyed with. *Nada.*

"Thanks, Maya."

Lishan grabbed a granola bar from her emergency stash. She was hungry, but she couldn't take the time to head outside just yet. She called Elizabeth Walker.

"Good morning, Lishan. You're not calling me at gunpoint, are you?"

Lishan managed a quiet laugh. "Not yet. Just checking in. I have some additional news, if you feel it's pertinent and worthy."

"I imagine you wouldn't waste my time if it weren't. Shoot."

Lishan relayed the murder story of the night before. She also included details about her conversation with Howard Perkins, which she hadn't mentioned previously. She decided not to keep telling people about the night at the garage.

"I know Howard. Excellent journalist. Too bad he disappeared from view when he retired. I'll bet he's living vicariously through you now. And Mazzini... unfortunate to see a reformer lose his chance, though I imagine he's done some good, ultimately. Can I use his name?"

"Yes. I imagine it will fuel the fire," Lishan said.

"And Howard's? Presumably not, but he always did live on the edge. I'd like to, if it's okay. We did favors for one another over the years. His name in print, especially regarding Conner, would add additional credence to the story."

"Yes. I asked him. He said he didn't know what value his name would bring, but he did smile at the thought of being a bellows, he said. He had run-ins with Conner over the years, and having his name associated with the *coup de grâce* made his face shine."

"Perfect."

"I think I'll head to Kramerbooks. I'll wait there for the newspaper drop. Thanks, Elizabeth.

"The thanks go to you, Lishan. It takes courage. Got a front page to massage with an editor. Lay low, Lishan. Bye."

- - -

"Damnit! That riffraff of a reporter. And what about Ferrali? Did he just roll over? Who in the hell is that chief whatever attorney who thinks she can just do whatever she damn well pleases?" Jack Conner was livid. His team of legal counsel—including two Yale grads and one ex-circuit court judge—was meeting with him in Conner's suite at the Ritz. Conner was pacing a hole in an expensive Sultanabad rug.

The army of attorneys and one judge had arrived just as Conner finished his breakfast. He was in no mood for this.

Tom Danforth was the first to speak up. It wasn't that the others were timid, but his experience as a judge taught him the meaning of expediency, especially when someone of importance, someone with deep pockets, was waiting. "I called the U.S. Attorney's office ten minutes ago. He has been unavailable for..."

"Damn him. Give me your goddamn cell phone." Conner knew just what number to call when things were not going his way.

"What in the hell has kept you?" Conner never did try to hide his annoyance and anger.

The response was not what Conner had expected. Ferrali was angry, and defensive. "I've stood by you for the past seventeen years, Jack. Don't give me this crap. You've done some fairly stupid—if I may use that word—maneuvers, and I've barely been able to keep you out of jail more times than I can count. This time you may have gone too far."

Conner's eyes widened. His voice quieted, just a little. "What do you mean, 'too far'?"

"I mean just that. You've pushed even the limits of what *I* can do. But I'm working on it. My division chief, Maya—that damned harpy—has forgotten who's the boss, and she's interpreting the law outside of your favor. You know, Conner, she has a good case against you. You might not be quite so lucky this time. And I'll be damned if I'm going to lose my job over you."

"Oh? So the time you lied, under oath, about the FDA fast-tracking one of my new drug apps, to protect my shorts—that doesn't count? And that time when you casually lost the files for the harassment complaint against me?"

"Are you threatening me?" Ferrali said, as his eyes narrowed. "You are, aren't you?" The cell phone's display went blank.

"That bastard hung up on me. Shit. I need him."

Conner redialed.

"Okay, if it's an apology you want, you've got it."

"Is that the best you can do?"

Conner fumed. "No. Okay, I'm sorry. I'll have one hundred thousand put into your account by day's end. Now get me out of this."

Conner yelled at his staff. "Out. Everybody out."

The disappointment showed on the men's faces. They were likely expecting to be treated luxuriously for being there so early. A breakfast buffet at the Ritz would support their importance in the world. Ashes to ashes.

As noon approached, Lishan prepared to leave their hotel on her way to Dupont Circle. She hadn't assumed the disguise yet, which she had picked up when Chris had taken her to her apartment.

I'm so tired of this, she thought. *Can't I just be a little more like me for a change?* Lishan didn't put on the thirty pounds, or the heavy makeup. Instead, she opted for a coat with a high collar to help hide her features, then a Castro cap to top it off. *This'll do well enough,* she thought with one last check in the full-length mirror.

Catching the rail to Dupont Circle, she arrived at Kramerbooks in time to secure a small table in the bookstore café.

The bookstore was an icon in the area. While waiting, she could peruse the books—see if there were any about Conner. She knew there was always fodder about the FDA.

Biding her time with a latté, a sandwich, and some research would pass the minutes that seemed to drag by. She used to pass the time here with Erik. She felt a tear, wondering if those days were gone.

At a few minutes after twelve, she saw the newspaper rack for *The Washington Mirror* being filled. She could barely contain the anxiety she felt, nearly knocking over a small round table with two young women sipping their coffees, which then spilled.

"Oh, I'm so sorry," Lishan said, her fervor like a sixth cup of coffee. "That newspaper rack has an article that I need to read. Sorry. Here. Replace your drinks, plus pastries." She put a twenty on the table.

They protested, but she wouldn't hear of it.

The newspaper. Lishan stopped breathing for a few seconds. "Arrest Warrant Issued for Conner Foods' CEO." The subheading delivered the finale: "Murder and Toxic Foods Cited."

Lishan paid the 75 cents, buried her head in the article and walked slowly toward her table.

"Hey!"

It was too late. The warning sound from one of the same two women didn't make it in time. Two refills spilled.

"Oh...! I'm so sorry, again. Here, let me..."

"No. It's okay. Must be why you gave us a twenty to begin with. Could you just sit down, tell us what's going on? Self-defense you might call it. Plus, your earlier comment caught our attention."

Lishan hesitated. She desperately wanted to read the article. She thought of a solution. "Okay, on the condition that I read this out loud to us. It's important to me."

The same woman spoke up. "I'm Laura." She offereding her end of a handshake. She turned to her companion. "Eb, this fine person must either be a JD or a journalist. She's on trial here but already attempting to call the shots. What do you think?"

"I would say we lock her up, but not until we finish drinking two full cups of coffee, which we have to hold with both hands."

Lishan broke a smile. "Okay. I'm outnumbered. This article is crucial to my life, my family, and a few friends. I haven't read it yet. Perhaps it will all become clear then." As she sat down, "Eb for Ebony?"

"Two points for you, honey."

"Journalist, if you must know. Apologies for my aberrant behavior." She read the headline out loud, followed by the story's text.

> Yesterday, Criminal Division Chief U.S. Attorney Maya Rosenstein issued an arrest warrant against Jack Conner, CEO of Conner Foods. The allegations include first and third degree murder, and attempts to sell dangerous, substandard foods, with unnatural shelf lives, which have reportedly resulted in illness and death.
>
> Journalist Lishan Amir, along with Niesha Amir, well-known retired journalist Howard Perkins, and author Alan Frazier have put what they feel is the final lid on several decades of effort to pin criminal charges on Conner, including illegal influence Conner may have had with the FDA.

Lishan stopped for a breath.

"You, I take it, are the said Lishan?" Ebony had leaned in close, clearly engrossed in the story. "We're familiar with Conner. One of our professors had us follow his shenanigans, noting how he's evaded the law. Until now?"

"Yes. I'm hopeful. One of his henchmen—a guy named Mazzini—finally decided to change his life before his misdeeds caught up with him. He was a little late, but at least there are a few of us who know of his decision to provide evidence against Conner, which we recorded. Mazzini was murdered last night." Lishan took another breath. "May I?" she said, returning to the newspaper. Both women nodded.

> Conner is considered a prime suspect in the murder of two of his staff—a strong-arm employee who went by the name of Mazzini, and a former production manager and private investigator, Beck Conner. Mazzini was murdered last night on Highway 97, minutes before he was to turn himself over to authorities into a Witness Protection Program. From within the U.S. Attorney's office, it was noted that, while Mazzini's death was unfortunate on numerous accounts, documents and voice recordings of Mazzini's statements incriminating Jack Conner were obtained prior to his death.

Lishan looked up. "The U.S. Marshals Service is in the process of locating Conner in order to arrest him."

"Are you in danger? If you need a place to stay..." Ebony turned to her friend.

Laura nodded, though visibly shaken by the prospect of being involved in a murder case. Then she smiled, as though clearing cobwebs. "Of course. How can we help?"

"Your offer is kind. I don't think I'll need to take you up on it, though. But, thank you."

Ebony continued. "Better to repair the FDA than do away with it, don't you think? Remember when Newt Gingrich attempted to dissolve the FDA, leaving safety up to the companies themselves? If that doesn't give a clue as to what deep pockets will do." Ebony handed a scrawled phone number to Lishan, "Just in case," she said.

Lishan stood, leaning over to hug each of the women.

"Yes, greed. Again, thank you. Are you here often?"

"Most every day," Laura said.

"Take care, you two." Lishan headed toward her table, refreshing her coffee on the way.

Disappearing once again into the article, she didn't want to miss a single nuance. It appeared to all be in order. *Journalism,* she thought. *It can be the people's voice if avarice and corruption don't water it down.* She decided to call Maya.

"No, I haven't seen it yet. Can you read it to me?" Maya's enthusiasm was palpable.

After the reading, Lishan couldn't help but ask: "What do you think?"

"Excellent. Excellent! Now, you and your auntie just need to stay out of sight."

"Do you need any assistance with the material for the hearing? Likely a fatuous question, but I don't want to leave anything to chance."

Maya gave it serious thought. She, too, knew that any oversight could be costly. "You know, I believe we're in good shape. If anything comes to mind in the next forty-eight, you'll be the first to know."

55

Maya knew she'd find herself in the U.S. Attorney's office before the shadows at her windows grew much shorter. Her prophecy—though it was more of a conviction—was realized in a matter of minutes.

"No, Nathaniel, we can't just drop this. It would be unfair to the public. Conner is a crook. I'm, shall we say, dumbfounded that he's gotten away with all he has." Maya heard herself push the accusation. She tried to hide her concern.

Nathaniel didn't miss it. "What are you insinuating?"

"Nothing." She paused. "No, that's not accurate. I just know he's unscrupulous, and he's slipped through our grasp too many times. Ultimately, that doesn't look good for you, for the department, in the public eye. He is responsible for the deaths and illnesses of workers in his factory and others he tired of."

"We don't know that."

"Yes, in fact we do. Look, I know he's your friend..."

"You can dispense with that line of reasoning right now."

"I would like to think you wouldn't compromise your position, your values," Maya lied. They both knew it.

"So bring me up to speed. What have you got on Conner?"

Maya knew this crossroads, the fulcrum's placement, would come. Her concern, of course, was that Ferrali would sabotage any possible justice. That would leave Lishan and Niesha, and potentially herself, in a dire position.

She had made multiple copies of all the documents and recordings, going to the length of sending copies to two trusted friends and her safe deposit box.

As to Ferrali, she was prepared, but it still brought butterflies to her belly. Maya reached down to her briefcase. Pulling out the Conner folder, she spread it out on Ferrali's desk. She hoped to accomplish the task of convincing him that this was a *fait accompli*, to get his buy-in that this was the correct thing to do—perhaps for him the only thing he could do to stay out of jail himself.

"Look at these documents, emails, and the transcripts of incriminating recordings. It's just too much, Nathaniel. Conner is a danger to the public. If you read the health literature these days, there is so much evidence pointing to artificial sweeteners, modified fats, and chemicals as causes of diseases in this and the last century."

"But that's not enough to hang a guy like Conner." Ferrali did his best to act angry, but he was beginning to doubt how long he could hold the charade.

"If he were simply a victim of greed without foreknowledge of his actions, then he would just get a slap on the wrist—which is essentially all he ever felt before. But his actions are premeditated. He has acted with the full knowledge that his new 'fats' were not passing the safety tests—that they were dangerous. And we can't overlook his harassment of the people like Fatima Habiba or, most especially, the death of the P.I., and the murder of Mazzini last night."

"We don't know that he was responsible for their deaths. Those two lived dangerous lifestyles, with a myriad of dangerous types no doubt after their necks."

Maya paused, looking straight into Nathaniel eyes. "Okay, let me convince you." She played the recorded telephone conversations.

Fifteen minutes later saw Maya resting her case.

56

Nathaniel Ferrali was upset beyond his imagination. His second in command had a case that was well prepared and seemingly watertight. He found himself at one of the more significant forks in his life's path. For too many years, he had been on the take by a couple of wealthy CEOs, the hundreds of thousands of dollars and free Caribbean trips just too much for his and his wife's greedy egos to pass up.

His thoughts raced in dizzying circles. Now what? The evidence before him was clear. Damn Maya—and Conner, who went too far this time.

Maya was just too good. He should have hired that yuppie, that social climber who would have thought twice about bucking the boss. But not Maya. Her reputation and eminence were clearly not to be jettisoned just to placate a dishonest CEO and a crooked Justice Department official on the take. How foolish could he be? Why *did* he hire her? Then he remembered her roots, the power of that lobby.

He would have to come clean for this case. But Conner wouldn't go down peacefully. Nathaniel knew his kind. The whole ship would sink if the captain gave up. He pulled out his cell phone.

"Nicole. We need to talk. Conner's going down." Nathaniel knew he couldn't proceed without discussing this with his wife. They were both in this too deep. She was not legally in jeopardy, as he was, but she stood to lose her lifestyle. And he knew she wouldn't stand for that.

"I'll be in your office in fifteen minutes. It's not bugged, is it?"

Fair question, Nathaniel thought. "No, it's not. I had it checked three days ago."

This gave him time to think, not that he hadn't brooded over this countless times before. But the money—and his and Nicole's love affair with it—always dictated their course.

He knew Conner had no scruples. In Conner's mind, if he went down, everyone deserved to go down with him, by the mere fact that they had let him down, hadn't protected him from this fate.

The door slammed—not its usual sound. He knew it was Nicole, and she was...perturbed.

"I saw that hussy Maya in the hall. She's behind this, isn't she? *Isn't she?* If she weren't here, you would just handle it like always, wouldn't you?"

Nathaniel just looked up, then out the window.

"Look at me, you spineless..." She stopped. Her husband had just stood, hatred in his eyes.

It had been years since they'd enjoyed each another. The money was good. The affairs were entertaining. "Till death do us part"—a line they had both replayed in their minds, on more than one occasion—slid from his lips.

"What?" she demanded. She sat down, softening—conniving, more like it. "Can the files disappear? You've done it before."

"Too many people have become involved...too quickly. No, they can't just disappear."

Nicole understood the gravity. She was no newcomer to deceit and its layers. She was good at it. She and Nathaniel had met when she was being prosecuted for embezzlement to the tune of $1.2 million. She knew she needed his backing if she were to escape a jail sentence. At 135 pounds, five foot eight, with implants, she kept herself defined in a seductive manner for just such an occasion. He succumbed, lied within his office, shredded documents, and Nicole went free. That was ten years ago.

"What is your plan? Or don't you have one?"

Nathaniel looked up. *Why have we stayed together these past years? Trophy wife, perhaps.* And for her, he thought, it was the prestige of his position—the money, the kickbacks. All of it would disappear if this Conner case blew up.

"That's why I called you. I knew you would have some devious approach to the situation. It's your M.O., after all."

Nicole bristled. While she knew he was right, having it spewed in her face was a bit much.

"As I thought. You have no clue. Maybe your president can send a Tweet with some advice for you." A wry smile replaced the anger on her face. Nicole stood, paced the length of the office, and then returned to her seat. "*You're* in trouble, aren't you?"

"Me? Just me?" Nathaniel glared. "It's just like you, isn't it? I couldn't have expected less. Just leave. You're doing me no good whatsoever. In fact, quite the contrary." Nathaniel walked briskly to the door. Opening it, he smiled. "Good day, Ms. Crin-shaw."

Nicole narrowed her eyes, stinging him as much as she hoped she could. Crinshaw, indeed. Her maiden name. The door slammed again, as much as the auto-closure unit would allow.

Nathaniel drew a breath. It was just him now, wasn't it? Now he had to give his situation serious thought. If he took Conner's side, it likely wouldn't hold up against the evidence against Conner, and Nathaniel would look like he was bending the law. But if he came clean—told the truth—perhaps the public would find compassion, as they often did with a criminal or iniquitous public official who turned himself in. Yes, that would be his position. His life as U.S. Attorney would be over, but he had enough friends who owed him, several of whom would no doubt offer him a position as senior counsel within their Fortune 500 status. And he'd be rid of Ms. Crinshaw once and for all. Perhaps he could sue her, bring up her embezzlement case if the statutes hadn't expired.

Nathaniel smiled. It wasn't all bad.

57

Lishan knew she had to make a viable plan for her safety, and that of those close to her, over the days ahead. She had to buy sufficient time for the media to spread the story so the public was informed. Then it would be more difficult for Conner to take any criminal action, given the publicity. Lishan knew it wasn't enough to stop a criminal like Conner, if he was bent on destroying everyone involved. But it was a start.

She pulled out her cell phone. It saddened her to think of the time that had passed with a fence between her and Erik. But she needed to consider his well-being, his safety.

With her phone held between her two hands, her thumbs were quick to send a text. It was time, she felt, to put the past in the past. "Erik, hi. Truce?"

Several long minutes passed before she heard the "Working Up a Black Sweat" message tone. One text message back: "I'm thinking."

Lishan fingers were quick. "Wrong answer." Lishan's fury fueled her adrenals. She decided to cool down by spending the next hours looking through the bookstore. She realized it was an opportunity she didn't often take advantage of, given the time constraints of work and the rest of her life. She'd forgotten how sweet it was to just linger in the aisles.

Hunger caught up with her. *Seven o'clock. How did it get to be so late?* Finding a table, she ordered a glass of 14 Hands cab and one of her favorite dinners—Tuscan Chicken Paillard. She loved the thin layers of chicken, pounded to perfection. She re-read the article, contemplating how her memoir might read.

Her phone rang, an interruption that annoyed her but also frightened her. *Auntie!*

"Hi, Auntie. Have you seen the paper?"

"Yes. I'm sure you have. Where are you?"

"Kramerbooks. All of this danger has been suffocating me. I had to get out, be around people."

"How do you feel about the article?"

"It's good. The publisher, Elizabeth Walker, was personally involved. Do you think it'll help, Auntie?"

"It'll help the cause, but you're not out of danger yet, not until every one of those crooks is locked up."

"I know. Auntie, I'm just going to hang out here. The distraction is good for me. I'll call you later, okay?"

They exchanged concerns before hanging up.

The band was setting up in the mezzanine in the bookstore/cafe. The lead singer, pushing his dreads out of his way, called down to Lishan, "Aren't you on a major record label?"

Lishan looked up, smiled, and shook her head.

"Come up, so we can talk—if you like."

Lishan paused, then decided why not. She bussed her dishes, then found the stairwell, enshrouded as they often were behind clutter in old buildings full of books.

"Lishan. Local reporter." Lishan extended both hands, embracing the single hand proffered.

"Jimmy. Jimmy Lingo. Reporter, eh?" Jimmy hesitated. "Oh. I know who you are. *Intrepid* reporter. You're the one who sticks her neck out, going after the big boys. We've never met, but I follow your articles whenever I feel like buying a mainstream paper. Glad to meet you."

"As well." Lishan smiled. "Jimmy Lingo and his Dreads Band? I've heard your work. I like it. Love it, in fact. You speak your mind. Too few of today's musicians take on the issues like they did a few decades ago." Lishan took a brief look around. "Will you be a regular here?"

Jimmy laughed. "No. Can't be puttin' down stakes for this cat. I like to keep on the move, spread the love." He motioned toward a small, round table in the corner. "What brings you here, if I might ask? Good chance I'll get the scoop that'll be in the paper tomorrow, am I right?"

As they sat, Lishan looked around, giving Jimmy the impression—a correct one—that it was to be a private conversation. "Something like that." *What can I tell him? I don't know this guy. If I trust my intuition, he's okay.* Lishan was feeling alone, the burden of the Conner story on the front page with no one to share it with. *Why not?* she thought.

"Actually, no, I'm not getting a scoop tonight. *This* is the scoop of my life, if I survive it."

She showed him the paper's front page, the Conner headline. He read down through the first two paragraphs, enough to give him the gist.

266

Jimmy moved in closer over the table. Probably in his late forties—difficult to tell sometimes with the Rastafarians, who kept themselves in good shape with healthy foods, dancing, singing, and loving 'till all hours. There was wisdom and peacefulness in his manner. He wore a medallion with *Jamaica* inscribed in it.

He looked up at Lishan, taking in the seriousness in her face. He read the rest of the story, concerned.

When he looked up again, it was obvious he now understood the gravity of her situation.

"Someone needed to do this. You're courageous, I'll tell you that. Conner doesn't usually let bad press about him get out, and this front-page headline's going to cost him. He's not going to like you mucking with his blueprints for entitlement."

"He's already made that clear. There have been threats on my life—real threats. I probably shouldn't be here, but I had to get out. Crowded as it is, I think I'm safe enough. I'm tired of thinking about it, though."

Jimmy nodded, knowing to let her guide the conversation from there.

As the evening pushed on well toward midnight, their conversation during his breaks ran the spectrum from as light as David Sedaris humor to as dark as Russian literature. Lishan stayed through the sets, enjoying the music and the camaraderie. Before they parted for the night, a stroll along the nearby majestic homes allowed them to wind down.

"Where will you stay?" Jimmy wasn't extending an invitation—simply concern. "With your auntie?"

"Yes, though in consideration of her safety, I may just find a room for as many days as need be." She thought about trading phone numbers. *Why not?* she thought. "What's your number?"

After trading texts, followed by a sincere hug and a kiss to the cheek, they went on their separate ways to wherever home was for the night.

🖐✍

At half past midnight, it was late to call her aunt. But Lishan knew Niesha would worry otherwise. She planned to walk a mile to a B&B Niesha had taken her to when Lishan was grieving the loss of her parents. Lishan wanted downtime—no talking, no explaining. But she was exhausted.

"Taxi, miss?"

The voice coming from the Diamond Cab that just pulled up coaxed her in. It was just too inviting. The call would wait until she arrived at her lodging.

"The Aaron Shipman House—bed and breakfast, Logan Circle."

The driver nodded.

It was a short haul to Logan Circle—less than five minutes without traffic. After a couple of minutes, Lishan noticed that the driver had picked up speed and started heading in a slightly different direction.

As her fear escalated, she decided to send a text. Just in case. *Just leaving Kramers. In a Diamond Cab. Think I'm in danger. Help. Lishan.* Before she could decide who to send it to, the cab began slowing by a park. It was dark, unlit. In a hurry, she snapped a photo of the back of the driver, capturing part of his face in the rearview mirror, then sent it to her last contact— Jimmy.

Rudy yelled at her, reaching back to take her phone, but she moved away. Then her attention shifted to a tall figure approaching in a gray overcoat.

Lishan could see the silver Lincoln Escalade parked in front of the taxi. Her eyes grew round as she recognized the approaching male. Jack Conner. She thought about leaving the taxi, but the driver had already gotten out, covering the driver's side rear door, while Conner opened the door next to Lishan.

"Hello, little girl. How nice to see you again."

Lishan bristled. "You won't get away with this."

"Ah, such a classic line. I suppose a person resorts to clichés when faced with the unthinkable."

Lishan melted into the far corner.

"I just wanted to see your face, one last time. You know, for old time's sake. I'll be at my villa, while you...Let's just say you won't be quite as comfortable as you've been. In fact, you won't be comfortable at all. Maybe you will, though, depending on your beliefs about reincarnation."

Conner reached over and pinched her cheek. Lishan wasn't fast enough to stop him, but she followed with a glancing uppercut to his nose—a potential deathblow she learned in martial arts—but her punch wasn't solid enough.

Conner arched back, surprised. His nose hurt like hell, blood dripping on his coat. Then he just laughed.

"Goodbye, Lishan. Too bad you won't be any more trouble to me. It was quite a sport, really."

Conner got out of the taxi, standing close to ensure Lishan didn't leave the confines of the backseat. Rudy was already in place, ready to drive off.

Conner just smiled and waved. He loved winning.

As Rudy sped off, Lishan could feel her life dangling before her. She couldn't quite believe it. *This is how it ends? Bastard.*

As Rudy picked up even greater speed, Lishan noticed there was no metal or plastic guard behind the driver's seat. She took a deep breath and lunged toward his head, reaching around each side of his head, poking into his eye sockets. Rudy's strength extended to his face, and he clamped his cheeks as tight as he could against his eyebrows to buy him a few seconds. In the process, he grabbed her wrists, instinctively bringing his knee up to hold the steering wheel straight.

But his loss of visuals along with the excess speed was too much for the curve up ahead. They were passing through a neighborhood. He hit the center divider and bounced to the right, sideswiping several parked cars before slamming into a parked Porsche 911T. The airbag deployed, distracting Rudy and giving Lishan the moment for escape she needed. She was out the right rear door and running behind the wreckage, hoping to get around the curve before Rudy could get a bead on her.

The airbag slowed his exit from the car, but he could just glimpse Lishan as she rounded the curve. Rudy fired off two rounds. But he knew his chances were slim at that distance with his short-barreled pistol.

A few lights turned on in the neighboring residences, then extinguished as people decided it best to remain in the dark.

Lishan ran as quickly as she safely could. Falling and injuring herself could be her fatal mistake. She stopped to look back, surprised that Rudy was only about one hundred feet behind her, quickly closing the distance while she stood for those few seconds. She took off again, dodging slightly left and right, hearing a windshield shatter to her right.

She didn't dare stop again to look behind her, though the uncertainty challenged her anxiety all the more. Finally, she heard sirens, thankful that the neighbors didn't take kindly to collisions and gunshots in their neighborhood.

As two Metropolitan Police cars arrived, both squealed to a stop where they saw Lishan, who quickly ran behind the closest car. The two officers, spotting Rudy, drew their weapons as he took shelter behind a car.

But Rudy was no slouch, holding NRA titles in marksmanship. He shot the arm of the closest officer, one who apparently misjudged the capabilities of the slightly heavy, older man they intended to arrest. While the alarmed officer momentarily withdrew from sight to assess his wound, Rudy lobbed a grenade under the black-and-white. Seconds later, there was only one police car, and one policeman, left.

The grenade put a new perspective in the minds of the remaining officer and Lishan. Standing behind a car was no longer necessarily a safe bet. They saw Rudy begin to ready another grenade, pressing them to run behind another parked car. But they heard no explosion. Instead, a shotgun blast came from a second-story window. The policeman looked up to see a barrel protruding, held by an elderly, silver-haired woman, one eye squinted.

The officer ran up alongside a parked car from where he could see Rudy, who was holding both shoulders where they were bleeding. Rudy inched along the ground toward the grenade, not giving up.

The officer sprinted to Rudy and pulled him away from the grenade, not wanting to disturb it. Rudy's gun lay next to it. A quick frisk found another handgun and a switchblade.

Within a few minutes, six black and whites had converged on the block, along with an ambulance. News of a downed or slain officer traveled fast.

Over the next half hour, Lishan gave her story, along with the grandmother who had taken Rudy down. The officer filling out the paperwork leaned up against a shiny black Shelby sitting in the driveway in front of grandma's house.

"Hey, don't scratch my car," the grandmother yelled.

The officer smiled at her verve and made a notation or two on the form about a "feisty elder," and her hot car. Then he asked Lishan, "Where can we take you?"

Lishan thought about home—wherever that was, tonight—and then her aunt. But for the remainder of the night, she just wanted some ease.

"The Quincy Hotel, on L, if that works for you. If they don't have a room, I'll find one nearby."

As they drove off, another ambulance appeared. When the paramedics gathered up Rudy, it appeared he was still alive.

The MPDC officer was pleasant and exceptionally under-standing. Upon arrival at the hotel, he asked if she would like him to wait. Lishan declined but thanked him for his generosity.

54

Lishan finally let herself feel relief as she entered the lobby. Then she heard the reminder on her phone. Jimmy had called, asking if she was all right. After receiving the mysterious photo of a taxi driver and the message, he had called the cops.

Ah, Lishan thought to herself. *I need to call him, but I must call Auntie first.*

After checking in, she realized she had no bags, but it was no matter. The king studio room had two robes—all the comfort she needed.

Lishan felt tears as she sat on the bed, but she wasn't ready yet to let down her guard. She took in the quiet, her space for the night.

She placed the call to Niesha.

Upon hearing her niece's voice, well after midnight, Niesha stood abruptly. "Tell me you're okay."

Lishan spoke as quickly as she could so her auntie's fears would not gain too much ground. "I'm alright, now, Auntie. I'm at the Quincy. Rudy Conner tried to murder me in a taxi, but he failed. He's in jail. Jack Conner accosted me while I was in the taxi. Then he left. I know he's leaving the country. I'll explain all the details later."

"Lishan! Are you sure you're okay? Shouldn't you come over? You know where I am." Niesha finally slowed. "Okay, you stay put. I'll alert Maya about Jack Conner and Rudy. You call the minute you need me. No exceptions."

"I'm just exhausted, Auntie. Yes, I'm fine. I've stayed here before, kind of a home away from home when I'm not at your comfortable place." Lishan begged off the phone. She just didn't want to explain the entire drama on the phone. She also didn't want to be alone.

She started to text Jimmy but decided a text message was too impersonal, given her time with him earlier.

"Am I correct that musicians are always up until four in the morning? This is Lishan."

"You discovered our secret, yeah. Is it all *irie* with you, Lishan? Should I be worried?"

272

"I suppose I'm alright. I just wanted to call you after sending that obscure photo." Lishan gave the short version of the past hour. "Thank you for calling the police, and also for such a sweet time tonight."

"Thank you. And yes, a sweet time. All is not right with you at this late hour, is it? Just ask if you would like my help, my company. I'm a good listener. Any time. Ten minutes from now. Doesn't matter."

Unequivocal compassion, she thought.

They spoke of making a lunch date sometime soon, then hung up.

Lishan lay back on the bed, her breathing finally slowing. A few minutes later, a whim made her smile.

"Ten minutes have gone by. Would you be up for joining me until that bewitching hour, helping me sort out a few things, like Erik, relationships, where I'm headed? Is that fair to you? I can't sleep."

"Fair? Yes, of course. What brand of nourishment may I bring?"

Lishan felt a mild giddiness at the level of refinement and gentlemanly manner of this man.

"Let's see. There's coffee in my room, but no baguette, cheese, or dry red wine." She could hear Jimmy's smile.

"I know just the late-night deli. How shall I find you?"

Lishan began with cryptic directions in reference to where they had been earlier—unnamed over the phone. She was still nervous about her phone being tapped. Then she remembered—Rudy had already known her whereabouts. Perhaps Conner did as well. Yet, with Mazzini gone and Rudy under wraps, she felt she could breathe just a bit easier for the night. "I'm at the Quincy, on L. Let me know when you're entering the lobby, and I'll come down and run interference."

She imagined two strikes of a ship's bell when Jimmy appeared in the lobby, carrying a cloth bag of Jamaican colors—black, green, and yellow—containing the goods.

Lishan suddenly said, "Can we sit for a moment?" Her breathing had become laborious, hesitant.

He sat next to her, holding her hand to help her feel comforted. They sat there, on a lobby couch, until her breathing eased.

As they ascended to her fourth-story room, a sense of relief finally overtook Lishan.

"Comforting room," Jimmy offered, earnestly, as he took in the colors, touching the fabrics. He unloaded a baguette, a block of Pecorino, and a Hess pinot noir along with some miscellany.

"What are those?" Lishan's inquisitiveness had her peering over his shoulder.

"Ah, Jamaican specialties: patty and coco bread. The deli owner keeps a Jamaican section. And I brought a small roll of our 'no worries' Rasta weed, but only partake if you are comfortable with it. It is a wonderful sorting tool, though. Speaking of which?"

With an array—a feast, really—in front of them spread on the Queen Anne coffee table, they settled into a floral-patterned loveseat.

"Yes, sorting. As I arrived here tonight, I found some of my concerns of the past couple of weeks temporarily behind me. Erik, though, I just don't know. I don't know what you gathered when we talked at Kramer's? I know it was hard to hear at times."

Jimmy turned toward Lishan. "I have a sense. Talk to me, dear."

Lishan gave a troubled smile. "I always believed Erik and I would be together, but I realize that I, for one, have held back. Is it something in him, or in me, that causes me to question? Perhaps I've subconsciously kept a few bricks in the wall these past few years, I don't know. In our last brief phone conversation, he hurt me, but it wasn't, or didn't appear to be, simply a fleeting error. He just didn't seem to care about me in that moment."

Lishan paused, as though searching. "Also, I don't know if he's been hypercritical—he professed being hurt when I slept with someone else, as though it were something he wouldn't do, yet I believe he's had interludes with more than one student of his, and he hasn't told me."

"Can you imagine living without him?" Jimmy's demeanor was tender, full of heart.

"I don't know. The fight and flight has kept me on edge, but I also have doubts I need to understand. I draw him in, yet I push back. I think I'm afraid, but I don't know whether it's worries about myself, or him. He's been as romantic as our platonic relationship has allowed, yet he's presented an unexpected and upsetting anger on a few too many occasions. Then I divide this muddle by the death that almost enveloped me. What am I doing?"

Lishan's cell phone rang. "Damn," she said lightly. "Oops," she added, though Jimmy didn't express the slightest ruffle. "It's Erik," she announced, searching Jimmy's face for direction.

"Maybe this will help in your search. Go ahead."

"Hi," she answered.

"Hi. I called to apologize."

"Oh. I'm surprised, given your last call. But thank you."

"What are you doing? Where are you?"

Lishan hesitated, but she felt okay about her actions. "I'm talking with my friend, Jimmy, trying to sort out my life. Someone tried to murder..."

"He's there with you...now?"

Lishan could hear the annoyance already in Erik's voice. "Well, yes he is. We're just talking. I..."

Again he cut her off. "Where are you?"

"I'm in a hotel. I don't know if your phone is tapped. I..."

"And you won't tell me where?" Anger was building, yet again, in Erik's voice.

Now it was Lishan's turn. Her voice rose, firm and controlling. "This isn't about you, Erik. This was about my attempt to keep my location under wraps. If you..."

"Is he staying..."

"Quit interrupting me. Your rudeness is unbecoming."

"Are you sleeping with him?" The tone was accusing.

Lishan's irritation heightened. "Listen, Erik. He came by for awhile so we could talk. He's helping me. Did you hear me say I was almost murdered?"

"You didn't answer my question."

"No." Lishan's face tightened, anger seeping out from her eyes.

"I don't believe you." Erik was now enraged, his mind losing control. "Everyone I ever loved lied to me. All those homes I lived in...they all lied. Lied. Lied. You are such a tramp."

"*Stop!*" Lishan's anger was full force. "Mr. Andersson. It's not that I mind a reference to whoring—'prude' I'm not. But your intent to bully me, to harm me emotionally, is *not* okay. I feel sorry for you." Lishan drew a deep breath before continuing. "I wish you well, Erik. Goodbye." That was it. *Fini.*

Lishan looked over at Jimmy. "You heard his last? It was so loud."

"Yes. I'm thinking your boundaries and your sorting just came together."

Lishan let out a single laugh. "Curiously, I feel no tears. Not one, though I know they'll come. I was in a relationship some years ago with a guy who was sweet as could be most of the time, but once or twice a week he would get angry—very angry, mostly without any provocation from me. Later, after he calmed from each outburst, he blamed it on his childhood, which I believed and had compassion for, but he did nothing about it. I'm not planning a repeat. I remember an expression about returning to a restaurant over and over, though the bad food never improved."

Lishan's gaze shifted to the wall in front of her, though her focus was miles away. She stood and walked to her messenger bag, withdrawing her journal.

"I need to erase Erik from an appointment. Do you mind if I make a note?"

"Closure. I understand. Take your time." Jimmy walked to a window, looking out over the D.C. landscape.

The thirteenth. It was to have been a special day. Impermanence, the Buddha said. As she erased Erik's name, she looked over at Jimmy.

Lishan's tears finally came, and she cried while Jimmy held her. A long yawn prompted her to check the time on her cell phone.

Lishan sat up. "Jimmy, I don't think I can stay up much longer. I don't know how you do it."

"I sleep in and often manage a siesta midday." Standing, he gathered his sandals and his cloth bag containing his wallet and a stash of personal items. At the door, he turned to face Lishan.

"You have my number. I would encourage your using it, no matter the reason. Most importantly, though, keep yourself safe. We need your voice in the world, especially since many people in this country are, unfortunately, silent."

At the door, a comforting embrace closed their hours together before Jimmy walked to the elevator.

On impulse, Lishan called to him in nearly a whisper, "Do you have any special plans on the thirteenth?"

Jimmy turned and smiled warmly, withdrawing from his bag a small journal in which he wrote a note with a small heart next to it.

咠凡

After a delectable blend of sweet and savory for breakfast the next morning, Lishan prepared for the Senate Committee on Health, Education, Labor, and Pensions hearing she was attending later that morning. An Internet search afforded her the additional details any worthy journalist should be aware of before attending meetings and interviews. She didn't have a change of clothes—her attire from the previous night would have to do.

As the coffee peeled back Lishan's eyelids, she decided on a taxi. She caught her breath as a Yellow pulled up, but she felt that particular drama in her life was over after last night. As she arrived in the Senate hearing room in the Dirksen Senate Office Building, she looked for the least conspicuous seating—she had nearly forgotten her life was potentially in danger, but the crowd brought it all back. She spotted Maya in the back right of the room and took a vacant seat next to her.

They exchanged events of the past couple of days, followed by Maya's pointing to two U.S. marshals lingering in the wings, in case Conner appeared. Maya said his ego was of a size that gave him a false sense of security.

The chairman had just called the committee to order and made his requisite opening remarks. Lishan sat, poised, ready and hopeful for an execution of substance.

"In today's hearing, we will examine whether the Food and Drug Administration must alter its nutrition labeling to, once and for all, provide the public with information that's truthful, easy to understand, and void of doublespeak. Specifically, we're here to charge the FDA with further modifying its regulations about trans fats and food additives. The public has long been denied a straightforward label that informs of the true and real ingredients in products on our country's shelves. Those companies who label the front of the package as being a 'zero trans fats' product, when in fact trans fats—a.k.a. partially hydrogenated oils, for one—*do* exist in the product, must no longer be allowed that deception. As to food additives, monosodium glutamate, for example—an excitotoxin that causes headaches and other severe problems—has more pseudonyms unrecognizable to the average consumer than I can count beyond my fingers and toes."

This prompted light laughter, as the chair was known for his visibly counting—on his fingers—small numbers of things.

"How this deceit of the public continues unabated is beyond my comprehension. Or is it?" The chair had the tone of rhetoric, seemingly customary in high-ranking positions in government. "It is my esteemed hope that those voting members present to-day have the clarity of intellect and the ethics representative of solid family values to leave any puppet strings behind and stand up for the good of the public."

A murmur ensued. As he paused for a sip of what appeared to be water, Lishan drew whatever substance she could from the grandiloquence and jotted it down. She was hopeful his carefully chosen wording was indicative of his true feelings.

The hearing continued, with apparently substantive dis-course on the merits and drawbacks of present-day labeling regulations. Lishan wrote "apparently substantive" in her side-bar notes since the opposition contradicted many of the "facts" presented.

When one of the speakers made mention of Conner's Mod X3 Connola Oil and its dangers, as brought to light in a news leak yesterday, a loud disruption occurred in the left rear of the room.

"That is absolutely false! It would revolutionize food stor..." began the tall figure until a neighboring male, who looked like Secret Service, quickly pulled the man back to his seat. No one noticed the one-way ticket to Cinque Terre that fell from the tall man's lap.

"Too late," said Maya. She stood, catching the attention of the two marshals, pointing at the outspoken man. Looking down at Lishan, she simply said, "Conner," adding, "nice disguise."

In less than six seconds, both marshals had seized Conner, handcuffed him, and began parading him through the front of the room and through the double doors.

"These two marshals have been wanting to perp walk Con-ner for at least a decade. Now they've had their day," said Maya, sitting down.

"Do you imagine he'll avoid jail and continue with business as usual?"

"No, not this time. Too much evidence against him—we have enough to substantiate probable cause. He'll try for a mistrial, then an appeal, but the public has had its fill of CEOs getting away with... murder."

After the camera flashes and uproar quieted, the meeting resumed. At the 138-minute mark, the chair called for a vote on whether to report the bill, with its changes to trans fat and food additive labeling, to the Senate. The ayes carried, mostly along Democratic lines, but this time with a larger handful of Republican defectors. The battle was not yet won, as Lishan knew. The Senate and House had to approve, followed by the president. But the proposed changes to the FDA were out the gate.

Lishan was inspired. She would see to it that the public stayed informed, regardless of the self-described D.C. oligarchy.

One mark for the public.

"Will he get out on bail?" Lishan asked, fear driving the question.

Maya had confidence in her composure as she gave Lishan's question some thought. "No. For capital crimes, especially complicity with the injury of an innocent child and the poisoned students, no judge—not even the ones beholden to Conner—would risk putting their reputation on the line with all the evidence against him. He'll be in jail within the half hour. No bail for him or his oversized ego. He's not going to see the light of day without looking over prison walls for many years to come. This I can promise you."

$\mathfrak{E}\,\mathfrak{P}\,\mathfrak{I}\,\mathfrak{L}\,\mathfrak{O}\,\mathfrak{G}\,\mathfrak{U}\,\mathfrak{E}$

An ethereal painting of her calendar, a red star on the thirteenth, dissolved as she awoke. *Where am I?* crossed her mind. *Ah, yes, the Quincy.* She had stayed here the past few days—chilling, she told her friends. Besides, home was nonexistent.

She had two suitcases in her room. Auntie had gathered additional clothing from Lishan's apartment, answering Erik's questions with a simple "She's okay."

Lishan felt a hole in her soul. Was it her vagabond state? She opened her journal, the one with Vermeer's "The Girl With The Pearl Earring" on the cover. She began writing, nearly stream of conscious.

I miss Erik. I keep thinking about what he said, "All those homes." Was he a foster child, in homes where he wasn't loved? That would explain so much. And what of Jimmy? Nice fellow. Yet my history with Erik counts, doesn't it? Perhaps he'll have an epiphany, come to his senses, mature beyond that last bump. I'm not infallible, but neither am I necessarily at fault. Have I truly done something wrong? I have, in Erik's mind, which counts, but that doesn't make it my truth. I know I'm lovable, and I can love. This is about Erik, not me. I'm no longer confused about this. I can meet Erik where he is, but can he? I'm not the same woman I was before my life was put in danger. This I know.

Lishan sat back, rereading her entry. Growth. Understanding. Movement. Strength. A decision was in order. She reclined, Bose headphones in place. Sade Adu again—*Is It a Crime?* In the silence, her turmoil continued. One more, Sade. Tell me what to do. *The Sweetest Taboo.* Lishan cried until the song ended. Drying her tears, she could not decide. She knew she needed to take a step. No guarantee presented itself. She stared at her phone, the keypad—the step.

Texting: *"Jimmy, hi. Decisions to make. You helped me so much, for which I can only thank you. I can't do the 13th, but know that I see the beauty in you. Be kind to yourself. XO. Lishan."*

Texting: *"Erik. I'm working on forgiveness, on understanding. Not just for you, or me, but for each of us. I understand, as well, about "All those homes" in your life. It's okay. If you believe, then Quincy Hotel. Rm 403. I am here. The sheets are silk. Delay is inadvisable. Lishan."*

LETTER TO THE READER

I would like to take this opportunity to personally thank you for reading my work. My intent in writing *Silence Her* was to challenge each of us to speak up for justice, and to draw you into the storytelling world.

I would appreciate your taking a moment or two to review my book on Amazon. Your honest reviews help authors to continue bringing you the best possible stories in the future.

Works Cited

[i] Dr. David Graham. Lucas Catton, Ed. "FDA Overhaul Needed to Quell Drug Threat." January 13, 2007.
http://www.opinioneditorials.com/freedomwriters/lcatton_2007 0113.html

[ii] Klemm, Rolf D.W., MPH, Dr PH. Johns Hopkins Bloomberg School of Public Health. "US Food & Nutrition Policies: The Actors, Structures & Instruments." 2006.
ocw.jhsph.edu/courses/FoodNutritionPolicy/PDFs/Lecture2.pdf

[iii] United States Food and Drug Administration. "Foods / Healthier Americans." 5/27/2009.
http://www.FDA.gov/AboutFDA/ReportsManualsForms/Report s/BudgetReports/2007FDABudgetSummary/ucm112799.htm

[iv] United States Food and Drug Administration. "Guidance for Industry: Letter Regarding Point of Purchase Food Labeling." October 2009.
http://www.FDA.gov/Food/GuidanceComplianceRegulatoryInfo rmation/GuidanceDocuments/FoodLabelingNutrition/ucm1872 08.htm

Douglas Fetterly is a freelance writer and novelist with a passion for literature, love of adventure, and propensity for social consciousness in his stories. He has traveled extensively, including Russia, Kenya, Egypt, Ghana, Europe, South Pacific, Mexico, Canada, Cuba, and Asia. Living on or near the water most of his life—at times on a sailboat or houseboat north of San Francisco—helped him keep perspective through life's trials. Interests include surfing, sailboat racing, ocean conservation, backpacking, indie films, guitar, more surfing, and the treasure of his kids and grandkids. Most days he can be found surfing with his wife at a variety of O`ahu surf breaks, or writing at a local café. He has enjoyed storytelling classes, dancing, singing in community choirs, and earned a Bachelor of Arts in English Literature.